The Pharaoh's Curse

Also By Kyro Dean

Rogue Royals: The Baron's Ghost

Rogue Royals: The Earl's Assassin

Glister

Fires of Qaf: The Covenant of Shihala

Fires of Qaf: The Seal of Sulayman

Fires of Qaf: The Haunting of the Immortal Killer

Fires of Qaf: Eve of Fyre

THE PHARAOH'S CURSE

ROGUE ROYALS: BOOK 2

KYRO DEAN

EIGHT MOONS PUBLISHING

Copyright © 2023 by Kyro Dean

All rights reserved.

No portion of this book may be reproduced in any form without written permission from the publisher or author, except as permitted by U.S. copyright law.

Cover illustration copyright 2023 by Midjourney and Eight Moons Publishing, LLC.

Cover design copyright 2023 by Eight Moons Publishing, LLC.

Published in the United States by Eight Moons Publishing, LLC.

Printed in the United States of America.

www.eightmoonspublishing.com

To all my readers: it takes a village.

Contents

Blank page		IX
1.	Chapter 1	1
2.	Chapter 2	5
3.	Chapter 3	10
4.	Chapter 4	19
5.	Chapter 5	25
6.	Chapter 6	33
7.	Chapter 7	42
8.	Chapter 8	52
9.	Chapter 9	60
10.	Chapter 10	72
11.	Chapter 11	82
12.	Chapter 12	93
13.	Chapter 13	97
14.	Chapter 14	106
15.	Chapter 15	111
16.	Chapter 16	120
17.	Chapter 17	125

18.	Chapter 18	132
19.	Chapter 19	139
20.	Chapter 20	147
21.	Chapter 21	154
22.	Chapter 22	163
23.	Chapter 23	171
24.	Chapter 24	179
25.	Chapter 25	190
26.	Chapter 26	201
27.	Chapter 27	207
28.	Chapter 28	212
29.	Chapter 29	218
30.	Chapter 30	225
31.	Chapter 31	233
32.	Chapter 32	241
33.	Chapter 33	250
34.	Chapter 34	260
35.	Chapter 35	265
	Glossary of Aegyptian Arabic	277
	Glossary of Aegyptian Gods	280
	Glossary of Victorian Slang	282
	About the Author	284
	Thank You!!	286

One

Zarina flipped the crumbling skull over and hefted it from one hand to the other. It was what, three thousand years old? Probably some high priest or Aegyptian noble. In other words, a right snooze. She chucked it over her shoulder, where it hit the wall with a crack and burst of bone powder.

There had to be something of greater value hidden around here, or at least something more interesting. Her airship was on its last balloon after her encounter with that ruddy pirate, Rushing. The red-haired Britannian had nearly sand-sunk her. She'd be stranded for good if she didn't find enough treasure to pay for the costs. And being stranded in the Aegyptus desert could only mean death.

Death.

The haggard dog that lived in her shadow.

Zarina double-checked the latch where a trailing, clear tube hooked into her breathing mask's patchwork of copper and brass. She exhaled in relief. Secure. Of course. She wasn't stupid enough to let the poisons leak in.

She pulled close the long, maroon vest she wore to fight off the cool of the tombs and ran a hand along the pocked hieroglyphic walls, her fingers rising and falling with the crumbling dimples. She paused to trace around a priest's particularly sharp nose then touched the bridge of her own.

The resemblance was undeniable.

She moved on, her hand gliding over passages from the Book of the Dead and warnings for grave robbers. *May those who defile Horus be torn into a thousand pieces that float down the Nile to the bottom of the sea.*

Zarina snorted, and the flow of fresh air hissed inside her mask. It was all a bit dramatic, but what was family for? Her mother always said Prince Meryatum's line was a paranoid bunch, and this was his very tomb. A twinge of pain tightened her chest. Eighteen years and she still missed her every day.

She swallowed the chilly memories of her mother's murder and adjusted her green-tinted goggles against the glare of the gas lantern—goggles that prevented her from getting blinding headaches because of her lovely inbred bloodline. Just another example of how she'd be in a grave soon if she didn't find something she could hock. She waved her lamp toward the center of the crypt where her umpteenth great-uncle still rested in his burial rags.

"Sorry old man," she said with a shrug. "A girl's gotta do what a girl's gotta do. Besides, if you haven't crossed over yet, my borrowing a few things won't make a difference now."

Muffled yells echoed down the narrow shaft she had crawled through, reverberating around the tomb. She turned and dropped to the floor, listening. Voices this far out in the desert could only mean one thing.

Grave robbers. Land pirates. Filthy sand snakes.

But how had they found her? No one should know where this tomb lay.

Fragments of light shimmered down into the darkness. They were coming.

Zarina dug into her pouch and pulled out her buriers: small, brass beetles coated in iridescent green and designed by her ancestors to dig into small spaces. She put their backs to the heat of her gas lamp. Their gilded legs began to circulate, scooping back and forth in scurried, halted movements. She moved back behind Meryatum's tomb and pressed herself into the shadows.

From the corner, she counted three bricks across and two up from the bottom to the set stone behind which lay secret chambers. The buriers left her hand, traversing ancient stone in search of soft sand.

Gruff voices grew louder, the flicker of fire stronger. Zarina crouched down, snuffing out her lamp and tightening the latch on her breathing mask. She exhaled a curse.

Her breathing tube went straight from her ship to where she hid, leading them to her like broken earth behind a sidewinder. And what if they stepped on her tube? She'd be forced to unplug, to breathe in the tomb's foul air. A few minutes of that, and she'd be too sick to move. The odor of ancient must and formaldehyde was already leaking through her mask.

Her life was a seed that only sprouted trouble.

She banged her head softly against the rough stone and squeezed a handful of shifting sand. What was the point of being heiress to Ra's godly fortune if the blood that gave her that right also made her the only person she knew too weak and sickly to enter the tombs without aid?

Oh, right.

To appease the gods' cruel sense of humor. That was the point.

But what else could she do? Leave? The robbers were so close she could practically smell their cumin-heavy breath from down here. No. She would have to wait for them to come, for her buriers to finish digging. The thud of footsteps joined growly voices, and the soft crumble of sandy granules tickled the air near her.

The buriers needed to move faster. Shay's will, they *had* to. If she were caught down here with a band of lawless, slobbering, carnal scoundrels . . .

She shuddered away from the imaginings and pressed herself deeper into the shadows. To die down here at the hands of men could not be her fate.

A tall ruffian too skinny for his robes alighted in the tomb. Two more pairs of dirty feet tumbled in after, jostling her tube that lay in the dust beneath them. Each man carried a flickering light and wore a nasty, bearded grimace and a navy blue stripe along their hems that the green lenses of goggles turned brown.

Adajin's men.

Ya maraary, not again. Zarina scrunched herself smaller, trying to blend her sand-covered skin into the matching walls behind her. How did they keep finding the tombs? Hadn't she just dealt with his stupid men last week?

The warm metal of the buriers pricked against her skin and re-nested in her pouch. She reached her fingertips into the freshly dug crevices, shifting the brick behind her. The block's sides were thinner than the rest, made to be moved. But the weight still strained her muscles, still pulled at the tendons in her elbows as she quietly shifted it out of place.

Why did her ancestors have to build everything so sturdy?

She shifted her hands around the edges. Just a bit more and the hole would be wide enough that she could climb through. Just a bit more and she could escape these terribly ugly men and hide in the haunts of the tomb's maze.

The wall released the brick with a gust of cool, dry air that brushed past her cheek. She caught the rough edges, shifted, then flinched as the brick's weight fell back against the stone with a muffled *chink*.

The men quieted.

Ya rab! Would nothing go right today?

She held her breath. Hands found her tube, tugging against her mask as they pulled themselves closer. Zarina dropped the brick. It pinched her finger in a shot of grainy pain, and she stifled a yelp.

"Over there," the hardest voice said.

She kicked her legs back into the blackness of the hole and shimmied herself through. It would be impossible to see once inside, but blind was better than dead. Already she could tell the air was cleaner inside. Maybe there was a tiny opening that could lead her to another way out.

The scuffle of boots neared. She squirmed faster. The last of her vision faded into the dark when a thick hand caught her own. A shock of cold spread under his hard fingers. Running, not fighting, was how she stayed alive. She shook her arm, tried to pull free, but it was no use.

The man yanked her back into the light.

Two

Zarina struggled, kicking, and spinning, and bracing her knees against the edge of the stone around the hole. But she was weak—her in-bred ancestry ensured that. One hard tug sent her sprawling back into Mery's tomb, where three leering faces caked in sand and sweat stared down at her.

"Looks like we found the little marmoset what killed our men last raid," the hard voice said.

Zarina bit her cheek to quell her heart's quaking. She glared at them with an upturned chin and shifted to her knees. As the last queen of the desert, she'd fry in Aegyptus's heat before she let them shame her. The goddess Ma'at would see to that.

The shortest of the men tilted back and forth on his feet, his beady eyes gleaming in the shards of lamplight. "Adajin will be pleased by her."

Three to one. And all three bigger and meaner than she was. Her throwing stick and short dagger would be useless, like breath against a sandstorm. At least breath was something she had. She inhaled warm outside air to clear the honey from her mind. Her mother always said a clever woman could spin yarn from a donkey's leg. What was her donkey's leg? Throwing stick, ruby dagger, mask . . . and the pouch around her waist. A pouch filled with the last of her last resorts.

Had it come to this?

Even if she survived these men, the shadow that killed her mother lived on to hunt her, too.

The middle-sized man with a nose like an eggplant tipped his belly toward her and squeezed her cheeks between his filthy fingers. "I'm pleased by her, too."

Her stomach lurched. Last resort, indeed.

She yanked her face free and resisted the urge to spit. Adajin's hired grunt snarled and stepped back, kicking sand in her face. Under the cloud of million-year-old grit, she let her hands fall crisscross in her lap—one hand on her air tube, the other inside the pouch. Her fingertips brushed over prongs and cylinders, the silky metal of her sand buriers and the bumpy blue wings of her Finder. She shifted the sacred blue scarab to the side and fished through tubes and gadgets before finding the smooth glass of their mark.

The hard-voiced man leaned closer, exposing narrow teeth crammed together like the houses in Cairo. "By Allah's strength, we will tear you apart."

"And by Ra's, I will blind you." Zarina ripped out her glass naphtha bomb and threw it hard against the stone floor.

The brass band encircling the deadly sphere bounced once before the imprinted glass shattered and colored smoke filled the air. Rosy particles billowed throughout the room, and the men coughed as dust filled their lungs. Zarina pressed her mask to her face and blinked through her goggles. The greenish hue of her current lenses rendered the pink smog mongoose brown.

Clumsy feet shuffled toward her. Arms reached for her through the haze. She ducked and weaved through the advances, her crouched frame the height of their legs. She kicked a shin and used her hand to goose-pinch the back of a pair of scrawny knees. The men's growls grew thicker, angrier, and short-breathed.

"You desert thief," one coughed near her ear.

She turned too late.

Arms snaked around her, squeezing her tight. Hot breath and crowded teeth clamped around her ear in shocks of biting pain. Zarina dropped an elbow into his stomach as hard as she could. She torqued her body and let out a gasping scream. He bit harder, piercing her skin. A racking cough shook his chest. His mocking sneer turned sour, belabored. She pushed at his weakening arms and found room to slip out. He staggered forward. She touched her ear, the iron of blood marring her finger a brown that could only be red before her lenses.

She stepped back as his large body hit the dusty earth. Pink spit trickled from his mouth, pooling in a dark puddle on the floor. Disgusting. She wafted through the smoke, finding the other two bodies in similarly defeated positions: eggplant nose draped across Uncle Mery's tomb, and beady eyes prostrate on the ground by the shaft. The man possessed the good sense to run, just not the oxygen to do so.

Zarina hesitated, sweeping her eyes across the pink-covered carnage. "What do you think, Uncle Mery?" She slapped her hand on his sarcophagus. "If there are more thieving snakes above, I'll have a better chance fighting them off without a sack full of treasure. Though, if there are only one or two, I might be able to give them the slip and take to the skies if I have the treasure in hand."

She listened hard. Silence answered.

"You're right. My ship can't outrun anything right now. If there are more men above, I'm dead either way. Might as well spare myself the inconvenience of lugging up loot until I know what's up there."

She stepped over Beady Eye's lifeless body and peeked her head into the shaft, blinking at the glimpse of sunlight near the top. A hand grabbed her shoulder tight and pain shot through her shoulder. Fear ran like a fork down her spine.

A fourth robber? Had she been so stupid to miss one?

Zarina dropped to the floor, breaking his hold, and rolled to the side. She scrambled back to her feet, blinked, and took in the green-hued man through her goggles.

Tall, tanned, and muscled—a mammoth to the peons she fought before—with a face shrouded in a thick burlap that covered his head and shaded his eyes.

That must be why he stood despite the pink granules coating the room. The stick of her dust failed to find his lungs. She released the dagger from the sheath on her braided belt and crouched low. Her only chance with the behemoth would be staying out of reach.

She dodged and bobbed, waiting for him to strike. The man crossed his arms, silent.

"Come on." She goaded him with a flash of teeth. "Fight back."

She had to get him to move. There was no other way she could catch him off balance.

Zarina took a swipe at his shoulder. He leaned back. She pounced, dashing around his back and pulling on his freed arm. He teetered, tipped—then found his feet. She was too close, too slow. He reached out and shoved her back. She toppled to the ground so her hands scraped the roughly-hewn stone. Angry droplets poured from her palm, the blood of her ancestors weeping from her in a family tomb.

How appropriate.

But what was his game? Was he playing with her? Amused by her feeble attempts before he pounded her to a pulp? She pulled herself up and bit through the pain. She would not be made a fool.

"I said fight back." She ran for him, dagger at the ready.

He caught her, spun her around, and shoved her face-first against the wall. Rock crunched against her face mask. He twisted her elbow behind her back and wrenched it up and up until pain bolted from her shoulder in every direction. She gasped, refusing to let go of the knife clenched behind her back and struggling against his hold.

"You've gotten sloppy," he said, his clear baritone as hard as the metal pressed against her lips.

Zarina froze.

That voice. Those muscles. The sun-kissed skin. She should have known.

Her heart pinched.

"Farak?"

He released her arm, and she spun around.

He pulled the covering from his head. Large brown eyes, creased by the desert sun, stared back at her under thick black lashes. It was him—even with the scarf covering his nose and mouth, he was exactly as she had always remembered.

And his presence meant her doom.

Three

Zarina swallowed, sand and vinegar stinging her nose. She hadn't seen her Guardsman in seven years. Hadn't heard his voice or watched his left cheek dimple when he smiled, hadn't even known if he was alive. And with how they left things? So awful and awkward and—none of it mattered. He shouldn't be near her. She tightened her grip on the dagger to gather strength.

"Farak, What are you doing here?"

"What I've always done," he said. "Getting caught up in your trouble."

His voice was harder than she remembered, colder. But it was still his, and her moral resolve wavered. Zarina clenched her fist, the cold metal of the hilt digging into her fingers. She had to stay strong.

She cleared her throat. "You know the terms of our parting. There's only one reason I would ever want to see you again."

Farak's intense gaze sifted across her face. He leaned over, placing a tattooed hand on the wall behind her, and bent down so his nose nearly touched her own. "Remind me."

Heat flushed her cheeks. "If you don't remember, then I shouldn't have to . . . to—"

"Say the words."

She opened her mouth, but the syllables stuck to her sand-parched lips. It had been so long, her request seemed foolish—nay, impossible—now. But the hope behind it had been all that kept her going the many moons since they parted, and the only thing that stayed her hand from using her sacred blue Finder to call him back.

As the last descendant of Ra in a long line of queens, her family was fated to be hunted by assassins until the day they died. Along with a throwing stick and map, each daughter of Nefertari received a sacred cerulean beetle that would call a bodyguard to protect them until they met the same fate. What made it even more terrible, was that the Guardsmen were cursed, too, forbidden to act on any love they felt toward their queen lest both their souls be damned.

But that didn't mean things had to stay the same, did it? Could love overpower the gods? Had Farak finally forsaken his oath and come to be with her?

She took a steadying breath and savored the smell of jasmine and reeds that clung to his skin. Behind it, the stinging scent of alcohol burned her nose and pulled her from her stupor.

"Have you been drinking?" She studied the lines of wear and worry that marked his face as the last of her flowery pink smoke bomb settled to the earth and on their clothes. A few specks sat like sunspots on his eyebrows. "You never drink."

He pulled back as quickly as he appeared. "You say that like you know anything about me."

"We lived together for eleven years."

"And have been apart nearly as long."

"Then why have you come back?" She peered into his eyes, hoping for an answer—*the* answer she wanted to hear—but they shone back all business and distance.

Her heart ached.

It had not been like this all those years ago. The brown and bronze had once looked at her with warmth before she left him in the middle of the desert. But if he was still mad at her after all this time, if he had not abandoned his oath to be her lover instead of her Guardsman, things must be as dire as she feared. There could be only one other reason he had returned.

Her left hand darted to the silver throwing stick she kept tucked into her belt. A gift from her mother taken from the sacred library in Cairo—the last gift before she died—and a reminder of their shared fate. She gripped the cool metal, heart thrumming.

"The assassin? He's coming, isn't he?" She whispered the words through a dry throat. The formaldehyde and bad news turned her stomach sour.

"If the assassin knew who you were, you'd be dead."

Relief at the grim truth loosened her grip on the throwing stick. Death came for everyone she cared about—her mom was already gone and Farak would be next—but at least it wasn't here yet. Because once fate caught hint of her in the wind, there would be nothing she could do to stop it, and she had already lost so much trying.

Love was the last thing she had left, and it was powerless against the gods.

She turned her head from him and stiffened. "Then you're not welcome here. Leave."

"You don't own the desert, Zarina."

"I think we both know I do." She angled her dagger toward him with a flippant tilt.

"Your family hasn't ruled these lands since the last hippopotamus hunt."

"Ra is my family, and the desert will always be his." She said it forcefully to hide the hypocrisy in her words. Had she not just been hoping Farak had come to steal her away from Ra's grasp?

"You cling to Ra, still?" Farak's words were sharp. "After everything?"

"Don't you?" She challenged his glare for one second—two—then dropped both her voice and her eyes, staring at the sand-strewn floor through her green-tinted goggles. "That's the only reason you came, isn't it? Your godly calling? Your *duty*?" She spat the last word before sealing the rest of her disdain with clenched teeth.

Bitterness sat like a scorpion between them, neither of them wanting to move for fear of being stung.

Farak broke first, crossing his arms over his broad chest and pulling himself to his full height. The white, billowy shirt he wore did nothing to hide the bulging muscles underneath, and the blue-green glow of foxfire beads lining his pants and sword gave him an ethereal, imposing stance.

But he would never hurt her, not physically. That was part of the curse. The curse he was so honor-bound to uphold, and the curse she had tried so foolishly to free him from.

"You abandoned me in the desert to die seven years ago." The venom in his voice bled into her heart. "Why would I come here for you?"

His words stung far more than any serpent's bite. She had been wrong on both counts. He was not here for her, not out of duty nor out of love. He had not chosen her at all.

Her lungs struggled to breathe. The gods were cruel to orchestrate such a chance meeting. Or had obscure fate done so of its own accord, a rolling wave triggered by a curse pushing, pushing, pushing them together until they met their predestined end?

It didn't matter—not anymore. She would be happy Farak took a step toward his perceived freedom, even if it was futile, and even if it gutted her.

She forced herself to smile. "Right. Good for you. Yes, good. So what *are* you doing here? It's not like you work for Adajin." She raised her fist to punch his arm playfully like old times.

His jaw twitched.

"You can't be serious?" Zarina dropped her fist, the bubblings of anger rising. "You chose Adajin over me?"

"What did you think I was doing all these years? Living off air and waiting for you to return? After you made your position so painfully clear and stripped me of my duty, I found myself in need of an employer. That is not something you can begrudge me."

"I will absolutely begrudge you working for Adajin. His men are muck, not worthy of the bottom of my shoe."

"Then that's right where I belong, no? With the men you deign to step on?"

"That was your fault, not mine." Zarina ripped off her breathing mask, risking the toxins in the air so she could yell freely. "I offered you everything, and you refused."

"What you offered me was a choice between condemning our eternal souls and fulfilling my duty to protect you just as generations of my ancestors have done before me. How is that fair?"

"Don't you speak to me of duty." The word sent rage rippling through her small frame.

She never wanted to hear him talk of duty or honor or fate or curses ever again. Not when they so clearly meant nothing to him. Zarina hefted her ruby-encrusted dagger and spread her feet into a fighting stance. If they were both so bound to unforgiving gods, what she did next mattered little. So much for being happy for him. She might as well learn just how far his *duty* would go.

"Are you going to fulfill your oath, now?" she challenged.

Farak put up his hands, eyes widening. "Zarina, don't do this."

"Your choice." She lunged, cutting his shirt sleeve as he dodged out of reach.

He stepped away, and she followed him along the wall and around Uncle Mery's tomb. Twice more, she ripped the thin muslin of his shirt with her small blade, and twice more, he refused to fight back. Already, her lungs were struggling with the tainted air. Her vision blurred around the edges.

She lunged again.

"Zarina." Farak grabbed her wrist with the pass. "Stop this."

He twisted her hand back. Pain throbbed in her wrist and up into the nerves of her fingers, so the blade fell and clanged on the floor. Precise, careful, just enough pressure to get his way without causing lasting damage. It was how he always operated, and it made her blood boil.

She had been swimming upstream and only moving toward a waterfall. Farak was still fated to protect her, even when he did not want to. A slave to a will not his own, just like she was. And he always would be.

She swung her left fist up and hooked Farak square in the jaw with everything she had. Jarring pain seared her knuckles. Her face drained of heat.

Had she actually hit him?

He let go and touched the forming welt.

She stared at him. At her hands.

"I—I—"

"Be quiet," he snapped.

His words stung. Her heart twinged. And her head swirled with toxins, but not enough to hide that she had done wrong. What was the matter with her?

She hid her pain under a thin veil of pride. "If you think I'm going to—"

"Hush," he commanded.

"That's rude, even for you."

"*Iḫras*," he growled, clamping a hand over her mouth.

The force of his words, of his hand covering her lips, was too much. She blinked back tears, and pushed her fingers against his, trying to pry away his hand.

He leaned in close, his dark eyelashes brushing against her hair. "Listen."

The word, so simple and full of danger, was his signal that trouble loomed near. Zarina gave up the struggle and closed her eyes, leaning on his arm as a rush of wooziness hit her. She swallowed to settle her swirling stomach, then tuned out the desert's swirling dust, along with her and Farak's heavy breathing.

Then she heard it. In the distance.

The soft whirr of an approaching ship.

The seed of worry panged in her liver. A ship way out here in the middle of the desert? How many visitors was Uncle Mery getting today? And worse, how many of his visitors were there to kill her?

She turned to Farak's worried face. "More of Adajin's men?" she asked, straining to hear the faint motor.

"No. We were a scouting party, verifying locations. Everyone else is celebrating Eid al-Adha. Everyone local, at least. But those motors don't sound local. Too much whine. Too much pitch."

"The Brits?" She tucked her foot under her dagger and kicked it back up, grabbing its hilt in one swift motion. "*Wlih*. I could use some fun."

"Then do so without me. You've already given me enough trouble." He waved his hands at the bodies behind him.

"*They* attacked *me*."

"I don't think my boss will care."

"I used to be your boss."

"So it was."

They stared at each other, Zarina hardening her eyes to match his.

"Why are you being so difficult? Do you want me to beg you to stay?"

"That's a good start." He met her challenge and straightened his shoulders. "Beg me."

She flinched. How could she ask him to honor his oath and protect her when that was the very reason she ditched him those many years ago? After she'd punched him, too. She wanted so much for him to be free of her and fate but had been a fool to ever think it possible. That was the thing about the will of the gods; mere mortals could do nothing to fight against it. All she could do is run for as long as possible and wait for her end—which would not be today.

Her liver gurgled with pain. Wretched donkey legs. Could she not just get the yarn for once?

She sheathed her dagger, popping the hilt closed, then open and closed. "Forget it. I survived for seven years without your protection, why would I need it now?"

Still, with him near, smelling of spices and hovering over her like a safety net, her mind sat frustratingly empty. He made her feel weak and invincible all at the same time. It was a terrible burden. A terribly addictive burden.

"Fine." He glowered. "I'll just go like I planned in the first place. Good luck with your *surviving*. You'll be lucky if you make it out alive, breathing in tomb air."

"Wait!" she yelled before she could stop herself. As much as she hated it, she could not let him go. Not after finding him and the way her heart had shifted to make room. She needed him. But she would not beg. Nor would she use the power of the curse to force him.

"I'll pay you," she said, straightening her shoulders.

"You're broke."

"I won't be by the time the sun moves closer to sleep."

"What are you talking about?"

"The treasure."

Farak's eyes widened. "What have you done?"

"I used my family's map to scout for treasure, same as you." She ignored the judgment in his voice. "Help me carry the loot up and get past whoever's headed over, and a third of it is yours. No honor required."

"Zarina, you should not do this."

"Why, so Adajin can have it, instead? It's my birthright."

"You steal from a god."

"And what have you been doing with Adajin's men? I take what's rightfully mine. Ra is in me, his blood is my own. And I am the last descendant, as you well know. If he cannot part with earthly things to save his own children, then what's the point?"

"To avoid the gaping jaws of Ahmet."

Zarina shuddered at the mention of the monstrous god of the underworld who ate unworthy souls. Hints of the dark teased the corners of her ever-blurring vision. It was just the toxins, she reminded herself, but the hair on her arm raised anyway.

"I have taken from Ra before, and I am not sorry. The gods hold my fate in their hands and squeeze me daily. Taking my inheritance is the only way I can avoid my fate a while longer yet. You understand this, don't you?"

Farak's hard shoulders twitched beneath his shirt. "You could just run. Your ship's quick, or at least it was when I took care of it. You'd be gone before that whining clunker makes it over."

He always aired on the side of caution, on the side of cowardice. And it had saved her life a half-dozen times. But not this time.

"I can't."

"You're just as stubborn as ever. It's going to get you killed."

"It's not like I want this life of running. I did not choose to be born cursed any more than I chose to have this ridiculously large nose." She threw her hands to the side before shrugging in defeat. "I stay now so I can run later. My ship's in bad shape. I need the treasure to fix her up, to stay ahead of . . . everything. I can't leave without it. Especially since Adajin's men have pilfered so many of the other tombs. He'll have the rest of my inheritance soon enough. This is my last chance to get her running again. And I need your help. Just this last time." She flicked her eyes to his and poured everything she had into them.

The corner of his lips twitched. "This really isn't a good time."

She swallowed her pride and did what she said she would not. "Please?" She whispered the word for the first time in seven years. "Not as my ordained bodyguard or as a friend. As paid help, and only until the job is done. That's equitable, right? Free from bad blood?"

Heavy silence lingered for a lifetime of moments, the churning whirr of the mystery ship growing ever closer.

"It would be best not to engage," Farak said, but he ignored his own advice and drew his curved kilij. The foxfire beads adorning the hilt cast long shadows along the painted walls and highlighted the stark difference between its long, simple blade and ornate hilt.

She stepped forward to hug him with open arms. He pulled back, cold and distant. She wrapped her empty hug around herself instead. Why was she still like this around him after all these years? Why did her feelings, her wounds, run so hot? And why did his run so cold?

"So you'll help me?" She coughed the words, the powder-covered room making its way into her lungs.

"One last time," he groaned. "Now, put your mask back on, and let's haul treasure before we're the ones dead in this tomb."

Four

The bitter vinegar inside her mask bit at Zarina's nostrils as she ducked into the small hole in the wall in search of treasure.

Farak unsheathed his kilij and handed her a gas lamp. She had to crouch in the room, the ceiling only a couple of meters above the ground. The light from her lamp danced across the floor and something dark glimmered in the back. Onyx maybe? She moved forward, illuminating the shadows and a dozen mummified cats.

"Yich. Apparently, Uncle Mery's side of the family was more eccentric than I thought." She navigated through the field of felines on nimble toes.

Farak ripped another stone away from the wall and crawled in, shoving the statues aside as he went.

Zarina ran a finger over a miniature boat replica that looked much like her own vessel. Next to it sat a sarcophagus the size of an apple crate. Three scarab beetles were painted on top. She picked it up and peeked inside at the beautiful, dried beetles in shocks of purples and greens that were only made richer by her lenses.

"Now's not the time for jewelry shopping." Farak's voice dripped with snark.

She tucked the box under her arm. "There's always time for a good pair of earrings. Now focus. Only high-value targets. We won't have a chance to come back here once we leave. Not when Adajin realizes his men never came back."

She slipped on a gold bracelet with an engraved image of the protective Singular Eye and turned toward a row of gilded benches in the likeness of jungle animals. "Those would fetch a hefty price."

"And take a dozen trips of two men each to carry them up. Be practical."

Farak shifted through crumbling crates of long-deteriorated figs and dates. He lifted the heavy lid of a wooden box with a shattering *creak*. Jeweled bracelets and silver amulets tipped to the floor, revealing a gold burial mask that winked with every hint of light in the room.

"*Sadad dink.*" Farak smirked. "Found the money."

Zarina pouted at the abrupt end to her treasure hunt. "You always could find a viper in tall grass. Let's go."

Farak shut the chest with a thud and pushed it out of the secret room. His muscles tensed, and he froze. "Something's off."

She shook her head. "You're not on that booby trap nonsense again, are you? We've never actually encountered any, you know. The only reason people talk about them is because of the ones we leave behind ourselves."

"Not with the tomb. With the ship outside. I don't hear the engine anymore."

"What?" Zarina poked her head out, her arms full of beetles and bracelets. "How could they get here so fast?"

"I don't know, but we've got to go. Any chance of them playing nice vanishes once they see the loot in our arms."

She nodded and dashed toward the shaft, but couldn't shake the dread filling up her heart. Outside hovered a now silent ship faster than the desert winds. Her mother's old stories surfaced in her mind and sent chills down her neck. "It's not the Brits, it's a ghost ship."

"Don't be ridiculous."

"It's the ghost ship my mother warned me about, the one that killed my great-grandmother and her great-grandmother before her. Quiet as the desert and a deliverer of death. It's carrying the assassin, and it's here to kill me."

Farak grabbed the loot from her arms and hoisted her up the shaft. "Then I suggest we run."

Zarina scrambled out of Uncle Mery's tomb and back up the shaft to the main hall in the Temple of Luxor. Farak squirmed his way out behind her.

Out in the sun that could melt the moon, she cupped her hand over her eyes. The white light of noonday shone unphased through the lenses in her goggles. The throb of a headache pulsed behind her eyes. Stupid blood curse that gave her migraines in the light. She needed something stronger for the full noonday sun. She slid off her breathing mask and loosened the knot in her headscarf that bunched around her neck. With deft hands, she pulled the light muslin fabric free and draped it over her hair and forehead.

Momentarily shaded, she twisted each lime-green lens and popped it out from her goggles' frame. In their place, she mashed lenses of a dark red and snapped them back on. She blinked a few times to adjust to the crimson hue, tapped the glass to make sure they were secure, and tugged her scarf free from her head so the desert breeze could cool her skin.

Off in the distance, an airship floated ever closer. A light-colored balloon bulged under a deep even deeper scarlet tethering, its moorings clamped smartly at the sides. A steam plume blew in short, pretentious puffs, like a sweat-streaked jollocks who was out of breath. The ship's motor was out, forcing the propellers still despite the running furnace.

Farak, too, shielded his eyes from the blinding white of the sun overhead. He untethered the binoculars hanging around his neck and tipped them up. "There's not one cannon on the deck of that ship. Not a single heat-glass. The cowardly foreigners probably hid their weapons below deck."

"Or it's the assassin who prefers more subtle methods than brute force weaponry."

Farak's deep voice rattled her from behind. "Either way, you can't run fast enough on the ground, and the skiff I came in is too easy a shot. Your ship is still our best bet."

Her airship hovered eight meters off the ground, moored by thick, braided ropes hooked around a pharaonic statue whose face had long worn away. Her figurehead—a large replica of Ramses' head—rose from the wood and attached itself to the top of the front mast. A limp net draped over the side and brushed the sand with the hot desert breeze. She gripped the netting and hesitated. What if the mystery ship was listing because the assassin lay in wait on the deck of her ship?

She held her breath and tucked her knee-high boot into the first gaping hole. She should not let Farak see how fearful she had become after years on her own. Only baby goats cried for protection, and she was no goat. Still, her knee refused to move no matter how she commanded.

"If you don't mind hurrying up," Farak said, making no attempt to hide his frustration, "I'd prefer my share of the treasure without shrapnel in it. Lest you forget, the Guardsmen serving your family for the past two thousand years have had equally dismal fates when up against the curse." He cupped a hand once more to his eyes and stared warily at the approaching shadow. "If there's a chance that ship carries the assassin, I want to be rid of it as much as you."

His words burned through her fear, and she made quick work of climbing up the netting. He spoke the truth, and it had always torn her apart. That was part of the reason she forced him away all those years ago, to spare him the agony of her life. To save him from their impending death. And yet, the second they were together once more, she dragged him right back in.

Royal hypocrisy flowed freely through her veins and cruel fate through her life stream.

"Good news," she said in forced cheeriness. "You're not my Guardsman anymore. Not the blood-oath kind, anyway. So you should be safe." It was a pitiful excuse she did not believe any more than the gods would, and she clung to it fiercely.

"The assassin won't know that. Nor care, I think. Not with us here together. For now, my survival depends on us sticking together whether we like it or not."

"Which means you don't like it." Zarina rubbed her right palm raw over the coarse rope to distract from the sting in her heart.

Farak said nothing, his toned arms trailing just below her feet.

With a hollow heart, Zarina tilted her head back and scanned the edge of her deck. She tightened her grip on the rough cord and hefted herself up. A hot breeze blew through the light fabric of her billowy pants as she climbed over the top. Her vest flapped and snapped against her ankle, and she took care not to step on the breathing tube that still dangled from the straps around her neck. It was a hassle but was the best way to get fresh air from the skies down into the tomb, even if it was a work hazard.

Zarina slipped off her mask and hung it over a nearby pole. With the kick of her boot, she flipped a lever. Heavy chains rattled in the hull of her ship, and the long line of her mask's breathing tube recoiled faster than the dart of a scorpion's tail. She unsheathed her dagger and scanned the deck.

Every barrel stood where she left it, every mooring knot tied in the same place. There were no signs of someone else being there. Not that there would be. There was a reason the assassins always won in the end. Why her family always died. He was smarter than her, whoever he was. More prepared. A mongoose to her cobra. And it didn't matter how she fought back, how hard she bit. In the end, he'd eat her up.

Farak joined her, thumping the box of jewelry onto the wooden planks and pulling out his curved kilij. She flicked her fingers toward the stern and tilted her head aft. He nodded, and they split, scouring the nooks and crannies of each end of her ship like they had done a thousand times.

"Clear," she called across the deck.

"Same." Farak sheathed his weapon.

She hurried over to the steering wheel and cast her gaze past the giant metal bird that flew at the base of Ramses. While the rest of the ship followed traditional Aegyptian craftsmanship with its sleek lines, bowed ends, and narrow body, the bulky figurehead was thoroughly foreign. A recent prize from her long-fought battle with the last Britannian pirate who dared loot her sea of sand.

"Farak, hide the treasure and cut the moors. We'll be more imposing in the air, and the altitude will give us better eyes on their cargo."

He stared at her, calculating. She winced. It was too easy to fall back into old habits, to boss him around like his life was hers. Now, their roles wove together in a tangled tapestry that Farak wanted no part of. With their new independence, how was she supposed to act around him? All the boundaries she once relied on blurred into a mirage.

She swallowed through the tightness in her throat. "Please?" She uttered the word for a second time and held her breath. She had never groveled so much in her life.

He glowered at her for a moment longer before relenting with a swig from his flask. "As you'll have it."

Her airship rose high into the cloudless sky. Light glinted off the metal casings that held the balloon to the ship, and heat waves roiled and rolled across the shimmering sand below. The foreign vessel continued to approach, listing with the breeze. The red tint of her goggles made everything seem more dangerous—more violent—and it kept her mind sharp.

A bang cracked the sky, and the previously silent motor roared to life. The ship turned swiftly, pulling up beside them on its broadside.

"Ambush!" she cried.

Five

Her heartbeat pummeled her veins. Would the enemy ship attack? Unleash a row of cannons and blistering fire? Each of her muscles tensed for action. Her ship was in no shape for battle. Though this time she had Farak. And that made all the difference.

"Farak, angle the heatglass west, northwest. Keep it covered until we're ready. We don't want to burn them until we have to."

"As you'll have it."

He rolled the giant, six-lensed magnifying glass across the deck and anchored it near the railing. The foreign vessel slowed. Zarina kept one hand on the wheel, the other on her dagger. The wind kicked up and blew her scarf across her shoulders and to the side where the beaded end flapped smartly. She waited for a signal, a sign from the other ship that fighting would commence.

A creak.

A shrill cry and screech.

She gripped her dagger with white knuckles. Was this where she met her end? At least it was in the freedom of the sky, not buried in a tunnel under a pistoria like her mother. She scanned the foreign vessel's deck for the source of the noise, for whoever was in charge.

A rusty pulley squealed, swinging with gusts of hot air that escaped the balloon.

A bubble of adrenaline burst and dribbled down her neck as sweat.

"*Ya lahwy,* what's going on? Why pull up on their fighting side if they're going to sand-sift out?"

Zarina nudged the helm, bringing their airship's upturned point to within a few feet of their adversary's. Farak moved away from the heatglass and stood a bicep's length behind and to the right of her, his hand on the hilt of his sword. It was his go-to position when faced with the first sign of a threat. Zarina shifted from one foot to the other. She was not the only one falling into old habits.

She cleared sand from her throat and raised her voice, "Who's in charge here? I demand to speak to the captain."

Silence. Pent-up frustration heated her skin far more than the sun. She slammed her fist on the railing and scanned the deck for an outlet, someone to yell at, to fight with. Her eyes fell upon a few bedraggled crewmen in sweat-soaked shirts, courting the shadows of the far end of the deck and avoiding eye contact.

The men were pale, wearing thick shirts and pants far too hot for this weather, and apparently deaf, considering their inability to follow her barked orders. Idiot foreigners filled this ship, not mercenary pirates, and definitely not assassins. Her heart released the fear bundled up inside, though tension still knotted her muscles. If they were hapless foreigners, what were they doing out here? Luxor stood in the middle of the desert, nowhere near Alexandria, or Cairo, or any known trade route.

"Oy!" she yelled over the gritty whip of wind. "You sun-leeched Brits. Who's in charge?"

Silent, salt-stained faces stared back at her.

She cocked her head toward Farak. "Maybe the heat has addled their temperate brains."

"It's a possibility." Farak frowned. "Even for Euros, they seem quite pasty. Perhaps they're lost over the desert sands. They wouldn't be the first."

Oh, she hoped that was true. A thirsty Euro would sell his soul for a glass of water. Or his ship, if she were lucky. Despite its clap-trap craftsmanship, their Britannian hunk-of-flying junk would fetch a pretty piastre--or forty--on the open market.

She scanned the crew. They *were* paler than the average Euro. Almost ghostly pale. Like they had just come from across the sea and straight through the desert. Or like they had never lived at all. Maybe this was a ghost ship. And where was their captain?

The heat of the sun pounded down on her neck as a chill crawled up it.

She needed to get out of her head and away from her imagination.

"Oy!" she tried again. "Show me your captain or I'll fry your faces off."

Farak sighed in the silence that followed. "That wasn't very diplomatic of you."

"Wasn't it, though?"

"Not a wit."

The wide-eyed sailors turned towards the sound of scuffling coming up from their lower decks. A lanky, glasses-wearing man in a sleek, tight-fitting suit spilled out from the cabin door. Scrolls and sheets of loose paper filled his arms. He tottered toward her, losing papers to the breeze. Despite the odds, he made it to the front-most balustrade a stone's throw away from her ship.

"My sincerest apologies," he puffed. "I ran below deck to grab a few things and got carried away, I'm afraid."

Zarina scowled. She could barely see the man's face through the pile of scrolls in his hands, though his speech was Britannian English. She hated talking in the foreigner's tongue, but her mother had forced her to learn for just such occasions. The only way a Brit would leave was if you told them bluntly in their own language.

"What are you doing out on the sands during Eid al-Adha? No permits were issued today. Only pirates are about." She said it as a warning.

"Ah, praise the Queen, you speak English. And no permits but one," the man said. He rifled through his papers, spilling more onto the deck until he reached a scroll bound and marked with a melty wax seal. "A special favor for my uncle. Stern man, but easily persuaded on all things Aegyptus. And he knows people who know people. You know how it goes. I'm Richard, by the way. I mean, Lord DeClare, Viscount of Pembroke." He shuffled an appendage free for a handshake though they were nowhere near close enough to reach, balancing his papers on one lifted knee, much like a crane. "I always forget the proper etiquette. Not that I know what that would be here. I know more about ancient than current Aegyptus. What etiquette do you follow for introductions?"

She crossed her arms and settled back on her left foot. "Our etiquette is avoiding them altogether."

His hand wilted. As all Brits go, this prattling man was particularly annoying, like a sweat bead in the eye.

"Ah, but you need no introduction, Princess Zarina Nefertari."

"Son of Mother Nut," she swore. "How do you know who I am?" She tried to stare him down, to bore into his soul and rifle through his secrets, but she still could not see his eyes through his armful of papers.

The man bent to pick up the documents slipping free from his charge and dropped a scroll that unrolled down the deck of his ship. "Oh, it's all the buzz in Britannia. I heard it from a cousin who heard it from Lady Harriet Spencer who mentioned Lord Sheffield of Portsmouth. Though where he got his information, I don't know. Honestly, the second I heard that an actual descendant of the most beloved of The Great Wives, Queen Nefertari herself existed, I dropped everything to find you. And *voila*! You'll excuse my French. The rumors said you were a short thing with a thin Aegyptian ship and stolen bird figurehead." He peered past her to the shiny raven. "I'd say that's about right. That, and you're wearing the sign of the gods on your wrist. Only ancient royalty owned things like that."

Zarina spun the bracelet she just borrowed from Uncle Mery as the Britannian man droned on and on. Of course, the one time she took something for herself it would backfire, her past once again sealing the fate of her future.

Farak moved up a step to her right flank. Threat level moderate: a reasonable chance for conflict. And she couldn't even enjoy it. Sewing chaos with Farak at her side lost its fun when people discovered who she and her family members were. Not that she had any family left.

The second every one of her female ancestors' identities got out, the fate of them and their Guardsmen had been sealed: assassination by an unknown force sent by the mischievous god, Apep, sworn enemy of Ra. It was to be her fate, too. And Farak's, if the records held true. Stay hidden and alive long enough to have a female child who can live her life in fear, learn the family secrets, have her own female child, then die by the assassin. She had done everything she could to avoid that fate: refusing the arranged marriage to her sickly cousin who died from natural causes (the lucky sheik) and living as a lowly air thief who ate locusts for breakfast to avoid identification.

She had even given up Farak.

Zarina shuddered. She did not suffer loneliness, bitter bug legs, and flaky wings in her teeth for naught.

Until now.

Her time had run out. All of Britannia knew who she was. It could not be a coincidence. That meddling Rushing pirate must have figured it out and spilled the secret. It made sense. Rushing's hair was a red so bright it triggered a migraine even with her goggles on. No one with hair like that could be trusted, especially a foreigner.

Zarina glared at the lanky man. Why was he still talking? "Go away," she interrupted him mid-sentence, then turned her back decisively.

He barely paused enough to breathe. "Oh, I can't leave now. I just found you. I have so many questions. How did Nefertari die? Where is her tomb? Do you know where all the tombs are? Does your family still follow the same burial rituals? Are there secret pyramids still active today? Do you have any family recipes or kernels of ancient corn?"

"Enough!"

She flipped back around and fully unsheathed her dagger. The gold and rubies caught the sun in threatening bursts of light. She squinted through a forming headache and leaned over the deck, jabbing the dagger at Richard. "No more stupid questions. You Brits are such idiots with your Aegyptomania and focus on a past that isn't even yours. You are not welcome here. Go drown in the Nile, for all I care, just don't be here when I come back."

"But—"

"Ah ah!" She gave one last jab. "No talking. Just leaving. And shut up about who I am." With that, she turned and headed below deck, kicking the heatglass as she went.

She entered the small room at the bottom of the stairway and pressed her hand against the smooth olive wood of the door. If a random foreigner could figure out who she was and find her in the middle of the desert, it was only a matter of time before the assassin showed up too.

No matter what she did, the curse still dictated her entire being. Her past, her present, the end of her future. She dug her nails into the soft wood, releasing a hint of its sweet aroma. She needed a plan to crush fate itself under her sand-filled boots.

After a hot summer's hour, Farak's heavy boots thudded toward the stairs.

"They put up a fight but they're gone," he said, bending his head to fit in the hallway under the deck. The sleek, fast frames of Aegyptian ships came at the price of space, both personal and cargo.

"Put up a fight?" She turned, a quirk to her lips. "Scroll boy?"

Farak crossed his arms, bulging his biceps. "A little one."

"You just pretended you couldn't speak English again, didn't y—"

"Yes, I just pretended I couldn't speak English. But I also unsheathed my sword and took a chunk out of his railing for good measure. Are you happy now?"

"I am." She smirked. "We need to get to Alexandria to turn our loot into coin before the assassin beats us there. Everyone knows that's the only port to fix a ship like mine, and if Rushing told the world who I am, she probably gloated about the damage she caused, too."

"I'm not going with you," Farak said, sliding the box of jewelry out from under one of the planks on the stairs where he hid it. "You survived the encounter with the ghost ship. My contract's up." He picked a few silver pieces and one gold out of the box.

"No way. The deal was for the day."

"It's Eid al-Adha. Holiday hours."

"That's not fair." She slammed the top of the jewelry box closed in a puff of dust that nearly nipped his fingers. "We didn't even have to fight anyone."

"And I want to leave before I have to. Darkness follows you, Zarina. And you made it clear that was a burden you wanted to suffer alone."

She huffed, searching for a way to keep him on. Selfish or not, she didn't want to be alone anymore, not with her name out in the wind. "It would be faster taking my ship to Alexandria. Your skiff must move like a pigeon."

"No."

"So you're just going to leave me? When you know the assassin is coming?"

His face hardened like glass. "That's no longer my concern."

The coldness in his voice and the truth in his words wore her down. "Weren't you the one who once insisted on fulfilling your duty at all costs?"

"Weren't you the one who said it didn't matter?" His bronze eyes challenged her. "That I should be free to make my own choices?"

She clamped her teeth over her response. She had had this conversation with Farak many a time before they split and knew how it ended. Only back then, they were fighting on opposite sides. But what was the worst that could happen if she persisted? Farak was no longer hers to lose.

"I believe the gods pushed you into my path for just this occasion," she said, reaching a hand out. "All our separation taught me was that we can't escape the curse, can't fight against fate. So why try?"

"Why try?" Farak grimaced and pulled away from her touch. "To make sure the last seven years haven't been a cruel waste of time. You're as tempestuous as the wind, Zarina. Which is it? Do you believe in the gods and curses and an unchangeable fate? Or do you believe we have the right to choose our fate? It can't be both."

His muscled frame loomed, and his question cast a shadow over her resolve.

She believed the first and wished to believe the second, but the gods loomed too strong in her mind and heart, and a history of death over generations told her fate had to be real. But none of that changed how much she wished she and Farak weren't a part of it all.

Only love had been able to tempt her soul toward eternal torment for defying the gods, but that was as much a lie as her freedom to choose. Neither Farak nor her had escaped their impending encounter with the assassin, even after all this time and changing everything within her power to do so. How could they ever fight against fate when the gods held all the cards?

Zarina took a deep breath and met his fiery eyes, all the more intense from her red lenses. "Ahmet's judgment, Farak. Would you just come on?"

His face remained rock-still.

"Please?" Zarina breathed the word through her dusty throat for the third time.

She softened her eyes and knit her brows together. It was the face that made him cave in the past. The face he could not resist. Until the one time he did.

Farak popped the flask off his belt and downed a heavy sip of bitter-smelling boozah, looking away from her pleading. "To the Port of Alexandria but no further. If Adajin sees you anything but tied up, the assassin will be the last of our worries."

Six

The fading light filtered in from the crack in her door. Zarina sighed and rubbed her bare eyes against the sway of the airship and the temptation to sleep. Farak had sent her below for the night to do just that. But that would be folly. Fate found her far sooner than she had hoped.

Weeks. It had only taken three weeks after her mother's identity got out for Apep's assassin to crush her in a sand tunnel beneath crowded city streets. And her grandmother? Four days of constant running before the assassin pushed her off the top of the Sphynx.

A knock rapped on the door, shooting tingles across her shoulder blades. She froze.

"Zarina?"

It was Farak, thank Ra, his deep baritone unmistakable. Warmth pushed away any remaining tendrils of fear. He had stayed with her through the night. Then cold—prickling and swift—surged from her belly button. What kind of terrible, cowardly person was she to drag Farak nearer to his death only to keep her from her own? The worst kind. A daughter of Ra.

She could not feel happy about Farak staying. She would not.

"I'm up."

She swung her feet off the bed, enjoying the buzz from the motors that tickled her feet through the floorboards. Her boots were a pain to put on, but nothing chaffed her more than sand between her toes. It was everywhere: in her hair, her pits, even her teeth. Could she have one place where it didn't irk her?

"We're nearing Alexandria," Farak spoke through the door. "Should we make preparations to land or wait and see who's in port today?"

"Land," she said, tightening her laces. "With my name out there, I have to hurry and get my ship fixed. The assassin waits for no one."

Farak's footsteps thudded upstairs, and she peered into a tarnished silver mirror. Time for braids. The higher the threat level, the tighter she fastened her hair to her head. It was a safety protocol. It also intimidated the Euros, who thought women should always be flowy and soft. Maybe this would help keep that persistent man from earlier off her back. She tugged hard on a strand of hair. Thinking of him nipped her brain like a swarm of gnats.

Zarina entwined various silver and copper beads and trinkets into the even weave that fell down her back. When two dozen or so braids nested at the nape of her neck, she used her scarf to rope them into a thick knot, so the tasseled end brushed her shoulder blades. To finish, she hooked on a pair of iridescent scarab earrings with legs that dangled below her jaw. Family legend said they were Nefertari's favorite pair. At least they had that in common.

"We've crossed the Nile." Farak returned. "We should be there in a lizard's lick."

"Ay. I'm heading up now."

She snagged her goggles and pouch and lifted a few lenses—the various shades of red for the intensity of the sun outdoors and the shades of green for man and fire-made light indoors. She didn't need them yet, the morning light gentle enough, but she wouldn't risk being stuck in a sun-filled city all day without them. Getting a light-induced migraine during a potential assassination would be just her luck.

As novel and grand as a royal heritage sounded, descending from a line of queens only ever brought her trouble. She was, after all, a descendant of the sun god who couldn't bear to see its light. The laughing gods were cruel like that.

She took a deep breath and kicked her door open, then marched up the few steps to the main deck. Helium hissed out of the balloon in the gentle blue of the early morning sky. It was one of the few things Zarina could look at without her goggles and one of her favorite things in the world. She peered over the glossy wood rail to the city below, enjoying the natural color of things before she had to put on her lenses.

A trickle of peddlers wound their way past merchants just beginning to set up shop on the dusty streets. It wouldn't be long before their songs of fish and trinkets took over the morning silence. Already the thick smell of bread mixed with the salty fish on the passing breeze. Her stomach growled.

Farak appeared to her left and leaned on the rail. "What's your plan for the city?"

"Why?" Zarina turned to him with a smirk. "Worried about me?"

Farak's forehead wrinkled into a pinch.

He would not make this easy on her, and that made what she had to say harder than swallowing a mouthful of honey. "I could use your help today. I know our deal ends at port, but I need you longer than that."

The wrinkles smoothed into a hard mask. "While it's nice to be asked for once, I do your bidding no longer."

No, he didn't.

Her eyes combed the city streets, looking for reds and oranges, yellows and blues. The counting helped calm her. Farak would not do her a favor, nor did she deserve one. With her portion of the loot from Uncle Mery, she had enough to fix up her ship and very little to spare for provisions. But in a big city like this, she needed the extra eyes more than the bread in her belly.

Zarina took a deep breath. "I don't expect it for free. I can pay you more."

Farak's eyebrows lifted. She had piqued his interest. Now, she just needed to reel him in.

"Full wages for the day. Then you can be done, no strings attached."

"You said that before."

She extended her thumbs and pointer fingers and touched them together to make a triangle. "Ra's honor."

Farak's eyes narrowed. "I have a benefactor."

"Adajin? Please. I know you don't enjoy doing his dirty work. The stink of your breath tells me that."

"If people could leave his service as easily as yours, he would not be such a menace," Farak growled. But it was half-hearted, and Zarina took hope. "His family may well be as old as yours and twice as ruthless."

"Then don't tell him." She waved off his concern. "Stop in to kowtow to your new master while I'm at Rana's and join me after that. It's like getting paid twice for the same day. I imagine that flask full of boozah burns a hole in your pocket."

Farak shifted his weight next to her. "You're seeing Rana?"

"Who else could flip this much treasure in a day? Besides, she and you are my only friends. Or were." She snuck a look at him, but his face sat, unmoving. "And she knows the black market better than I do this ship. Why wouldn't I see her?"

He paused. "I didn't know you two were still in contact. Have you been to the city often?"

Zarina let her eyes linger on a stand of swollen melons down below. "Hardly at all. But she is the closest I have to a sister. She will welcome me. And you are welcome to come with me, of course. To say hello."

"And get even more mixed up in your troubles?" He slapped the railing. "I'll pass."

Zarina pressed her palms into the wood. She had hoped seeing Rana would tempt him to stay on for the day; his refusal surprised her. They three had been on many capers as children, and Rana always seemed to hold a special allure over Farak.

In fact, the fateful day she met Rana was the day after both of them had lost their mothers; two lost souls in an unforgiving city. A week later, Farak had found them running like the wind outside the pistoria from a handful of teenage brutes. Farak had rounded off half, and she and Rana had fought the rest like the little scraps they were. With the world out to get them, they had fought like scraps ever since.

That day had been a coming together of all three of them into a sort of dirty, motley not-quite-family surviving in the heart of Cairo.

Fear of being found out and killed by the assassin eventually drove Zarina and Farak away from the cities, but they had always stayed in touch, coming together periodically in Alexandria where Rana had moved to be closer to what remained of her family's trade. It had never mattered how much time passed between visits, they were always thick as thieves and close as ever.

Farak's refusal to see her poked at the suspicious part of Zarina's liver.

"Shall I give Rana your best, then?" she asked, watching his face for a giveaway.

He grunted.

"Then we can meet up after I'm done." She put on her best smile. "I can't pay you your share of the treasure's value until sundown, so you might as well get paid to help me while you wait."

"You're as persistent as the sun in summer and twice as deadly." He sighed and took a swig from his flask, turning it upside down when he found it empty. "It won't be easy to keep track of you in the crowds."

"I know."

She hid her victory smile and kept her eyes on the scene below, searching her path to Rana's. Any foray into Alexandria posed a risk, but Rana lived in the center of the city. Getting there and back would require stealth.

"You should cover your face with a niqab." He walked to a supply crate on the upper deck and lifted out a hand full of rough, black cloth. "And mix up where you store things on the ship. In seven years, nothing has moved a cubit."

She frowned. The fabric head scarf he held was horribly hot—a thick version of those worn by more traditionalist Muslims. She wasn't any sort of Muslim. Believing that a bunch of bickering gods decided her fate was one thing, but the thought of only one laughing deity in charge of her impending demise was too cruel, no matter what religion it came from. The swath of cloth was also the drabbest of black, and black didn't look good on her no matter what lens she had on.

He did have a point, though. Hiding her face would be safer. If Farak couldn't keep track of her, she should at least make sure no one else could, either.

"It is a shame there aren't two of you. Then this whole sneaking around mess would be a lot easier."

"You're cruel, Zarina."

She raised a brow before dread settled in. "I'm sorry, Farak. I forgot about your twin brother."

"Convenient."

"It's not like I ever met him. How could I when he died as a baby?"

Farak's statuesque face held, which was worse than a scowl. He wouldn't even show her how he truly felt. Wouldn't even deign to waste anger on her.

"You're right," he said curtly. "His short life was meaningless. Killed by the plague as a way for the gods to correct the curse. One princess. One servant. No brother. No point. Just a leftover kilij meant for his hands."

"I didn't mean it like that," she whispered.

He squeezed the hilt of his kilij. The hilt from the sword meant for his brother that his mother had combined with the blade from his own. A symbol so he could remember always, though apparently, she could not.

She bit her lip, then took a risk and laid her hand on his. "Fate is cruel to us all."

He let her hand linger and lowered his eyes to hers. She held her breath, and he parted his lips. Then he sealed them shut and pulled his hand free.

"You should unbraid your hair and remove your goggles."

Back to business.

She sighed and squeezed the hardwood of the railing beneath her fingers. "You ask too much, Farak. I'll cover my braids with this itchy abaya if you insist, but if I go without my goggles, I will be blind, a sleeping aardvark to be hit with a throwing stick."

"They set you apart."

"I'm aware."

"Too much." He touched his foot to hers, the gentlest of nudgings that sped her pulse.

Had he meant the touch, so tiny and personal? Not if what he said was true, and their meeting again was by chance. He had chosen to run from his fate instead of return to her, and she must remember that.

Still, she missed this, missed him. The knots inside of her grew even more snarled.

Farak pulled at the fabric, concern etching his brows and the soft line just above his lip. "If you drape the edges of the abaya enough, you can shield your eyes from the sun."

How could she say no to that? To him and the look of worry creasing his face? She had been smart to leave him behind all those years ago. The tension in her fingers released.

"You win, Farak. I'll wear the coverings and keep my goggles tucked away along with the ruby dagger strapped to my thigh. But I'm decidedly unhappy about it."

She snagged the garments from his hand and began the tedious work of wrapping herself within. After a great deal of flapping, she caught a glimpse of Atacama blue and pulled her head through to the sky. Farak stood with arms crossed, his face crinkled with a hint of amusement.

"I look hideous, don't I?" She pouted.

"Yes."

"Farak!"

"Since we're on your ship," Farak breezed past her indignation, "I request my mother's dagger be returned."

"Dagger?" Zarina asked.

"The one with the snakes on the hilt. I know you know which one it is. It was conspicuously missing from my bag when you so kindly dumped me in the desert."

Zarina kept her eyes on his face, refusing to look at the trunk behind him where it lay nestled in an oiled cloth at the bottom. It had been her only memento of him, and with how things were going, probably would remain so.

"I don't seem to recall—"

"Zarina!" It was his turn to bark.

A horn bellowed down below, signaling the opening of the Port of Alexandria's docks.

"Times up," Zarina shot a sorrowful look at him and dashed up to the helm at the head of her ship.

Airships crowded the harbor in the dry cool of early morning, each vying for the first shot at the city's stores. But Zarina had to be at the front of the line for the refueling stations or get trapped in the city all day, waiting for her turn in the queue. This was especially true considering the repairs she needed. Tom Tom's shop filled early and quickly with requests, and when it came to her ship, no one else would do.

She gripped the helm and pulled the tasseled end of the ship's blow horn twice. The docks returned her signal with two short bursts of their own.

"Farak, you ready?" She yelled over the whipping wind to where he handled the balloon's intake valves on the deck below.

He leaned his weight into the release, a thick brass lever wound tightly in leather strips. Helium *shooshed* out the top of their balloon, speeding them toward the ground. Her stomach flipped, and she leaned into the helm for grounding. They leveled off thirty *kassabah* or so above the harbor. A dockhand in large goggles and thick gloves reeled a silver pulley gun around and took aim.

"Brace for tethering," she called out. She turned the point of the ship toward the harbor, losing sight of the pulley gun below.

A crack snapped the air. The gun shot a metal anchor the size of a sarcophagus at the massive metal hook on the front of their ship, just below the raven. But instead of gripping the hook and reeling them in, the metal claw missed its mark and headed straight for the deck railing.

Zarina cursed. "Down in front!"

She spun the wheel hard to the right, so Farak swayed precariously over the side. But his calloused hands well knew the shift and tilt of ships and grabbed the nearest rope. He swung over the edge and back around, landing neatly on the rough wood of the deck.

"Turn around. Shore up. The tether didn't take," he called.

"Ay. I swear they were aiming for my head." She turned the wheel so the metal bird faced the docks once more. What was with the dockman's aim? She'd never seen such a wretched shot in all of Aegyptus. "Farak, release gas from the front quarter pocket, so the tethering hook is more visible to the ground. Those *hemars* couldn't spit on the Great Pyramid if they were standing on its doorstep."

Farak's biceps bulged with the weight of the lever as he released more air. The gun cracked again, shooting another anchor directly at their broadside.

"*Ya kharaashy.*" Zarina spun the wheel full tilt.

The bow swerved sharply as the hook sliced the air nearby. She slammed into the helm, and stabbing pain rolled up her shoulder. Ropes swung overhead, and rain barrels tipped and tumbled across the deck. She righted the ship with a spin of the wheel and dashed to the railing. Down below, a hooded figure hovered where the dockman once sat.

The assassin.

Her heart shivered. "Farak, dive!"

Seven

THE SCREAM OF RELEASED helium sent chills up her spine and across her shoulders. Wind blustered by, tugging at her braids. With the shadowy servant of Rerek aiming at her ship, her fate loomed ever larger.

Farak called over the chaos, "Turn and fight or run for cover?"

Zarina bit her cheek, holding tight to the helm. What could she do against the assassin when he was directed by fate to be her end? Haphazardly shooting the heat lens down at port would only start an air brawl which could hurt innocent people. Her heart already carried the burden of the pain she brought Farak, killing peasants would only make things worse.

Fighting fate would only hurt people and end in her demise.

She took a deep breath and yelled, "Run! Our best chance is splashing down in the harbor on our own and hoping the port authorities will keep the assassin back."

"You'll be fined," Farak called back.

"Ay. But we have no choice."

Just like in every aspect of her life.

Farak's face crumpled into his tale-tale sign of disapproval, and she bit back her annoyance. "The dockhands will be furious."

"It's not like I plan to come back," she shot back.

"You barely have enough treasure to pay me and Tom Tom as it is."

Zarina shot him a glare. "Is that what you're worried about? Getting your cut?"

He focused his attention on pulling in a line of rope.

"I said I'd pay you, and I will." Though how she wasn't entirely sure.

None of that would matter if they died, and she still had to cross a quarter of the city without being lampooned. Fate may take her in the end, but for now, she would keep the gods' eyes to her back and run.

She dipped her ship past a blocky beast with thick sails and a monster balloon. Crewmen on the boxy deck spat curses and cries of indignation as her trailing helium blew their airship off course. Flat rooftops grew larger with their descent. The bread in a cart took on oval clarity. The red of a shawl popped like desert flowers.

"Pull up," Farak boomed from the deck.

She shook her head. Braids whipped and stung her cheeks.

"Zarina," he warned.

"I can't. We have to get lower, or we'll be hit by the assassin."

"You'll dash us to pieces on the next roof." Farak's words were thick with incredulity.

He did not trust her. And why should he? Before they parted, she had relied on him far too often to make the difficult decisions. But she had learned a trick or two in his absence, like how to trust herself.

"It will work. I learned it dodging Huns in China."

"You've been to China?"

A line of sheets drying atop a roof flapped free, and a barrel scraped the bilge.

"Now," she called to Farak.

He pushed his whole weight into the levers, cutting off the stream of gas and jarring the balloon as it leveled off. The nearest rooftop sat just a jump's distance away from the bottom of their ship. Cries of alarm bloomed in the streets wherever their shadow touched. She spun to check the harbor behind her. She could just see the glisten of the gun from afar, twisting, twisting to take aim once more. They needed more steam power, more speed.

Zarina set their course dead-on for the port and locked the wheel before jumping over the balustrade that surrounded the upper deck. Her boots thudded on impact, and she tripped on the very robes that she had put on to save her. She regained her balance and grabbed the heatglass from where it rested, dragging it to the edge of the boat where a large hook hung for lifting cargo onto the deck.

"What are you doing now?" Farak called as he tied off the sails.

"I'm going to hook it to the boiler room lenses on the side of the ship to magnify the heat power from the sun and give us a steam boost. We're a harder target down by the rooftops, but we still have half a city to go before we're able to land in the port. If we don't gain some speed, we'll never make it."

"That's reckless," Farak chided, but he was by her side in three paces. He grabbed the knot that held the hook to lower her down the side of the ship and pulled it from her reach. Did he always know what she was going to do before she did it?

"I can do it myself," she barked at him and jumped to grab hold. Two leaps later, she yanked the ball of rope back toward her.

Farak's grip tightened around the knot. "We don't have time to waste."

"It's *my* ship. You haven't been on it in seven years. If anyone is going to waste time getting in the way, it's you." She ripped the roping from his grasp.

Farak crossed his arms and furrowed his brow. "As *I* said before, nothing on this *jahanami* ship—including you—has changed at all. Everything is exactly as it was."

Zarina's scrambling fingers worked to untie the thick rope as she ignored the prick in her heart. "Things have too changed . . . this knot is significantly larger than it used to be."

"If you don't want my help, why are you paying money you don't have to keep me around?" Farak's gaze turned to her, golden and serious and asking far too much. "What other purpose do I serve for you?"

Her fingers slowed to a crawl. What could she say to that? She didn't even know herself, not anymore. He was there to help, yet she couldn't bear to let him do the work for her. To risk his life and save her like she was helpless. Even if she was.

She yanked and yanked on the coarse strands of rope, banging the knot against the railing when they would not pull free.

Farak sighed and scooped the ball of rope from her grasp once more. In three swift movements, he smoothed the tangles and freed the hook. Why was he better at everything than her? Even half-drunk.

Farak looped the cord around his elbow and hands. "Ready?"

Zarina refused to look at him as she removed the thick lenses of the heatglass from their stand, tying a rope to the metal joints that held them together. She hefted them over her shoulder, then kicked her foot free of draping fabric and slipped it into the crook. With a huff, she gripped the rope tightly.

"Hoist."

Farak stepped back and pushed her off the edge with his foot. The rope unspooled with a *zhhhhhip*. Halfway down, she reached a row of eight circular glass magnifiers that channeled the sun's heat inside the hull to boil the engine's water. Right on cue, Farak pulled hard. She stopped and swung against the side of the airship. The lenses of the heatglass clanked against the wood and reeds, and she cringed.

"*Ayyaa*. Do you want to crack the lenses?" she called to a Farak overhead.

She placed her boots solidly against the side of the boat and pulled the heavy heatglass off her back to inspect. Still intact, praise Nut. She twisted one hand more securely into the rope and used the other to work the six glass lenses over the largest magnifier that lined the side of the hull. She clipped the edges together and angled the glass so that it would catch the full sun.

A beam of light burst from the bottom and into the magnifier. Intense heat radiated across her hands and face and into the boiler room of the ship. A headache spiked in her brain, and she shielded her eyes. Despite the agony beneath the bridge of her nose, she could feel the rumble of the ship steadily gaining speed.

"Don't leave the magnifier on too long," Farak's even voice called down.

"I'll leave the heat on as long as I like."

"You'll push the ship too fast. She'll fall apart in the breeze before we even land."

"She'll hold." Zarina chaffed with his criticism. He must see her as a wet-feathered duckling straight from the egg.

"I don't agree."

"I don't care. And if we do fall apart in the sky, then the assassin won't be able to sink an anchor into us. Win-win."

Farak tutted like a *jida* trying to correct her grandchild, and the sound carried down with the fish-soaked wind. Zarina cringed. Farak was usually right about these things. Hopefully, her already damaged ship could handle the surge. If not, they'd crash to the earth in a blaze of glory much like the mythic Bennu, only they would not rise from the flames to live once more. Even worse, they'd both die knowing she had been wrong.

The rhythmic bouncing of acceleration threatened her grip. She needed two hands to hang on properly and one to shield her eyes. An impossible feat. Unfortunately, her goggles were tucked beneath heavy layers and out of reach. Stupid. She should have planned better. Not that she'd tell Farak that.

Zarina flipped the itchy fabric of her hood over her hair and ears, tugging it down as far over her eyes as she could. The shadowy reprieve lessened the pain stabbing her brain, and she gave the rope a hard tug to tell Farak to hoist her up.

One yank upward, and a smashing quake rocked the boat. She plummeted several feet, her stomach lurching into her throat before Farak tightened the rope. Further down the side of the hull, the port's anchor had speared wood and papyrus in a splintery wound. Despite their best efforts, they had been hit. A thick rope tied to the metal end pulled taut, halting their progress and tethering their ship to the assassin's gun.

"*Haga tehar'a el dam.* There will be nothing left before long." Careful to keep her eyes covered, Zarina dug through her robes and managed to pull her dagger free. "Swing me left, Farak."

He grunted with the effort, swaying her closer and closer to the point of impact. The ship's engine squealed with steam, straining against the hold of the port's pulley gun. If they weren't careful, they'd burn the motor and be stuck floating in the breeze with no way to defend themselves. The assassin could just haul them in and slit their throats at that point. Or hurl a cannon ball at their balloon and crash them into the ground.

Just another reason she shouldn't have left the magnifier on.

She needed to cut the rope and release the gun's hold on their ship.

With a final swing, she leaped off the end of her rope and landed on an exposed point of the anchor. The metal burned the pads of her fingers with the sun's heat, but she held on despite growing blisters. She raised her dagger like a priestess before the slaughter and stabbed the blade down into the thick rope. Wiggling it side to side, faster and faster, she sawed her way through the braided reeds.

The ship groaned and creaked, being pulled in two different directions. Her dagger's smooth blade would never cut through in time. What else could she use? Zarina paused her sawing and dug once more through the insufferable robes. Her hands touched the cold metal of her throwing stick, and she ripped it free. Another inherited gift, the piece wasn't like any other she had seen; one side was smooth like most throwing sticks, but the other was uneven and jagged like the end of a key.

It would do.

She flipped the silver stick so her hand held the smooth end and hacked at the rope's frayed ends with the jagged tip. Stinging sweat dripped into her eyes. Her headache threatened white spots on the corners of her vision. At last, the individual threads began to snap one by one. They would be free.

Now to survive the abrupt release. She tucked away the dagger and stick and glanced up; the way back to the deck was too steep, too far. She wouldn't be able to make the climb.

Farak worked to swing the rope over. Twice it swished by, a granule too far for her to catch.

"Hang on," he cried over the churn of the motor. "I'll swing it by once more."

Could she afford to wait? For all the divine blood her ancestors claimed ran through her veins, she was no immortal goddess. She'd fall like a piece of sandstone and shatter on the city below. She shifted her feet to find a more solid position and took stock of her options.

A shimmering hole into the boiler room pocked the wood above the embedded anchor just big enough for her to fit. If she positioned herself carefully, would she have enough time to jump through when the ship shuddered free?

Zarina pulled sharp wood away to make the opening as big as possible. Her odds were not good. No, her odds were like seeing the sun in a sandstorm. But she had to try. There were only a few threads left on the rope. She worked quickly to brace her hands on each side of the hole, to place her feet just so along the inside of the anchor to provide the best leap-off point. Then, she held her breath.

When the last cord snapped, she kicked hard. The ship burst free, shooting her through the hole with a loud *crack*. Sharp reeds stabbed at her legs as she plowed through papyrus, but she managed to pull herself into a room brighter than the sun itself.

Her lungs heaved in painful rasps. White consumed and blurred the edges of her vision. She pressed a hand to the inside of the hull to try and hold her balance. Only small patches of grainy wood materialized in the glare of the boilers. She tried to hold onto the glimmer of brown, to fight the agony.

Why was she so weak?

She fell to her knees. The growing heat of the boiler room warmed her cheeks and jarred her bones as it pushed the ship far past capacity. Farak's desperate cries reached her ears. He must think she had fallen to her death. She should call to him, tell him she was okay. But the light hurt too much; she could barely breathe.

Wahsiratah.

Her muscles shook, too weak.

She reached a shaking hand up to cover her eyes, but her thin fingers did little to help the burn. The light seared like a thousand suns, and the floor beneath her shuddered and cracked.

Then a darkness, cool and black, consumed her.

The underworld.

Had fate found her at last? She searched for Anubis through the pitch, for the boat that would take her to the afterlife to see her mother. Cool water lapped at her arms, her legs, her tightly woven hairline.

Where was the boat?

She cupped her hands to her mind's eye and peered at pitch, waiting. But something was off. The sound of footsteps, the smell of jasmine and bitter. Her body lifted from the water. It was cozy, at first. A refuge from the blinding heat of her life and the chill of death. But it could not be real.

Soothing dark and growing curiosity renewed her strength. She was not ready to be torn apart by the monster Ahmet, to have her heart weighed against the feather of Ma'at and found impure. Not before she could make things right with Farak. He deserved that much. She kicked hard against the arms holding her in the dark and back toward the painful light. Her heels found a stomach. A spleen. She dug her elbow and fingers in, aiming for a liver.

"Zarina," the dark called.

She would not listen, would not let Ahmet take her. "*Rech-kwi tju, rech-kwi ren-ek!*" She recited a protection against death and thrashed harder.

"*Ya 'iilhi*, Zarina. Stop."

Through blurry light, a face emerged, creased in irritation. The rush of her pulse quelled in her ears, and she forced her clawing fingers to quiet. The hands that held her were calloused and worn, not clawed like a monster. The face, set with worried bronze-gold eyes, was Farak's. She wanted to stay there, wrapped in his jasmine-smelling arms, but she could not rest on this journey if the assassin forced her to start the next.

"Have you settled?" he asked, his voice soft for the first time since she found him.

She nodded, still in his arms as their breaths mingled as one for a moment, two.

Zarina soaked up his closeness. This was the Farak she remembered. Her Farak. The reason she ran from death. She wanted nothing more than to stay this way for a thousand moons, to confess her feelings had never changed.

Farak shifted her and peered gently into her eyes. "I thought you had fallen." He whispered his admission as if he were afraid the desert would hear and whisk his words away.

She pressed a hand against Farak's warm skin, the shape of worry in his eyes too much for her. These moments meant nothing to him, she must remember that. It was only her heart that beat like a camel stick against rock.

Her fate was twice cruel: to have an assassin out to kill her and to have to live in that terror alone. Though in the dark, where not even the Eye could see, one thought haunted her most: it was not fate but her that brought misery.

"I'm harder to kill than that," she said, looking away. "Though Ba Pef refuses to let me rest on this black day."

Farak set her down, and she wobbled. He laid a heavy hand on her shoulder to steady her, the tattoo of the Singular Eye on the webbing between his thumb and pointer finger a reminder of their tied fates. And with that symbol, her resolve shifted as easily as the sand. He *had* saved her from the light, just like he used to. But did he do so out of old habits? Or did he still care? She glanced his way, took in the bulge of his muscles and the warmth of his skin, and felt spectacularly small.

She should say something. Her fight with death, real or not, taught her that. If nothing else, she needed to apologize for leaving him behind, for ignoring his wishes in the hope that it would save his life, even if it cost her own. With the assassin on her trail, her hourglass would soon run out, and it was the only way she could unburden her heavy heart.

She opened her mouth.

"That was stupid." Farak's face settled into its usual judgemental stoniness. "You shouldn't be so careless in the future."

Zarina smashed her lips over the forming apology, a sting in her newly-opened heart.

"Stupid or not, it was necessary." She brushed his warmth from her arms and stepped further from him. "You're welcome for saving your life."

"Ay, after first putting it in danger."

The chill of guilt and blame blew between them. "Let's not waste time quibbling about the past, or we won't be alive to do so later. How's the ship faring? Did we make it to port?"

Farak's stubbornness relented to the situation at hand. "We're in it now. What's left of the balloon is the only thing keeping us from sinking into the harbor and not for long. The sea has found the boiler room. If salt gets into the tanks, you'll have more than a hull and balloon to repair. I say fuel up and leave. Repair your ship in Cairo."

She flinched. "Can't do that."

His words were as gruff as his glare. "You want to stay in Alexandria?"

"I don't have a choice, Farak. It's either a day on the ground here to fix my ship, or the rest of my very short life on the ground when she gives up the ghost on the way to Cairo because I didn't repair her."

Her words were true enough, even if they concealed a greater truth. Cairo was off-limits, and Farak should know better than to suggest it.

"But the assassin—"

"Will never leave my shadow, now. Trying to wait him out is no use. My days of hiding are over. I can only run as far and as fast as I can and never stop."

His eyes met hers, unfiltered by colored lenses or duty or care. She rose to his challenge. She would not go to Cairo. Not ever.

He broke first and replied tersely, "As you'll have it."

Relief slipped down her back. She turned and headed up to the deck. A sharp *pop* and heavy *slosh* followed her steps. He was drinking again. Already a taboo in Aegyptus's Muslim society, it was a knife in the back of his pharaonic oath. The oath she tried to force him to break. The oath he chose over loving her, and the reason she left him in the desert.

He claimed he wasn't here for her, that she was nothing to him. But if he was really free from his blood duty, what turned him into a belligerent drunk?

"Don't drown your bitterness too deep, Farak—I own you for the day." She winced. That had not come out right.

He replied by gulping down the rest of his bottle and tossing it with a *clink* that rattled and rolled across the wooden planks of the floor.

At the rate he drank, alcohol would kill him before any assassin did—and he, her. She just hoped her wounded heart was strong enough to survive it.

Eight

Zarina ambled between the market stalls, staying directly in the center of the run-down ruts of well-traveled earth. She clenched her fists to keep her itchy fingers from wandering toward the cottons and silks and burlaps hanging in bright folds from each stand they passed. It would do no good to draw attention from the singing merchants and their persistent mongering, not when she needed to keep a low profile.

Why else would she forgo the safety of her goggles and wear such a suffocating outfit? Not planning to use the disguise very often, she had overlooked the silky, breathable hijabs most women wore and had only spent the bare minimum. The fabric was thick, scratchy, and usually used for cleaning rags. A heavy hood covered her hair, and a muslin veil sat just below her nose. Her back itched with heat. She slowed near a stand selling savory incense and wafted tendrils of scented smoke toward her.

Frankincense and cassis, with just a hint of cardamom.

She smiled.

Just because she was drenched in sweat didn't mean she had to smell like it. She breathed in the spicy air and released.

Zarina slipped her dagger from her belt and tucked it in her sleeve. With one swift motion, she flashed the silver blade to see behind her. Farak's reflection bounced back, his wavy image in the background a stall or two behind. He would follow her to Rana's, then break off to kowtow to that wretched Adajin before meeting her later. Despite his covert presence and capable muscle so close behind, she jumped at every clatter and cringed with every cry of fish and spices—with every clinking bracelet.

The assassin had yet to show his face on the streets, choosing instead to stalk her every move, waiting to strike. The impending doom did little to soothe her fraying edges, but what choice did she have? Tom Tom was none too happy to take her mess of a ship on, and the only way to pry it from his calloused fingers would be to pay his price in full. That meant Alexandria. That meant vulnerability and crowded streets and Rana.

Rana's shop lay one cart and a left turn ahead. Thank Ra. The heavy treasures from Uncle Mery's tomb weighed on her aching, bruised muscles. Zarina scanned the stalls, casting a glance behind her.

All clear.

She darted into a dimly lit shop covered in paintings of the Singular Eye. In the safety of the shadows, she pulled the hood off her head and snapped on her goggles. A granite sculpture of Hathor, Rana's patron goddess, and her gilded cow horns graced a small table in the corner. Shelves full of cheap trinkets lined the walls, and a tangled waft of coriander and bay leaves clung to the air.

Zarina took a deep breath and held the warmth of familiarity inside her. Despite grandstanding to Farak about her and Rana's unbreakable friendship, doubt had crawled its way in. It had been many rainy seasons since she had come to see Rana. Too many. And the black city rumors encompassing Rana told of a slippery woman who stirred the winds and disappeared in the swirling sands. But everyone involved in the black markets carried rumors of equally dark reputations, and she had never been like that with Zarina.

The soft clack of wooden beads announced company, and Rana entered through a curtain leading to a back room. Her midnight blue headscarf hung around her shoulders, revealing thick, black hair that fell in a loose braid down to her belly button. A gold and sapphire flower clipped back the tendrils framing her face, centered too with Hathor and her protective moon and horns, a symbol of safety and womanhood. She wore a long skirt in the same blue as her scarf, patterned with a rich weave. A dozen gold bracelets clinked on her arms and ankles every time she moved.

If Zarina were a more worldly woman, she'd envy Rana's soft curves and full lips. Even Farak had been known to swallow hard in her presence. As it were, Zarina had no time for jealousy. Besides, she and Rana owed each other their lives.

Zarina cracked a grin when Rana's moon-like eyes found her.

"Zara, *Nuur 'innaya*." Rana swooped into the room and pulled Zarina to her. "It has been too long, too long."

Zarina pushed back for a breath at the sudden show of affection, then sank into Rana's embrace. Why had she worried so? Rana's glow never dimmed, and neither would their friendship. She was the closest thing to a sister she'd ever have, and that was the one thing her mother had always wished for her: to find a place to settle and have a real family, a real sister. Zarina had always wondered what having the bond of a true family would feel like, but her closeness with Rana would have to do. She had no family left.

"I had some troubles out on the sands. I'm sorry for being away these many sunrises. Mekal hasn't been treating you badly, has he?"

Rana leaned back, keeping a hand on Zarina's shoulder, arm, or hand. "He's temperamental as always."

A lean, grey cat covered in sleek, black spots hopped onto the corner table. He maued in protest and rolled his arched back through to his tail.

"Ah, Mekal." Zarina rubbed the cat's chin. "The best guardian in all the Two Lands."

"And don't I deserve a guardian?" Rana flashed her dazzling smile and chuckled. "No mouse in Alexandria stands a chance. Come, sit, Zara. We have much catching up to do."

Zarina's smile fell a coin's worth. Nothing sounded better than relaxing with Rana while the world bickered around them, but it wasn't the world she was hiding from. She plucked Rana's hand from off her own and gently let it go. "I'm afraid I have no time."

Rana's full lips slipped into a pout. "This is a business visit, then?"
Zarina nodded.

Rana sucked her bottom lip in and let it go with a pop that melted away her look of sorrow. "Then you've come to the right place. What is it you seek?"

Ever the actress, Rana was always teasing others with her display of emotions. Rana may always have her back, but that didn't mean Zarina knew what she was feeling at all. That was the most reliable thing about her. She brushed away the thought and grinned.

"Now that you mention it, I'm out of naphtha bombs and haven't had time to make them myself. Do you happen to have any in stock?"

"Up to no good again, I see. " Rana clucked her tongue at Zarina. "Yes, yes, of course, I have some."

She slipped into the back room and pressed the tattered end of a floorboard, so it popped up just enough to reach a delicate hand inside. She undid a second latch and opened the board up further. Inside, lay four rows of tiny glass orbs filled with swirling gases and deadly powders. Each was sealed with a brass band around the center and had the images of Hathor and Ra etched into the glass, one on each side.

"*Aibtisamat Rae.*" Zarina hefted a pink globe and smiled. "I'll take the lot." She slipped one of each type into her pouch. "Though I'll have to grab the rest later, I can only fit three in my pouch, and my ship isn't ready yet."

"So much." Rana clicked the floorboard shut once more. "Has my Zara found good fortune? For how else would she pay for all this?"

"That's the other reason I'm here. I need to use some of your connections." Zarina dug through her robes and pulled out a golden face mask, the finest piece from Uncle Mery's chest.

"*Ya khabar abyad*," Rana crooned, taking the mask with gentle fingers. "So exquisite. You've outdone yourself this time. Where did you find such a treasure? The street lord Adajin seems to be the only one bringing in artifacts anymore."

Zarina hesitated. This was not her first time using Rana's reputation to trade off-market goods over the past few years, but that was before Adajin had started looting her family tombs. She couldn't name the obvious treasure-hunting spots any longer without drawing suspicion. But how to justify knowing where Uncle Mery's tomb lay hidden?

"I suspect I found them in the same places Adajin does."

Rana puckered her lips. "Why are you being coy with me? I thought we were partners, even if you don't come to visit very often."

Guilt weighed on Zarina's heart, and she took a breath far too big for her lungs. She couldn't afford to lose Rana. Besides the newly mercurial Farak, she was all Zarina had. And even that teetered on the rocks because Zarina had been too worried about what, or who, she'd find if she came to visit, that she stayed away too long.

Maybe she should tell her? The secret locations were out anyway, with Adajin's inexplicable knowledge pilfering them all. She glanced at the doorway and pulled Rana to the back of the room.

In the shadows of the shop, she pulled out a roll of papyrus from a hidden pocket on the inside of her shirt deep within her itchy robes. A silver clasp of the Singular Eye bound the tanned scroll in a tight roll.

"*Najah bahir*," Rana breathed. "What is this? A mystery."

Zarina pressed the center of the eye, and the lock released. She unrolled the scroll to reveal a map of the Two Lands, as the pharaohs saw it long ago.

She pointed to a yellow star amid a cluster of others in the temple of Luxor. "I found it there."

Rana's delicate fingers ran along the painted images of kings and temples, queens and tombs. "Where did you get this?"

"My mother, who received it from her mother before her and so on. It's a family secret, and you may be the only semblance of family I have now."

Rana's large eyes left the papyrus and found Zarina's. "You're in trouble."

Zarina's throat closed around her words. "What?"

"Roll it up. Put it away." Rana pushed the scroll toward Zarina.

Zarina slid it shut and stashed it back under her robes. Had showing the map to Rana been a mistake? She hadn't mentioned the assassin to her, so why was she acting so skittish?

"What's going on, Rana? You're not one to dabble in fear or suspicion. I thought if anything, you'd want to sell the map."

Rana's eyes flickered to the doorway and back to her. "The price of some things can only be death. Access to limitless wealth is one of those. Does Adajin have a map, too? Is that how he has come into so much wealth?"

"What? Don't be ridiculous." Zarina shifted uncomfortably.

Rana touched the horns of the Hathor statue with closed eyes and whispered a prayer under her breath. When she finished, her eyes shot open. "Who else knows about the map?"

"No one. Just me, you, and Farak."

"Farak?" She eyed Zarina through narrow slits. "You haven't said his name so casually since you two parted."

"He is back in Alexandria, and we are in a temporary truce. You didn't know? I thought, with him in the city under Adajin, you would have seen each other around."

It was a thought that had occurred to her more than once over the years. Farak and Rana curled up together, ruling the black market. It was ridiculous, really, but loneliness does strange things to the mind. It was one of the reasons she visited Rana less and less over the years; she feared finding him there.

Rana's eyes softened once more. "No. He has come by to see me even less than you."

Zarina nodded in the strained silence that fell between them.

Rana clucked her tongue. "You don't think he is the one, do you?"

"The one?" Zarina's dusty throat tightened. "What do you mean the one? Like *the one* the one, because I don't—"

"The one who whispers secret locations into Adajin's ear. He's surely seen your map, no? With all your years together?"

"No." Zarina waved a hand to silence her friend. "No, absolutely not. Not Farak. He wouldn't do that to me."

Rana looked over Zarina with sharp eyes, her dainty nose upturned. "As you'll have it, *Nuur*."

Zarina swallowed, and her grainy spit scratched its way down into her chest. Rana read the situation wrong. She said it herself, Farak rarely came by, so she couldn't truly know him, not like Zarina did. Or the way she used to, anyway. The distance between them had grown with each year they were apart. But there was no way Farak could betray her that much, could betray the gods who gave him and his family purpose and the strength that made him so imposing. There was a difference between refusing to be by her side and actively working against her. It was a step too far off the eternal cliff into the Nile's gate to death.

Not even Farak could fight the gods.

And still, her stomach churned as the thought of Farak's potential betrayal needled its way down into her soul.

"Come," Rana said, hoisting Zarina's mask up so it gleamed in a stretch of light from the doorway. "We must look to the future and not the past."

"So you think it'll sell, then?" Zarina asked, grateful for a change in subject.

"Yes, yes, though I cannot pay you your portion in advance this time."

Zarina bit back the curse tickling her tongue. "I need the money today, Rana. I cannot compromise on that."

Rana pouted, her large, brown eyes the perfect topper to her puckered lips. "I'm sorry, Zara. I spent all my free monies on cards."

"Ah, Rana," Zarina sighed. "How many times must I tell you to stay away from those gambling houses? It never goes well for you."

"Well, it would if those men weren't downright cheats. I swear Sadiq keeps cards up his *djellabas*."

Zarina paced in front of the shelves, tipping a dusty urn to see its insides. Empty. Like her coin pouch. What good was a treasure map if she couldn't sell anything she found? Rana so very rarely let her down. How was she supposed to refuel and repair her ship now? And if she couldn't, how would she escape the assassin? Or pay the harbor fines? Or Farak? After her sharp words with him on the airship, he would not forgive her for this. She had to get paid today, even if it meant stepping out of the shadows.

"Just show me who you normally trade with, and I'll do business with them directly. That way I won't need your coins."

"I wish I could," Rana sighed. "But my clients are all secrets. They don't like leaving a trail. You understand that. I'm afraid it would go very badly for both of us if I tried such a thing. And getting them to trust you would take days of persuasion—time, it seems, you do not have."

Zarina swiped the golden mask back from Rana. "Maybe I should just trade this with the dockhands for the fuel and repairs I need. I would get short-changed for sure, but that's my fate. The sun rises always on someone else."

"No, no. What a waste that would be . . ." Rana skirted behind her, pulling the ends of Zarina's braids. "I'm sorry, Zara. I've disappointed you. Let me think. I know I can figure something out." She tapped her chin and squinted her eyes. "Ah, it has come to me. A wealthy, foreign man is in town searching for items for his collection. He's not one of my regular clients. I heard about him from Sadiq."

"Sadiq the cheater?" Zarina crossed her arms and leaned back on her left foot.

Rana cast her hands into the air. "I did not say he was a liar. And this is the only solution I have if you want your money today."

Zarina would rather deal with a viper than with foreign traders trying to give her dust for her family's legacy. They'd pinch the dagger from her hand if she failed to keep a watchful eye. Desperation was like a sand trap, a slippery slope leading to forced choices and death. But today it was a necessity.

"Take me to him," Zarina said.

"*Marha*," Rana said with a clap and a smile. "It's been too long since I went to the market with a woman."

NINE

Zarina tucked the hood back over her forehead, so her goggles barely peeked out. Without her Guardsman's protection in tow, she had given into worry and decided to wear them with Rana. If the edges of her head covering fully shaded her face, they should give cover to the silver rims too. At least, Farak was off with Adajin, which meant he couldn't chide her about how she should be more cautious, or how her goggles were too obvious, or how her ship hadn't changed in seven years.

She balled her fists. Who cared what he thought?

She should not let others ruin her perspective. The world looked rosy through Zarina's pink lenses, the colors more vibrant and the contrasts more distinct, and she would focus on that instead.

Rana, too, draped a blue muslin scarf across her silky hair but kept her face veil-free. It was the perfect balance between respect for the local culture and what she truly believed—which was the power of the old gods like Zarina. Rana moved with ease through the crowd, offering well-wishes and mischievous smiles to her fellow merchants. Zarina did her best to follow.

There was a whole world she was a part of that Zarina couldn't comprehend. A world built on deals and lies, slights of hand, and very carefully chosen words. She simply didn't have the patience for it like Rana did. Besides, that dark world was trying to kill Rana when she met her for the first time back in Cairo, and that had left a bad taste in Zarina's mouth ever since.

Rana trailed her hands across the fabric veils and piles of robes they passed. Zarina followed suit, not wanting to stand out or invite more attention from the vendors. The coarse threads of cheaper wares roughed her fingers. But as they went, the fabric got softer, the cotton finer. They were entering high society, and more and more of the people in the streets were shooting her suspicious, hooded looks. While hijabs with their basic head scarves still punctuated the crowd, face veils were a rarer occurrence.

As the majority of residents shifted to foreigners, her costume became more of a liability. But she couldn't take it off, now, and her silver-rimmed goggles wouldn't fare any better. Upon close inspection, she wouldn't ever look like she belonged anywhere but the desert dunes. But while she would stick out more, so, too, would the assassin.

"Here we are," Rana said. Her delicate finger pointed lithely to a manor a few paces ahead.

Like his pretentious counterparts, the dapper owner uniquely designed its facade to represent his origins. Flanked by a towering Asian temple on one side and an austere domed figure that might be Prussian on the other, the Britannian manor offered simple, if not boring charm. Rectangular windows covered its square face, and a chestnut door sat solidly on a modest porch. The small-leafed bushes that lined the foundation were entirely out of place in Aegyptus' severe heat, and it showed in their yellowing, crispy foliage. It must have cost a fortune to import all this ridiculous foreign material, which meant Rana was right; whoever lived here had more than enough money to make the trip worth her time.

Rana fluttered up the steps, looking more like a sunbird than a human. She pulled a thick rope that set off clicking gears. A small jackal statue climbed up the wall, following the chain. When it reached the top of the door frame, it fell, catching against a metal tether that swung the jackal so it rapped against the doorframe.

It was a clever, entirely unnecessary piece. Such were the Brits.

The door opened to reveal a maid with a loose, cream skirt and hood tucked neatly around her plump face. Her sleeves were rolled up at the elbows. The wrinkly woman tipped her long nose up and down in an inspection of Rana. Her puckered mouth eased, and she nodded her in. For Zarina, she offered a pert twitch of her lips and a sideways glare. She clearly didn't believe Zarina's disguise. It was probably the goggles. That, or her complete lack of humility.

Why hadn't she listened to Farak? No, why couldn't she think of these things for herself? She didn't need Farak to survive. And either way, it was done. Zarina added the suspicious woman to her list of potential problems.

"This way," the old woman said, waving them into an ornate living room.

They passed through a narrow walkway that seemed a complete waste of space, pictures of stodgy old men in stiff uniforms lining the wall next to doors that led to who-knew-where. The one at the end opened up and a tall Britannian man emerged, his gray eyes shrewd and his coppery-brown hair loosely swept over his forehead.

With a disapproving scowl in their direction, he turned back toward the room and gave a swift bow. "It was good meeting with you, Lord DeClare. I look forward to our future business."

"As with you, Lord Sheffield," a stodgy voice emanated from the room.

This Lord Sheffield clipped his heels together and bustled past them, careful to shove himself closer to the wall than to touch them like he feared they had the South Plains Plague. Rana eyed him studiously as he passed, a quirk to her soft lips as she took everything in. When he tried to dodge past her, she stepped in his way. Twice more they did the little dance before the man huffed and shot her a scathing look before disappearing out the door they had come through.

Zarina lifted a brow and Rana shrugged. "It is fun to play with the gentry, no? When they are not the ones we need to do business with."

They followed the tired maid through the same door the lord had left through. Dizzying patterns covered every kirat of the walls inside, leaving no time for the eye to process what it had just seen.

What was with the Brits and their unceasing patterns? Were they afraid to let their minds rest?

A plush couch sat upon an intricate carpet in the middle of the room, and on the couch sat a tall man, lean and severe, with tightly combed hair and a tightly wound sneer to match.

"What is it you want?" He spoke in jilted Arabic and offered them only the smallest of glances, his eyes otherwise trained on a book written in letters she could not read.

"If you please," Rana said and swooped into the room. "We heard you are a collector."

He turned a page without looking up. "I have no time for knock-offs and badly made trinkets."

Zarina glared and loosened her veil. Not even her rose-colored glasses could make this man appear more pleasant. "What we have are not badly made anything. They're sacred treasures plucked straight from ancient tombs. The only hands they've been in since the ancient priests who placed them there are mine."

The man turned another page.

She clenched her jaw. She may be sullying her ancestry by hocking the treasure she found in Uncle Mery's tomb, but she was still the last heir of the ancient queens. The sand and sun and secrets of Egypt lived in her veins. They were both hers and a part of her.

She raised her fist and took a step. "How dare you come into my desert and accuse me of peddling trash?"

Rana's hand breezed in front of her, and she shook her head. "*Sayidi*," she addressed the man far more politely than Zarina would have. "We do not ask for too much of your time. A bold collector, such as yourself, should know that diamonds are often found in the dust. What harm is a little look? Hm? Surely, the find of a lifetime is worth putting down your very interesting book, no?"

The man lifted the corner of the next page, hesitated, then shut the book and stood up. "Get out."

"You cannot kick us out this way." Zarina stormed forward. Her hood billowed off her head, revealing her tight braids, but she didn't care. "You're as much a collector as I am a camel. You're a fraud, worth less than the trinkets you detest." She raised her palm and aimed for his book.

"Desert sand," he said and caught her hand, pulling it over her head. Knots of pain pinched in her shoulder joint. "There are a million liars and cheapskates in Aegyptus. Why should I believe you're any different than the rest of them?"

Fire seared her muscles in agonizing stripes. She should have waited for Farak to finish with Adajin before entering this strange house that smelled like empty silo.

Why did she keep thinking of him?

Tears surfaced in the corners of her eyes at the man's words, at the pain in her shoulder, at the injustice of everything.

Zarina ground her teeth over the well of sorrow threatening to drown her out and balanced on her tip-toes. She stared into the man's eyes and refused to struggle. She could not win this fight, just like so many others. It would be better to pretend she was unphased and hope for a blessing from the gods.

"*Sayidi, sayidi,*" Rana's voice chimed, soft and urgent. "We do not want trouble. If you're not interested in what we have to offer, we are happy to leave."

The man lifted Zarina's hand higher, and the knots in her shoulder radiated out in pinpricks of heat. White spots shot across her vision.

She took a tight breath and exhaled her rage. "If I am just sand, then let me go lest my anger turns to glass and I cut you down."

"You dare insult a Lord of the Court?" The man's smooth face darkened to a tint redder than her glasses.

She grinned at him defiantly. "You are lord of nothing here. The desert belongs to someone else."

"Uncle?" A male voice said from the doorway behind her. A voice she had heard before. But from where? "What are you doing? Put her down."

Zarina braced for the drop, but the man set her down so the heels of her boots eased into the rug.

She yanked her hand back and bounded away, turning to see her rescuer.

The man was tall, lean, his face only glimpses of familiar. Zarina bit her cheek. *The Brit from yesterday.* His curly, mud-brown hair stuck up in every direction, catching warm hints of light. Soft eyes, colored by her goggles to that of a scarab's sheen, hid behind flimsy glasses, and his slight, limber frame carried itself with a hint of resigned unease.

His appearance walked the line between man and child, surreal and real, only winning over abject adulthood because of the pleasing set to his lips and the surprisingly square jaw that sat beneath them.

Though, there was a softness to his eyes both wholly unfamiliar and startlingly whole. She could not place the look exactly, but she was sure she had seen it somewhere before.

Zarina lowered her brows and stared at his face, trying to recall his name. What had it been? DeClare something. And he called the man his uncle? She scowled. How many DeClares were in Aegyptus? And why had the gods brought him here?

"Rich . . . will . . . ad? Rich . . . alala?" she asked in English, careful to muddy the ending of what she hoped was his name. It was better to sound tongue-tied than wrong. "What are you doing here?"

"My apologies, Princ—I mean, Lady Nefertari. My uncle can get carried away. I told you he was a stern man. I'm staying with him for my duration in Aegyptus." He offered a stilted bow. He had traded in his suit for loose khakis and a breezy white shirt with the top few buttons undone, allowing a glimpse of his smooth chest and angled clavicles, both parched with sunburn from his foray into the desert the day before. "After we parted yesterday, I was certain you'd disappear forever. And yet, here you are."

She nodded, taking his words in, but he spoke his foreign tongue so quickly, she was sure she was missing things.

She slid her tongue over her top lip. No speaking until she was sure what to say. Why did a foreigner pretend to care so much for her, anyway? And why was he looking for her to begin with? He was the reason the assassin found her. That made him dangerous. But so was leaving without the money for her ship. Rana had barely managed to get her this contact. What if there was no one else? Was begging this man to look at her wares worth the danger or humiliation?

She shifted her gaze between the young DeClare and his stern *khali*. There was no way either of them could be the assassin, but in case they were in contact with whoever tried to kill her, alive and crippled with no ship was better than immediately dead. She scowled. Her life was just one terribly forced choice after the other. But for now, she needed to find a way out. She side-stepped further away from Khali DeClare.

"*Yjb 'an nadhhab alan*," she whispered to Rana and eyed the door.

"But *Nuur 'innaya*." Rana looped a hand through Zarina's crossed arms and spoke in gentle, lilting English. "We cannot leave, yet. You did not tell me you had such a handsome friend."

"He's not my friend," she said flatly.

How could he be when she did not even know his name? Why had she thought Rana would be any good at helping her leave this place? All she wanted to do was make friends with her enemies.

Richalala DeClare's face crinkled into a sheepish grin. Of course. Men were always blushing themselves silly in Rana's presence. Though his gaze did not wander the tempting landscape, but met Zarina's eyes instead.

Rana giggled and pulled Zarina closer to him. "You jest, I am sure. Such a strong specimen, this." She plucked his sleeve and his collar, disregarding any notion of personal boundaries.

Zarina adjusted her goggles. Was Rana laying on a thick layer of charm to secure a future client, or was Zarina missing something?

Rana held on to her arm while she introduced herself to the foreigner, using the opportunity to continue trying out her broken English.

Zarina narrowed her eyes. Rana's interest in him had to be business. Didn't it? Maybe?

Richalala was tall, sure, but instead of bulging muscles like Farak, his arms were winnowy and long. And he smiled way too much. Who had reason to be so happy?

"Oh my, I did not mean to put myself between you two," Rana said, her grin annoyingly coy and directed at Zarina. "I see you cannot stop looking at Lord De Clare. I should have known. Such a handsome couple. The gods would surely approve."

Zarina's cheeks flooded with heat. His awkward smile deepened. This was an utter disaster.

"*Ayaa*, enough Rana," she said and swatted her friend. "They are not lords here. And the gods care not for the people who traverse the desert sand. We should go."

"Not yet, not yet," Rana shrugged her off. "We have yet to ask Lord DeClare if he's interested in your goods. That is why we came here, no? Because you need money, no?" She fluttered her eyelashes at them both.

Zarina grimaced. Rana never listened.

"You need money?" Richalala's cheery countenance shadowed. "What goods are you talking about? Oh, no." His eyebrows furrowed into their most serious stance yet. "You're not selling those pieces from the tomb are you?"

Zarina hardened. "What tomb?"

"I found you outside those ruins with that gold bracelet of the pharaohs on your arm." He pointed to where the edge of her bracelet glinted beneath her robe. "Considering you were where the famed Temple of Luxor resides, it isn't too much to conclude where you had just come from."

Zarina scowled. Maybe he wasn't all dumb Brit. That made him even more dangerous.

"*Laki alaka.*"

"Uhh . . ."

"What's it to you?"

"Those artifacts need to be donated to a museum, not sold to some private collection only a few people will see."

Of course. Fate would now leave her to fight with an altruistic pest who wanted to preserve the cursed treasure of the gods. An indirect emissary of divine beings who had been trying to kill her bloodline for centuries. How fitting.

Zarina smirked. "My goods, my decision."

"*Your* goods?"

"You know who I am." She pulled her shoulders back and stared him down.

"How long have you known about this, Richard?" Khali DeClare interrupted.

Richard. So that was his name.

Khali DeClare stood diagonal from her a tomb-length away, but his presence filled the entire room. His tone was as sharp as the point of his nose. "You know my life's work is everything ancient Aegyptus, and yet you keep this from me. I will not tolerate liars in my home."

"Ah, Uncle William, it's nothing like that. I only just learned about it yesterday." Richard's air of confrontation relaxed in stark contrast to his uncle's. Where his Uncle William grew rigid, he rested at ease. Even in his eyes.

"Yesterday is not today, so why am I only hearing about it now?"

Richard's cheeriness held annoyingly fast. "Because I only just arrived this morning."

Zarina cleared her throat, impatience like scarabs pinching between her toes. "Do you want to see the treasures or not? I have neither the time nor the desire to follow all your tiresome English words."

"Yes, of course," Khali DeClare said. He sat on the couch and motioned her over.

She marched past Richard. Even his pout had a joyous look to it. A smile pout. A smout. An annoyingly puckered smout. She cast her gaze ahead to business, putting him from her mind.

In front of Khali DeClare, she slid the first of her treasures out. The silver bracelet, even tarnished, sucked the breath out of the room. It was a test. Many rich men with far less greed in their eyes had tried to rob her before. She would not risk showing him the golden mask until she gauged his reaction to something far less valuable.

Khali DeClare opened his palm, and she placed the bracelet in the center. He pulled the blackened metal just below his nose, inspecting the jewelry with apparent cynicism. But with each glint of light, his furrowed brows rose higher.

"Remarkable," he said with a shake of his head. "Truly amazing. You were right, desert mouse, this piece, at least, is no fraud."

"I want three mahbub for it. No less." Zarina squared her shoulders, preparing for battle.

"No," Richard said, marching across the room and placing himself between her and his uncle.

Zarina glared at him. "You want me to take less?"

"Actually, yes. I want you to give it to a museum for free."

Zarina choked on her sandy spit. He might as well have asked to burn her ship.

"No." Khali DeClare stood, his hand clasped possessively around the bracelet. "Enough with your prattle, nephew. I accept your terms, mouse." He reached inside his coat and pulled out a purse.

Zarina eyed the way the heavy coins pressed through the leather. So much money. More than she had seen in years. It was everything she needed to go into hiding. The first signs of good fortune she had seen in years.

"Zarina," Richard turned to face only her. "You *don't* want to do this." He lifted his eyebrows twice and glanced back behind him.

"*La ijre.*" Zarina smirked.

"Foot? Your foot or mine? And what? My Arabic is terrible," Richard said with a crinkled nose.

"It means I couldn't care less about you and your museums. I will sell to Khali DeClare."

"No." Richard grabbed her arm and lifted his eyebrows twice more, this time screwing his lips to the side. "You want to give it to a museum," he said through clenched teeth.

Zarina ripped her arm from his hold. How dare he grab her so? If Farak were here, he—he would do nothing because he didn't care. Her stomach hollowed. The DeClares were proving to be more trouble than they were worth. If she could just get her hands on that pouch . . . .

"Ah yes," Rana swooped in from behind, crooning in agreement. Every part of her flowed, adding power and charm to her words like the Nile pulling boats wherever it wished. "Yes, you do want to give away the treasure, *Nuur 'innaya*. Think of the fame. Of the honor and attention you'd receive." She winked at Zarina and clasped her hands.

Zarina looked into Rana's dusky blue eyes. A handclasp in dire circumstances was their signal to trust the other. But why would Rana agree with Richard? Fame and attention were the last things Zarina needed.

She glanced between Rana's warm eyes and Richard's twitching eyebrows. Leaving her fate in the hands of this foreigner could only bring trouble. But she did trust Rana. She had to. She cast her a wary glance.

"Yes," she said slowly, the words sticking like burrs to her tongue. "You're right. Donating my treasure is most definitely what I want."

"No," Khali DeClare pushed Rana and Richard aside. He ripped open a set of books on the shelf that turned out to be a door and pulled a second pouch from a safe inside. "I'll double the price. That's well over what it's worth. I've traveled in and out of Aegyptus for years, waiting for legitimate treasure to find my doors. I will not let you leave with them." He shoved the bag into Zarina's waiting hand.

The weight of the coins washed relief through her nerves. "I thought you didn't want my desert trash?"

Khali DeClare's face stretched tighter and more distraught. "I'll triple the price, then. And beat any offer on whatever else you have."

She smiled at the khali but clenched the leather tightly, worried Richard might snatch it from her grasp.

Instead, he dropped his arms and looked comically crestfallen. "Ah well. You seem convinced. At least posterity can say I tried."

Zarina blinked twice. What just happened? Had this been their plan all along? Rana had never once let her down. But why had Richard helped her out? If he wanted those items in a museum, why press his uncle's bid higher?

"Agreed," she shook Khali DeClare's cold hand with a wary glance toward Richard. "But you will need more bags of gold for what I've brought you. I expect to be paid in full before I step back into the dust."

"Done," Khali DeClare said.

Within the hour, her pockets were emptied of her ancient inheritance and replaced with three bulging bags of clinking coins, minus Rana's finder's fee. A happy Rana chittered at her side as she left the musty silo-house to head back to her ship. Warm sun winked in crimson bursts on the glass of her goggles and threatened Zarina with a headache. Her black robes soaked up the heat, but a faint breeze meandered with them down the street, offering some relief.

"Wait!" Richard cried, stumbling out of the house and into the street behind her. "You haven't said goodbye."

Zarina grimaced. "That was intentional."

Rana elbowed her through the robes.

"But aren't you curious why I did it?" he asked, his eyebrows twitching again.

Zarina hesitated and hated herself for it. Why did she care why a Brit did anything? And yet, in a life filled with everyone trying to do her in, his behavior indeed seemed curious.

Richard smiled and tucked his hands in his pockets. "Because I'm the inheritor of Uncle William's fortune. So when he dies, I can donate the artifacts to a museum myself. Isn't it great?"

"I will never understand you and your desire to worship what has already passed away. Only the gods live forever."

"Don't you see what I'm saying?" Richard stepped in front of her with one of his long strides. "You can get the money you need, and I can still preserve history. It's the perfect arrangement. I'll even help you get the best prices, as you saw in there." He smiled smugly for a moment, but even then his lips had an innocent turn. "So don't go trading your family heirlooms to anyone else, okay?"

Zarina narrowed her eyes. It wasn't goodwill after all. He just wanted her treasures all for himself.

She opened her mouth to tell him off when a bang cracked the air behind her, and the street exploded into chaos.

Ten

THE DEAFENING CRACK REVERBERATED down the street.

Several terrified woman uttering prayers to their god pushed past her, separating her from Rana. Zarina ducked behind the nearest stall, and the crowd scattered in screaming disarray. Her breath caught in short gasps, and her heart thundered in her chest. Was the assassin trying to make a move in the middle of the market? After the stunt with the port gun, anything was possible. Of course, after generations of the assassin stealthily attacking from the shadows, she'd get a bold one who came after her under Ra's very eye.

Her best bet was to keep her head low and stay out of sight. But where was Rana?

She scanned the flurry of hijabs and robes, merchants protecting their most fragile wears, and mothers scooping children from the road.

There.

Across the street.

A flash of blue silk and cobra black hair disappeared behind a pair of earthen pots. Rana was safe. And where was that blundering Brit?

The crowd swelled with fleeing people, and a barrel crashed to the ground next to her. She flinched and pressed herself against the wood of the cart she hid behind. The throng of people only added to the chaos, but she refused to join in. Refused to panic.

Had Farak finished with Adajin and come her way yet? The late morning sun still clung to the eastern sky. Was that too soon? They were supposed to meet down the street from Rana's as soon as he kowtowed to the street lord properly, and she was nearly there. If he was close by, he'd have an eye on her, even if she couldn't see him, which meant it was best she stay put until he came to her.

Though if he wasn't here, she'd be wasting time as trouble approached. And did she even want him there with death looming closer than ever? Her mission to escape her curse and his said no, but deep inside, she knew the real answer.

Her finger twitched toward her fat pouch and the blue Finder burier nestled within. She had only ever used it once, the day her mother died—as was custom—and Farak had appeared, a child just like her, having left his own mother and family to follow its path back through the desert and right to her. She could do the same now . . . prick her finger and activate it with her blood, then send it scurrying to his location. But that would also force him into another eternal compromise, and she told herself she'd never do that to him again.

Zarina left the burier where it lay and scooped a handful of hot sand, then flung it to the side. Sure, she had been miserable the last seven years, but Farak being back made her life—and death—far more complicated.

And what about the foreigner? He had saved her with his uncle earlier, but a street brawl and god-driven killer seemed hardly within his capabilities. Useless. She needed to focus on getting out of the streets without getting lost in the fray. If the assassin was about, he'd be coming directly for her.

She eyed the passersby carefully through her pink lenses, but what was she even looking for? Her assailant had worn black in port, but that narrowed things down not a wit. She focused on the faces in the crowd, looking for evil eyes or crooked noses—she had always pictured the line of her family's oppressors as people with big, oddly bent sniffers. It was the only taste of justice she could muster.

Thick fingers slid over her shoulder in a tight grip. She yelped and scrambled forward. Dread squeezed her heart. A second hand snaked around her other arm and held her back. Panic crept up her neck and cut off her breathing. She writhed and twisted, trying to break free.

"Zarina," Farak chided, "hold still."

The death grip on her shoulders transformed into stays of safety. She relaxed her muscles and let a crouching Farak pull her to him. She took a deep breath of his jasmine and reeds.

"Are you hurt?" He turned her around and scanned her puffy robes with a critical eye.

"I'm intact and flesh-wound free, but I lost Rana in the crowds."

With Farak around, the knots in Zarina's muscles loosened. He was too comfortable, too capable. She couldn't help it, and her heart tightened with guilt and burned with anger. Why did her Guardsman have to be him?

Farak's keen eyes flickered over every person, every cart, barrel, and cranny near them. "Coming to the market was a bad idea."

"Was it?" She tucked her hand in a pocket and pulled out a leather bag that tinkled with coins and bulged fatly around the middle.

"Rana came through?" He nodded appreciatively. "She could sell sand in the desert."

"Would I waste my time with a *tāgir* who couldn't?"

"No. Now, stop distracting me." Farak turned his attention back to the streets. "We need to focus on how to get you out of the market, or it won't matter how heavy your pouch is."

"What's going on, anyway?" Zarina asked. "I heard a shot, and everyone started running."

"Adajin."

Zarina growled. "I was worried all this time about being murdered by a skilled assassin when, in reality, it will be at the hands of a clunky street gang? Adajin will not leave my life be. You have no idea how infuriating it is to have every moment of your life ruled and ruined by an entitled and hapless idiot."

Farak shot her a heavy-lidded glare, his mouth smooth and straight, ungiving.

She swallowed and looked away. The contempt in his eyes could not be for her.

She pressed the issue at hand. "What does Adajin want, anyway? Is my fortune so poor, I stumbled upon a street war while trying to avoid an assassin?"

"This is no street war. It's targeted. Aggressive. Personal."

She swallowed hard, her heart rate picking back up. "He can't know about his dead men already."

"He could if I told him."

"Farak!" She clenched her hand into a fist, forcing it to stay by her side. "Why would you do that?"

A group of harried women jogged past, their robes flapping behind them in the desert heat. The street was almost clear now. Maybe she should have gone with the crowds.

"I had to tell Adajin something when I came back alone." He dropped his voice to a whisper. "Two on your left."

Zarina peered over the wooden stall. Sure enough, a couple of squinting men trudged down the street, scanning crevices and kicking over barrels. She ducked low and craned her neck around a nearby stack of crates.

"Three more coming up on the right," she whispered. "And you could have told him the two men left for Graeco, taking the treasure for themselves."

"He'd find the skiff the men and I took outside Luxor. I wasn't going to risk my neck for—for a flimsy alibi. We're outnumbered and overpowered; what do you want to do?"

His words belied his truth. It was *her* he didn't want to risk his life for.

She sunk to the sandy earth, leaning her back against the splintery wood of the sun-bleached cart. Several color-splashed scarfs slipped down next to her. Why couldn't she have hidden behind a stall selling something more useful? She picked one up and let the smooth fabric slip through her fingers. Nothing in her life ever went right. Not even Farak. How could he have betrayed her so easily?

The smooth silk danced between her fingers, unnaturally pink. Her rosy goggles sharpened the dark creases in the folds instead of accenting the bright. The light.

She was a hypocrite.

Wasn't Farak betraying her exactly what she wanted? Maybe not *exactly* . . . .

She had hoped all those years ago that he would abandon his obedience to the curse by choosing to be with her. He had gone a different route, had denied the gods' decree that he always protect her but never love her by stabbing her in the back. At least he got the second part right.

But what did that mean for the curse? Farak had taken an active step of defiance. Did he think he could fight the gods? The thought was ridiculous. As desperate a hope as her mother's had been to find a family. As Zarina's had been seven years ago.

There was no fighting fate.

That didn't stop every bit of her insides stinging with pride, burning with rejection.

"You're right, Farak." She forced her voice steady. "Good call."

He raised an eyebrow. "You were just sinking your fangs into me, and now you're agreeing?"

"I am many things, Farak."

"Like fickle?"

She rolled her eyes at him. "But I mean what I say. I told you when I left that I wanted you to be free. Though, I would have liked your newfound freedom to have come without a betrayal." She did nothing to hide the sadness in her eyes.

His bottom lip twitched, and the sun-marked creases in the corner of his eyes grew deeper. "I cannot be your friend, Zarina. I should never have been in the first place. But for curse's sake, I'm on your side here. Trust me on that. Now, what do you want to do?"

Her crimson lenses amplified every muscle tick in Farak's face as he broke her spirit. She plucked at the scarves next to her sweat-soaked robes. What did running matter, anymore?

"We will fight off the street gang," she said, clutching the purple of a blue scarf.

"Terrible idea."

"I didn't ask for your opinion." The words came out sharp, hard, but that didn't matter. Reconciliation was off the table. "It is only temporary—a way to clear a path so I can leave Alexandria. Get up. We'll charge left, try to break through the two men before the three on the other side catch up."

"You mean six."

She jerked her head right. The group of men had assuredly doubled. "*Ya dahwety.*" Could she catch a break for once? "Fine, six. Ready?"

"Zarina." Farak used his commanding voice--the one he pulled out when he thought she was being particularly impetuous and needed correcting. But he was neither her friend nor her royal guardsman, and she would listen to him no longer.

"*Wahid,*" she said, beginning the count.

"Please, don't."

"*Itnan.*"

"You're *Majnun.*" He pulled out his curved kilij and crouched into a running stance.

"*Talata.*"

They jumped up from behind their cart and barrelled toward the thinner part of the street. Her feet faltered. Farak, too, slowed. The two men in the street before them lay face-down in the filthy sand. A deep red circle soaked into the back of each of their white robes, unmistakably gruesome despite the merry orangey-pink of her goggles.

"What happened?" She eased toward the first man and toed his hair with her boot.

Farak spun around, but the six men from the other side of the avenue were also down in a pool of blood.

His voice broke the eerie silence. "Run."

Zarina scooped up the hem of her robes and bolted down the nearest alleyway. Farak ran an arm's length behind her.

"Take the next left," he said from behind. "We will head for Rana's and hide there."

She shook her head. "I can do this myself."

"Don't be foolish, Zarina. I know this city far better than you and—" He growled. "You missed your turn."

Zarina kicked her feet heavily into the sand as she ran. Stinging pride aside, she couldn't afford to ignore his advice, not when her life rested within reach of the viper's strike.

"Ten paces more, then left," Farak guided, his voice tighter this time, challenging her to disobey, begging her not to.

She crushed her teeth over a retort and nodded, giving a number to every footfall. "*Wahid. Itnan. Talata. Arba'a. Hamsa.*"

But the number six parched away in her mouth. At the end of the street, blocking her from the safety of Rana's shop—a hooded figure blotted out the sun.

"Farak," She tried to scream, but only the husk of a whisper escaped her lips.

She grasped for her dagger. Her throwing stick. Anything. But the robes were too thick. The coarse folds too many. She dodged left into a narrow crevice between two shops. Farak sprinted past her and dead-on toward danger. The assassin took flight down the emptied street, not wanting to clash with Farak's size and strength dead on.

Zarina wiped sweat from her eyes. Why did Farak do that? His wages for the day weren't worth this. She breathed heavily, catching half-breaths. Cold stone pressed into her back and stomach from the walls, cooling her nerves.

His life was not worth risking for a sickly, selfish, ungrateful girl. He must know that. That's why he betrayed her, why he didn't want to be friends. She had to fix it. To stop him. To accept her fate on her own.

Zarina slid back out into the blinding light of the sun and dashed down the street. She stumbled and tripped on her robe, pushing past the frustration. If only she had time to take these dreadful things off. But she couldn't stop. She had to have a hand in her fate, had to free herself from being indebted to someone who despised her, otherwise, the weight of that guilt would send her straight to Ahmet the moment she met her fate.

Ahead, Farak dodged and weaved among the stalls, chasing the assassin. The few people left in the streets scattered from their path, barring doors and slamming windows shut. The black-cloaked killer had the upper hand despite Farak's bulk, always one step out of his reach and moving faster than lightning.

What if she could round the assassin off from the other side? If she ran fast enough and took the side streets, she might make it. That is if her feeble lungs could hold up long enough.

Zarina ducked left, running as fast as her feet would carry her, across and up, racing to get ahead of the assassin and Farak. Every opening into the streets she passed revealed a shot into their melee.

A glinting dagger-fling at Farak.

His hands trailing the dark cloak.

A stumble.

A dash.

The spilling crash of lemon crates.

Her lungs squeezed smaller, shortening her breaths. Would she get ahead in time? Too much farther, and they'd all be into the lower burrows: a section of the city that twisted into an impossible maze.

Another glimpse into the streets saw Farak and the assassin clashing dagger on sword. A delay. A halt in their sprint. She would make it to the end of the street on time, but what was her plan? Throw herself at the mercy of the assassin? She wasn't suicidal yet.

Zarina turned into the final alleyway where a dozen cages filled with hooting baboons lined the shaded side. She dodged the first set of bared fangs and skidded to a stop. Horrible beasts. Horrible and ugly and for once of use.

She grinned and grabbed a handful of hot sand, then poured the tiny granules over the first lock. Next, she took out one of her metal buriers and let it loose into the rusty opening. Over and over, Zarina repeated the process until a dozen clicks from a dozen locks pocked the air.

Zarina scooped her buriers back into her pouch and dug her throwing stick from her robes. Then, she braced herself and, with a deep breath, gripped the top baboon cage. Pink-tinted teeth gnashed at her fingers, and she flinched. Baboons were nothing but blue-butted bad tempers filled with disease, and she was counting on that.

Zarina gave the cage a push. The wooden shell clattered against the others and knocked locks free to the ground. In a crescendo of hoots, the baboons burst from their cages like rats from a bag of wheat.

Rabid beasts scattered in every direction, snarling and grunting. Zarina raised her throwing stick and screamed, corralling them toward the streets ahead.

One turned and eyed her with hungry rage. She growled back and swung the jagged end of her silver stick, hoping to scare it off. The baboon snarled. She swung again, heart pounding. She refused to die at the hand of such a nasty creature. Why did Ra consider them sacred? Maybe because they were more like her than she cared to admit: Cursed.

With rebellion bursting from every pore, a great part of her wished for the fangs to attack so she could beat out her rage. The mangey primate screeched. She did, too, pouring out all her frustration at life and Farak and the curse of her bloodline.

The baboon lunged.

She tried to swing but was too slow. Instead, she fell back into the dirt and braced herself, using the throwing stick as a shield to keep it back. Its dirty fangs wrapped around the metal. Rotting flesh and mangos soaked its breath. Sweat stung her eyes, sharp pebbles her back.

The throwing stick slipped in her fingers. Could she hold the baboon back with just one arm?

The creature hissed, hairy fingers grabbing at her braids in answer to her question: she'd have to.

She pried the first thick finger free before giving up and using one of her hands to dig for her dagger, but the ruby hilt was too far down, strapped tightly to her thigh. She tried for her pouch next. Her muscles shook. Her stomach clenched, revolting against the rotting breath. She reached inside the leather bag and pulled free a smoke bomb with a gasp, unable to see the color. There was no way she could cover her mouth and nose, so she took a deep, baboon-tainted breath and threw the sphere hard against the primate's red nose.

The naphtha bomb exploded in a spray of lotus pink.

The baboon shrieked, falling back and clawing at its nose. Blood leaked from its nostrils. Its black pupils dilated.

Zarina flipped over and jumped to her feet. She swung one last time with a cough, then left the shrieking animal. Tears streamed from her eyes, and the smell of flowers and chemicals made it hard to breathe. She wiped her face over and over but kept moving forward. Thank Babi that hadn't gone worse, but now she needed to find Farak.

She rubbed aching ribs and stumbled as she tried to catch her breath. A yell—Farak's—sounded around the corner.

Of course, not even a narrow escape from the blood-thirsty and putrid fangs of baboons earned her a rest. She gripped her throwing stick tighter and dashed around the corner. The edges of her vision blurred—the pink powder and lenses making for painfully vivid scenery.

Four baboons circled Farak, the others hooting and scurrying over and under the stalls that lined the street. Her pulse quickened, and dread scraped the bottom of her empty stomach. Her brilliantly stupid plan could be what killed Farak in the end, not the curse.

And where was the assassin?

Eleven

Zarina darted down the dusty Alexandria streets toward Farak, hoping to distract the baboons and give him a chance. She was close enough to hear their raspy grunts when the horrible sound of shattering wood caught her ears from behind.

Zarina spun around, kicking up dust. The hooded figure was like the desert's night sky—dark and enveloping and dizzyingly real. She swallowed hard. He must have slipped around the other side of the alley after the baboons flooded the streets. So much for her brilliant plan. The only thing she accomplished was separating herself from the one person who could protect her.

The hooded man pulled out a gun. Her heart seized. *Ya kharaashy.* A throwing stick was worthless in a gunfight. Her dagger equally futile. And her bombs? Her weak lungs were still coughing up the last one, vision blurring around the edges.

She spun her stick round and round, faster and faster so the crooked end blurred in a whirl of glinting sun. Maybe she could distract him? Bide time until Farak showed up?

Or not.

The dread in her stomach threatened to hurl out of her mouth. He was fighting another wild battle in the street behind her and hated her guts. She was on her own, as she should be when meeting her end. As her mother and grandmother had been before her.

The assassin raised the barrel and locked its sites on her. A gloved finger slid onto the trigger. Her courage shifted like a desert storm. She threw the stick with a grunt. It flew through the air before scuffing the dusty streets and rolling with a clatter in front of the assassin. Not even close. The assassin looked down, the infuriatingly small tip of his nose peeking out of the hood.

It had to be now.

She charged at the figure, her feet slipping over loose earth. Too loose. Her feet lost their grip and tripped over her robes. She landed with a thud and the ripping of fabric. Her face smacked the earth, and her lenses shattered. Pain radiated up her nose, welling in her eyes. Little pieces of pink glass brushed her sealed lashes and sunlight speckled her inner eyelids with blots of purple and blue, white and bright.

If her fate wasn't sealed before, it was now.

She covered the back of her head with her hands and tensed in expectation as the warmth of blood trickled out of her nose.

"Ahrrraaa!" A cry echoed above the distant hoot of baboons and her own heavy breathing.

A *bang* cracked the air, and she recoiled.

Waited.

No pain. No stick of blood.

The angry sound of scuffling and heavy blows tumbled down from further up the street. She tried to look. Sun scalded her eyes, her brain. She smashed her eyes shut and felt her way forward, turning into what she hoped was the side of the alley and heading for cover. Her finger caught a sliver of wood. She pulled it back in a prick of pain. Then, pushed forward until the cool shade of a merchant's cart eased the headache behind her eyes.

Zarina fumbled for her pouch. She needed to see. To get back in control. Her fingers trembled, and she dropped the first lens she pulled free. Then the second. She cursed and gripped the third tightly until she popped it into the frame of her goggles. Moss green. It would do, though the verdant tints were better for lower light. She fumbled for another and snapped it into the other side. A lighter green, the shade of lime. Good enough. She squeezed the bridge of her nose to alleviate some of the pain and looked up.

Pale, sweat-streaked skin. Disheveled hair. Glasses sitting askew on a stark Britannian nose.

"Richalala?" She blinked through the uneven hues softening the light. For the love of Nut, why couldn't she remember his given name again?

"Richard." He pushed up the glasses, breathing in short, heavy gasps. "Are you okay?"

She nodded, scanning the street for trouble. "Where did the assassin go?" She swallowed the fear and dusty saliva building up in her mouth and glanced at him. "And why are you here?"

"You still hadn't said goodbye." He bent over and spit blood, pain shading his normally smiling face.

"You're bleeding." She jumped up and ran to his side.

His nose wept, a river of blood following the dip of his lips and coating his teeth in iron. Several bruises marred his cheekbones, and—her stomach twisted—blood poured from his now punctured shirt. Her mixed green lenses made the bright red two shades of awful brown, and she swallowed down her shaken nerves.

He saved her, this foreigner from the cold of Europa. He owed her no debt, no allegiance.

So why did he risk his life for her when she could barely remember his name?

Zarina hesitated, her hands hovering uselessly around his side. He needed help. A doctor, maybe. But the only *almaealij* she knew of in Alexandria worked from a ship in port. Too far. She tucked her hands deep into her robes and untied the silk scarf she'd pocketed from earlier. She whipped it out with a flourish, bit her lip, and pushed it over the ragged cotton of his shirt.

His breath caught. He reached for his side, his hands sliding over hers, skin on skin and skin on silk.

She blushed but held firm. She owed him this much, no? Holding his blood in was the least she could do after he kept hers from spilling all over the street. Their shared heat was that of survival.

She should offer thanks or something. But what? She'd never given more than a slap on the back to Farak before.

"Ouch," Richard said, the twisted form of a smile plucking at his lips. "If you push any harder, you're going to do more damage than the picket ball wedged in there."

"Picket ball?" she asked, nose scrunched.

"It was a joke. The pain's so bad, I think the bullet's still in there, is all," he offered a strained smile.

Zarina flinched, slipping her hands out from his. She should really inspect the wound, but that sounded too close, too intimate. "Sorry. I, uh . . . I'm not used to caring for other people. It's usually the other way around. The whole princess thing, you know . . . ." She trailed off and looked away. She sounded despicable.

"Right." Richard winced another grin and slid to the earth, his back against the alley wall.

Cold sweat poured from his hairline, and his skin waned closer and closer toward translucency. Port or not, she had to get him to a doctor. She had to save him. The curse of death was hers, not his.

Another cry scratched the silence in the streets behind her. She jerked her head around, and adrenaline banished the shakes racking her hands. Farak. She had forgotten about him. About the assassin and the baboons.

Zarina took a step toward the street and stopped. She owed Richard her life, and by saving hers, he might lose his own. But the same stood true for Farak. Her heart ached, but as she battled the logic and debt of heart and hand, her soul's habit was with Farak.

"Stay there," she said.

She shot the Brit an apologetic look, grabbed her throwing stick, and bolted out into the sun-glazed street. At the end, where the lane turned into chaos, a bloodied Farak knelt on one knee. Black robes lay splayed upon the ground before him. Empty.

"Farak, are you okay?" Her pulse quickened as her feet slowed.

Blood poured from his shoulder, but his skin was still the warm olive it always had been. Some of the pain in her liver eased. The assassin was gone, vanished once more, and with him, their only chance at keeping the upper hand. But hope etched the edges of her searing headache. If the robes fell, maybe Farak had seen the face of whoever hunted her. Maybe, after over a thousand years of her family running, she'd finally have a face, a name, to put with her curse.

Her feet crunched on the coarse sand as she approached Farak from behind. He dropped the cloak and scooped his satchel from the street, hastily shoving its spilled contents back in. She stooped to help, grabbing stray foxfire beads and tinkering tools, a greasy rag, and his flask—though she was tempted to throw that one in the gutter.

The blue sheen of a scarab that looked almost like her own cerulean burier caught her eye. Its brass legs wriggled in the air as it tried to flip over. After two attempted flips, the mechanical beetle succeeded and began its journey toward Farak. Zarina reached for the bright metal, and he snatched it away with a look that could kill.

She had messed up this time. With the baboons and port.

"Farak . . . ." His name stuck in her throat.

He shoved the contents back in the leather pouch and turned his back to her. Blood dripped down every taut ripple in his muscles. Her liver ached, and she stood, taking a few steps back.

Silence ticked between them, heavy and loud. The sun beat hot rays upon her hair.

She cleared her throat. He froze on his knees, only his fingers tying his bag back onto his belt. A baboon bite wept on his shoulder, the flesh jagged from yellowed teeth.

Her fault.

Wasn't everything?

"Farak." Her tongue parched in the heat, but she muscled the words out. "Thank Ra you're okay. I mean, not okay. You're bleeding, but otherwise . . . ." She faded off, then tried again. "That's the assassin's cloak, isn't it? That means you—you saw him, right?"

A slight dip in Farak's head told her he heard what she said, but he gave her nothing more.

"Farak . . . ." She bit her top lip and reached a hand out to touch him before pulling back. "Why aren't you celebrating? You chased away the assassin and saw who it was. There hasn't been a break like this in a thousand years!"

Dusty wind tugged at his hair, accentuating his rigid body and silent lips.

"Farak... Say something. Give me *something*. Why are you being so quiet?"

He whipped around and onto his feet in one fluid motion. "You just attacked me with a pack of raging monkeys. Let me breathe!"

"I—I was trying to help," she said weakly.

"Help?" he growled, his hand squeezing the strings of his pouch. "Does it look like you helped?"

"I—"

"Why would you run toward the very person trying to kill you, you foolish woman?"

She bristled. "To take responsibility for myself for once. And because at that moment, the assassin was trying to kill *you,* not *me.*"

"One always leads to the other."

"Then tell me what you saw!" She stomped up to him and stabbed his chest with her finger, head tilted all the way back to see his face towering over her. "Tell me about the assassin so I may know who hunts me and stop them."

"Stop them?" he sneered before his voice dropped and he looked away. He rubbed the bridge of his nose and sighed. "You can't dam the Nile without flooding the plains."

"What in Nut's name does that mean?"

He snapped his gaze back to hers, eyes intense. "It means when you try to defy fate haphazardly, you make everything worse. For everyone."

It was what she had feared all along, that her desire to escape the will of the gods was only hurting others.

Zarina took a step back, his words burrweed on her heart. "Are you saying I should hop on the soonest boat and pick up Ahmet on the way to death?"

"Of course not," he scoffed, wrinkling his nose. "I'm saying we can't do things impulsively. We have to think. Make a plan. It isn't just the gods who watch your every move."

"How can I make a plan when you won't tell me what you saw of the assassin?" She spat the words, anger bubbling up. "Why are you being so cagey? You'd tell Adajin if he asked. You tell him everything."

"Don't be petty, Zarina."

"Tell me what you saw!"

They stared at each other, the faint rustling of the braver citizens poking their heads out to see if the danger had passed.

Farak broke first, turning away from her with a sag in his shoulders. "I saw nothing."

"Lies," she countered. "You had the cloak. You—I know you saw something. If not his face, then his clothes or weapons. A mark on his skin, the color of his hair. Something!"

"I saw nothing," he snapped, hand brushing the handle of his kilij.

Her eyes widened.

So did his.

Uneven footsteps crunched behind her. Blood froze in her veins, and she whirled around, brandishing her silver stick.

"Woah." Richard put up his hands in defense.

"*Ya msebty el sowda.*" Zarina threw her stick at him. He ducked, and the metal landed just past him in the street with a muffled *clink*. "You are the most forgettable man in the entire world. Stop appearing out of nowhere."

The sun highlighted the sickly hue of his skin, and her stomach dropped. She shouldn't be so callous to him, not after what he did for her.

She tried again. "Are you sure walking is a good idea?"

She took a small step toward him, not wanting to distance herself too much from Farak. He held the secret of the centuries whether he would admit it or not, and she would keep an eye on him at all costs.

Richard smiled something weak and leaned against a baboon-ravaged fruit stand. "Just getting my blood pumping. Though that may be the wrong move right now." He swayed slightly and pressed his fingers into the sun-bleached wood. "Is that an actual throwing stick?"

He bent down feebly and scooped up her weapon so he could hold it just below a squinting eye. "Fascinating. This looks authentic. Another heirloom like that bracelet on your arm? You know, I've read that these are essentially useless in battle. I suppose I'd have cause to worry if I were a duck or other small creature. Though yours has an interesting pattern cut into the end. I haven't seen that before."

Zarina adjusted her mismatched goggles. Was he making fun of her or had he lost too much blood? It didn't matter, she still owed him a debt and tempered her tone with begrudging gratitude. "I just used that useless stick to chase away a bloodthirsty baboon. And now isn't the time to be talking about heirlooms."

"I can shut him up for you," Farak offered venomously.

"Sorry." Richard's wide smile fell into something sheepish. "I get that a lot. I tend to go on and on when I find something interesting. And you," he said, with a spark in his pained hazel eyes, "are utterly spell-binding." He held her gaze before turning with a faint blush that only made him look paler. He readjusted his glasses with a red-stained hand and cleared his throat.

Farak's muscles tensed into rocks between his shoulder blades. "If you came here to woo a princess, you're desperately out of your league."

"Actually, I came to offer my services."

Zarina snorted. "Services? You're a bleeding man from Europa, what could you possibly offer the heir of Aegyptus?"

"Information." He pulled his shoulders back with a hint of pride she hadn't yet seen in his overly-green eyes, then quickly winced from the effort. "As a highly respected foreigner, I know everybody who knows everything about everybody else. And whoever I don't know, my uncle does. You clearly rubbed someone the wrong way. Let me help you figure out who and offer you protection and finances in the meantime."

Zarina studied the peculiar man with shrewd skepticism. He spoke in fancy and flattering words, but many eager scholars had come searching Aegyptus for ancient secrets before, all of whom valued the information in her brain more than they did her.

"Why would you do this for me?" she asked.

"Hm? Why else?" he asked as casually as if they were discussing the ever-constant weather. "Because I like you and you need help. That's what friends do, right?"

His words, so painfully simple, heated the sands of her heart into jagged glass. *That's what friends do.* Which is why Farak wished they never had been.

"Your information will do little good if you die in the marketplace," Farak sneered from behind.

Zarina shot him a glare. "Not everyone has boozah on hand to wash away their blood or brains."

"I'm happy to share." He strode forward and grabbed Richard by his one good shoulder, then ripped back his shirt. Using his teeth to pop the cork he poured it over Richard's wounds.

Richard gasped.

Farak barked out a laugh. "It's a mere flesh wound, yet this Euro whines more than a dog with worms for a belly."

Zarina clenched her jaw and pushed Farak aside, but what he said was true. No bullet lay lodged in Richard's skin or muscle. It must have just missed his shoulder, grazing skin as it went. How humiliating.

It was the final confirmation, the grain that tipped the scale. If Richard made Farak upset, she would keep him around. Ensure the gulf between Farak and his curse only widened and spite him in the process. It was perfect. If he wanted nothing to do with her, she would make sure it was clear she felt the same way.

"I accept." She snatched her stick from Richard's hands and tapped it against her palm.

"You can't be serious?" Farak turned to face them. "We don't have time to waste on this—this—suited centipede."

"Rana likes him."

Farak's face fell and with it what was left of her heart. Something *had* happened between those two; that was as clear as the dimple in Farak's chin. But what? A deal gone bad? A romantic tryst? Her steely heart twinged at the thought. Not that she cared. She couldn't care.

Zarina clenched her fist around her throwing stick, the metal warm from her touch. After everything that had happened between them, weakness still ate at her resolve. Death by assassination was beginning to seem like a mercy.

Yells wafted down the street, stirring her cooling blood. Farak's soft features hardened.

He rotated his bleeding shoulder. "More of Adajin's men. You need to hide."

"When do I not?" she muttered.

"What?" Farak asked, popping open his flask.

She glared. "Are you seriously going for the boozah right now? A little bit of action never used to make you drink in the past"

He glowered back at her and doused his wound in the smelly liquid, stoic despite the sting. "*You* are why I drink."

She ground her teeth. "Come on, Richard, Rana's shop is around the corner and up the street. Hopefully, she's found safety there and can help us hide."

"Yes ma'am," he said, half saluting her.

She turned on her heels and sprinted down the street, then stopped when she remembered his current state. She came back and looped an arm under his, staring pointedly at Farak. Then she hobbled with him down the street. Farak lingered behind. Would he follow? Her stomach sank with every footfall. He hadn't been wrong back in the tombs. Farak was a wild cannon now, someone she didn't recognize.

After a moment more of worry, Farak's heavy footfalls caught up, releasing a knot in her side she hadn't realized was there.

"You should leave Rana out of this." He turned his hardened gaze on her, his steps in time with her own.

Any trace of hope remaining in her stomach soured. "I am not the curse, Farak, though you seem to think I am." Her bitterness seeped out through clenched teeth. "And I will involve Rana if I want to. I need her."

"It is not your birthright to use people, Zarina. If you need to treat someone like their life doesn't matter, have it be me."

His words spilled like sand into every crevice of her heart, slowing its beats and turning her steps into sludge. "You think so little of me," she said, "and after I tried to save you." His judgment, his disapproval of her was too much. It had always been. "It is not using her if she wants to help. But since *you* so obviously feel used, you're free to go."

She untangled herself from Richard and took a bold stance. Farak took a step back, the street dusting his shoes with the unexpected stop. She met his challenging stare and pulled several gold coins from her pouch, then threw the money at his feet. They *clinked* to the earth, the largest rolling in a spiral until the image of Cleopatra lay face down in the dirt. It was far more than he was owed, but she didn't care.

He looked at the coins. At her.

She squared her shoulders and choked out the words. "Your services are no longer needed."

"You're dismissing me?" he whispered. "After the assassin, the baboons—You're casting me off... again?"

She turned her back to avoid the crushed look in his eyes, to lessen the pain slipping down her throat and filling up her heart. If he had managed to see who the assassin was, the secret would go with him, but so would the anger between them, his choosing Adajin or Rana or anyone else over her again and again. Seven years had not been long enough to heal the wounds between them, and now they only grew deeper.

She didn't need the information, not for the price. Besides, she worked better in the dark. That had always been the case.

She crossed her arms tightly against her trembling chest and stared away from Farak and at the last of the baboons making a mess of a fish stand.

Over the growing yells of Adajin's men in the distance, the sand sifted and crunched behind her until Farak's heavy footsteps faded into nothing. She turned, the salt of tears threatening the corner of her eye. The gold coins she had thrown lay untouched upon the earth.

Dirty money, stained by the curse. Just like she was.

She turned back toward Rana's shop. "Come, let's go." She scooped Richard back up and headed towards Rana's, leaving the blood money in the filth where it belonged.

Twelve

Zarina dashed into the cool shade of Rana's shop. They needed to hide, and Richard was slowing her down. Adajin's men were breaking down doors and scouring every nook and cranny, and it wouldn't be long before they came there. No place obvious would keep her safe.

"Rana?" she whispered, a sudden anxiousness over the silence settling in her bones.

She jumped when Mekal landed on the table nearest her. He maued expectantly, and she placed a hand on his head to quiet him.

A door creaked.

Zarina moved to pull her throwing stick free, but a weak and raised eyebrow from Richard changed her mind. She did the quiet work of lifting her robes to reach her dagger. Richard blushed conspicuously and looked away from the bare skin of her legs. She pulled the ruby hilt free, her heart racing like the desert winds.

Was Rana here? Or someone far more nefarious?

Zarina placed one foot in front of the other and headed into the back room. A pitcher lay overturned on the table. The rug to the cellar lay kicked to one side, so she braced herself and grabbed the handle.

Wahid.

Itnan.

Talata.

She wrenched the door open. A spear thrust out.

"Woah!" Richard cried, pulling Zarina back.

She dropped to the floor, and the end of the spear splintered the wall just above her head.

Her attacker rushed out of the opening, and Zarina kicked her legs out. The person fell, the dark folds of a cloak spilling out over the wooden planks. She readjusted her hold on the dagger and jumped behind the assailant. In one fluid motion, she thrust the attacker firmly on their knees and put the blade to their hooded throat. A victory, at last. But against who?

"*Nuur?*" Rana's voice trembled.

"Rana?" Zarina yanked her dagger away and took a step back.

A thin, shaking hand pulled the hood off shiny hair that smelled of lilies and jasmine. A blue-flower clipped back dark ringlets, Hathor's moon and horns glinting in the light.

Zarina released her and stumbled back.

What had she almost done? Now that the cut of fear had passed, she could clearly see the cloak was azure, not black.

"I'm so sorry," Rana said, her voice soft. "I thought you were Adajin. I stiffed him on some vases several moons ago and everyone knows he's been in a bad mood lately. I thought he may have heard that we are familiar and come to collect on his grievance. He hates no one in the city more than you. What did your ancestors do that his hate is so strong? I fear he will stop at nothing to find you. And me now, too, no?"

Zarina spun Rana around into a tight hug. "Nevermind all that. After we lost you in the market chaos, I've been so worried. *Eh akhbaar?*"

"All is well now that you're here, *dewa-net jer*," Rana said, twining her arms around Zarina.

She could feel the flat side of Rana's dagger pressing against her back, just as hers pressed into Rana's. They had both been prepared to fight to the death, to kill each other, thinking each was someone they were not. Even as they embraced, their blades still hung at the ready. Ra cursed her life with fear, and she had thrust that curse upon everyone else.

Would Adajin take his anger at her out on Rana like she feared? Would the assassin?

Maybe *she* was the curse.

Zarina's liver ached. She loosened her grip and pulled away.

"Farak said you were helpless in a fight without him." Rana's coy smile returned. "I see that that is not so true."

The reminder of the blood money left on the sand soured their reunion. "When did you speak with Farak about my fighting skills?"

"And you brought Richard?" Rana turned her hazelnut moons on him. "A pleasant surprise."

"Richard? Ah yes, that's right." Zarina twisted to where he stood behind her; her unlikely savior from an unfortunate spear wound and the assassin's bullet in the marketplace. She stepped up to him and focused on his face.

He blushed under her scrutiny, but she would not allow herself to forget his name again. Ever. Not if Rana could do it after just one meeting. She ran her gaze over the dips in his brows, the curve of his hairline, and noted how the different hues of her lenses cast each of his light eyes in a different shade of gemstone green. It had been years worth of sunrises since she had the desire to learn anything about someone else, much less remember it.

She searched her brain for something, anything to keep her from forgetting. "The end of your name sounds like *sharir*."

Richard raised an eyebrow. "What does that mean?"

"It's Arabic for evil."

He winced.

"Not that that means anything about you. You didn't name yourself, the gods did." She smacked the hilt of her dagger against her thigh as hard as she could. "Not that the gods think you're evil. It's not a sign or anything. It's just a way to remember your—" She sighed. She was just making things worse.

Screams echoed from the shop next door, and gruff men yelled orders. Wood cracked and glass shattered, along with their momentary sense of safety.

Death did indeed live in Zarina's shadow, but she could not mourn that fact right now. "Rana, we need to hide."

"Yes." She nodded solemnly and pulled her towards the back. "Come with me. We must hurry."

Rana led them into a back alley filled with barrels of grain and crates of foul-smelling ducks that quacked noisily at their approach. Zarina glanced behind them. Men poked their heads out of doors and yelled curses. She picked up her pace, pushing Rana faster, and pulling Richard along.

But with every footfall, Farak's words and the ghost of Rana's dagger on her back haunted her. Was she using Rana? Involving her selfishly in a fight that was not hers? They had saved each other long ago, but did that give her the right to risk Rana's life forever? Her pounding heart bled with the thought.

She clasped Rana's hands as they skittered between crates and dashed through doorways. "We should split up, Rana. You owe me nothing. You don't deserve this."

Their delicate fingers intertwined. "I'm not leaving you."

"They will find us in the streets no matter where you take us."

"I'm not taking you through the streets."

She rounded a corner and yanked Zarina and Richard into a dark storage room full of sharp-smelling spices and a heavy water urn that took up the entire space, its clay lid etched with flowers. With a wary glance at the doorway, Rana pulled free the same blue barrette from her hair and pressed its metal petals into the largest flower on the urn. The piece clicked into place, and the ground beneath them pulsed with a gentle hum.

Zarina shifted as the urn rotated backward, clay grinding sand until her nerves pushed through her teeth. The urn stopped just as suddenly as it had started, revealing a shadowy hole in the floor beneath.

A secret entrance into the dark. Zarina froze, fate teasing her, testing her, tempting her to defy it. To hide. To fight. To run. To stay.

She looked to Rana's wide, beckoning eyes and swallowed as the bellows of Adajin's men closed in.

Thirteen

Zarina hesitated. If this was a tomb, there could be gases that would make her weak enough for the assassin to squash her like a cricket. Then again, sick was better than dead. Richard placed a hand on her shoulder, and she took comfort in the small act.

For the first time in a decade, she had someone new to rely on, even if he couldn't quite be trusted.

"Down. Quickly," Rana said, shoving her toward the opening.

She inhaled one last lungful of dry, clean air, held her breath, and stumbled down into the dark. Richard breathed heavily behind her, and Rana's dainty steps entered last. Then, the grainy churn of sand boomed in the dark as the urn shut closed above them. Zarina blinked three times before a green-tinted flicker bloomed to her left.

She stood upon a narrow set of stairs that wound down and across, leading her further into the dark. Eerie gas lamps fluttered on as she passed, and the few foxfire beads in her pouch glowed a gentle blue that looked two shades of seaweed green. Already, she could feel the wheedling of an impending headache from the different hues of green. She should stop and find their matches, but that would have to wait until she made it off the staircase; the uneven steps and fall into a bottomless dark made a switch too risky.

She took each step carefully, running her hands along the smooth walls that curved precisely with each step. The work of a master craftsman, but not one from her family. She would surely know if that were the case. Had there been another ancient family of mechanists whom she didn't know?

Or was the machinery that sealed the entrances added after Aegyptus's first steamvolution?

"What is this place?" Richard asked.

Rana's voice rang clear in the quiet of the cave. "Ancient tunnels built below the city back when Alexandria was Rhacotis."

"Is that what the city was called before Alexander the Great took over Egypt?" Richard's voice pitched with excitement. "Fascinating. May I pick your brain, write an account of this place?"

"No." Rana's usually soft voice took on an edge. "You pick flowers, not brains. And very few know these tunnels exist. I expect you to keep it that way."

"How do *you* know they exist?" Zarina asked. And how come she didn't? The mystery only added to the pain building behind her eyes.

"My father. And his before him. You are not the only one with family secrets. These tunnels have been hiding truths and providing safe passage to my family for centuries. But mostly I use them for my other-market business. The entrances connect all over the city."

Richard ran his hand over the sandy wall next to a sconce. "Is that who maintains these tunnels? Your family?"

"Just me."

Zarina scrunched her nose. "Did you know about these when we first met? If so, why didn't we hide in them instead of barrels like dying fish?"

"My father only shared them with me just before he passed, a year after our meeting, *Nuur*. But these tunnels are not for playing."

In the silence that followed, Zarina blindly led the way down the narrow staircase. She had always assumed Rana was alone, but she had failed to think about her family or what they may have left her. She had also never thought to ask about Rana's father—or any father for that matter. Hers was just a bedtime story her mother told of the handsome rogue who lived in Cairo and put mischief in her eyes. To Rana, however, a father was someone real.

Zarina rubbed the tips of her fingers together, guilt nipping at her. She should have known more about Rana's family.

Then again, she couldn't even remember Richard's name. So what kind of friend did that make her?

If she watched carefully and strained her eyes in the dark, offshoots of different paths would appear to the left and right along the way, some clean of debris and well-worn, others covered in loose dirt, undisturbed dust, and nests of spiders. It made sense. One person could not maintain all these tunnels alone. But where did the well-trod paths lead, and why were some abandoned?

"How have you kept these tunnels hidden all these years?" Zarina's feet found the safety of the bottom floor and her muscles relaxed their grip on her bones.

"A mixture of family secrets and well-placed entrances below ancient water sources. The urn we entered through has been rooted to that spot for thousands of years."

Zarina tugged at the straps on her goggles. "Sounds like a lot of work for some empty caves."

"If they were empty caves, that would be true," Rana's soft voice scolded in the dark. "But a web of freedom through the entire city is a high-value commodity. Can you imagine what Adajin would do to this city if he found out about them?" Rana slid to the front and ushered her through a small opening to the left that hid in the dim light. "There are always men like him around. Men who cannot be trusted."

"Don't tell Farak, then," Zarina muttered.

"That is the second time you've mentioned Farak today, *Nuur 'in-naya*." Rana's round eyes glimmered in the stretch of light reaching from the lamp she held.

"He was with us just before we met up with you," Zarina turned, looking away from Rana's gaze. The headache growing in her temples wasn't just because of the light.

Rana's delicate voice guided them through a long tunnel that felt even darker. "But he was not with you when you arrived. You did not leave him in the desert again did you, *Nuur*? Only the gods can survive a snake bite twice."

"They had a fight," Richard told Rana from behind, unsettling Zarina's nerves. Even after he saved her life, she had not grown used to his presence. "About you."

Zarina cringed. Richard buzzed more than a bee. Distracted, she bumped her knee into a large wooden door tucked into the shadows that obstructed their path. Rana removed the flower pin from under her blue scarf and clicked open the moon-and-horns-shaped lock with a heavy twist of her wrist.

The room they entered sputtered to life, gas lamps casting shards of light upon intricately painted walls. Pharaohs, priests, and queens all dressed in white re-enacted events of life and death on every kirat of plaster around them. Animals and monsters, both real and horrifyingly imaginary, pocked the spaces between, with the Nile winding its way around the entire cavern.

Richard let out a low whistle.

"What is this place?" Zarina breathed out.

"A tomb long forgotten." Rana walked the perimeter, lighting the room as she went. "When the tunnels were built, my ancestors discovered many such places and incorporated them into the maze. We will rest here until the commotion on the streets has quieted. There's water in the urn on the left."

Zarina itched to take out her map and double-check the location. How could there be a tomb in Alexandria? Had the star rubbed off over time? Or were there other royal families that failed to survive fate's heavy-handed death sentence and frittered away into oblivion, their tombs and glory along with them?

"This is amazing," Richard said between excited breaths. He pushed the glasses up on his nose and dug out a pad of paper from his pants pocket. He licked the end of a pencil that appeared from some fold in his shirt and went to work copying the images laid out in the room.

Zarina ran a hand over a relief of Ra holding up the Singular Eye, Ramses the Great standing below him in a marsh. Painted figures flickered and danced in the light, six queens barely darker than the plaster lined up below, her ancestor, Nefertari, included. The principal wives of Ramses the Great were not uncommon sights in the tombs, but having them all together in the same image was something she had not seen before.

She blinked and dug through her pouch for new lenses, ever dependent on the colored glass to keep her headaches at bay. How could she read the walls if looking at them sent her mind reeling? She pulled the other lime green lens from her pouch and snapped it in place of the moss green, squeezed her eyes shut, then looked back up at the wall.

Ra and Ramses remained, but where there once stood six queens, the brush of the Nile took its place. And the Singular Eye had closed, now just the crescent of a setting sun. Zarina blinked. Squinted. Had she imagined it? She moved closer to the wall and leaned in, trying to detect traces of what she had seen. Nothing. No smudges or texture to indicate that something hid beneath. Did the green lenses make the difference?

Zarina dug a hand back into her pouch and pulled out the darker, moss-colored lens. She cast a wary glance at Rana and Richard, who leaned over the sketchpad together. Was she crazy for trying this? What did she expect to find? She popped the hilt of her dagger once. Twice. Then pushed the right side of her lime-green goggles onto her forehead and slipped the moss lens in front of her right eye. She sealed her left and gazed back at the wall through the improvised glass.

Nothing.

Just Ra and Ramses over the marsh. What was she missing? Or had the pressure from being chased by an assassin her whole life finally cracked her?

She switched, closing her right eye and opening her left, then looked again. Alone, they revealed nothing but painted reeds. But she hadn't been looking through one lens the first time she saw the queens. She had been looking through both. With a deep breath, Zarina kept the moss-green lens to her right and the lime goggles over her left and looked through both.

Once more, the regal shapes of six queens appeared, the rays of Ra shining on the left-most and the rays of Ramses on the right. The faint and flickering images pulsed and receded, and she closed her eyes to think as her hands went through the mechanical work of switching the moss lens permanently into place and pulling her goggles down once more.

This was no mental trick. Those images lay hidden, revealed only with two different lenses. Who left them? Other mechanists like her own ancestors? But that would indicate royal heritage—only the descendants of the pharaohs held the secrets of the steam and cogwork necessary to run in a cave system like this. Were there more clues hidden in other tombs? The tombs she had been visiting her whole life?

Zarina retrieved a glowing foxfire bead from her pouch. The soft, radiating wood shimmered against her fingers in the dim light of the tomb. She looked once again at the queens and pushed the bead against the top of the first's crown, pressing hard as she traced the lines down and over.

"*Nuur 'innaya,* I don't believe you're supposed to add your own art to the walls." Rana tsked at her elbow.

"This isn't my art. These images are already here. I can only see them with my off-colored lenses."

She finished with the feet of the sixth queen, took her goggles off, and stepped back. The women radiated blueish-green and hovered half a meter tall each like ghosts rising from the dead.

"The six primary wives of Ramses the Great." Richard touched his finger to the glowing lines left by the bead. "You're a genius to trace it in phosphorescence."

Rana leaned in close enough, her nose touched the wall and came off with a hint of glowing blue. "But why would the priestly craftsman hide the queens? They were beloved."

"I don't know." Zarina backed away. And why was Ra's light shining on one and Ramses' on the other? She had not traced that part of the mural with foxfire because it sat too high on the wall.

"Are there any other hidden paintings?" Richard asked, eager as a shepherd awaiting the arrival of lambs.

Zarina turned like a grain mill, slow and steady around the room, peering through her goggles. Every meter or so, she lifted her goggles off, checking for discrepancies.

"Here," she called when she reached the back wall. "Queens again, painted in a different hand. Only the six are paired up in two lines."

"Bloodlines, maybe?" Richard offered. He streaked a finger through the traced images on the first wall and rubbed the glow between his fingers. "Ramses married his first two wives, then a daughter from each after they passed. That would account for two of the pairings. The third set could be the two Hittite princesses Ramses received in trade negotiations to stop the wars."

Zarina huffed out the musty smell building up in her nose. The tomb seemed drafty enough, and Rana had clearly entered many times. The likelihood of toxins was low, but it still made her nervous. She focused on the mystery to keep the worry at bay.

Richard may be on to something. Nefertari's image lined up with her daughter Merytamun's, both well-known figures of her family tree. "Their need for ancestral purity is why I can't look at the light and why I have this infernally long, straight nose."

But the rest of her words fell away as she tilted her gaze higher. Above two sets of queens, Nefertari's included, hung a black upside-down boat with two lines descending, one short and one long.

The symbol of death. And off to the side nearest the final queenly set, cloaked in shadows, a serpent with a knife.

The vengeful god, Apep.

Richard placed his hand on her shoulder, and she jumped. "Are you okay?"

"I . . . ." What could she say to that?

The god that wanted her dead hunted her even in this random tomb under the earth. And if there were others—if more tombs held similar secrets—maybe they also held answers. Answers that could lead her to the man who hunted her. To the man who killed her mother. For once, she could hunt the hunter. It was something she had only started dreaming of when Farak caught the assassin's cloak. Maybe she could find the killer without his information. It was a taste of hope in the bitter cup of her life.

"*Nuur*, you are deathly pale. What is it?"

"Nothing." She clipped the word.

Rana puckered her lips. "I do not believe you, but I will wait. You always tell me your secrets in the end."

Why *was* she keeping secrets from Rana? Richard was one matter, a foreigner she just met. But Rana? Her friend of over a decade and trusted confidant. Seeing the images of the queens, the symbol of death, and the god who wanted her dead—it was all too much.

Indecision racked her tiny frame in trembling shivers. After everything she went through, after everything she had believed and felt and done, she had not been able to escape her fate. The selfishness of self-preservation reared its ugly head within her. Part of her wanted to tell Farak. Maybe he would know why this was here. Maybe his family knew of the secret tunnels already. His lineage was as ancient as her own and passed on their own sets of curses and secrets.

But the very thought of sharing anything with Farak sent her blood boiling. Even if he did have answers, he wouldn't tell her. He just lied about the assassin. He betrayed her to Adajin. The serpent, Apep, could kill him for all she cared.

Zarina gave a stilted nod. "Is it time to go up? The flickering lights in this room are wearing me down."

"I will see." Rana disappeared into the darkness of the tunnel they had come from.

"This place is amazing," Richard said as he sketched more on his pad. "Secret messages hidden by color pallet variations. I never would have dreamed. And I wouldn't have found them without you." Richard looked up from his pad and met her eyes. "You're amazing."

"Go back to your sketches." She waved him off, but his words hit something buried deep within.

Why hadn't Farak ever talked to her like that? It didn't seem so hard. Why could a stranger say nicer things than her childhood companion, her first love? Her heart pinched with the admission. She *had* loved him. She still did, in a beleaguered way. But he did not feel the same. His love had been his work, his calling, for that was all she was to him.

Rana's slender frame and petite, glowing nose appeared back in the room. "It has quieted. I would take you to a different entrance, but I feel I've already shown you too much. Let us go up and take our chances."

"Thank you, Rana," Zarina said, taking her friend's cool hand in her own. "For everything."

Rana's smile lit up the darkest corners of the tomb. "Of course. We owe each other that much at least, no? After all we've been through. Come, Richard." She swooped over to where he stood and plucked the pad of paper from his hands. "Oh my, it is lovely. Zarina, look."

"I don't have time," Zarina said, toeing the edge of the doorway. She needed to get above ground, to take what she'd learned and turn it into answers.

"*Nuur*, I insist."

Rana thrust the book in her face, and Zarina found herself staring into familiar eyes. Her own eyes. Richard had not been drawing the room, at least not the whole time. He had been drawing her. Heat bloomed in her cheeks and ran down her neck. She was supposed to be avoiding attention, not sitting still long enough for some Brit to sketch her likeness in detail.

Richard eased over and took the book back, tucking the creased pages into one of his many deep pockets. Despite her mismatched lenses and the poor lighting, she could see the blush on his cheeks.

He cleared his throat. "Zarina's right. We should get going. There's much to discuss."

Fourteen

—·—

The urn churned slower than a dry water spigot. At last, the hot sun of late afternoon crept into the dark where they lay hidden. Rana stepped out first, looking both ways down the street.

"The birds sing of safety."

Richard followed Rana out and stepped into the open air. "Seems she's right. Let me check 'round the corner just to make sure."

Before she could protest, he bounded down the street in a dust cloud, well-recovered from his minor flesh wound.

Zarina shook her head and shielded her eyes as she stepped into the dry heat. The sun was hot and hight, laughing at her. She bent her head and switched her mismatched greens for red lenses, then assessed the situation. After their fight, Farak most likely went to Adajin. She badly wanted to say good riddance. But something had occurred to her as she marched up the damp steps back into the land of her inheritance.

If she wanted to stand even the smallest chance at surviving her curse and protect those she cared about from getting hurt, she had to find the assassin before he found her. And to do so, she needed answers about the tomb she just discovered.

She refused to inquire further of Rana about the secret tunnels and hidden messages, not after she risked her life thrice this day alone in a fight that was not hers. And while Richard often sounded more like a book than a human, he seemed just as surprised about the caves as she. That left Farak, and she would rather die of thirst a hand's reach away from a cistern than ask him for help. So who else could possibly know of ancient secrets? Her stomach twisted as tightly as her braids.

The very same man Farak just returned to.

Rana's gentle hand came to rest on Zarina's shoulder. "What will you do now, *Nuur*? Alexandria has turned her back on you. You will not escape trouble here forever."

"I must seek the one who seeks me."

Rana raised a quizzical brow, worry creasing her round moons.

"Adajin."

"I do not understand." Rana's pout resurfaced. "The sun does not seek the moon, for if they ever met it would mean both their doom."

Zarina laid a hand on Rana's. "Something much darker than night hides in my shadow, Rana. Adajin knows where my family's hidden tombs are. How? He must have a source. Or family legacies like you and I. I do not know how he finds his knowledge, but it has to come from somewhere. And I need it."

"Is this about money?" Rana's usually sweet voice took on the hard edge of skepticism.

"No."

Rana's puckered lips flattened. "Then run. Get out of Aegyptus. Leave the desert and whatever ghosts haunt you. You can be free. Safe. You can stay alive. Please leave, for me." Her delicate fingers pressed into Zarina's skin.

Her plea strained Zarina's already weary heart. How badly she wanted to keep running, to take to the winds and never look back. But she did not believe for one sand granule that her fate would leave her be if she left Aegyptus. The gods were not bound to this desert alone, and vengeance was a force only quenched with blood.

She turned to Rana with heavy brows and an equally burdened heart. "I cannot. There is too much here. Too much of me, of everything I know. And I could not leave you, either," she added, trying to lighten the weight between them. "We are family."

"What is family?" Rana touched a finger to Zarina's lips. "I think you and I hardly know. Besides, you did fine these many seasons without visiting me at all, *Nuur*."

Her words stung, and Zarina bit her lip, pulling it back from Rana's gentle touch.

Rana sighed, a flower wilting under the desert sun. "Your life is not worth sacrificing for money or memories. Not for fame nor glory nor fortune. Not even for a bodyguard who does your bidding."

Zarina pulled her hand back and cast her gaze to the floor. How could she make Rana understand without bringing her further into the blackness?

"If you will not leave," Rana's voice grew impatient, hurried, "work with me. Join the other-market. *You* said we are family, yes?"

"Yes." Zarina met Rana's gaze and found desperation.

"Then forsake your cursed heritage and embrace mine. Truly be my family. A blood oath. Inseparable. I will even leave Aegyptus with you. We can take fate with a dagger and carve it into something our own."

"I can't." Zarina's chest ached, the gritty air of guilt crushing her down, down, down.

She reached toward her longtime friend, who pulled away.

"Rana, *ohkti*, you are my family. But I cannot poison your blood with mine, nor can I abandon my blood and the journey that lives within it to take on yours. And I can no longer put you in danger. You've already done enough. More than enough." She reached once more and caught Rana's soft hands before they could pull away. "I want you to be safe. I bring only danger. You must see this."

"Then you accept the fate the gods handed you without question?"

"I accept that my fate is mine alone to fight."

Rana's brown eyes flickered between softness and something much sharper. "Then it seems I cannot save you."

"No." Zarina sighed, and a pinch of guilt escaped. "But I can help save you from my shadow."

Richard popped around the corner, sweat soaking the fringe of his wildly curly hair. "We gave them the slip. None of Adajin's men are within a several-block radius. So what's the plan?"

"To find Adajin." Zarina pulled herself from Rana and straightened her shoulders.

"Wha—?" Richard shook his head. "But . . . didn't we just—?"

Rana brushed past Zarina and tugged at Richard's collar. "Yes, *Nuur* makes no sense, but her mind is made up. We are left in the dust behind her."

"Actually . . . , Richard can come if he wants."

Two sets of honey-brown and gemstone-green eyes flashed to her, and she shifted uncomfortably under the scrutiny.

"I simply can't put you at risk, Rana. But the Brits serve different gods than we do, and I need his resources." It was the truth, but it didn't change the look of betrayal on Rana's face.

Richard nodded, tapping his chin. "I'm not sure what fictitious deities have to do with anything, but rest assured, you'll be safe staying with me. Or, my Uncle William and me. We have gobs of rooms filled with nothing but mummies. You wouldn't mind sleeping next to one of those, right? And if Adajin is in control of the city, then a Brit official or two are being paid off somewhere along the line. My uncle will know who. Or will know the who who knows the who. Or the who who knows the who who knows . . . ."

Zarina stifled a groan as Richard carried on. She did not *want* to stay with Richard, even after all his kindnesses. He was still a stranger. And strange. But having the resources of someone unattached to Aegyptus's curses was an unexpected wind she could not overlook. These were peculiar times, indeed.

She swallowed her pride and looked to Rana with as much confidence as she could muster. "See, I'll be safe with Richard."

"It's improper," Rana said with a full-lipped pucker.

"Since when do we care about propriety? I spent my youth with no one but Farak. And you've had some adventures with him, too, I'd dare say." She shot Rana a forced grin, both relieved and hurt when the corner of Rana's lips tipped into the shadow of a smile.

Something, sometime, had happened between Rana and Farak, it was the only explanation. Why were they keeping it a secret?

"So, what do we do next?" Richard asked. "I've never been a rapscallion before. It's all quite exciting."

Zarina gave Richard a tight-lipped once-over. He was far from the always-ready, ever-formidable Farak, but his willingness happened to be exactly what she needed, even if it came with too many words.

She considered her options, the blue Finder in her pouch tempting her as it always did. If Farak was with Adajin, she could activate it with a prick of her finger and be off across the city in no time. But she would not use that tool of fate, not even to escape it. They would have to find another way to figure out Adajin's location.

She looked to Richard. "Is your Uncle still the man who knows every man?"

Richard nodded with a bright smile. "Sure is."

"Then we're going to need him to accomplish the next step."

"What's that?"

"To find and infiltrate a den of thieves and come out with answers."

Richard's skin paled to near transparency through her dark red lenses, but his resolve held. "What do I need to do?"

Fifteen

Zarina pressed herself into the rough plaster of the incense shop across the street from Adajin's headquarters. The soft blue hem of the headscarf Rana had lent her cut off the sky from view. The creamy fabric was a welcome change from the coarse black thing that had tripped her up in the streets. She chose only to wear a hijab this time, leaving her billowy pants and tight vest exposed to passersby. That, plus her goggles and their red lenses made for quite a site.

In port, it wasn't such a scandal with all the foreigners passing through, but deep into Adajin's traditional territory, her carefree attire drew stares. Still, it was worth the risk. Her disguise earlier that morning failed to protect her from the assassin, and she felt more comfortable being able to run when things went awry—which they always did.

Richard ambled across the street, the perfect hapless bystander stumbling into places he should not go. She held her breath and popped her dagger open and closed from its sheath. Would he look at her hiding place as he passed and blow her cover?

Would he flee like a crane before a croc?

At least his blustering about connections was no farce. He had found the location of Adajin's headquarters—his real one, not the front he put up for government inspections. Apparently, his uncle *did* know everyone worth knowing.

Richard strolled up to one of the guards, gesturing wildly with his hands. On cue, one of Adajin's men seized him by the front of his shirt. Richard flailed and kicked, stirring up a ruckus.

Zarina ducked under a passing cart full of fish. She kept her breaths short and quick to keep the tangy smell of tuna and hake from her nose and tongue. She scurried along, half-crouched, until she passed the scuffle and broke free down an alleyway on Adajin's side of the street. Hopefully, the rank smell wouldn't linger on her clothes. Rana wouldn't be caught dead hiding amongst dead fish and neither would the expensive hijab she loaned her.

Hidden once more in the shadows, Zarina headed around the back and slipped into the lackluster fortress with a barrel of garlic and a flustered cook.

"What are you doing here, street cat? Are those pants?" the cook tutted disdainfully, her ruddy cheeks puffing. "Disgraceful. Out you go. Shoo." The woman took up a flour-coated spoon and chased her around the barrel.

Zarina danced one pace ahead and pressed a finger to her lips to shush the woman, who lunged at her once more, but her bones were frail and her lungs filled with age. She panted, her lips pulled down by the sheer presence of scandal.

Zarina kept her voice low. "I'll be in and out, no problems." She bit the inside of her cheek. It was a mostly true statement, or it would be true if everything went according to plan.

She slipped a silver coin from her purse and held it up so it caught the light. The woman froze. Zarina reached across the barrel to press the cold metal into the woman's leathery hand. Would it be enough? Should she have gone with gold? The woman inspected the coin between two shaking fingers, bent to the floor, and hurried away. What was it with the help in Alexandria? So much loyalty to such terrible people until they had no loyalty at all. Were souls bought so easily?

She grabbed a drab apron and swung it around her waist. Maybe exposing her pants had been a mistake. Zarina wound through the bustling kitchen and out into an empty hallway that smelled of soured grain. She pressed her ear to door after door.

The barking yells of a perturbed Richard caught her ear from down the hall. They were coming from a room with an extra thick door whose wood had split in several places, parched from thirst. She pressed in and listened.

"Get off me," came Richard's muffled yells. "Do you have any potion of stew and lamb?"

Zarina frowned. That couldn't be right.

She teased the handle open, pushed the door a breath's-width. Through one crimson-tinted eye, she surveyed the room. Richard stood directly in front so she could see only his left side. Adajin sat before him, surrounded by a gaudy amount of guards, loot, and veiled women. A shameless display of power by such a tiny man. She scanned the menagerie of twisted faces that lined the walls. No sign of Farak.

Ya lahwy.

Adajin sneered cruelly at poor, battered Richard whose cheek shone a shade of red just lighter than the blood on his lip. "Do *you* have any notion of who *I* am? You're the one in my house."

"I didn't ask to come in. Your thugs—foozler and gibface here—took me against my will." Richard jutted his chin at the dim-witted muscle standing next to him.

Zarina smiled. So there was some oomph to Richard after all.

"Everyone knows you can't come this far into the city without running into the Lord of Alexandria. So if you weren't coming to see me, the question begs, who or what was worth risking the run-in?"

Zarina tensed, ready to flee. A gnarled feeling filled her belly. If Farak could betray her, anyone could.

Richard flashed his unflappable grin. "Why, a partnership of course."

She breathed a silent sigh of relief. Richard was sticking to the plan, trying to lure Adajin into a deal he couldn't refuse while she searched for the source of Adajin's inexplicable knowledge.

And it was working.

All the guards that would normally cause her trouble had slipped into the main room, wanting to see Adajin harass one of the foreigners—a quid pro quo for how hard the occupation of Britannia had made all of their lives.

Zarina removed herself from the door and turned to the locked room behind her. She blew sand into the keyhole and pulled out a digger.

"A partnership?" Adajin growled in a laugh that trickled out the cracked door behind her. "You drastically overestimate your weight in this country, my foreign friend."

Richard's voice came through clearly. "I could say the same for you. Sure, you have muscle who tame the streets, but there's a reason you haven't captured the port."

Adajin scoffed, and Zarina placed one of her brass diggers against the nearest gas lamp nested against the coarse wall. She cast searching glances up and down the hallway. It would only take a moment to heat the gears and get them moving, a moment she prayed she had.

"Your power ends at the water," Richard continued. "You need foreign contacts, protection from Britannia's intervention to get any farther. A few lowly police aren't going to help you cross the seas, no matter how many pounds you slip in their pockets. You see, we Brits have a terrible habit of sticking our fingers in all the pies."

A shuffle down the hall sent her pulse crashing. She slipped the warmed and wriggling digger into the lock and scurried into a shadowy recess, then sealed her eyes shut. Maybe if she couldn't see the danger, the harm would pass her by. It was how she coped, running and hiding from tomb to tomb with her mother. And it had worked—until Cairo.

The heavy footfalls of a guard passed. She squinted at his back, relieved his head was even thicker than his neck. She exhaled.

Ayyya. Too close.

She waited another moment then dashed back to the locked door. Her digger scuttled out of the keyhole with a soft scraping sound and landed in her hand. She tossed it in her pouch and grabbed the handle.

With a look both ways, she dashed inside. Her eyes struggled to adjust to the shadows. Her red lenses weren't right for this light, but she didn't have time to change. If things went right, she wouldn't be here long, anyway. She squinted.

A single desk sat at the far end of the dark room, its edges chipped and the varnish fading. She swung around the back side and ripped open the two drawers. Straining against the light, she leaned down farther. Shipping passes and rubber stamps filled the first—counterfeits to help get his goods into ships in the port. The second contained nothing.

She ran a hand along the bottom and frowned before her fingers found a catch. She smirked and dug her nails into the small dip, then pulled. Beneath a thin sheet of wood sat a map just like the one she inherited, little stars over family tombs hidden in the desert sands.

How did he have this? Only she and Farak carried maps like these that she knew of. Did his family have one, too? Or did Farak . . . ?

She pocketed the map and slammed the drawers shut without thinking, then winced. That would be a step too far, even for him. She double-checked the stone walls for any hidey-holes or secret chambers, then declared the room a wash.

She slinked back across the hall and took another peek at Adajin and Richard. A group of men traipsed in from a back door, their curved swords clanging. Their hulking leader was a sunkissed tan with fierce bronze eyes.

Her heart stopped.

Farak had gone full Adajin. She could not longer deny it.

Zarina bit back a grainy curse. Farak's natural ability to rise to the top of any ocean always left her feeling like she'd drown without him pulling her up. Only now, he wasn't offering his hand but kicking her down with his boot.

The clink of metal falling against wood told her the digger had finished, but she could not pull her eyes away. Farak knew she and Richard were working together, and the glassy coldness in his eyes was something she had not seen before. Something terrifying. She had not thought things through. Not well enough. Farak had always been the planner and her the one to never listen. Hadn't that been what happened in the streets?

Sweat beaded on her brow, her lip. Farak hated Richard. So what would happen to him, now?

"Farak," Adajin's icy voice beckoned her old bodyguard to the front. "Any news of the filthy marmoset causing problems in my city?"

Marmoset? Zarina scrunched her nose. Why did they keep calling her that? Adajin was nearly as small as she was, his face far more rodentesque.

Farak crossed his thick arms. "You tell me. That's her new *habib* your men are roughing up."

Habib?

Zarina's cheeks stung with heat. Richard was the farthest thing from a lover she had. How could Farak say that considering their history? After opening her heart those many moons ago to ask *him* if he would be her *habib*?

Wobbly, weak tears of memory threatened the corner of her eyes. She crushed her eyelids together and took a seething breath. If it were true, Richard would be a far better lover than Farak ever would. That *alwaghad*.

An agonized grunt from Richard pulled her attention back to the center of the room. His pale skin and wily hair lay on the dirty floor, the line of blood trickling from the corner of his mouth like the Moses-plagued Nile.

"Will she come for him?" Adajin asked Farak. "For her new foreign toy?"

"No." Farak's eyes emptied with a darkness that pushed Zarina back from the door. "She only cares for herself. But he might be able to lead us to her."

Zarina winced as pain spiraled out from her heart and burned her lungs. It was her fault. She created this Farak who worked for Adajin. Who said cruel things and kept secrets. It was the only explanation.

Which was all the more reason to find the assassin and end it all. But now she needed to find a way to save Richard *and* look for secrets. She was only taking steps backward. How could she move forward again?

"He says he can strike a deal between Britannia and my men." Adajin lifted the hair out of Richard's eyes and pinched his chin with rough hands. "True or not true?"

"True," Richard said through clenched teeth.

"Not true." Farak countered. "He has no more power in Europa or Britannia than a fish does on the sand dunes."

Adajin sneered and squeezed tighter, forcing Richard's mouth open with a painful cry.

"He does have money, though. And information on Zarina." Farak offered casually. "If that's important to you."

"You know it is," Adajin said and threw Richard back on the hard floor. "Or you never would have come to me as a drunken mess claiming you knew where the treasure of the gods lay hidden."

Zarina's knees trembled. She pressed her palms against the splintered door to keep herself up. Her mind reeled. Her skin burned with fury. Farak *was* how Adajin found her family's sacred tombs. Farak was how Adajin hunted her. Farak had given Adajin everything. Had given him her.

She sank to the earth, her resolve to fight weakening, and tucked herself in as small as she could, wishing to disappear. Farak—her fated protector, the one who showed up soon after her mother died, who swore to protect her, who cradled her in his arms just that morning and told her to trust him—had handed her over, unbidden, to the gaping jaws of death long before fate had forced them to meet again.

"You know, Farak, I almost threw you out that day." Adajin's distant voice mused through the pounding in Zarina's head. "But here you are, throwing out others for me. Life's circular like that, you know. A more loyal henchman I have yet to see."

Loyal.

Zarina spat the bile burning her throat and pressed her fingers together so hard, her knuckles turned as white as Richard's. How was she supposed to fight Farak and escape her fate?

An agonized cry from Richard lifted her chin.

Through a tiny crack at the bottom of the door, she watched Adajin land a swift kick in his ribs. Zarina cringed and looked away. How many lives had she ruined by trying to keep her own? Richard didn't deserve that. Neither did Rana or—

Another thudding kick and cry from Richard.

Why so much violence? Her life was filled with it, with betrayal and lies and bad men hurting innocent people. And what for? Her lineage meant nothing to anyone anymore. Yet the violence would find her as it always did. Farak would point the way.

Another pained grunt from Richard twisted her insides.

Bile climbed up her throat, and she clapped a hand over her mouth to keep it at bay. As a child, she had been the innocent one harmed by the curse, but she had also been the cause. The innocent one who barely escaped while her mother died behind her with echoing screams. And why? For trying to live? For trying to give her daughter a normal life?

That's why they had been in Cairo. Her mother had been skipping and singing all the week before, telling her they would finally settle with the same roguish man who happened to be Zarina's father. They'd rekindled their love, she had said, had defied fate and chosen each other. With a wide smile and that tell-tale mischief in her eyes, she had promised Zarina they'd finally have *a place to call home, a place for family, and perhaps another little girl to be your sister.*

She died that day.

Only pure cruelty could execute such unjust punishment. The same cruelty Richard endured on the other side of this door. And only a coward would stand by and watch without doing anything about it.

Her mother was not a coward, and neither was she.

But that meant she could no longer run. That she had to choose something and follow it through. Ignoring fate hadn't worked for her mother and had turned Farak into a monster. And running from her curse had only given her a life full of sorrow.

So what did that mean for her?

Shaking, Zarina climbed to her feet and looked up and down the hallway. At one end hung a gas lamp whose white light flickered red against her goggles. She slid the iron-framed box off its copper hook. The weight of it strained her tired muscles and plummeted to the floor. Zarina caught it just before it clattered and stifled a cry as the hot glass pressed against her skin. She yanked the lantern away from her and held it out, rotating her arm back and forth. A red welt grew in the shape of an upside-down boat.

Death had marked her.

She ripped her eyes from the omen and pushed the silky blue of her hajib farther up her arm to keep it from rubbing, then hurried back to the door. If she was going, she'd take as many of them with her as she could.

She flicked the lantern off, placed it on the floor, and pulled a hex key from her pouch. With four expert twists on four worn screws, the back panel came loose. She pulled from her pouch a pair of linen gloves dipped in wax and set to work removing the hot, chemical-soaked mesh core.

Richard cried out from the other room.

Her fingers flew faster.

She ripped off her apron and rubbed the core up and down the coarse fabric to spread the chemicals, then plopped the mesh in the center. With practiced dexterity, she enveloped the mechanism with the apron and tied a neat knot on top. Zarina sifted through her pouch until she pulled out an etched glass sphere with purple-that-could-only-be-blue powder. She would normally use her second pink bomb, but naphtha killed, and she didn't want to hurt Richard. Instead, she would blast a hallucinogen through the room and take what she came for.

Her weapons secure, she clipped a papyrus and muslin mask around her neck. The ammonia and heather tincture inside bit at her nose, the fabric painted with a protective image of the Singular Eye. She yanked the lamp's starter, flicking the catch several times against the fabric.

A bright flame bloomed, eating away at the chemicals in a white-hot blaze. Zarina hefted the top knot of the homemade fireball and kicked open the door. She lobbed the weapon into the center of the room and threw the blue bomb in after it. Then she slammed the door shut.

The explosion shook the room with groaning cracks.

When the majority of the noise ceased, she creaked the door back open. Crumbling plaster fell from the ceiling. Men cried out, snarling and weeping, and smoke blossomed in heavy clouds of blue and black.

Zarina smiled and donned her mask, then stepped into the room. She would not run from nor rely on anyone ever again.

She was there for justice.

Sixteen

Zarina threw herself to the floor and crawled through the havoc engulfing the room. Hot plumes of blue and grey clung to the ceiling, disorienting men with noxious fumes that conjured wild delusions before forcing blissful unconsciousness. Several had already collapsed, drool and incoherent mumblings spilling from their lips.

She kept her small frame low to the ground, nimble enough to avoid panicked feet. Ahead lay Richard, his hands cupped protectively over his head. She would get him out of the mess she made; he deserved that much from her after all that had happened. She would not be the destroyer of innocent lives like the assassin.

Zarina elbowed her way forward and slid next to Richard. She touched a finger to his, and he flinched.

"Richard." She pried his hands from his head. "Don't be such a Brit. Let's go."

He peeked out between wisps of hair. "Ah, God bless the Queen! Zarina, I was so worried."

"Worried about me? You were the one getting your ribs kicked in."

"Ah, that?" He shot her a ragged, lopsided grin. "It's my honor as a gentleman to take a beating for you."

She raised an eyebrow. The toxic fumes were clearly getting to him. If she didn't hurry, she'd be lugging his giggling, limp body all the way out.

He gave an awkward chuckle. "You're cute confused. And what about you?" His normally aloof eyebrows furrowed into a thin line.

"What about me?" She worked to untie his wrists; a good excuse to look away.

The ropes slid from Richard's wrists, and he placed a gentle hand on her shoulder. "Are you okay?"

"Of course, I am." She pulled away from his reach.

He shrugged and lifted himself onto his feet. "If you say so."

The doubt in his voice stung. She yanked Richard back down into a crawl beneath the haze. "If you stand, you fall. Stay down and follow me. If we linger, the toxins will knock you out, too."

"You mean these pretty blue specks?" He blew a swirl of smoke from his face. "It's like snowfall back home. Only it tastes like . . . ." He stuck his tongue out. "Oh, no. Burnt cheese. This isn't like snowfall at all."

Zarina shook her head. "Save your breath and my ears. You're ranting like a child."

She led Richard back toward the door she came from, careful to weave through the unconscious bodies and the more dangerous scuffling boots. The smoke cover would be gone soon, and they needed to be out of there by then. Hopefully, with all the chaos, they could sneak back out through the kitchen and make a run for it before the toxins really did a number on Richard and he started hallucinating.

Halfway to the door, the guard with the thick neck crashed to the floor on top of her legs. She cried out, straining and pulling as she tried to wheedle her shins and feet free.

Richard crawled to her side. "Hold still, I'll roll him off of you."

"Just leave." Zarina pushed him away. She could deal with her problems on her own. She was the protector now. She couldn't have anyone else die because of her. "You need to get out before the dust settles and you start seeing things."

"Nah." Richard winced, shifting his weight under the man, then gave the broad shoulders a heave. "I'm not going anywhere without you."

Zarina wriggled her feet, but they refused to budge. "I'm not worth your life. Just leave."

Richard readjusted his position, huffing and pushing. At last, the pressure lifted long enough for her to pull her legs out. Richard grabbed her waist to help her find her knees, and her cheeks warmed. Why did he insist on ignoring her commands and touching her and smiling all the time?

She hurried forward to put distance between herself and his surprisingly trim arms. Luckily, the doorway stood empty ahead. Zarina jumped up, dragging Richard along with her, and surged forward. She shoved him through the doorway first, but before she could follow, she ran straight into muscled abs and muslin lined in foxfire beads.

Farak's bulging arms swooped around to ensnare her, and she ducked, stumbling backward to stay out of his reach.

She spread her boots in a fighting stance, unable to look him in the eye. "Move."

"You've made a mess of things this time," Farak said through a thick burlap cloth he had tucked over his nose and mouth.

"Get out of my way."

She unsheathed her ruby dagger and bit her cheek to stifle the memories. Had she not just done this with Farak yesterday? Though, then she had been testing his loyalty. She needed no such test this time. He had made it clear exactly who his master was. Blood would be drawn in this fight.

"Why did you even come here?"

"None of your business."

Zarina wanted so badly to turn away from the sharp gold of his fierce gaze, but she couldn't risk taking her eyes off his hand, his muscles; one twitch uncaught could spell her doom. If he was even physically capable of harming her, that was. She still wasn't sure what parts of Farak's forsaken oath held—how much control the gods had over the unwilling—and she didn't want to find out.

She clenched her jaw, every muscle twitching with expectation. "I'm glad I did come, though. I hadn't realized Adajin was *your* new *habib*."

Farak tensed, his hand hovering over the hilt of his sword. "There is only one way this ends without destroying everything."

"Everything for you or for me?"

"I told you to trust me."

She eyed his hand warily as the gap between fingers and sword diminished one granule at a time. "I do trust you—to backstab me. I heard everything, Farak. You sold out the gods. You sold out me. You might as well have just knocked me out and handed me over to Adajin in person. Dying at his hands is worse than the assassin's."

Farak's lips twitched.

"Ahmet take you," she spat. "That's your plan right now, isn't it? To hand me over?"

Farak swung like a crocodile in the Nile, swift and unexpected. She blocked just in time, his giant blade glancing off her tiny dagger. She stepped back and held her knife at the ready. The small weapon would not be enough. She brandished her throwing stick with her other hand. It wouldn't do much damage, but her ancestors crafted it to withstand heavy blows, and the unique grooves fit perfectly in her hands like it was a piece of her, a part of her fate. Farak swung down again, testing her limits as the metals clanged and sliced against each other.

"*Khayin*." The word stung as she said it. "You've ripped my heart out for the second time, but I will not let you do so again."

She thrust forward, he stepped back. Jab. Anguish. Jab. Betrayal. Jab. Why?

Why had things ended up here?

She thrust and stabbed and swiped with the glint of her blade again and again, pushing him towards the door. She would not win this fight; Farak was bred to kill, his family picked by Ra for millennia for their strength and determination. But if she could get close enough, she might be able to slip out the door and run.

Farak jerked out of the way with her next jab. She fell forward, no resistance to catch her. He stuck his foot out and caught her leg. She tumbled to the earth. Electricity jarred her elbows, panged her arms. He turned and raised his sword. She lay, vulnerable. Their eyes met. A crease distorted the brazen confidence in his eyes. Why was he hesitating?

Sinewy arms seized around Farak's neck and a mop of curls stuck up from behind his back.

Richard's face popped into view. "Run, princess! Lest the lion catches you with his razor teeth!"

He was hallucinating. Hard. She scrambled to her feet, no time to warn Richard that his captive was far more dangerous than a mere lion. Farak crocodile-twisted, flinging Richard to the floor. She bolted for the opening. Farak blocked her path. Zarina dodged to the left, but he was there, too. She swiped her knife close to his chest, nipping the coarse fabric to reveal his iron chest beneath.

Then he grabbed her wrist, eyes dark-red and menacing through her goggles, and smashed her nose with his fist.

Seventeen

F ARAK HIT HER.

Warm blood seeped out her nose and down below her mask, taking her soul with it. Zarina wiped a smear on her sleeve. She staggered back.

He actually hit her.

She blinked against the blue light streaming around them and through the twist of agony snaking across her forehead. She had been so stupid, holding onto the naive and hypocritical hope that the bones of his curse could not be broken by choice. That Ra would protect someone who couldn't protect herself, that he would stay Farak's hand should he choose to rebel.

She had never been so wrong.

Fate would not force her or Farak's hands, just condemn them for eternity if they failed. Was there comfort in that? The Zarina who left Farak in the desert said *yes*. The blinding bursts of pain in her face said *Ra no*.

Farak ripped her mother's throwing stick from her hand and shoved it into his belt. He grabbed her arm harder than he ever had before.

She shook her throbbing head, unclasped her bitter-smelling mask, and took a deep breath. A hallucination would be better than this, and maybe the toxins would lessen the pain in her nose and the agony in her heart so she could think, if but for a moment. The rush of sparkles in her mind released some of her fear and sparked her instincts.

Things could not end this way.

She jumped and angled her feet, sliding on her heels and under Farak's fighting stance. He held, bent awkwardly toward the floor. Richard seized the opportunity, jumping once more on Farak's crouched back.

"I've got it by the mane," he crowed. "Watch its claws and run for the hills."

"Enough," Farak growled.

He reached a hand behind his back and grabbed Richard's shirt, throwing him off like a pup by the scruff. Richard hit the door frame with a groan and sank into a heap.

Zarina writhed in Farak's grasp, blood splattering on the floor as it poured from her nose. "I will not let you take me to be Adajin's dog."

"I don't see that you've left me any choice." Farak's voice wrenched with frustration.

"You're a traitor." Tears stung the corners of her eyes, hot with lingering chemicals and freshly made wounds. "You sold me out along with Ra and your family's legacy. Do you hate me so much?"

The words sounded sorrier than her pride would admit, and the fight left her body. The toxins riddled her brain with fuzz and blurry bursts of color. She was the only one in her long line of ancestors who had gotten her bodyguard to betray her. She snorted a blood-soaked scoff and sunk to the floor.

Farak's unrelenting grasp chafed her skin. She couldn't even smell his jasmine anymore. Just the scent of smoke and death.

"Well done, Farak," Adajin's voice snaked through the thinning haze. He wore a bronze and gold face mask, much like her own and yet nothing like hers by a dozen mahbub.

"You did this!" Zarina leaped to her feet and lunged at Adajin, but Farak held her back.

Adajin sneered. "I did nothing to you that you hadn't already done to yourself. Farak told me how you treated him. It's no wonder he wanted to destroy you and your fortune."

She spat, covering his sandal in her bloody rage.

Adajin's sneer deepened, framing his teeth in ugly rivulets of hate. "I plan to nail you like a masthead to my ship and sail you around Aegyptus for killing my men." He turned to Farak with a lazy wave. "Take her and the Brit to holding."

Farak nodded sharply and hoisted her up from the floor. There was no telling what Farak would do now that he was truly free. Free from her. From his feelings. From mercy. He was no longer bound by oath or blood or curse. His fate was sealed to damnation the moment he hit her. He could hurt her, could draw blood, and conjure pain. He already had.

But why did he torture her so, handing her over to Adajin? He could have cut her down, killed her with one swipe of his sword, and been done with the whole thing. He could have hit her hard enough to break her nose and sent her reeling, but underneath all the blood, the ridge stood as long and straight as ever. He hit her with just enough force in just the right place to accomplish his goal: to cause her agony without making her pass out so she could witness his loyalty to Adajin, to imprint the manifestation of her careless actions on her brain forever.

Without the guidance of the gods, Farak was just another corrupt man out for her treasure. They all were. Or so she wanted to believe.

But what about Richard?

Farak kicked the still-ranting Brit and lugged him to his feet with his free hand.

Zarina lifted her head.

"You used to be a just man, Farak. Now, you're as cruel as Adajin."

"As you'll have it," he grunted, looking away.

Farak slung her over his shoulder, tightened his grasp once more around Richard's scruff, and dragged them both through the door.

Zarina snarled and kicked at him. Twisted and thrashed and screamed like a child in a lion's maw. It was no use.

With each of Farak's determined footsteps, the crimson blood from her nose seeped deeper into his shirt. And with every one of his breaths, she slapped and bit and scratched a mark into his tanned skin until pain and exhaustion left her limp.

In all her sleepless, star-pocked nights throughout her lonely, terrified life, she never once imagined this to be her fate. The gods' final joke: to have the last heir of Ra killed by the very bloodline sworn to protect her.

Apep had long sought his deified father's throne but was no match for the sun god. So instead, he aided the foreigners invading Aegyptus and pried it from Ra's hands through war and politics and foreign religions. The only thing Apep had not fully destroyed? Ra's human bloodline. If he couldn't rule the desert sky and the earth beneath, he'd never allow a mortal to. But to use her god-appointed bodyguard to do his dirty work? The whole plan was carefully and cruelly devised for the god of chaos.

She never saw it coming.

Neither did the omnipotent Ra—though he clearly wasn't omnipotent at all. That or he didn't care about the sand mouse who held his blood. Maybe he was as forgetful as the desert sand and all the cities lost to it.

But if the gods could be so blind, maybe Apep wouldn't see her coming, either. Something deep inside—the light of Ra, the human instinct to survive, the burning heat of revenge—would never let her give up, even if her heart had frozen.

If the blood streaming from her nose proved anything, it was that—god's will or not—her fate could be fought. Farak had done it. So could she.

Maybe going after the assassin was her problem all along. Maybe she needed to go after the true source of the problem and aim for the gods. But even as she thought it, a cold crept up her spine, and she was sure Ahmet listened. Would he hear the unspoken words in her heart and find her guilty?

What did fighting her fate even mean? How could she fight something incorporeal and unseen? Something so much bigger than herself.

She would have to figure that out later. Right now, she needed to get out of Farak's grasp.

Zarina lifted her head to inspect her surroundings. Farak carried them down a dark hallway somewhere near the back of the compound. His broad shoulders and flexed muscles proved immune to her flesh wounds, his heart to her pleadings. She turned a pitying eye on Richard's weak efforts to break free from Farak's hold as his rantings shifted from lions and safaris to mud dragons and rampaging hippopotami. She grimaced. He could *not* hold his poison. He would be of no help. She was on her own.

Farak dipped under a large wooden rafter, which allowed for an opening. The time was now.

Zarina arched her back upwards and dug her fingers into the beam to gain a solid hold. Caught off-guard, Farak loosened his grip, and she used the opportunity to yank herself up, wrap her legs around his neck, and squeeze.

Farak dropped Richard and grabbed Zarina's legs, trying to break their hold. She tightened her thigh muscles and pushed the rest of her energy into crushing his neck.

"Zarina," he choked out gutturally. "Stop this."

She squeezed harder. She would not listen to what he had to say. Would not let him sway her with lies.

He tried for his sword, but haggard, half-conscious Richard climbed up and wrapped his hands around Farak's waist. It was just enough to deter Farak while he gasped for air.

"Zarina." His face reddened, and his words were hard and empty of breath. "You must stop."

His pulse throbbed against her skin, and she could hear the growing pain in his words, but he did not sound desperate. He never did. Not now and not when she left him in the desert. The weakness she feared crept into her muscles, fueled by guilt. Her legs loosened a hair's width, allowing him to capture a ragged breath before she tightened once more.

"I have to, Farak. I will never stop fighting for my life. You know this."

"You . . . don't." His face purpled, his lips an undeniable blue despite her red goggles.

"I will not let Adajin take me. He will kill me far more slowly than any assassin. You know this, too."

"I—can— help—you."

"If you want to help me, tell me about the assassin."

"No," he choked.

"Tell me!" She squeezed harder, yanking on his hair. "It is your duty."

"I can't—"

She growled. "You protect the assassin with your dying breath, Farak. You hit me, drew blood, and sentenced us both to Ahmet's jaws. I will never trust you again. Of all the things, you must know this the most."

"Escape—" His eyes fluttered, and he released her leg and pointed toward a door at the far end of the hallway.

Zarina hesitated, her grasp iron-tight.

It couldn't be that easy, could it? The door probably led to a maze filled with Adajin's men. Or a broom closet, giving Farak just enough time to free his sword. But what if it was true? Even after everything, the ice in her heart had not consumed their bond entirely. She did not want to kill Farak. Trusting him, taking a chance on the door would give her an escape. An avenue to look Ra squarely in the face and ask why? Because it was the gods who caused her problems, who played with her fate. It was them she hated more than the sand in her spit.

Farak's eyes fluttered, and he stumbled on his feet. A door slammed nearby, shaking her nerves. It was now or never, and if this was a trap—if she was stupid enough to have let Farak deceive her once more, then she deserved the death that would follow.

Zarina released him, swung her legs back, and kicked square between his shoulder blades so he fell forward onto the rough floor. She alighted upon his back, and he grunted with her weight.

"Go," she said, grabbing the collar of Richard's shirt.

Richard scrambled forward, and Zarina knelt, trying to grab her dagger and throwing stick off Farak's belt. She cursed. He lay upon them.

"Zarina?" Richard called, hesitating.

She clenched her teeth with a growl, glancing between the two, then stood up and dashed toward the door. Farak groaned on the floor, breathing in heavy gasps as he pushed himself up.

She shoved Richard against the wall next to the door Farak had pointed to. Holding her breath, she kicked the door open. Sun and relief warmed her skin.

Freedom.

She smiled and took a hot, fish and bread-soaked breath. Farak had told the truth.

"Guards!" Farak called from inside the hallway. "The prisoners escaped. West side, first door. Capture them, by Adajin's command. Dead or alive."

Chills ran down Zarina's spine. He had just been trying to make it to his next breath, the same as she.

Truth or not, Farak was no friend.

She pushed Richard into the streets and toward the alleyways on the other side.

"Run!"

Eighteen

Zarina scoured the crates below her bed for witch hazel and bandages, her bruised nose pulsing though they were free from goggles. It had taken until the deep azure of night to walk to her ship, and even then, the stars winked and laughed at her, certain they would not make it. Tom Tom would be finished with repairs by sunrise and had gladly taken a whole mahbub from her pouch as payment, but she would not feel safe until the wind of high skies blew through her hair. At least she had been allowed to stay on the ship overnight. To breathe in a bit of familiarity after the day she'd had.

And then there was Richard, beaten and bruised and still coming down off his high.

"That was quite the rorty adventure, wasn't it?" Richard puffed between words as he lay on her bed. His blood had already stained her sheets and he kept trying to turn to talk to her, wincing every time.

"Rorty?" The foreign word felt like pebbles in her mouth. She rubbed her thumb under the lip of her goggles and gently pulled them off, then rubbed a thumb along the tender bridge of her bruised nose "We're just lucky we made it out alive."

She glanced at Richard, then let her gaze linger. Maybe she had been wrong about Rana earlier. There was something to Richard now that she could see him in natural light. Something she didn't mind seeing. He caught her gaze and grinned.

"You could cut glass with those cheekbones of yours."

Heat flooded her face.

"It's not a bad thing," he chuckled. "They're strong and beautiful."

Her tongue failed her, and she turned hastily to search for the fine muslin bandages she kept for broken ribs and bleeding wounds. She moved aside the chest with Uncle Mery's beetles and found the spool far too soon. She still needed a minute to breathe. She had been told her tongue and her nose were sharp and had always taken that as a bad thing. But sharp to Richard was a good thing. Or it was to high Richard, at least.

"You were off the chump back there, by the way," he said from the bed. "Though the scurf deserved it, for sure."

"Basic English, please, Richard. And slower."

"That was . . . ."

"Better English, then. I have no energy to translate your toxin-laced monkey words." She tore a piece of the muslin to dab at her nose before moving closer to bind Richard's torso.

Heavy breathing filled the silence.

She pulled Richard into a sitting position, then hesitated. "Your shirt's going to have to come off."

"Umble-cum-stumble," Richard nodded. He grimaced and raised an arm to no avail, then tried to twist sideways and shake the shirt off but ended up coughing up blue-stained spittle.

Zarina sighed. "Enough of that. I'll . . . I'll help you. Just hold still."

With a memory of the tenderness her mother used when kissing her scraped knees as a child, Zarina grabbed the hem of Richard's shirt. She lifted it against his smooth, warm skin, following the curve of his back and the sinewy muscles underneath. His skin shone a deepening purple and blue around broken ribs. She bit her lip and reached the strong line of his shoulders and paused. The definition of his biceps kept the shirt from pulling over.

She sidled onto the bed behind him, putting a knee on each side of his back. With a deep breath, she straightened the fabric back down, then slid it up and up and up. She was closer to him now than she'd ever been, her breath swirling through the wisp of his hair and onto his neck. His back pressed against her, and the smell of lye and soap and Aegyptian rain tempted her to linger.

But she could not. Not like this.

Zarina had tried to be the bringer of justice and had only caused more pain. It had been a stupid idea. She was the source of everyone's pain. The only way to protect others would be to remove herself entirely.

She grimaced.

Did that make the assassin the hero in this story?

She hurried to slip the rest of Richard's shirt off, tossed it into a ball in the corner, and slid off the bed in a flurry of heat.

"Is it bad?" Richard asked. His bright gemstone eyes looked to the floor. A hint of color warmed his cheeks.

She tore a few long strands of muslin and soaked them in witch hazel. "That depends. Do you mean bad like the marketplace when you acted like you were dying and had hardly a scratch?"

"Hm." Richard puckered his lips. He closed his eyes and tilted his head up. "I daresay this hurts more than that, but I don't want to be made a fool. I've led a pretty sheltered life if you can believe that."

"I can."

Zarina pressed the muslin into a swollen cut that ran just above the line of his belt. He breathed in sharply and shot her a pained grin.

Once the rise and fall of his chest slowed, he asked, "Ever had tea?"

"Of course, I've had tea." Zarina scowled. "Everyone drinks tea."

Richard sighed. "I love a good tea. I'd give just about anything for some rose hip tea right now. With a hint of orange, perhaps."

Zarina hesitated. His liver still fought the toxins from earlier, that much was clear, but his voice and eyes were clear.

"I like Koshary," she relented. "It's light and black with a hint of sugar and milk, sometimes a dash of mint." She imagined sipping the bitter-sweet liquid, and her breathing slowed, tension leaving her body. "I have not had it in . . . too long."

She slid her tongue along her blood-stained lips as sorrow parched her heart. She used to drink that tea with her mother and then with Farak. He would make it to comfort her in the dead of night when her nightmares woke them both with her screams. When she left Farak behind, she left that comfort with him, too, and suffered her nightmares alone. Now, Farak was her nightmare, and she was his.

"I'm sorry," Richard said after a sharp inhale.

"For what?" Zarina lifted the gauze to give him a reprieve. The wound she worked on was deep and long, puckering bright red with the start of an infection.

"For your bodyguard going rogue back there. That's a shoddy bit of luck."

Zarina dipped the thin fabric in the bucket of water she had pulled from a barrel, then pulled it clear and twisted hard. "Luck had nothing to do with it. It is my fate catching up with me."

Richard snorted.

She slapped the damp rag against his back and felt only a twinge of guilt when he winced. "Fate is not something to be laughed at."

"That's exactly what it is," Richard said, recovering his grin.

"You don't believe in the gods?"

Richard pursed his lips and tossed a hand to the side. "I don't believe all-powerful beings puppeteer the trivial details of our lives. The whole idea of fate is rubbish."

She glared straight into Richard's eyes and shook the sopping muslin, so flecks of watered-down blood speckled his shirt and hers. "Fate is real. It has controlled my life since before I was born. That cannot be denied."

Richard's grin widened. "I'm not buying it."

"That does not change the shadow I live under." Zarina struggled to control her temper as she placed the muslin along the swollen, angry red of his shoulder. "If fate does not exist, why has an assassin hunted me from birth? Why did my mother die young and violently? And hers before her and so on back millennia? If fate has not done this to me, then my suffering is a product of the nonsensical and absurdly prolonged cruelty of man. That's worse."

"So you've just given up, then?" Richard's light eyes met her own, gentle and disarming behind the bruises.

"I never give up." She padded at his wound, her fingers working in increasing agitation. "That's why I'm still alive, and why I've decided—"

She took a breath, the words ice cold in her mind. "I've decided to stop running and fight my fate every day."

Richard grabbed her hand. "What exactly *is* fate to you?"

His inquiry, the warmth of his hand against her cold, caught her coming retort and twisted it apart. "It's—Fate is—" She bit her tongue as she grasped for the right words. "Everyone knows what fate is," she finally huffed and pulled her fingers from his own.

Richard leaned back on a hand so his torso stretched in front of the lantern before her, the moon across an ocean of black. He tilted his chin toward her, his smile warm and genuine despite a split lip. "It sounds like that's your problem. Everyone knows what fate is but you."

"I know what it is." She ripped another piece of muslin and dunked it in the bucket. "I know more than anyone."

"Is it immutable, then? Unchangeable and permanent? Or are you fighting against it, believing that you do have a say in whether you live or die?"

"I—" Her voice dropped away, and with it, her confidence.

Which was true? She daily suffered the curse of poor bloodlines, only being able to have a daughter and owing her Guardsman her life but being forbidden to share her love with him. But she had chosen to fight against her fated death and the lot handed down to her unasked and undeserved.

Were the curse and fate given by different hands? Or was one an extenuation of the other?

Richard leaned in, his sincere smile so close she could smell his scent of soap and rain. "I think fate is what you make of it yourself. You should fight, but not against some deified idea. You should fight against whoever is trying to kill you. A person. Flesh and blood. They have the answers, and I promise you it's not some mystic and unknowable force. A person is behind your misfortune, and the only way you're going to change your future is by finding them."

A coursing, surging strength ran from her heart and through her veins, encompassing his accusations, his heat, and the strange desire she had to slide once more behind him and whisper secrets in his ear.

She did not pull away, but let her lips linger just below his. "You have no idea what a curse from the gods feels like. What it's done to generations of my family. You cannot know; you Brits are a baby civilization. You know nothing of the ancient ways of angry gods who control this desert."

"And yet..." Richard's green eyes sunk into her own, lily pads tethered to the Nile.

She swallowed, her throat thirsty for a drop of rain. "And yet, what?"

"And yet, you so badly want what I say to be true. I can feel it in you, you know, that deep ache for freedom and willpower. Of wanting something so badly it hurts."

He was right, and she wanted to both swim in his gaze and hide from it. But he was also wrong. He made all her religion and beliefs sound wrong and twisted, which wasn't true either. She gathered great strength from her heritage and ancestry. Could she have one without the other? Could she be proud of where she came from and deny the parts of it that controlled her, too?

Richard did have a point about the assassin being something tangible—something that could have the answers she needed to understand her fate.

"Even if the assassin could bleed," she whispered, though she wasn't sure why, "I did not find anything I did not already know at Adajin's. I am certain the identity of my attacker lay in those hieroglyphics from the tunnels." The words spilled from her faster and faster. "There was more to them than I revealed. The queens again. Death and a servant of Apep ready to strike with his dagger in hand. But I don't know what they mean. Rana seemed just as surprised as we were about their existence. And Farak...." She let her voice drift off.

"What about Cairo?" Richard asked.

Zarina bit her cheek, and the iron of blood coated her tongue. Its bitter, earthy flavor chased away the spell Richard's eyes had cast, and she pulled back. "What about it?"

Richard's usual grin appeared, widening the haggard split in his lip. "The Aegyptian National Library is there. I practically live there whenever I come to stay with Uncle William. There's a bang-up restricted section I've only ever been in twice. The stodgy old keeper doesn't like Brits poking around too much. I bet your mysterious symbols are hidden somewhere in those dusty ol' scrolls."

Zarina's stomach twisted and knotted like the rigging on her ship. "Does it have to be Cairo?" But she knew he was right. There was more in Cairo than the National Library that could help her in her quest.

"Ay," Richard drew out the word and popped up a brow, but she refused to give anything else away. "It's our best bet. I thought, considering your time restrictions, you'd want to get things done quickly."

Her time restrictions? What a stupidly delicate way to describe the blade aimed at her throat. She pushed the iron around in her mouth. The gods were mocking her with a forced return to Cairo. But if they couldn't foresee Farak's betrayal, maybe they would not see hers. Either way, the worst had happened. She had to find the assassin and learn the secrets he held, which meant a return to the place where her hope of family ended.

Richard took her hand in his, startling her from her thoughts. "You don't have to live in the shadows anymore. I can help make sure of that."

"I don't need your help," she said, but she let his hand wrap around her own and softened her voice. "We should finish tending to your broken ribs so you can get some rest before we head out."

Richard smiled. "And where is the fire in your eyes taking us after the cock crows thrice?"

"To Cairo." The words stuck in her sand-blasted throat. "My home away from home, the lair of liars, and den of death."

Nineteen

The wind brushed Zarina's cheeks as her ship rose higher. The azure of fading night kissed the acacia beams and dipped and rolled over hatched papyrus. Thank Renenet she once again graced the skies and flew between the clouds.

Tom Tom had outdone himself this time; her ship looked better than the day she and Farak pulled it from a buried tomb near the sands of Abusir and repurposed it for flight. It was one of the few benefits of her ancestry—thousands of ancient and more recent documents detailing how machinations worked. Now, if only she could keep her ship in top condition. With Cairo in their future, the odds were worse than a gazelle winning a lion fight.

"Ah, look at her." Richard leaned far over the railing and gazed at the city below. A solid night's rest had eased the grimace he tried to hide every time he moved. "Isn't Cairo something?"

He turned to face where she stood at the helm, a grin playing on the corner of his still-cracked lips. The inexplicable tug of desire she had to be closer to him had faded to a shadowy ache that she worked to push farther down.

"Is it?" Zarina shook her head at the dusty smog rising over Cairo.

The first hints of sunlight burst from the sky overhead, but not one ray could penetrate the stink hole below. The pink of her goggles did little to change the color of the air.

She groaned. "I can't wait for the soles of my boots to land upon its soil."

"Is that how you say you're excited to be there?" Richard cupped a hand over his brow as if it would help him see through the pollution.

Zarina eyed his bent frame, so slight and battered against the waking sky. One push would be all it took to end him; like a ceramic bowl elbowed off a table that shattered into pieces. So careless. So carefree. Richard did not have to think of all the ways he could die. He was free to think of how he could live. Like Rana. And now Farak. Everyone but her. Maybe it would be easier to pretend fate did not wait for her with a scale that would judge her soul. But how could she? An entire eternity of her soul at the hands of Ahmet seemed far worse than knuckling under here. And that was what Richard didn't understand and what Farak no longer believed.

Still . . . Richard's words floated through her, lazy and suffocating. *I think fate is what you make of it yourself.*

But believing so couldn't be worth the risk. Even if she was wrong about the existence of fate, what was she losing by adhering to the idea? Fleeting happiness in a desert that was cold and unforgiving anyway? Only love had ever felt worth the risk of being wrong, and Farak and fate ensured that could never be.

The potential loss of her faith meant if she was wrong, she'd lose her soul to blackness. She'd never see her mother again, the only true family she had ever known.

Zarina puckered her lips, watching the wind riffle playfully through Richard's curls. It was easy to claim fate and the gods weren't real when you grew up with silver spoons and an always-full belly, when you were taught that everything you had came from your own hands. He'd only ever understand fate if he went through what she had. If his life was threatened daily with its very existence.

She noted how far he leaned over the railing, how carefree he looked hanging over a potential death, and itched to nudge him—not to kill, but to teach. But what good would it do? A brief look into the eyes of Osiris would not change how he viewed the world.

Instead, she smirked. "Yes, that is exactly how you say you're excited to be somewhere. Use it freely, and Aegyptus will welcome you."

Or quite the opposite. But Richard had lived a life of ease. A little revilement by offended locals could only help tip the scales of injustice in the world. He was part of Aegyptus's occupation, not part of the people oppressed by it. He would be fine.

A horn bellowed below, signifying the start of trade. Already, vast merchant ships carrying spices, and animals, and fruit, and indentured servants swarmed the skies above Cairo.

"Prepare yourself," Zarina said to Richard. "Unlike Alexandria, Cairo has no rules to govern the merging of traffic between the skies and the city below. If you keep leaning over the edge like a child, a passing ship could take off your nose and your head with it."

Richard pulled himself upright. "The National Library is in a noble's mansion in the eastern suburbs. That way." He pointed toward where the top of the sun peeked above purple sand dunes. "It's easy to find. The mansion is more like a palace, all balustrades and towers. Plus they cover the top walkways in dandy flags. It's quite a sight."

"I know where the library is. Its foundations are older than your entire civilization," she said, but the bite of annoyance had gone from her.

Richard was like a child, talking of rainbow flags like they were a bag of warm lavender bread on a cold desert night. She wanted to scowl at him, to turn her nose and *scoff*, as the Brits would say, but something in his innocence kept her pessimism at bay. She hated his easy upbringing and uncomplicated family tree, but his light and optimism disarmed her—made her wish she had a childhood filled with doting khalis and flag-filled festivals instead of dark tombs and stories of death.

A swift ship half the size of hers raced by, its sails flapping just past the tips of Richard's outstretched fingers. The morning rush at its finest.

"Here we go," she said and gave the helm a hard twist.

The ship's graceful curves about-faced and plummeted toward the city. She grabbed the wheel in a sudden stop and swooped between crisscrossing traffic. Red-sailed ships filled with blue-suited Aegyptian *shurta* puttered by all looking purple. Their eagle eyes scanned the skies as they patrolled the area looking for heavy-laden hulls they could board and exploit, all in the name of a 'safe' Aegyputs.

Zarina gave them a wide-berth, arcing under and up. The ship dipped toward the earth, responsive to her smallest touch. She smiled, then heard it, cheerful and brash and terribly foreign.

"Oy, bobbies!" Richard waved fanatically across the railing directly at the *shurta*. "Captain!" He beamed and waggled his hand back and forth like a flag of surrender.

"Richard," she spat his name. "*Iḫras*. We do not want their attention."

She cast a glance backward to make sure they were clear of passing ships and saw something far worse. Her heart seized.

A flash of black, an aura of death.

Sinister and pressing and then completely gone. Had she seen the assassin? Or was she imagining things? She scanned the kaleidoscope of sails and painted ships.

Nothing. The figure as dark as the night sky had vanished.

She turned her head slowly, sure she would catch something in the corner of her eye when a rusted metal skiff blasted by their front.

Zarina yanked the helm, spinning it left toward a smoke-chugging behemoth from the mines of Ethiopae. "*Ya msebty!*"

She ripped the ship back the other way. A jarring rumble tore through her ship as the scratch and tug of tearing papyrus and splintering wood raked against her heart. They broke free from the behemoth and limped through empty air to a shuttering stop. She left the helm and ran to the port side. A jagged gash marred the light wood of her hull with black.

"Ayyy," she snarled and slammed her fist against the railing.

Richard leaned over the side, his curls clinging to the breeze. "It's just a bit of a scratch, then, innit?"

"What?" She wrenched her head in his direction.

"Well, it's not like your ship sails on water. A little breeze never hurt anyone, did it? And look at that—" He leaned over the side so far that one of his feet hovered in the air. "The scarring looks like the Nile, don't you think? Kind of like the scratch I have on this arm." He raised his right sleeve to show her a flexed and wounded bicep. "That's got to mean something."

"The Nile leads to the gateway of death." She kept her voice flat and her eyebrows flatter, ignoring his toned muscles. "Is that what you were hoping it meant? That we are on our way to death?"

Richard's foot landed upon the deck with a thud, and he slumped into a thoughtful pose, one elbow below his square chin. "You're rather high-strung, aren't you? Probably all that royal inbreeding."

Zarina released her fist and gripped the smooth wood of the railing until her knuckles cracked. "The whole Britannian gentry is one marriage away from ruddy-cheeked, jutting-chinned, cousin-brother babies all named Nigil. You should be preparing for your actual future instead of following me. Go scour the lands for a pale slip of a thing with whom you can have your own gap-toothed baby instead of traipsing across Aegyptus."

"You know, my mother almost named me Nigil," Richard said with an unruffled smile. He stretched his arms into the air, revealing the bandages from yesterday's beatings. "And we Brits don't all have gap teeth."

"Enough of you do," she muttered.

"Only the lucky ones." He winked.

A ship flew by close enough to touch, all angles and sharp edges, its sales a bright yellow. A school of silver mechanical fish nipped and bit the air with every turn of the motor's cogs. The blue-turbanned crew shook their fists as they passed, angered by the airspace she took up sitting idle in a sky with no rules.

"Aya! Get your own bit of air, you greedy waste mongers!" She shook her fist, then huffed down the steps into the hull to put patch her wounded ship. "Come on then, if you're going to blather on anyway, you might as well help me fix the ship. We may not be taking on water, but wind will rip through here and down to the boiler as soon as we start moving. We'll fall to our deaths far faster than a ship would sink."

"I think you forgot to say please," Richard said, following on her heels. "That's a bit of bad manners, that."

"And yet, you followed."

He chuckled. "Since you're so wise, perhaps I should take your advice: travel around the world looking for a—what did you call it—ah, *a slip of a thing*. You know, to shore up my future."

She pulled open the door into the storage hull, but Richard shut it just as quickly. She flipped around, her back pressed against the smooth olive wood. His hand lingered on the door above her. He leaned in, smelling of cinnamon and ink and the morning breeze. She held her breath and looked up into his seriously playful eyes, worried he'd hear the panic in her heart.

"Would you . . ." His whispered words brushed against her cheeks, while his eyes searched for something she was afraid he'd find.

Trepidation and heat snaked down her back, but she couldn't move.

"Would you put in a good word for me with Rana?"

The ice holding her in place shattered into daggers. "Excuse me?"

"Rana, that lovely bit of jam you had with you earlier. I don't know much about her, but she seemed interested." He straightened, freeing her from his warmth, and tugged at his collar just as Rana had, probably remembering her lithe fingers and fluttering lashes so near his skin.

Zarina snapped. "You're right, you don't know anything about Rana." She shoved him back and ripped open the door and bundles of papyrus stored in shelves on the side to stuff into the hole. "She is much too much for you to handle. A crocodile in a well. She'd eat you up, and then me for suggesting it. Besides—" Zarina's grip on the papyrus eased. "—if Farak can't even win her over, she certainly won't spend her time on the likes of you."

He slouched against the beams of the doorway, his feet crossed and shoulders relaxed. "A bit of Othello, that is. But I don't mind you growing sweet on me."

She had read enough of Britannia's Shakespeare to know being compared to one of his characters was probably an insult. But for him to choose Othello?

"Are you calling me jealous? *Manaf lileaql*," she huffed. "The only green-eyed person here is you."

"All right, then, what about you?" Richard abandoned his leisurely pose and grabbed his share of bundles, helping her tie them into the gap. The yellow smog of Cairo disappeared from view, and the angry yelling of shippers stuck in the reeds.

"What about me?"

"What are you doing to prepare for your future?"

She tried to shake off the anger needling at her skin. "My future holds only death. I do not plan for anything but survival. Not anymore."

"Bah," he said with a wave of his hand. "You're just proving my point. You're high-strung. A worrier. All quick-sand and sunburns. All 'the Nile means death'. You know as well as I do that the Nile can also symbolize rebirth and growth." He patted the newly-patched hole as if to make a point. "This can be a sign your life will change for the better. It's like you're trying to be unhappy." He leaned in once more and tugged on the ends of her knotted braids.

Zarina yanked her head back. His sense of boundaries was as bad as Rana's. "I do not wish to be unhappy, my life allows for nothing else."

"Mhm," Richard said half-heartedly. "Is that why you choose to ride around in a death boat?"

"Excuse me?"

He tapped a hand on the beam above his head. "This is a funerary ship you pulled from a tomb, right? It looks like one. That means its job is to ferry souls down the Nile to the gates of the afterlife, which makes you—" He poked her shoulder softly, then tapped her chin when she looked down. "—the lucky captain of a death boat. You're waiting for the assassin, shovel in hand, to dig your own grave."

She opened her mouth, then, for a lack of words, closed it again and turned toward the stairs. She needed fresh air.

"You're so busy making decisions for everyone else," he continued, following her, "that you don't have time to make them for yourself. Like how you wouldn't let Rana help even though it should have been her choice."

"I was protecting her," she snipped. "And I make decisions for myself." She stopped on the last step, so Richard ran into her from behind. She turned to face him. "All the time, in fact."

"Ah, so they're just poorly-made decisions you haven't thought through."

Zarina chaffed. He was beginning to sound like Farak.

"For instance," Richard pushed on, "we're spending all this time hunting down the assassin, but when we find him, what are you going to do?"

"Ask him for answers and stop him from killing me."

"Ay." Richard smiled. "But how? Are you going to invite the bloke for a pint and ask him nicely to set aside his lifelong mission?"

"No," she said defensively. "Of course not."

"Then what?" he asked.

The weight of his question settled in her liver. What could she possibly do to the assassin to keep him from killing her?

She knew the answer, and it was soaked in blood.

"I'll figure it out." She turned and headed up the steps. "You tend to your own walls."

"You know," Richard said, keeping pace behind, "I'm not sure you'll know what to do with yourself once we figure all this out."

She opened her mouth to reply when feet thudded on the boards above them. Her eyes darted upward before flashing to Richard.

His smile disappeared—her safety along with it.

Twenty

Zarina flipped around so quickly that her braids stung her cheek.

"You distract me, Richard. Now the assassin could be on my ship."

"More likely a copper come to harangue you for holding up traffic." Richard's furrowed brows eased.

She glared at him. "I do not want the *shurta* on my ship either. Do you know what they do to locals around here?"

He listened for voices, then flashed his easy grin. "Shall we go see instead of speculating about things that haven't happened? I know that's a favorite pastime of yours."

She glared at him hard before stomping upstairs. It would serve him right if she was speared the moment she reached the deck. Teach him not to be so glib.

But there was no justice for her today. A tall officer in the distinctive Aegyptian azure blue that showed royal purple in her pink goggles hovered on the edge of her decking. His dark eyebrows were as thick as cattails over an angry-red face—though she wasn't sure if that last one was because of her lenses or not.

Richard had been right: the *shurta* had come to chide her. And rob her. And maybe throw her in jail. They wouldn't care one wit that an assassin was chasing her or that her boat was freshly wrecked. Since the Brits took over enforcement in Aegyptus, corruption had only grown worse. Their mere presence on her ship after an entire life of avoiding them only proved she had been right—the scar on her boat was an ill omen. Not something good.

"*Dabit*." Zarina nodded to the man, shoving what little respect she could muster through clenched teeth.

"Hey ho, ya bobby, where's your captain?" Richard slid to her side. "I haven't seen him in ages."

The policeman furrowed his brows, concealing serious eyes. He frowned and disappeared. A moment later, another head popped up, this time doffed in a dusty cap and a grass-thin mustache.

The man looked between the two, his grass blade twitching just so, then broke into a toothily-spacious smile.

Zarina couldn't help but shoot Richard a smug look and mouth the words "gap-tooth!"

He returned her silent victory crow with a wink, spoiling her satisfaction. He was supposed to be humbled, not enjoying himself.

"Richard DeClare," the captain said and slapped his own thigh. "What are the odds? What are the odds? I thought you were back in balmy Britannia for another year."

Richard sidled past, blocking her way, his limbs loose and everywhere as if the ship were his. Zarina's neck muscles pulsed in outrage.

"That was the plan, Cap., but I heard some news too good to be true and had to come see for myself." He shot a glance back at her, and she stiffened. "How about you? Doing sky duty, I see? And during rush hour. Still on Lord Cromer's bad side, eh?"

"Ah, that," the captain said, taking off his cap and rubbing the sun-bleached stubble of his scalp. "He's just upset me and some of the boys were drinking in the streets. The locals don't like anything to do with intoxication, I'll warn you now. Though, by the looks of you, anything more'n a glass of whisky would bowl you right over." He barked a laugh and flashed his gap-toothed smile with a wink in her direction. "Though I dare say, you look right awful. Tavern brawl? Or did you fall down the ruddy stairs? Ha!"

"Chalk this up to a wild game of cricket." Richard chuckled, and the men proceeded to guffaw and slap each other on the shoulders like the sun had gotten to their brains.

"So who's the nomad?" The captain asked, wiping tears from his eyes. "She looks like you plucked her straight from the desert. I've always wanted to do that meself. Find a grateful desert wench and show her what's what about a Britannian man."

"That's it." Zarina shoved Richard's arm out of the way. "If you don't have a real reason to stop me, get off my ship."

"Hey-ho, hey-ho." The captain put up his arms like he was placating a wild boar. "No offense meant. I didn't know you spoke English. A harmless mistake."

She glowered at the stupid man. Just because she wasn't supposed to understand didn't make his comments any less insulting. "Go away."

The captain's face fell. "Is this how you feel, too, Richard? After all we've been through, eh?"

Richard ran a hand along his collar and smiled awkwardly. "Aw, that? Of course not. She's having a bad day. Just fixed her ship and now it's all scratched up again."

The captain nodded and plopped his cap back on. "I see. Yes. Women do care about things like that."

Zarina nearly bit her tongue. "Things like what, exac—"

Richard clamped a hand over her mouth and rubbed the knuckles of his other into the top of her hair. "Isn't she something?"

She bit his fingers, and he yanked them away with a yelp.

"Ha. A desert rose, this one," Richard said and shook the pain from his fingers. "Anyway, we're in a hurry. Mind escorting us down? We're headed toward the National Library."

"That dusty old place? I don't get why you like reading about them creepy ol' Aegyptians and their cursed mummies so much." The captain twitched his grass blade as if the dust from the library were under his nose.

"Got to keep Uncle William happy. You understand. Now, will you help an ol' chap out? There's a bottle of port in it at my uncle's place, just don't tell the local officials." He grinned.

"Ah ha. Now you're talking." The captain jumped down into his ship, forgoing the seven or so steps he labored up the first time. "Just follow Cap'n Smith. I'll take you where you need to go."

The *shurta* airship pulled ahead and raised its red mast, signaling for nearby ships to move out of the way.

Zarina rounded on Richard and shoved her finger into his chest. "What in Ra's name was that?"

Richard's eyes widened before slipping once more into ease. "You seemed upset about all the traffic, I thought I'd help get you to your destination without any more damage to your ship. Rather dapper of me, no? Just coat me in metal." He grinned with boyish charm.

"What?"

"Because I'm your knight in shining armor." He tipped an imaginary hat.

"Anything in armor will burn in the sun and sink in the sands here." Zarina ground her back teeth together. "The sun shines without you, and so do I. I don't need you to get me through traffic, and I don't need you to fight my battles for me. Especially when you do so by kowtowing to a hateful, stupid man who thinks he's better than me."

The captain breezed by in his sleek *shurta* ship, shouting at them to follow. Zarina sighed. At this rate, there was no way she could get to the library quickly without looking like she was following the captain, even if she wasn't. The whole thing stunk of imperialist favoritism, something the local Cairens were loath to tolerate. Add them to the list of people who wanted her dead.

Richard waved Captain Smith off and turned toward her. "I wasn't trying to fight a battle for you. I did that yesterday." He lifted his shirt and rubbed a hand over his bandaged and taut abs. "I was trying to keep you out of fighting altogether."

"By calling the *shurta* over?"

"Exactly."

"The only thing they're good for is drawing attention and stealing my money. Oh yes, and insulting me to my face."

"Ah, I'm not worried about the money," Richard waved away her concerns. "Your face is no worse for the wear."

Her stomach growled at his insolence.

"And the attention was a bang up to the elephant distraction for getting you away from the cloaked man weaving his way through the ships."

"Cloaked man?" She swung around, scanning the skyline. Pain spiked in her temples from the sun and her fate catching up with her.

"Ay, like the one in the marketplace. He's been following us since early this morning."

Fear and anger burst inside her. "And you didn't say anything?"

"I worried it would only concern you. I mean, when you did finally see him, you hit another ship."

She grimaced.

"He wasn't close enough for any harm, yet, anyway. And now that the coppers are escorting us down, we're safe."

Zarina mulled over his words, a sandstorm swirling inside her. He should have told her. She did also hit a ship. And he did find a way to get them into the city without another port incident, even if it made for some ugly stares from the locals.

"I want an apology." She raised her chin with all the defiance of her deified ancestors. "For standing by while I was treated so awfully by your fellow Britannian just because of my gender and where I came from."

"I was trying to help—"

"There's a better way than tolerating cruelty."

Richard's smile fell, and his green eyes studied her face. "I'm sorry, Zarina. You're right, and I'll do better to unlearn such boarish behaviors." He fell to his knee and grasped her hand. "Forgive me?"

She pursed her lips tightly, but the heat was already fading. "For now."

"Grand." He popped up and twirled her around.

She yanked her hand away and rubbed it on her pants.

"So?" Richard leaned his elbows back on the banister, his demeanor as cool as if he'd spent a day at the beach.

"So what?"

"So are you going to trust me and follow the cap'n, or continue punishing me for your bodyguard going rogue back in Alexandria?"

Wind whipped her hair, the annoyed shouts of the *shurta* little pokes of irritation that told her to hurry. The tombs she grew up in were far more bleak than these sunny skies, but they were also far more quiet. Or maybe she had just been alone far too long.

"I'm not punishing you," she said at last. "I'm being realistic. Aegyptus is my home, the place of my birth and all those before me, and it will be the place I die, sooner rather than later if I trust the wrong people." Zarina jumped up to the helm and swung it in line to follow the *shurta*. "So help if you want, but don't expect something in return. You will not find it in me."

Richard mustered a somber stare, though mischief still tugged at his lips. "I do want to help. And I require nothing you won't give to me freely, princess." He hopped onto a barrel, kicking his legs up to recline. "Cairo, ho!"

She pulled the iron lever whose chain ran down to the steam release hidden in the boiler room. The ship picked up the pace, skipping from cloud to cloud until they were in the thick of Cairo's pungent smog. Richard said nothing, watching her with a quirked brow and soft eyes. She stared resolutely ahead, giving in periodically to see if he was still looking at her.

He was looking. Always.

She gulped and redoubled her efforts, keeping her line of vision away from his square jaw and wind-whipped hair. From his gentle eyes and relaxed demeanor.

But keeping him from her sight did not keep his words from her mind. The scratched Nile on the side of her ship hung heavy on her thoughts, its rapids twisting and twining as it carved new paths throughout her. Rebirth. That's what Richard had said. And she realized now that she did trust him, for better or worse.

He knew she was not some soft gentlewoman from the cold of Europa, a damsel in distress. She was exactly as the captain said, a nomad from the sand dunes, only she was not plucked from the desert by some man.

She *was* the desert.

She was Aegyptus.

She was Ra; all the divinity of the gods left on the earth.

And Richard was trying to support her in that—albeit clumsily—an agent free from fate and still devoted to her cause with all the understanding a foreigner could muster.

She could feel the assassin's presence everywhere now that she had stopped running. But with Richard at her side, she no longer feared her death. She would take his advice to plan for the future and hunt down the assassin so that when she found him, she could find the answer she needed, and then, if necessary, kill him and be free.

Twenty-One

Zarina switched out the red lenses of her goggles for her moss and lime-green ones just in case. She didn't want to miss any opportunity to find a clue and had no idea where they would be hidden. Fortunately, the streets were busy with harried statesmen and melting Brits far too busy to notice her. It gave her and Richard the space they needed to survey the library and make a plan.

The outside stood several stories tall, its facade a chipping white paint that stopped beneath pointed balustrades. Long, tired vines climbed up one side, and stark, dry earth rested below the rest. There were plenty of exits in case of an emergency, though some would assuredly break her fall by breaking her legs. There were even a few half-windows that poked out from the basement, greatly reducing her chances of dying in a sand trap.

She eyed those longer than the rest, shrouded in shadowy memories of her mother's end, of her bloodied hand disappearing beneath hot sand, of her tears.

So many tears.

Then a new understanding surfaced for Zarina.

Her mother had defied the idea of her fate by seeking a normal life and family for her and Zarina. She hadn't feared fate or death but had looked forward with hope and love. Which meant in the end, neither death nor the assassin had stolen her mother away. She had given herself to them freely for a chance at living. For a chance at love.

What did that mean for Zarina? Who did she love? As the last daughter left in a long line of heroines, she had no child to live for. Could she live for her mother's dream? For the women who came before her and another chance at love even if it meant accepting an early death?

"Ready?" Richard asked, the summer heat kissing his brow with sweat.

She nodded. "As I'll ever be. I'll keep an eye on the windows, and you keep an eye on my back. We get in and out as quickly as possible. No getting distracted by your love."

"My what?" he asked, a wrinkle in his nose.

"*Books*," she emphasized and smiled. "All the books. I don't want to die because your eyes were on a dusty spine instead of mine."

He grinned. "Fair enough."

Richard stepped into the shade of the large, cracked front door and pulled a frayed cord. A deep, bellicose chime rang out thrice before a squinty-eyed man lugged open the door.

His eyes opened a slit further as he took them in, Richard in his relaxed British finery and Zarina in her two-toned green goggles, her vest and pants and braided hair, all still smattered with blood from the day before.

"Ah, Lord DeClare, it has been more than a year," the man said with a pursed mouth. "Your patronage is always appreciated." He held out a hand but did not move from their path.

Richard swung out a small jangling bag of soft velvet. "As is your generous help." He placed the pouch in the librarian's hand. The man's spindly fingers closed around it, but Richard held on. "Ah. Ah. Help first. We need access to your restricted section."

The librarian's eyes managed to bulge through the tags of skin that folded over his eyelids. "I would prefer it if you chose a different avenue for your work today. Those scrolls are delicate. They crumble easily, my lord."

Zarina sighed loudly, and the man's narrow gaze snapped toward her. Her mother had told her the stewards of Aegyptian libraries were wise servants of Ra and the goddess Shay, versed in pharaonic histories and ready to serve his descendants. This librarian looked more like a dusty floor pillow.

"The ancient histories are also not for riff-raff," he said with an upturned nose. "Many of these scrolls were written by high priests for the very pharaohs themselves. We can't have surfs smudging them up. I request you leave your servant outside."

Zarina gritted her teeth. *He* was supposed to be serving *her*. Her mother never would have stood for such blatant disrespect. She had always been commanding and confident, a force to be reckoned with until the very end. Zarina channeled her mother's energy and took a breath.

She ripped the pouch from the man's hands and flung the coins helter-skelter down the foyer behind him. Each one *chink-clinked*, and rolled with painful poignancy, their echoes bouncing down the empty corridor.

The librarian's eyes shot open wider than she thought possible. She reached for her dagger, but the scabbard stood empty, her blade lost to Adajin's mortal temple along with Farak and her throwing stick. Instead, she grabbed the man's collar and lifted his slight frame off the floor. It took all her strength, but she refused to shake from the effort.

"Let us in, by order of Zarina Nefertari, last descendant of The Beloved Queen, protector of the arts, and loved by Shay, the goddess of wisdom and keeper of books whose very air you waste by breathing." The words felt strange on her tongue, the authority a mirage of power shimmering from an imposter's mouth.

The librarian's skin tags stretched to near invisibility. "I—You—-She can't be serious?" He asked, turning to Richard.

She dropped him to the floor, one hand still on his robes, and pinched his cheeks so she could turn his face to hers. "You will address only me when I'm in your presence. Richard can do nothing for you; he has devoted himself to me as you were ordained to do, lest you've forgotten after all these years of doting on books instead of queens."

She turned her gaze to Richard to confirm his loyalty, relying on the tentative tendrils of trust growing between them. He offered a resigned smile, though his eyes belied unease. She tilted her head, eyebrow raised. Had she done something wrong?

Richard cleared his throat. "Right O', Hamil. You best do as she says. You don't want a firebrand burning inside your library. Best to put it out by showing us your restricted section."

Hamil's mouth flapped open once, then twice more before he acquiesced. "I should expect such nonsense from a Britannian. You don't care for any country's traditions unless they involve tea. The goddess Shay will be mortified."

They followed him through rooms cluttered with artifacts behind glass and rows and rows of shelves filled with fading books and piles of scrolls. The smell of musk and vanilla and grass, all mixed with a thick coating of dust, filled her nose. At last, they arrived at a green and rust-painted door with what were probably yellow and cream flowers crawling across the front in raised wood. A heavy-set copper handle rested in the ancient door with a gaping keyhole below.

Hamil eyed her sideways before slipping in an ornate key and clicking the mechanism open with a thunk.

Cool, stale air brushed past Zarina's cheek as she stepped inside the small room that was older than memory. Two ornate sconces churned unbidden above them, their blue glass sides folding open and filling the room with a gentle light. Several dry scrolls and a few gilded books rested on two brittle shelves that sagged in the middle. Smatterings of Hebrew, Greacian, Aegyptian, and Arabic mixed and mingled among the scripts.

"What trick is this, you jackal?" Zarina growled, turning on Hamil.

"You asked for the restricted section. I brought you to the restricted section."

Zarina pushed him back against the wall, pressing an elbow into his throat. "This can't be all of it."

"It's all I've ever seen," Richard offered, trying to sidle his way between her and the idiot librarian. "They're the oldest texts I've seen on any continent."

She shook her head, meeting his worried stare with a fiery one of her own. His eyes searched hers, then he backed off, hands drooping to the sides.

She turned back to Hamil and pressed him harder into the wall. A choked harumph escaped his throat. "Either you broke your divine oath and sold out the legacy of the gods—in which case Ahmet will weigh your heart and find it so heavy with the black of your failure that he will feed on you for half of all eternity and not hunger a quip—or you're lying."

It was a line she had heard her mother use when a bread monger in Alexandria tried to stiff her three *zeri-mahbub* in change. It felt embarrassingly dramatic to watch as a child. Now, it seemed just right.

Hamil glared back, his sharp eyes sliding over her face. "If you were truly a descendant of Nefertari, you would see the machinations," he sneered.

She chomped her mouth closed over the retort she had ready and turned on her heels, surveying the room. The half-baked brick was right. Intricately laced into the stones of the wall were thin wires of copper, turned blue-green by her goggles and oxidation and time. She ran a finger over one, tracing it to a pinhole in the bottom corner of the room. She should have seen the legacy of her ancestors before anything else. But she was out of practice, running from what tied her to the curse instead of embracing it.

Zarina stood back, analyzing the inlay of wires and the shape of the room. They spun symmetrically toward the northeast where they coalesced around a gold ring a coin's width in diameter. She touched two fingertips to the hole and walked them down until she found what she was feeling for. The gentlest groove in the hardest stone. With the shadow of a smile, she dipped her finger under the tiny latch and pulled.

She waited for a clatter or clunk, something to tell her she had been right. But the hidden gears and pulleys worked smoothly, only the tiniest whisper of chatter sneaking through the stone thanks to expert craftsmen, generations of knowledge, and meticulous upkeep. Gears revealed themselves from the wall as they turned, the mechanism far more complicated than she had realized. The back wall was no wall at all, but a heavy door that slid sideways on metal tracks to reveal an illuminated opening.

"Ha!" Richard clapped his hands, rushing forward so his nose was just out of reach of the moving stone. "Would you look at that? You've been holding out on me, Hamil, you ol' chap."

Zarina returned Hamil's glare with a smug smile. "Don't challenge me again." She pushed him forward. "Now take us inside or get out of the way."

Hamil's face darkened even further, but he led the way with a sloppy wave of his fat hand. "I expected Nepthali's daughter to be regal and full of grace. Ra only knows what happened."

"I suppose we can thank the roguish father I never knew for that." She stuck her tongue at him and pushed him forward.

Inside the tunnel, the atmosphere was heavy with lives gone past. The blocks that made up the walls stood sharp, each edge cut with mathematical precision. The tiles lining the floor portrayed scenes of the family that built it.

Her family.

An image of Neferatari—a white-clad figure with a sharp nose and lantern in one hand—led the way around each bend. Well-known figures from Zarina's ancestry followed after her. Hehet, who discovered the power of steam when she vowed to move the pyramids to save them from the flood; Nephthys, who created a temple maze with shifting doors to thwart corrupt Nubians from defiling the home of the goddess, Isis; and Annipe, who first raised a boat from the Nile into the sky.

Zarina had always known this vault existed, though this was her first time inside it. The tomb of ancient scripts was the most well-worn star on her map, the gilded ink faded from fingers searching for it over and over as if it would save them. The tunnels in Cairo had been used by her ancestors to offer homage to Ra and provide a safe place to rest, hidden from the assassin. But it was not meant to keep them, the consumption of food forbidden so near to Ra's earthly presence.

It was to this place she had been traveling with her mother as a young girl of seven summers. And it was to this place they never arrived after the assassin found them trading for bread in a basement just a few streets south so they could eat before they came.

Neferatari's lanterns brought them around the last bend and into a room stuffed to the brim with papyrus scrolls bound in leather and golden scarabs. Gas lanterns flickered to life at their arrival and cast long shadows across Richard's eager face. She breathed in the scent of warm sand and jasmine, of cool, dry air.

"Where are the scrolls from the time of the Betrayal of Men?"

"The Betrayal of Men?" Hamil's voice dripped with dry disdain.

Zarina bristled. "The fall of the Middle Kingdom and the start of the New as you historians so inaccurately call it. Ra has only ever had one kingdom, regardless of which mortal rules it at the time."

"History is difficult to track on an eternal timeline," Richard offered, unbidden. "It's just a way for us mortals to distinguish between the various ruling families."

"Because those in power like kings and pharaohs are all history cares about," she replied sourly.

"It's true," he said with a playful grin. "I spend all my time thinking about one princess in particular."

"*Ayya,*" she punched his shoulder and turned back to Hamil to hide her blush. "I'm waiting, scroll keeper."

"The histories you seek are there," Hamil said, pointing to a ledge in a dimly lit corner far in the back. "Though be warned, some texts are best left unread."

"And some words are best left unsaid, yet you speak. Why do you hover, so? Go away."

Hamil hesitated, his expression as sour as an unripe persimmon. "Last time I left a queen unattended in these vaults, a treasure went missing."

"What are you talking about?" Zarina asked.

"Over there." Hamil pointed to an opulent display of headdresses and crowns, of bracelets and scarabs on the far wall. In the center, pressed into azure fabric, was the imprint of a beetle gone missing. "A sacred Finder suddenly disappeared."

"Who took it?" Zarina stepped across the room and ran a hand over the empty space.

"I don't know," Hamil harrumphed. "Another servant of Shay was on duty, and we've been commanded to keep the identities of Nefertari's descendants secret, even from each other."

"And you're sure it was a queen who took it?" Richard asked.

Hamil's bitter lips tightened. "Do you think we'd let just anyone in here?"

"You let in riff-raff." Zarina shot him a glare. "How dare you accuse the queens. I should gut you with the blade of my ancestors for such a traitorous remark. Now get out of my sight before I change my mind."

"And leave you here with the artifacts?" Hamil sputtered.

"Someone needs to guard the entrance and make sure no one finds us down here."

Hamil's chin puckered with disapproval. "Are you expecting someone else?"

"You know very well the answer to that," Zarina said, her voice low and dangerous.

Hamil's sneer melted, and he turned abruptly and left. She leaned through the doorway, making sure his pillowy frame was completely out of sight before returning to Richard and sliding the first scroll off the shelf.

The thick parchment was the color of mottled sand with Nefertari's beetle symbol sealed in the center.

Zarina pressed a finger to the center of the scarab's wings. The legs unclasped with a delicate puff so she could slip the parchment free. The thinly woven papyrus reeds crackled as they lay flat for the first time in centuries, but inside, the paintings were still crisp and vibrant and not what she needed. She already knew of the revolution that allowed Ramses II to take control of Aegyptus, claiming Ra lived within him. And she knew how Nefertari's descendency from the great pharaoh, Ay, made her even more beloved by Ramses and his people.

But before she could rule this scroll out, Zarina popped the dark green lens from the left side of her goggles and slid a lime one in its place.

She gave the scroll another scan before rolling it back up with soft fingers and pulling down another and another.

Richard, too, searched through the texts, distracting her with his "Ohs!" and "Ah has!" like he already knew what he was reading but had also never seen it before. It was Richard who declared he had found something of interest, first.

"Here," he said, his finger scrolling past a scene filled with egrets flying over the Nile. He stopped on an image of three queens. Each had a smaller image of another queen at their feet, the Aegyptian symbols for purified blood resting above two of their heads. "This is what I suspected earlier. That Ramses' six wives came from three lines, two pure Aegyptian, one Hittite."

Zarina pulled the bottom of the parchment down further, tearing a strand of reed in the process. She breathed in with a hiss, and Richard took the scroll from her hands with a scandalized look.

"I'll just hold this, shall I? So you can read without encumbrance."

She puckered her lips to fight him, but let the words fall. Now was not time to refuse the gracious out he gave her for being so careless. "Hold it still, then. I can't read if you're wobbling around in this wretched light."

She scanned the queens, moving a hair's breadth at a time and closing one eye every move to check for differences. It wasn't until the bottom, below the queens' feet, that she caught a wisp of difference.

"I think I found something!" she whispered excitedly. "Roll it down more."

What to the naked eye was the arch of a sunset transformed into the hidden lines of the Singular Eye. Below it lay three kingdoms. Aegyptus's Upper Lands to the south lay under the light of the first queen, Nefertari. The lower lands to the north lay under the next queen, Isetnofret. And a foreign land, excluded from the light of the Singular eye, lay at the feet of Queen Maathornefurer.

In the shadows of that foreign land came the serpent Apep. From that foreign land came death. And from the histories of that land would come her answer.

Twenty-Two

Zarina shut an eye. Opened it, then shut it again as she inspected the delicate parchment. Had there really been secrets hidden in these dusty scrolls in Cairo the whole time? Had her ancestors missed them all and for so long?

She couldn't help but smirk. It was pure irony that the inbred defects that required her to wear colored lenses to avoid migraines were what led her to the discovery.

Her eye caught the whisper of difference at the bottom of her page, and her heart picked up.

"Richard," she whispered, just in case Hamil lurked nearby "This queen, you can see her, yes?" She tapped on the foreign woman with a corn-textured cone as a crown.

Richard nodded. "The Hittite princess betrothed to Ramses to quell war."

"And do you see the dagger?"

"No." Richard moved closer, and Zarina slid off her goggles so Richard could take a look. "Fascinating," he whispered, the cinnamon of his breath brushing past her cheek. "I still can't get over the idea of secrets hidden in plain sight. Truly genius."

Zarina squinted her eyes against an oncoming headache and leaned closer to the musty papyrus. "What does it mean?"

"My guess is as good as yours."

Zarina sighed. "I thought you claimed to be an 'expert' on ancient Aegyptus."

"I am," Richard said simply. "But so are you. This isn't the whole puzzle, but two pieces of it. One which should not surprise us, and another that leads where we want to go."

She frowned and took the goggles back for another look. "Two pieces," she thought out loud, looking between the three pairs of queens, two in the light and one in the dark. "The one that should not surprise is that Ra does not give favors to the Hittite lands. That's why they are in the dark."

"Right-O," Richard said with a nod. "The Hittite lands were blessed by Pharaoh *Ramses* because of his union with the Hittite princess, Maathornefurer. Because of their foreign blood, however, they were not favored by the god, *Ra*, unlike you."

"A lot of good it's done me," she said and used her vest to wipe a smudge from her goggles. "The second piece..." Zarina ran a finger over the serpent and his dagger. "...is Apep coming from the Hittite lands. But that makes no sense. Maathornefurer was married off as an olive branch by Ramses to stop the war between the Hittites and Aegyptus, an arranged marriage that proved successful. Why would their peaceful union cause Apep to come forth?"

"Because the snake is not Apep," Richard said simply

"Then who else could it be? The rivalry between Apep and Ra is well-known. And it's clearly Apep's serpent form slithering forth from the shadows."

"Your family has done what all others do," Richard said with that air of patient indifference that was both infuriating and inexplicably soothing.

"And what is that?" she asked, not sure she wanted the answer.

"You've taken a true story and made it into a legend filled with bits of truth and bits of showmanship. Think about it. According to legend, Apep is the god of foreigners and has brought war countless times to Aegyptus' doorstep. If it were truly Apep coming to kill you, dagger in mouth, why would he be so secretive about his vengeance? And why would he wait so long to accomplish his goals? If anything, he's already won by filling the land with Britannians who, like my uncle, take and destroy everything that is Aegyptus for themselves."

Zarina's heart slowed as Richard's words swirled, both hot and icy and trapped within her chest. His logic made sense but also couldn't be true. She tilted her chin up stubbornly. "The gods work on their own time, and we'd be fools to question that."

"Perhaps, they do." Richard pulled the scroll to its end to smooth the wrinkles before rolling it up with adept, bruised fingers. "Grand histories often contain the important bones of truth. But for now, we have to look past the aggrandized showmanship in your story to find the answer. If your family decided to cast Apep as its oppressor, what trait or deed could they be representing in god form?"

"You mean, what quality did Apep imbue in his servants to invoke such hate?"

Richard looked at her, a quirk to his lips and a hint of collusion in his *mazeaj* eyes. "Yes, of course."

Zarina pressed her lips tightly together and glared.

He cleared his throat. "I'm sorry. I'm trying. Your ideas are strange and new to me, but I am now in your world, not mine—and frankly, I like it much better here. I will try to be more respectful."

She watched his earnest eye in the dim cast of lanterns a moment longer, then nodded once.

"Thank you," he smiled warmly, melting her cold. "Now, whatever imbued quality drives this story has got to be powerful enough to devote generations of people to both murder and protection."

"Protection?"

Richard gave her a pointed look.

"Ah," she looked to the shadows behind the shelf. "You mean Farak."

He nodded. "So are you going to tell me what all that's about now, or keep leaving me in the dark?"

She stiffened. "What what's all about?"

He raised a brow.

She sighed.

He wasn't going to budge. How long had it been since she last heard the story nestled in the crook of her mother's arm? She had never actually told it herself before. Without a daughter of her own, she had never needed to.

And with Richard, she wasn't sure she wanted to share. It was a story of her and Farak's closeness. Of their history. Of her shame and Farak's servitude. Of their forced fates and the tragedy that started it all.

A hand touched her own. Startled, she looked up. Richard's hand sat atop hers, light and warm and reassuring.

"I promise I'm an engaging audience," he said with a quirked smile. "And a good secret keeper. But I can't help you solve your, ah, fate unless you tell me the whole story. I'm certain the answer to your problem lies in the middle of all your stories."

His presence, his word, and the clarity in his gaze washed over her. And for the first time since she could remember, she felt free. Free enough to share a small piece of her soul.

"Farak's family descends from the sacred Pharaoh Ay's Great Royal Guard," she said, easing into the story she had heard a hundred times. "A group of men and women plucked from every caste for their strength and bravery and respected just below the pharaohs and priests. Even through the political upheaval between Ay's time and that of his great-granddaughter Nefertari's, they stayed loyal, a formidable force that brought death swiftly."

"So they're all just born loyal, then?" Richard sounded a mix between incredulous and entranced. "Explains a lot about your bodyguard's stodginess, yeah?"

She offered a half-smile. "Ramses thought so. That was until one night when he went to visit Nefertari and found the chief Guardsman, Rahemlen, in her room. He had confessed his love to her, and she had refused. Jealous with rage, Rahemlen sprung at her and wrapped his hands around her neck.

"Ramses entered a scene of sorrow and desperation, watching as the darkness within his untrue servant tried to extinguish the light of the woman he loved so dearly. He killed Rahemlen on the spot. Nefertari was equally unlucky." Zarina brushed a hand across her throat, feeling the ghost of a bruise that had scarred generations.

"Oy, that's more than a dollop of mischief, that." Richard managed a somber face.

"She lived a while longer but never recovered from Rahemlen's rage. When she eventually passed, Ramses called all the Guardsmen before him."

"He's going to kill them, isn't he?" Richard couldn't help but look excited. "Enraged kings love to kill. Our own King George—"

"Hush," she chided him, though his nonchalance lightened some of the dark in her story. "Ramses called all the guards together and decreed they would fight each other."

"I knew he wanted them dead. Was this like a fight to the death, last-man-standing type of brawl?" Richard whistled low.

"More like a fight until everyone is dead. Ramses' revenge. A culling to be inflicted by the guilty party's own hand. But Nefertari's daughter Merytamun pleaded on their behalf. You see, she loved one of the guards . . ." Zarina's voice drifted off. She had never felt a connection to this story before, but as she spoke she could feel the sorrow, the yearning and desperation of her ancestors.

Richard squeezed her hand. "You okay?"

"Ah, yes. The light is hurting my head," Zarina half-lied. "Merytamun's pleading worked. Ramses decided to spare the rest of the Guardsmen on condition that Merytamun marry him instead: a love lost for a love lost."

Richard shook loose his shoulders, sleeves brushing nearby scrolls. "I still get the willies thinking about the pharaohs marrying their own daughters."

She half-smiled, something genuine this time. "It is the way it was. Merytamun, for loving a traitor, was cursed to only have daughters who could only have daughters, and so on, lest they forget their place in his kingdom ever again. Then Ramses relegated the Guardsmen to the lowest caste in all the land, decreeing they forever serve queens they are forbidden to love. They made a blood oath bound by Ma'at, the goddess of justice and gatekeeper to eternal life, and were cursed to only bear a son when a royal daughter is born. One servant for every master."

Richard ruffled his hair before saying, "So Farak only exists because you do."

She nodded, guilt filling her lungs and choking out her breath. She was glad they were in the muted light of the library so Ra couldn't witness her shame.

"And he is supposed to die if you do, too?"

"So it has been with all the generations before," she could barely say the words. "And all for a woman they are forbidden to love. Not that they want to."

"Was it only Nefertari's line that was cursed?" Richard brushed to the next question, not seeing her pain, but it was better that way.

"No," she said, clearing her throat of the pesky sorrow that coated her voice. "Ramses no longer trusted any of the women in the palace and cursed his second wife, Isetnofret as well. The assassins extinguished her line millennia ago, and that line of Guardsmen with it."

Zarina's history, her confession of born guilt, sat heavy between them.

"What about Maathornefurer's line?" Richard asked.

"Hm?" Zarina ran a finger over the image of the Hittite queen.

"Were they cursed, too?"

She bit her lip. "Maathornefurer's line was spared the curse, marrying into the lineage long after both the primary queens had passed, though I assume her descendants have long faded into ignorant obscurity, not really belonging in Aegyptus and all."

Zarina plucked at the pages in a nearby book, the paper soft and worn. Richard leaned against the same shelf, chin resting on his fist and brows furrowed in thought.

"So Maathornerfurer's line could have sons but in exchange weren't protected by the Royal Guardsmen?"

One of the pieces of parchment with a sharper edge cut her finger. She gasped and pressed the tip into her mouth to stop the bleeding. "There were no Guardsmen left to give them."

"Three family lines are tied up in this thing, whatever it is," Richard said with an energized nod. "Yours, Farak's, and the Hittite queens'. And if it's enough to turn devout people like Farak into rebels and regal people like you into tattered nomads—"

"I'm not tattered!"

"Then just imagine what it's done to Maathornefurer's family."

Zarina rubbed her sandal under the edge of the dusty shelf. Her fate and the generations of tragedy behind it had always made her feel like she was lost in a sandstorm, reaching for something she could not find. But for the first time, down in the musty dark of the library with Richard, she felt she could see the hard edge of something real past all the grit. And for the first time, she could feel others reaching for the unknown with her.

Farak, worn down by a family oath he, too, was born into.

And a sharp-toothed darkness fueled by millennia of something far stronger than anything she'd ever felt.

She pulled her vest tight and shivered. "Fear makes for strange winds."

"What about that, then?" Richard asked.

"Fear?"

"Not necessarily." He rubbed his scruffless chin. "Any strong emotion would do. Which takes us back to our original inquiry: what does Apep symbolize for Aegyptus and your family that could motivate murder?"

Zarina pushed out her bottom lip and leaned back on her heels. "Chaos," she said with a shrug. "The embodiment of envy and the jealous pang in one's liver that leads to the path of evil. But why would Maathornefurer be jealous of Nefertari? The Beloved Queen was dead long before Maathornefurer's arranged marriage. It is why I never bothered to learn much about her or her sister. That, and they're not pure Aegyptian."

Richard finished scratching his smooth jaw, then patted through his pockets. At last, he pulled out his sketchpad from earlier. "This is why," he said, his gemstone-greens shining in the light. He flipped the pad open to the picture he drew of her earlier.

"Put that away," she huffed, uncomfortable warmth spidering up her cheeks.

"Don't you see?"

She could barely look at the soft curves in his drawing, the delicate way he managed to draw her nose and the forlorn look that lived within her eyes. "See what?"

"Ramses loved Nefertari, right?"

Zarina waved Richard off, her cheeks now as hot as the desert sun. She refused to read further into the matter-of-fact way he said such heavy words.

She averted her eyes and whispered, "Of course, he did. She was the one for whom the sun rises. Ramses said so himself."

Richard smiled. "Exactly. He built temples in her honor. Put up vestiges in her image all over the land. Added her seal on important documents and tabulae with his. She was his first wife, his most primary, and it sounds like the love of his life."

"So what does that have to do with Maathornefurer?"

"What do you think? You barely knew who they were, and you are versed in royal ancestry. The only reason I know they exist is one tiny document that talks more about the parade that came to drop off Maathornefurer than anything about her, personally. The second Hittite's name we don't even know, only that she was the first's sister."

"So she was jealous Ramses didn't love her enough to curse her and spent her life trying to destroy what he made?" Zarina scrunched her nose, aggravating her headache. "That's ridiculous."

Richard gave her a hard look, his lips curving just enough to infuriate her. She pursed her lips and stared back.

"Maybe not," Richard said at last, moving close enough his nose sat a touch away from hers. She held her breath, trying not to get lost in the scent of cool rain and the hot spice of cinnamon. "Ramses' love came with power and recognition. Those Hittite princesses left everything they knew to join a long line of wives in a country known for its god-selected blood purity. They knew they would never advance here and that their children would have no influence in Aegyptus or back home. They were stranded, left in the desert."

"And angry," she said.

The princesses took shape within her mind, their forlorn and anguished faces next to Farak's as she flew away those many moons ago, hands outstretched in a sandstorm as the gods left them to die. She pressed a hand to her stomach to ease the hurt.

"Ay," Richard said. "They were angry. Angry, unloved, and with nothing to lose. And there's no stronger force in all the world than revenge."

Twenty-Three

Zarina wished to linger in the onyx and sandstone tunnels, to hide in their cool safety a little longer. But Richard's eagerness would not have it, and he dragged her away from the hidden library and back under Cairo's smoggy sun.

It was her fault, really, for suggesting where they ought to go next. They had scoured the rest of the scrolls that looked like they might hold an ancestry of the Hittite princesses to no avail. Richard had been right, no one cared about the princesses once they had passed. It was sobering and alarming. How could a line of descendants that held a sliver of Ra's blood disappear so easily? Aren't lanterns supposed to shine in the dark?

Forgotten or not, a queen of Aegyptus is a queen of Aegyptus, and Maathornefurer would have been buried where all of them were. If there were any clues left to find, they would be in her family's most sacred tombs.

"The Valley of the Queens," Richard crooned to himself as their ship headed farther south.

The grainy wind tousled his curls on the deck below, and the sun brightened his sunburnt cheeks. Back in the skies and amongst the freedom the clouds provided, she couldn't help but smile.

Richard hung over the banister at the front of the ship, grinning widely. "Aegyptologists only just discovered some of the treasures there, and you've had a map to all of them this whole bloomin' time. I know a fair shake of Britannian gentry who would trade their mothers for a piece of that information."

Zarina scowled and leaned against the helm. "That's because Britannians give their women the same rights as cattle."

Richard glanced over his shoulder and raised a brow. "Aegyptus is no better."

"The ancient Aegyptians treated women equally to men. Women could divorce and marry whomever they wished, and land rights were passed through matriarchal lines. Hence why Aegyptus is mine."

"How's that going for you?"

Zarina snapped her head down towards Richard. "What?"

"The whole ruling Aegyptus and being married to whomever you wish thing," Richard said, his tone mocking and playful. "I was just wondering if it's everything you dreamed."

Zarina puckered her lips, then tugged the rutters of her ship in a hard right. Richard lost his balance and fell over the side, catching the railing just before plummeting to his doom.

"Woah, woah," he cried, panting.

With all the grace of an egret chick, he slid his legs back over and onto the deck. Zarina couldn't help but smirk.

He put some distance between himself and the railing with a pointed look directed at her. "A bit of podsnappery that was, trying to fling me to my death. I didn't mean any harm, I was just trying to feel about."

"And what can you feel at all with words instead of hands?" Zarina tugged her brows down, safe in her tease on the upper deck. A playful smile slipped from her lips.

"Is that an invitation, princess?"

She scowled.

He laughed. "My apologies, but I do enjoy seeing that apple red on your cheeks. I was just poking about to see whether or not you've thought about marrying someone and all that."

Zarina stiffened in the warm breeze. She could feel Richard eyeing her, all patience and innocent curiosity. Or was it innocent? She bit her lip and caught his glance before focusing back on the skies.

"I just wasn't sure," Richard continued, clearing his throat as he kicked a foot back on the railing, "what with you and your old bodyguard acting like scorned lovers and all."

Zarina slammed against the till of the ship—an accident this time. The ship whipped around, careening to the right. Barrels and boxes and Richard went tumbling toward the edge. She yanked the ship back on course but struggled to do the same with her thoughts. Fortunately, Richard had been ready this time and caught the railing, twisting about so he landed with his back against the wood. The whole thing made him appear far too collected as if he were casually waiting for someone to arrive on the deck of her ship.

"Farak and I have both been scorned," she sighed, "but we have never been lovers."

"Ah," Richard said as if he knew anything about anything.

The sun stood high in the sky, disintegrating all the shadows and places to hide. He strode up the three steps to the upper landing where she stood and leaned over the helm. "So there's no one else, then?"

"No one else to do what? Scorn me? Because there are plenty to do that." Zarina tried to keep things light, but Richard stood just before her, only the wood of the steering mechanism and a thin slip of sun between them.

"You deserve someone who loves you as much as Ramses loved Nefertari. Or Horace loved Isis. Someone who will worship you as the queen for whom the sun rises."

He placed gentle fingers atop hers, his gemstone greens catching flecks of gold in Ra's light, made all the brighter by the pink of her goggles. Zarina stood frozen, words gone and her hands helpless on the helm between them. She swallowed, a hot, dry thing, and bit her lip as she grasped for the desperate straw of communication.

"I—"

He leaned in, pressing his lips to hers. A warmth far hotter than Aegyptus' desert engulfed her. She pulled back with the whisper of a gasp, then leaned in greedily to smell his cinnamon, to see if the taste of his lips matched. His hand tightened over hers, but his mouth stayed soft, inviting and unassuming as all of Richard ever was, and she did not pull away. Soft fingers played with the tips of her braids and brushed against her jaw. Then glided down her neck, where they rested, her pulse beating against his.

At last, his lips parted and left her with a sigh.

Zarina pulled back, dazed. She blinked once, then twice, and the shape of reality sank in. "Farak . . ." she breathed.

Richard frowned, a sadness creasing his eyes that plucked at her heart. "I daresay my pride's been hurt."

A chill ran down her spine, quenching their shared heat. "No, you sun-baked perch, look behind you!"

The temple of Luxor had come into sight on the horizon, and past it, in the shadows of the Theban Hills, floated a giant, sharp ship that jutted to spear blades on each end.

Richard spun around. "Oi. You think those are Farak and Adajin's men?"

"I can smell his stink from here." Zarina scrunched her nose.

"They've beaten us here then, have they? But how'd they know where we were headed?"

Zarina shut off the engine so they slowed to a glide, then eased the till west. The sleek, slight angle of her ship should look like a mirage on the horizon to Adajin as long as they kept their distance. If they held their course due west, the Theban Hills that sheltered the Valleys of the Kings and Queens would soon give them cover so they could get closer.

"I don't know why they're here." Zarina punched the till. "There's no way they could have known our plans. We spoke to no one about where we were headed, including Hamil."

"So they're just tomb-raiding the one location we happen to be heading to at the time we are heading there?" Richard's tone sounded as doubtful as she felt.

Zarina scanned the sand below Adajin's ship where tiny specks of men milled about on the sand dunes. What *were* they doing here? She slipped her map from her vest pocket and scanned the thick cluster of stars that loomed over the valley of the queens. She rubbed the nub that stood over Maathornefurer's tomb. It was farther back into the canyon than where Adajin's ship hovered. So either he wasn't there for the same reason they were, or he didn't know where those tombs were.

"Nefertari," she muttered and moved her finger to the brightest star.

Richard peeked over the edge of the map, casting light shadows. "What's that?"

"Adajin has banked right over Nefertari's tomb." The realization thundered against her mind and struck like lightning through her frame. "This is Farak's doing. He is digging up my very heart. The source of my family."

"You think he's raiding Nefertari's tomb to spite you?"

"Not just to spite me, to finish me off. It is the greatest and last of my family's legacy. A sacred space we may only enter once a year at the Wadi festival to commune with Nefertari's spirit and be strengthened by the will of the gods."

"The Wadi festival?"

She nodded. "Or the Beautiful Festival of the Valley, a celebration of the dead."

Richard's fair brow scrunched in tight. "I thought the assassin was the one trying to kill you."

"He is, but earlier in the marketplace, Farak saw the assassin and refused to tell me who it was."

"Blimey," Richard breathed. "I don't get it. Why would he defend the assassin after they slaughtered generations of his family? After fighting with him so long to protect the heir of Ra?"

Zarina scowled, but Richard's words carried a new barb, one that tore through the veil of her mind and bathed it in Ra's light. She snapped wide eyes to Richard. "Not the heir of Ra. *An* heir of Ra."

"I don't follow, love."

"Farak is trying to change his fate!"

Richard ran a hand through his scraggly curls. "I thought you said you couldn't change fate."

"I don't know that *I* can. But Farak . . . maybe he learned the same thing we did—that the assassin is a descendant of Ra, however dirtied their bloodline—and now thinks he can please the gods by protecting them instead of me."

"Them who?" Richard scrunched his brow.

Zarina met his eyes, mind sparking with more understanding than her family had gained in generations. "Adajin."

Richard rubbed his arm, face twisted with unease. "Adajin, the dirty street lord, is a descendant of Ra?"

"And the assassin." She nodded quickly, all the pieces forming in her mind. "It is why Farak protected him even after learning his identity."

Zarina released helium from the balloon with a *hisssss*, so the ship hugged the hills more closely. While the assassin's secrets were coming into the light, they needed to stay out of sight as they neared the final hill behind the Valley of the Queens.

"The blatant attacks are the perfect disguise and the chaos Apep strives on," Zarina thought out loud. "Two ways to kill me while I looked over my shoulder for someone else entirely. He doesn't care how I die, as long as it's by his command and he keeps me in fear. And the timelines match up. The assassin didn't start trying to kill me until Farak joined his forces and handed over his sacred map, revealing information only Ra's descendants would know."

"But if that were the case," Richard interjected, thrumming his fingers on the sketch sitting atop the nearest barrel, "wouldn't there be another Farak somewhere? A scary brother protecting Adajin, too?"

"If Adajin weren't a male and born to Maathornefurer's line, maybe," Zarina said with a shake of her head. "But he was twice blessed not to be either. Though now that you mention it, Farak *was* born a twin. The first in all Guardian history."

"And how did the gods account for that embarrassing miscalculation?" Richard asked, a wiggle to his brows.

Zarina glared. "Curses aren't an exact science."

"They aren't a science at all."

She narrowed her eyes and stuck out her tongue. "Guardsmen aren't born by immaculate conception, the gods have to fit them in amidst human-laid plans and nature's tricks. His mother believed a set of twin queens had been born to match, but two weeks later, a plague ravaged his family, and his brother didn't make it. Farak always assumed it was the gods correcting against nature's mistake."

"Are we sure Farak didn't strangle his twin to death with his scary-strong baby hands because he looked at him funny?"

"You'd be less inclined to dismiss nature and the gods if it had killed your family like it has Farak's and mine."

She waited for Richard's sarcastic remark, but his eyes turned thoughtful. "You're right. I would be. It must be incredibly frustrating to have so much of your past tumble into your present."

"Thank you, it is." Zarina smiled and tied the scabbard of her new weapon on her braided belt. She finished and glanced up at the sky. "Farak carries his brother's hilt attached to his own blade so he can always remember the importance of life. He kills only to protect me." Her liver panged, and she ran a hand over the smooth wood of the till. "Well, he used to. Now he protects Adajin. Ra's princely heir."

"I still don't see how Farak could do that," he said with a shake of moppy curls. "Turn his back on you like that after all those years together."

Zarina paused, then lifted her head slowly to meet Richard's gaze. "It is much easier to take revenge than to seek understanding. To believe you are owed justice. And it is always easier to hurt someone who betrays your love than it is to help them."

Richard's usual smile fell. "I wouldn't do that to you."

"*Ana aelam an hadha sahih,*" she said and felt it in all of her. "I know this to be true."

How had she grown to trust Richard in such a short time? Or were these the feelings Farak said clouded judgment and made for bad choices?

"Ah, throw Farak to the fish." Richard's grin resurfaced. "Let's talk about something far more cheery. Like how you kissed me back just then."

"I did not," she lied, cold sweat slipping down her neck.

"Right-o. So, does this mean I can call you my saucy young prawn, now? My chickadee? My chuckaboo?"

"I'll chuck your boo if you don't quit it." She breathed it as a threat, but Richard chuckled.

"Damfino what that means, but I like the sound of it!"

She groaned. "You want to call me some childish nickname? Then help me. Free me. When the assassin is gone, you can call me whatever you want."

He laid back against the banister, a slack smile teasing her beneath annoyingly mischievous eyes. "Now, that's a deal, princess."

Twenty-Four

Zarina watched the sun set in a firebird burst of oranges, and crimsons, and glimmering golds. This could be the last time she saw sunset melt into twilight, and she tried to absorb it into her very bone and blood. Then, in one last shimmer of heat and sun, it was gone, and night wrapped around them. She closed her eyes and took off her goggles, then opened them slowly, taking in the dark blues and blacks of night, unfiltered by lenses.

It was stunning.

After five hours of travel, the night had come to take its claim to the desert. Zarina and Richard took turns listening to the winds that filtered past the hills for the sound of sleeping silence on the other side, waiting for Adajin's men to fall asleep.

When all was quiet, she jumped over the railing of the upper deck and landed on the wood below in a crouch. With a pointed smirk at Richard, she kicked open the two leather chests that stood against the wall that held the door to her bedchambers. She sorted through the blades, daggers, cimeters, and a few rusty kilijes wrapped in greasy cloth.

A thick blade with a serpent wrapped around the handle caught her eye. It was the one Farak had been complaining about. The one tied to his waist the day she had called him with her blue Finder. The day her mother died. She had deliberately told him it was lost, but here it was, at the very bottom of this chest, exactly where she placed it the day she flew away.

And it was perfect. Since he had dared to take her mother's dagger and throwing stick and use them against her, she would do the same to him.

She slid the dagger next to her empty scabbard and the loop where her throwing stick usually rested and felt a pang of loss. A pang of anger.

Next, she checked her pouch. One pink bomb, the gas swirling softly inside the etched glass images of Hathor and Ra. Her sand buriers and the blu scarab used for finding Farak—her hand hesitated over that one, its constant allure no less powerful, but she brushed by. She had a few tools for her machinations, a couple of foxfire beads, and both her map and the one Farak's she had stolen from Adajin.

"You ready?" Richard asked, pulling a knapsack tight around his shoulders.

Zarina poked the soft fabric of the knapsack. "What are you planning to do with that?"

"You have your bag of tricks." He pointed to the pouch hanging at her waist. "And I have mine."

"Do you plan to draw Adajin's men to death? Or flatter them into leaving you be?"

He wriggled his eyebrows. "You'll have to wait and see. Now, what's the plan?"

She mulled over her choices, listening for answers in the sighs of the desert. "We go down to Nefertari's tomb," she said at last. "Sneak in and lay in wait for Adajin."

She had never hunted anyone before, had never planned to kill, only doing so in the heat of battle to protect herself, and she was pretty sure Richard hadn't either. But the only way to make a new fate was to kill the first one. And she had never wanted it more badly. Not just for herself and her future, but to find justice. To create it herself if she had to. It was the only way to stop running and seek a new life.

Richard's confident facade slipped. "And then what? You'll be surrounded, trapped underground with no way out."

"I will slit Adajin's throat." The words felt rusty and bitter on her tongue.

"And probably die in the process." Richard grabbed a pinch of red earth from a nearby ledge and threw it at her.

She caught a speck and crushed it over her heart. "And finally live."

He watched her, the shadows of the night darkening his skin and the stars lighting his eyes. He opened his mouth, then shut it. "You don't have to kill someone to start over, Zarina. We can leave this place and move on. All it takes is for you to choose, for you to realize that you control your fate, not some deity or Farak or Adajin or anyone else."

"You're starting to sound like Rana," she said, gripping the top of Farak's heavy dagger. Pain radiated along the ridge of her nose, and she ran a finger under her goggles to relieve the pressure. "And it is not a choice, Richard. How many times must I tell you that?"

"As you wish."

They traversed the dry, rocky backside of the hill and rounded the bottom on the eastward side. Despite their earlier teasing, Richard had remained silent, his usual casualness turned into something rigid and determined. She cast a glance his way, enjoying his sinewy, hard frame against the soft moon. Hopefully, this ordeal would not change him too much, not in the way it must change her.

One fire flickered weakly in the center of camp, and three lanterns pocked the distance. Adajin's men standing guard. But there were none on the mountainside above Nefertari's tomb to block their way. Why was it that haughty men assumed a large feature in the landscape was enough to stop a woman in her tracks? It was nothing to her, she had simply to walk around. But a lack of Adajin's stupid men did not mean a lack of Farak, and she proceeded one foot in front of the other, wincing every time a pebble tumbled down the side until they stood above the entrance to Nefertari's tomb.

Adajin's men had made quick, sloppy work of the boulders that had blocked the entrance. Bits of rocks lay scattered across the ground, revealing a rectangular entrance, partially destroyed from the explosion.

"*Ya homaar*," she cursed under her breath.

It hurt to see something so sacred being treated with such disrespect. Especially when there was another entrance boulder-free just a few meters up.

Careful to stay in the shadows, she felt with her foot until she found the entrance her family had used for generations: a heavy rock, shaped like the pharaonic nose that graced her own face. With Richard's help, she twisted it hard, revealing a tiny hole in the center of The Seeing Eye. She scooped out her blue Finder burier for its second intended purpose, pulled out its antenna, then dropped the rest down the hole.

The soft scrape of metal against metal faded as the burier fell deeper into the mountain.

"Another bit of desert magic, eh?" Richard asked

"Magic is just science you don't understand." Zarina tsked, standing up straight. "Aegyptus has been far ahead of Britannia in the steamvolution for millennia."

"I thought all your country's progress and knowledge was lost after the first steamvolution because of the Great Euro-Afrikaan Wars and when Rome burned the Alexandria Library."

"What do you think sparked the second steamvolution? Secrets uncovered. Descendants opening up and sharing their family secrets—though many of us didn't." She winked then faltered, remembering Rana and her hidden caves. "You've seen by now that there are worlds of machinations your baby civilization knows nothing about."

"Hey, now—" he started, but the shifting ground beneath his feet cut him off.

The earth shivered twice with a soft moan, and Zarina watched the desert behind them to make sure neither Farak nor Adajin lurked nearby to hear. A circular slice of scraggly land decompressed into the ground and slid left, leaving a slim hole she and Richard could easily slide through, though Farak had always struggled to fit.

Zarina put a finger to her lips and leaned down to listen. Gruff voices garbled with metal emanated from the hole. "Adajin's men await inside."

"We'll just try again later, shall we?" He gave her an uneasy smile.

"No."

Maybe Adajin hadn't been foolish enough to leave the hills unwatched. Maybe he had set a trap, instead. Either way, she had prepared for this. She opened her pouch and pulled free the pink bomb, hefting it from one hand to the other.

She placed the bomb over the person-sized hole and hesitated, taking slow, deep breaths.

Richard slipped his hand over her wrist. "Shall I do it?"

"Bomb a room full of people?" she asked, scanning his face through the blue shadows. His eyes were true, willing, and resolved, but the set of his mouth faltered.

"Better me than you." Richard glanced nervously between the bomb and the hole. Her fingers twitched, and his grip tightened. "What if Farak is down there?"

Her knuckles strained. "Farak isn't down there any more than Adajin. He wouldn't be. True power comes from saving strength until it is needed. If anything, Farak and his new heir watch us now from the next hill over. We need to move quickly."

She half-believed it to be true and half-hoped it so with every grain of her being. They were both battling fate but doing so from two different angles. Farak had chosen his side, and it wasn't with her. Why was it still so hard for her to choose her own?

Richard's hand held firm. "So he won't go in the tomb, but he's willing to let Adajin's men die there in his place?"

"Adajin's men are not Adajin. He only cares about the heir. And Farak has killed far more than I. He does not find value in the souls of men, not when eternity is so long. He does what has to be done."

They stared hard at each other, a soft pleading in Richard's eyes. "You can choose not to believe in fate, Zarina. This fate or any other."

"But I do believe in it," she whispered, a prick of warmth in the corner of her eyes that she willed away with a sniff. "You must let go."

He swallowed hard. "I can't let you do this." He released her wrist and took a swipe for the bomb, but Zarina pulled back out of his reach. "If Farak is down there, you'll never—"

She dropped the crystal orb of swirling poison down the hole.

The bomb *tink-tinked* down the rounded twists and turns of the tunnel, searching for ground.

"Oy!" he said, swiping his hand over the hole like he had any hope of catching it. "Can't a bloke do something nice for his honeyboo?"

"Thank you, Richard," she said with an aching smile. "But it is not your fate we are trying to kill. I must steel myself for what is to come. Which is why I must do this." She stood from her crouch and kicked Richard onto his back. "Try to stay quiet, yeah?"

She took off Rana's blue naqib, pulling it free so its fringed ends tussled in the wind along with her braids.

"What's this?" he said, alarm marking his eyes, his cheeks in full bloom.

He tried to rise, but she pushed him back down. Then she knelt on his chest and slid her body next to his in the cold sand. He went still as she nestled in close. She turned his face toward hers so they were nose to nose, lips a granule apart, and smiled. His cinnamon breath stilled. His gemstone eyes scanned hers. Then she threw the naqib over them both and tugged it tight.

Richard's chest tightened. "I don't under—"

The muffled sound of an explosion rumbled beneath the earth, and a pink puff of deadly gas blew from the hole, the specks coating their clothes and skin in a soft smattering.

"Ah," he breathed, his muscles relaxing into something soft and warm. "You little marmoset."

"You do not yet trust me fully."

"I trust you. I just don't understand your world or how I fit into it, yet. But I want to . . ." His eyes deepened under long lashes, making her heart skip. Then his lips cracked into a grin. "I also do not trust your bodyguard and his scary, man-killing hands."

"His hands are only scary when they hold a blade." She ran a finger over her palm, remembering how often his hand had been her only line to safety. The only warmth she had on cold nights.

"Oi, I'm right here you know." Richard pulled his head back, pouting.

"Hm?" She pressed her palms flat against each of his cheeks and pushed them together.

"Much better," he muscled out between his squished lips. "No more reminiscing about your manstress."

"Manstress?"

"You know, your man mistress."

She leaned forward, her heart picking up a chorus in her chest. Their noses brushed together. Their breath mingled, cinnamon and lavender. "Worried?"

"That he's watching from the next hill as you so helpfully suggested?" He quirked a brow. "Absolutely, yes."

Her heart tugged, and heat filled her cheeks.

The wind finished scattering the soft trickle of granules. She pulled the silky cloth from their heads and let the cool breeze blow between them. But she did not move, not yet. Not when she wanted to linger in the safety she felt nestled close to Richard.

"You had me on a string, there," he said, clearing his throat. The warmth in his cheeks matched her own. "Not that I'm complaining, but couldn't we have just backed up from the hole a bit?"

She pushed up onto her elbow, one hand over his rapidly beating heart. "Ay, but I've been trying to ruffle that smile of yours since you got here."

She leaned in, tempted to steal a kiss to muster her courage. To feel his hands in her hair and the pull of his lips. But all the talk of Farak had wound her heart too tight and made her liver ache. Until she found a way to resolve her fate, guilt was a crocodile with its teeth in her heart.

She sighed and tapped a finger on Richard's nose, then sprang to her feet, pulling him along with her.

"Come on. It's possible Farak and Adajin heard the explosion and come for us now. We must get in before we lose the element of surprise."

"But your sickness," he said, and tapped her chin. "What about the fumes?"

Zarina shook her head. "Nefertari's tomb has been aired out every year since she was buried. The air is safe."

She swung her feet into the thin shaft and shimmied herself downward. Richard's face appeared above her, backed by the star-smitten sky. He looked stronger than when she met him. Or maybe she knew now what lay beneath his square jaw and trim frame. Knew what he saw with his green eyes and how his heart made decisions.

And for the first time since she impulsively decided to risk her life in the tomb for a chance at justice, she wondered if what Farak and Richard had said was true. Did she never think ahead? Plan things out? Would it matter if she changed that now? It was not her life alone that mattered. It had never been, but she saw that now. Her resolve wavered, but before she could climb back out, Richard's large feet dropped in above her.

"*Ayyya!*" she cried and tumbled down the shaft to avoid getting hit.

It took several uncomfortable twists to make headway in the tunnel after the awkward angle in which she had landed, but soon her eyes shone out through a pair of Nefertari's painted on the other side of a tomb wall. The dead bodies of Adjain's ugly men lay strewn across the floor. One hairy brute still groaned softly in the corner, and several gas lanterns lay scattered across the floor where they were dropped, lighting the opulence of the tomb with ghostly flickers.

She scanned the room, while her heart shrunk tighter and tighter, coming perilously close to caving in on itself. It nearly burst as she sighed in relief. Farak was not there. She had not killed him. She had not harmed the man who suffered from fate as much as she.

She took a slow breath. She could not be weak now, not question the decisions she made as she had on the surface. There was too much at stake. There was her future, the curse, Richard . . . and Farak. If any of them were going to survive this, she had to get the answers she needed from Adajin as soon as possible and end him if necessary.

The beetle she sent down waited for her on the wall over a small brass circle. She twisted it to the right and plucked it off to store in her pouch. The wall before them pushed open, revealing a crack just big enough for them to squeeze through. The lanterns from Adajin's men cast shadows across the room and illuminated the spectacular opulence Ramses bequeathed to his wife upon her death.

Richard stepped beside her, his mouth open like a man who met Rana for the first time. And could she blame him? The room's beauty still took her breath away every time she entered the sacred space.

They stood on the floor of rebirth, a level above Nefertari's sarcophagus in a large room filled with vases, statues, and tools needed for Nefertari's journey out of the underworld. A set of stairs rested at both ends of the chamber with a smooth landing that ran down the center of each. Every speck of wall and ceiling was covered in plaster and paint. White backgrounds and rich murals depicted her ancestor preparing for death in white gowns and making sacrifices to animal-headed gods. Moss greens and corals and golden yellows marked geometric patterns that climbed up the sides of columns. She tilted Richard's jaw toward the azure ceiling awash with an infinite amount of white stars that trailed into the darkness.

Zarina pulled out her goggles, savored one last look at the tomb in its natural colors, then snapped them on. The pink lenses were still in, skewing the blue shadows to shades closer to purple. Then she bent down and scooped up one of the gas lanterns, tweaking its nozzle so the light was less bright. Now that she knew who the assassin was, she didn't need her two-toned lenses distracting her with clues. She'd search for any lingering secrets once Adajin was dead, not before.

"I could never have dreamed . . . ." Richard's voice faded away.

"It was Ramses' masterpiece. The last gift he could give to Nefertari." Zarina brushed a hand across her ancestor's likeness and lingered on the nose. "I only ever come for the festival of rebirth." She shivered though it was not cold. "So be careful. I do not know what curse lies in wait for descendants who do not obey and bringing you down here most certainly crosses a line. Nefertari—" She closed her eyes and pressed her fingers into a triangle, "—forgive me and understand."

Richard laid a hand on her shoulder, his curls flopping as he turned his head to the side. "It's going to be okay."

She nodded once and waved Richard forward to the farther set of stairs. "Her tomb is down this way. If I am to die, I will do so with her. We will start and finish our fate in the same place."

Zarina waited for him to join her at the top of the descending staircase. She had never actually been to this part of the tomb. Communication with the dead happened in rebirth, not in the underworld, and the room below symbolized just that.

"This all seems rather morbid, don't you think?" Richard said as he stared with her into the black below.

She did not look at him. She couldn't take her eyes off the darkness. "Hm?"

"Well, first you're riding around in a death boat, and now you're descending into a room that is literally supposed to be death on this earth. If I didn't know any better, I'd say you have a flare for the dramatical."

"Just take my hand," she said and reached for his warmth.

He obliged and intertwined his fingers with hers so they could descend the staircase.

At the bottom, in the center of the main chamber lay a sarcophagus of granite, exquisite even when covered in a layer of dust. She laid a hand on the cold stone and adjusted her goggles.

"What color, Richard? I do not recognize it so easily with my lenses and the dark."

"Pink. A soft marbled pink."

She smiled at Nefertari's sense of style. Even in death, she was larger than life. Truly one from which the sun shone. But this newfound connection only made things harder.

Richard gave her fingers a squeeze, and she squeezed back. He was comfortable and safe. Hard and soft and always there for her. He did not carry with him the same guilt Farak did. Richard was here by choice.

"Are you sure you want to do this?" His voice barely broke a whisper.

"There is no other way."

They did not have to step over dead men down here. Even Adajin's scoundrels knew better than to travel to the underworld unless they had to. She sidled past the tomb to the wall that held the entrance to the stairwell. There, she found a dark corner blocked by a tall, jackal-headed urn of ancient grain and slid down to crouch in the dust.

Zarina looked around, analyzing the angles. Here, she had a good angle to throw the dagger at anyone coming down the stairs and Nefertari's tomb gave her a good defense if she missed and they attacked.

She nodded, satisfied. "We'll wait for them here."

"I'd offer you my coat if I had one." Richard plopped down next to her.

"What would be the point of that?"

"You know, to keep you from getting dirty."

"In the deserts of Aegyptus, everything is dirty all the time."

Richard tapped the block of stone behind them. "This place isn't so bad. Especially all painted up."

She turned and ran a finger over the white-washed wall, picking up streaks of sand, then shoved it in Richard's face. "See?"

Richard muttered something in reply, but Zarina stopped listening. She rubbed her finger over the spot again, then used the hem of her vest to wipe all the dust off in a flurry of motion.

"What are you doing?"

She finished clearing off the stone and moved a lantern closer. Sure enough, a hint of metal shined through a tiny divot in the center of a crack. A machination. How many times had she been in this tomb and never seen it? And if Nefertari's chamber was the ultimate secret of her lineage, what did that make this, and who left it?

She reached to press the metal when a crunch echoed down the chamber. She tensed and listened. A soft *tippa-tap* nipped at the silence. A small pebble bounced down the stairs and rolled into a crack.

Zarina blew out the lantern.

"Wind?" Richard whispered.

She shook her head, her blood pounding in her throat and liver.

"Adajin?"

A shadow in the stairwell grew darker, then vanished with the sudden white blaze of a gas lantern.

There was no time to wait and find out.

A sandaled foot stepped onto the cold stone at the bottom of the stairs. Zarina grabbed the heavy snake-handled dagger and sprung from the shadows.

It was now or never.

Twenty-Five

Zarina cursed. She couldn't see the figure well enough in the dark to throw her dagger. Instead, she lifted the heavy blade and lunged to the side of Nefertari's tomb, swiping for the darkness.

She aimed for the eery glow of the lantern and caught cloth. A *riiiip* teased the pressing silence in the room. The figure stumbled back. She tightened her grip on the dagger and swung again. Whoever she fought swung their lantern at her face. She fell back and stumbled. Ducked a swipe of glistening metal, then thrust the hilt of her dagger upwards against the holder's wrist.

Contact.

A cry in the dark.

The lantern crashed to the floor and burst into blinding white flames. In the flash of white and headache and confusion, Zarina saw only one face.

"*Nuur?*"

Zarina fell back onto her hands and cut her palm on the stony floor. She could hardly speak through her pain and surprise. "Rana?"

It had only been a day since they saw her last, and already she looked different. More vexed and haggard. More wary. Coy.

The lantern's flames died out just as quickly as they had burst forth, and only the deep of black and their heavy breathing lingered between them. Then a softer light shimmered on. Richard emerged with his lantern from their hiding spot in the corner. He had on his usual smile, but that did nothing to mask his rigid shoulders or the sharpness in his eyes

"Richard DeClare," Rana said his name with a purr. She turned, and the light illuminated her voluptuous lips and olive skin. "Whatever are you doing here? And in the dark with my *Nuur*? Mind and hands wander away from the god's sight."

Zarina pressed her bleeding hand to her vest, hoping the sting of pain would clear her mind and drain the heat from her face. "We go where the fates take us. Why are you here? You don't often leave Alexandria for secret tombs."

The shadows deepened the pout of Rana's lips, the elegant curve of her raised brow. The flickering lamplight played mischievously in her eyes and reminded Zarina once again why men fell for her so easily.

"I am here for Adajin."

"You work for Adajin, too?" Richard shook his head, one hand on his waist as the other held the lantern higher. "Blimey, what's a guy got to do in this town to get loyalty like that?"

"You misunderstand," Rana said, her pout deepening. "I am not here to work for Adajin. I am here to kill him."

"What?" Zarina and Richard said together.

Rana's eyes slid around the tomb, taking in every shadow, every painted star until they landed back on Zarina. "Adajin crossed a line he should not have and left me no choice."

"Is this because of me?" Zarina stood and took Rana's hand in the slip of light between them. Rana winced, and, guilt-stricken, Zarina eased her grip on the wrist she had just bruised.

No other reason made sense. Why else would Rana be here, now, at the same time as she? "Did he try to kill you in revenge for helping me?"

"Nothing like that, I assure you," Rana said and offered a coy smile. "In his angry search for you, he tried to expand his empire past where the gods allow. And we can't have that, no?"

"Ah!" Richard snapped his finger, shaking the lantern so light splashed around the tomb in sharp angles. "He found your tunnels, didn't he?"

Rana's smile dropped into something sharper, something tinted with annoyance and rage. She turned her eyes on Richard. "He cannot even make a bomb properly but throws them around like Baal, the god of thunder. He destroyed the ceiling to one of my main trading routes hidden in a pistoria's basement. The rubble sealed the passages, but it will only be a matter of time before he figures out what he discovered, no? I have been working tirelessly under moon and sun to fix this problem, and Adajin is the last piece left to eliminate before I can be finished."

Richard lifted his lantern higher. "And by working tirelessly, she means?"

"Hush," Zarina waved him quiet. She already knew more than she ever wanted to about Rana's world. They both had barely escaped it as children. Besides, it did not matter now.

Rana cupped Zarina's hand in hers. "It is a terrible sorrow for me to spend my days this way when I have other pressing matters, no? A woman never has any time." She sighed and tightened her grip. Pain shot out from the gash on Zarina's palm, and she winced. Rana continued, concern creasing her brows. "But you know this well, already, my Zara. Will you help me? You broke my heart when you forced us apart back in Alexandria, but apparently, fate felt as I did and brought us together once more. The will of the gods is no coincidence, I think."

Zarina ran a gentle thumb over Rana's wrist with one hand, extracting her injured palm from Rana's grasp. The offer tempted her, the terrible person that she was. How could it not? She and Rana's goals were the same for the first time since they were girls. And just having Rana here—another friend in the face of death—was a huge relief. Especially, since Rana was no stranger to death or murder. The black market left shadowy marks on people who dipped their toes into its inky subterfuge, and Rana was born fully in it.

But she had left Rana to keep her safe. Darkness follows revenge, and Rana didn't deserve to be caught in the middle of her and Adajin's millennia-long fight. Did Rana's more noble quest to defend her family's legacy cancel out Zarina's need for justice, or did darkness always win?

Richard leaned forward. "By the by, Rana love, how did you find this place or get in here?"

Rana released Zarina's hands and turned to face him. "Adajin's obtuse ship floats outside. It was not hard to find from there. As for my way in, I have secrets, too. This you know, yes?"

The weight of Farak's dagger dragged at Zarina's hip. She shifted from foot to foot. The iron was too heavy, leaving her off-balanced. She placed a hand on its hilt to halt its sway. "This is the Valley of the Queens. Even your ancestor's tunnels should not travel here. It is sacred and secret. Meant only for royalty."

"Royalty?" Rana raised a quizzical brow.

Zarina wanted to shrink the same she always did when people found out about her ancestry, but instead, she straightened her shoulders and stuck up her chin. "Yes."

"Then your crown must be wherever mine is because it's not on your head."

"A crown doesn't make it true."

"Indeed." The shadows played on Rana's face, revealing glimpses of hidden emotions, fleeting as fireflies in twilight. "You know everything Aegyptus has to offer, then, *Nuur*? There are no secrets left for you here, either?"

"Ah, she's got you there." Richard laid his arms across her shoulder. "We just found a secret contraption behind that urn there." He nodded to the jackal head. "She had no clue it was there based on the cute little tilt to her brows."

"Richard," Zarina glared. "We don't know what we've found."

"Exactly," he said far too brightly. "And who knows more about secrets than you, but Rana? Together, I'm sure you can figure out what's behind it."

"Yes," Rana nodded vigorously, so her hair spilled out around her face in soft ebony tendrils. "I shall help you with your puzzle, and then you can help me with Adajin. The fates do want us together, no?"

Zarina hesitated. "But what about Adajin's men? I'm sure some must have heard the bomb go off."

"They are dead." Rana waved her hand lazily over her shoulder and made her way over to the urn.

Zarina knew Rana's hands were dirty, but her casualness about the death outmatched even Farak's.

Richard whistled low, clearly impressed. "It's a good thing Europa women aren't so bloodthirsty. There wouldn't be one man still walking around with his head. I think it's the heat here. Everyone's a little more cranky when their pits are drenched in sweat."

Zarina punched his arm. "*Your* pits are sweaty."

"Indeed." he widened his affable smile.

She eyed Richard warily. He was acting relaxed, but his keen eyes were still on guard. His smile tightened under her gaze, and he gave her a slight nod. She nodded back once. She *did* trust him. Maybe letting Rana help her kill Adajin was a good idea. Once the assassin was dead, there couldn't be any secret left that still mattered, could there? So why not share the secret in the tomb? She had already let Richard in.

She slipped past Rana and Richard and ran her hand along the sandy, white walls, once more finding the mark. Then, she pulled a burier out to clean the groove, slipped her finger in, and popped it open. The wall behind the urn shuttered, shooting bursts of dust and sand in the outline of a hidden door. The ancient stone pulled back into a recess, revealing a thin passage.

Richard slapped the wall and peeked in, giddiness rippling through his frame. "Aegyptus never fails to amaze me. You dames really make a bloke wish he were cursed."

She shot Rana a grin and stepped past Richard. "You don't know what you're saying."

He took a step in, but Zarina blocked his path. "We don't know what's in here. If there are ancient bodies or a preparation chamber, the fumes could kill us."

"You mean they could kill *you?*" Rana raised a brow.

Zarina swallowed. "Always me. But they can make you sick, too."

Rana touched a finger to her bottom lip. "How long must we wait for the poisons to clear?"

"It depends on how big the chamber is, what's inside. It could take an hour or maybe—"

"Will you help me, Richard?" Rana interrupted. "I believe I've found something here." She pointed to the stones in the secret chamber's doorway.

"Of course," he said and stepped forward. He leaned in, his nose near the wall in an inspection.

Rana placed an arm on his shoulder and leaned in. Zarina scowled at the closeness. Why was Rana always touching everything? Everyone? Before she had a chance to separate the two, Rana pushed Richard in. He stumbled into the darkness with a yelp. Zarina reached for him and only caught air.

"How could you do that?" She rounded on Rana. "What were you thinking?"

Rana turned her head and shot her a coy, sideways glance. "Is that *really* your concern right now? When Richard is in the dark all alone? Perhaps with toxins or curses or who knows what else?"

"This isn't the black market," Zarina huffed and turned toward the tunnel. "People matter."

All she could see was the ghost of an outline. Was that even him?

"Richard?" she called timidly.

Silence. Then a startled gasp.

"Richard!" She leaned in on her toes, hanging on the rough doorframe as far in as she would go. She wanted to go in, to save him, but she was useless. Death by tomb poisons was a slow, terrible process, but the effects could be felt immediately.

"Can you walk?" she asked, voice trembling.

"Yes." His voice sounded from the shadows

"Are you dizzy?"

"Nope."

"How about your stomach? Does it feel uneasy? Like it's full of minnows?"

"Only because you're sweet enough to worry about me so." His head popped into the light. "But in a good way." He grinned at her, and she bit her lip, hoping Rana wouldn't catch her blushing. "Honestly, though, I didn't smell anything. The air doesn't have that stuffy must smell of a tomb that was sealed millennia ago. It's fresher. And the chamber's not big at all."

Zarina chewed on her lip some more. She'd rather face a hoard of hideous men trying to kill her than the invisible threat of poison. She took a whiff and held her breath.

Nothing.

No light-headedness or nausea. She sniffed one more time. But Rana just walked in.

"Come, *Nuur*, or you'll miss out. If this tomb hasn't been sealed for very long, maybe what waits inside is meant for you."

Zarina toed the line between known and unknown, scuffing marks into the sand. But what if, as preposterous as it sounded, the chamber *was* meant for her?

She held her breath and stepped inside. She had entered a small chamber, the size of a market stall and filled with just as many valuables. Rana followed on her heels with the gas lamp. Hand-carved wooden and stone stands displayed daggers and blades encrusted with jewels and boxes etched with long-lost wisdom. But the image on the wall is what drew Zarina's eye.

Nefertari stood, hands wide with the light of Ra behind her and a look of horror etched on her face. At her feet, Isetnofret lay in a pool of rust-colored blood. And behind her, Maathornefurer, in Apep's shadow, dug a knife into Nefertari's back.

Zarina swallowed, trying to keep her limbs from shaking. She already knew it was Maathornefurer who wanted her dead. But seeing it on the wall, declared so boldly by the assassin in the place most sacred to Nefertari's descendants, sent fresh chills down her spine. She had underestimated the assassin's reach. Had underestimated the lengths they would go to to have her live in fear. To kill her. She was outmatched. She should never have come.

"*Ya nhar eswed*," Rana breathed out. Her hand slipped into Zarina's, and her face paled enough to catch the light. "It is one thing to run from fate. It is another to see it laid so bare before you. There is only darkness and hatred here."

"What do you know of fate?" Zarina asked half-mindedly, her stomach sick.

"Only that you fear it." Rana pulled her hand back. "It is why you would not leave Aegyptus with me, no? This obligation to the ultimate unseen."

Zarina nodded, her eyes still trained on the painted horror before them. She pulled the two green lenses from her pouch and slipped off her goggles to replace them. Thrice, she tried replacing the lenses, but her hands trembled too much. She did not want to see what other secrets could be hidden on the wall. Not in such stark colors, in such bold lines.

Richard moved into the light and squeezed her hand, then gently pulled the goggles from her fingers. He popped the pink lenses out and slid the green ones in and placed them back in her weak palms. But she still could not put them on. Not yet.

Richard stepped up to the wall for closer inspection. He ran his capable hands over paint and plaster, over the knicks and dimples in the ancient wall, until his finger rested over the black circle in the very center of The Seeing Eye.

"Oi. It looks like there's something here. A keyhole, perhaps?"

"Another secret?" Rana said, knitting her delicate brows together. "There are only so many turns you can take before the way back is lost."

"Ay," Zarina said, stepping in front of Richard to get a better look. "But if the path you're on leads nowhere, turning onto a new one is your only hope."

Rana tugged at Zarina's vest. "Harpocrates warns against one secret too many."

"What do the Graecian gods have to do with me?" Zarina waved her hand away.

"Ancient wisdom is still wisdom, regardless of the source. You are reckless, *Nuur*, poking in the dark."

"No more than you shoving Richard to his death." Zarina shot Rana a look over her shoulder. "And what's going on with you? You practically live in secret passages. Why are you shying from the shade now?"

Rana dropped her hand, and her gold bracelets clinked together. "If I'm shying from the shade, you're running from the sun. You travel the desert without a home." Rana's tinkling voice turned hard. "You make no effort to make friends, and the ones you do make you push away!"

Zarina's shoulders sank. "Is this about what I told you in Alexandria? I was trying to protect you."

Rana scoffed, her disdain like a knife in Zarina's worries. "I don't need your protection. I run an underground empire. You run a boat. You think much too highly of yourself, yes?"

Zarina pressed her palms into the cool stone, each thumb under one side of The Seeing Eye. "Don't forget it is I who saved you those many seasons ago when we were girls in Cairo. You did not disdain my protection so easily then."

"My life is in much better shape than yours, *Nuur*," Rana said her nickname with venom for the first time in Zarina's memory.

"And yet," Zarina said, turning around and shooting her a tight smile, "we are both in an empty tomb waiting to kill someone."

"At least I know who I came to kill," Rana's eyes turned fierce and fiery. "You were just going to kill whoever came down the stairs first."

"Not true!" Zarina took a step toward Rana, but Richard's hands slid around her waist and pulled her back.

"Shall I remind you lovely ladies that we are hiding in a tomb with an army of thugs in the desert above us?" He nestled his chin over her shoulder and whispered, "We must use our inside voices."

"See, *Nuur*? Richard thinks you're reckless, too." Rana's usually gentle smile morphed into a smirk.

Zarina lunged at Rana, but Richard's strong arms held her tight.

"Tut, tut," he said. "Enough with that. Chuckaboos should not fight, not after so many years of knowing one another. You're more family than friends at this point, so I'll allow the tiff that just transpired. Heaven knows my Uncle William always gets in a row with—"

"Richard," Zarina warned through grinding teeth.

"Right-o. My point is, tighten up. Let's figure out where this key is, kill Adajin, and get it out of here. You can fight each other to your heart's content when we are back on the ship."

Zarina stopped pulling against Richard's hold, and Rana's anger melted into a sulky pout. Why was she fighting with Rana, one of her oldest friends? Being in the tomb, dealing with Adajin's men—her nerves were fraying, affecting her decision-making.

"Excellent," Richard nodded his approval. "Now look at this."

He held the lantern up to the keyhole. Both Zarina and Rana had to stand on tip-toes to take a closer look. The light lit the hole only so far before blackness swallowed it up.

"It is like no keyhole I've seen before," Rana mused.

"Too wide." Zarina agreed. "Too deep. It looks more like a scabbard for a round dagger."

Rana leaned back on her heels. "What would be the point of a rounded dagger? It would be entirely useless."

"Except for hitting ducks," Richard said with a grin.

"My throwing stick!" Zarina barked. "The end isn't smooth. It's patterned, like a key. But it's long and thick enough to fit in this wall."

Richard ran a hand over his chin. "Could be. Where'd you find it?"

Zarina's hand instinctually darted to the empty place on her belt. "I didn't find it. It was a gift from my mother. A family heirloom."

Rana tugged her shoulder so they were face to face. The displeasure that marred her features earlier had melted in the wake of anticipation. "Where is it now? Your stick?"

"I—" Zarina cast her eyes to the floor. She could not tell which frothed more in her stomach, dread or embarrassment. She squeezed the bridge of her nose just above her goggles. "Farak has it."

Rana sighed. "Farak?"

Zarina nodded, guilty.

"See? No planning." Rana huffed. "If Farak has it, we shall ne'er see it again. The secret is better left untouched, yes? Let us leave this place and tend to what really matters. We have been distracted too long." She grabbed Richard's shirt and dragged him back down the thin corridor, leaving Zarina in the inky shadows of the tomb.

Zarina ran her hand over the sandy keyhole. She would not abandon this secret. Farak would be here tonight, she was sure of it. She would get her throwing stick back no matter what it cost her. And then, Farak had better stay out of her way.

She took the foxfire beads from her pouch and held them up to the mural, then slipped on the green goggles. But first, she needed to see what secrets were left for her on the wall.

Twenty-Six

She could not tell which came first, Rana's scream or Richard's cry of pain, but Zarina flew out of the chamber with only a glimpse at the mossy and lime-green secret hidden in plain sight. A moonish circle with two horns covered The Seeing Eye, a hieroglyph that echoed with familiarity.

She knew that symbol.

She knew it.

But in the flurry of panic, she couldn't for the life of her remember what it meant.

In seven strides, she burst into the main room of Nefertari's tomb. She nearly stumbled back from the blinding lights that filled the chamber.

So many. So many lights.

Had this been Farak's doing? A well-laid trap to blind and burn her?

A burly man held Rana, who curled into a crumpled ball, her fierce eyes flashing out from her otherwise helpless frame. Richard lay on the floor, bleeding beneath Adajin. Her heart ached, and she wanted to run to him. To rip every last hair from Adajin's beard and stuff it down his throat. But the lights were so harsh and his men so many. If she did not finish this soon, she would be lying on the floor just as he did.

She squinted into the blast of fake sunshine and squared her shoulders, fighting back the searing ache in her forehead. "Let them go, Adajin. Your troubles are with me."

He smiled at her, the lanterns reflecting off rodentesque teeth. "Ah, my little marmoset, we both know that's not true. This one here—" Adajin pinched Rana's rosy cheeks. "—already killed a dozen of my men in cold blood while they slept in their homes."

Zarina's jaw fell slack before she ground her teeth together. "Lies."

"And this one—" Adjain kicked Richard with a laugh. "—is a foreigner and ugly."

It took all of Zarina's control not to try and dig her nails into Adajin's eyes.

She shifted her weight, feeling Farak's heavy dagger against her thigh. It would take a second longer to draw than she was used to, and a second was all the enemy needed to gain the advantage. She was also out of bombs. Add in her blurry vision and the pain in her temple, and she was a croc's tail from fighting fit.

Zarina stepped her way behind Nefertari's tomb, Adajin's men rotating like planets around the sun. A lantern sat in an outcrop behind her. If she was fast enough, lucky enough, her plan just might work.

"Let Richard and Rana free, and I will come with you willingly." She said it as boldly as she could, slapping her hands on Nefertari's tomb for emphasis so she could feel the cool granite's weight and thickness.

"Why would I make a deal like that when I already have all three of you?"

"Because I have this," Zarina dug in her pouch and whipped out the map she had stolen from Adajin—the one that looked just like her own family map. Concealed behind it, one of her buriers rested between two fingers. She held them both close to the lantern's fire, an implied threat to burn the parchment if anyone came too close. "I presume you know what this scroll is."

Adajin's cruel smile did not waiver. "It is the same thing I already possess."

"*Did* possess." She flashed him a smile. "I stole this from your desk in Alexandria. All you have left is Farak's memory of what's on the map. You don't trust the mind of a drunkard, do you?" The words hurt to say and blanketed her heart in guilt.

But he had chosen his side in his desperate desire to serve his fate, just like she had chosen hers. At least, he wasn't around to hear.

"Of course not," Adajin shook his head. "But I do not rely on his mind. Farak!" Adajin called without turning his head.

She blanched. Maybe he had heard her after all. She steeled herself against seeing him again, fearing the inexplicable pull on her heart that always came when he was near.

A shadow emerged down the stairs, protected by a blinding foreground of light. Even so, she knew it was him. The dark clung to every curve in his muscles like a finely-woven sheet. Farak moved behind Adajin and stepped into the light. Zarina couldn't help but gasp.

A thick cut carved its way through one brow, and purple and blue walked their way across his cheek. She had not done that to him, not even after he hit her in the nose. She searched Farak's eyes for answers, for recognition, but he refused to look at her. His lips tightened, and his face remained stony. She flashed her eyes back to cocky Adajin, blood boiling inside her.

"What did you do to him?"

"Not important." Adajin held up a hand, and Farak placed a roll of papyrus into his waiting fingers. He flipped it open with much aplomb, and Zarina had to swallow down another gasp. "As you can see, I have a map of my own. It looks just like yours, don't you think?"

Zarina glanced between the two, anger and dread fighting within her. If the map she found had been Farak's... how did Adajin have another?

Her heart skipped a beat. Maybe Matthornefurer's line had royal maps, too. It was the final piece of the puzzle and confirmed that she had been right.

Adajin had to be the mocking, murderous offspring of the family that had tormented hers throughout the ages. He was the source of her suffering and the answer to her need for peace.

The burier buzzed against her skin, energized by the heat of the lamp. Its tiny legs clawed the air, hungry for sand.

Zarina slammed her hands on the granite tomb so the paper lay on top. She released the burier, which disappeared quickly within the crack under the lid.

"So it was you all along," she said.

Adajin ran a hand over his thin, scruffy beard. "I'm not sure what you mean, but I'm always happy to take credit whether for good or for ill. Any kind of recognition is better than falling into oblivion, forgotten by all, don't you think?"

"You aimed at my ship in the port, tried to crash me and Farak to the ground!"

"All in good fun. You're quite the little captain, scurrying about on your ship. I thought I had you when you went over the side, but you were just up to more of your tricks." Adajin's playful tone turned deadly. "You have more lives than a bennu."

"And you tried to kill me in the market."

Zarina kept her hand on the tomb, waiting for the burier to return. In the meantime, she would confirm Adajin's evil so Ahmet would have no doubt when he weighed the cretin's soul. She had to brace herself for what must be done. For what she must do.

"I did lose a lot of men in the market," Adajin's cavalier demeanor fell. "Another reason the prices on your little band's heads are so high." His words were met with a grumble from the men surrounding her.

"I didn't kill your men," Zarina scoffed. "You did."

The discontent grew around them, and Adajin held up a hand to silence his men. "What would I have to gain from killing my own men?"

"You—" Zarina started her sentence twice. "Hiding your true identity!"

He ran his tongue over his front teeth. "See, now you have me interested. Who exactly do you think I am?"

She pulled herself as tall as she could. "You are Adajin, foreign-blooded prince of Aegyptus from the line of Matthornefurer, vengeful assassin, and betrayer of Ra."

Farak's eyes darted to hers at last, but she could not make out what hid beneath. A painful, white glow had begun to eat the edges of her vision from all the light. Rana squeaked, and a giant hand pressed over her mouth. Richard, too, began to stir. Just in time. The last trickle of sand fell from the tomb's edge, and the burier returned to her palm. She felt the weight of the sarcophagus's lid shift beneath her hand and pulled back to get out of the way.

The granite lid sprang open.

She grabbed the lantern behind her and threw it over Nefertari's tomb so it burst on the ground in a roar of flames, catching two of Adajin's men on fire. They screamed in a flailing ball of orange and white. Richard found his feet. He barreled toward another of Adajin's men, sending him sprawling into the flames, then threw another lantern onto the pile.

Zarina dropped to the floor, crushing her eyelids shut against the explosion of light. After the initial burst, she cracked them open for a peek. Chaos filled the room in a scatter of lit fragments and shadowy figures. She pressed her goggles against her eyes for a moment of relief, then slid out her knife and ran her blade behind a giant brute's knees. He cried out and fell to the earth, clutching at the crimson that flowed from his legs.

She rounded the side of Nefertari's tomb. Three men stood where Adajin once had. Where did he go? Rana was nowhere in sight, and Richard had another man by his neck as he rode him like a camel who'd just been branded with Nar.

Then there was Farak, in exactly the same place, watching her as he always had. She would not be able to move without him knowing; a skill of his she had once taken for granted.

She shifted to the right. His eyes followed. Then one of the men lunged for her. She sprang onto the rim of Nefertari's sarcophagus, cringing with every step and muttering a prayer. Burning Nefertari's tomb while she lay inside it was bad enough. Zarina was practically volunteering to be Ahmet's personal snack by trodding on her corpse.

The brute reached for her again, and she stumbled back onto the open lid. Her tiny frame added to the weight of the marble lid, straining the hinges. The metal groaned. Sand fell from the cracks. Then, the lid snapped off and plummeted into the fire. Zarina sprang out of the flames, her hijab a streak of orange behind her.

"Ayy!" she cried and ripped it off.

She crushed it into a ball and threw it at the man who had jumped upon Nefertari's tomb behind her. The silky fabric wrapped around his face, and he fell back, flailing in agony.

Zarina wiped sweat from her forehead and the edges of her goggles then whipped around. The white fire of the lanterns flickered green through her lenses. She braced for the next attack, but the other two men were crumpled heaps on the ground. She turned to Farak, who stood motionless in the same spot she left him.

She raised a brow. "Did you . . . ?"

He stared at her, face statuesque.

She shook her head, trying to pull her eyes from his. The fire played tricks on her heart, reminding her of the heat she used to feel when near him, though he had never felt the same way.

The smoke thickened in the room, creating a veil of deadly smoke that caught in her lungs and made her cough.

"Rana?" She called over the crackle of flames.

If Farak hadn't helped her, maybe it had been Rana. Though she could not be the cold-blooded killer Adajin made her out to be.

But Rana was missing from the scene of carnage around her. So was Adajin. Terror streaked down her spine. What if Rana killed him before she could confirm his identity? She had been so certain it was him until he had not been. She could never rest until it was confirmed.

Richard elbowed the last of Adajin's men in the face with a grunt and rammed him back against the wall. Blood soaked the white plaster, a red streak beneath Nefertari's feet. He nodded once, and her chest ached. He was bloody and bruised and utterly miserable. Fighting was not in his nature.

But here he was, fighting his nature for her.

She skirted the fire to reach him when Rana screamed upstairs. She and Richard met eyes. He dashed up first. She followed.

Farak beat her to the stairs and blocked her way, his kilij in one hand.

Twenty-Seven

Zarina backed out of Farak's reach as Richard's footsteps faded, leaving them alone. It was better that way. He needed to find Rana, to make sure she was safe. She could handle Farak.

"Move," she commanded.

"You should not go up there."

She dashed to his left, but he blocked her easily.

"Why do you care?" she asked, tensing her shoulders.

Farak bent his head, looking at her through his lashes. She turned her head to the side, and he tilted his head to match. "It is not safe."

"Not safe for whom?" she asked, finally meeting his eyes. Each gold fleck burned in her heart. "Who are you protecting? Adajin, the assassin?"

"You keep seeking things you do not want to find," Farak said.

She dodged right, grasping for the stairs, but he blocked her, snaking his hand around her waist and kneeling to hold her there.

She struggled uselessly to free herself, punching and slapping his shoulders. She gripped the handle of the heavy dagger that was once his but couldn't find the space to pull it free. Frustrated, she growled and flipped around, so she stood with her nose touching the tip of his.

Zarina dropped her voice to a whisper. "Do you think I will not find out who holds the dagger when it's plunged in my back? You are protecting things that should not be protected."

"It's you," he said thickly.

"What?"

"I'm protecting you."

She shook her head, refusing the pleading in his eyes. "You cannot say such things after everything you've done."

"It has always been you."

Her throat parched. She pushed his arms, and he let her escape.

"Was it me," she asked, turning on him, "when you gave Adajin that map of my family's tombs?"

"It was so I could find you after so many years apart. I didn't have the resources—"

"What about when you punched me in the nose?"

"You should not have been there." He stood and took a step forward.

She flinched, whipping the blade from her belt.

He slowly slid his kilij into its leather scabbard, then reached out for her, palms up. "Adajin would have done far worse."

"Worse than breaking my nose?"

"I didn't break it," he said flatly.

"How generous of you."

He swallowed hard, dropped one hand, and held out his other. "I had to make you bleed so Adajin would not feel he had to. A controlled blow to the bridge of your no—"

"No decent Guardsman would have to harm their queen to save her." She crossed her arms over her chest to keep her anger in and his hurt eyes out. "You deserve to be cursed."

His hand fell. His face did, too, into something horribly forlorn that tore at her heart.

"As you'll have it" was all he said, and that enraged her more.

She didn't want to see the weakness he kept hidden under his hard muscles and deadly swings. The pain in his eyes made her want to run to him. Why, even now, did she feel that way?

Every muscle in her body shook, and she threw herself at him. He kept his arms to the side as she beat her fists into his chest. Tears flowed, a mixture of confusion and hurt and generations of torment. She hit and pounded and thrashed and screamed until she sunk to her knees in exhaustion. The fading fire crackled nearby. Nefertari's legacy had been charred into an irrecoverable blackness.

Gone. Forever.

When she had nothing left and her piercing headache hid beneath layers of pain, Farak bent down and ran a thumb over her cheek, catching the river of her tears. She looked up at him, and the fire in her softened. His face was not one of pride or power. Revenge did not burn in his eyes or hide in the shadow of his brow. He looked as she did, and he smelled of jasmine.

She laid her forehead against his and gave him one more chance. "Farak. Please, tell me."

Farak laid a hand on her cheek, his eyes creased at the corners despite the giant cut that ran the length of his face. Instead of an answer, he leaned in and kissed her. And for all his hard exterior, his lips were gentle, inviting her closer with a tenderness she rarely saw. It was like she was seventeen again, on the deck of her ship with the wind tousling her hair as she begged Farak to love her.

Only this time, he stayed.

Zarina dug her fingers into his shirt and pulled him closer, breathing in the essence she had missed for so long. She felt powerful and safe and instantly guilty, but she could not stop. He wrapped his arms around her and pulled her to him, chest to chest in the desert sand.

A clatter startled them apart. Zarina fell back and Farak, breathing heavily, stepped forward. He threw one hand in front of her and placed the other on his kilij as Adajin tumbled down the steps, his face a mask of bruises and blood. Behind him stood Richard, ghostly white and staring straight at her.

Zarina winced, her cut palm dragging against the pebble-strewn earth. Worse than that was Richard's torn face.

He had seen her kiss Farak.

Her spoiled hypocrisy had reared its ugly head, and now he knew what Farak did; that she thought only of herself. Her stomach twisted upon itself.

She looked away from Richard's pain and up at Farak's tense back.

She wanted to believe his words with every part of her being, that he had done everything for her. Maybe she could trust him again. Maybe she always should have. She and Farak were born together, and they'd die together, too. There was something right in that. Even if it tasted bitter on her tongue. Maybe Richard was right and there wasn't a place for him in this world of death and curses.

She was working hard to challenge her fate, to not become the curse on the lives of those she cared about, but she had so much darkness still to wade through.

Zarina found her feet, and Adajin dragged himself onto his knees with a groan. He pulled a dagger from his belt and raised a hand to throw it. Farak braced himself for a potential blow, but it was Richard who stepped out of the shadows, swung his knapsack around, and knocked the dagger from Adajin's hand.

Zarina looked back and forth between her two protectors who locked eyes so fiercely.

Then Rana stepped down the stairs like she was strolling the market, face relaxed and at an easy pace. Her hair hung disheveled around her shoulders in thick, luscious curls. Even the trickle of blood that marked her bottom lip looked thin and refined.

"I warned you, Adajin, not to go digging." She landed at the bottom and raised a flowered dagger in the air. The blue gemstones matched the one on the clip that hung loosely from her hair and carried the symbol of Hathor.

"Wait," Zarina cried, running out from behind Farak.

"You wish him to live? The man who has tried to kill you?" Rana asked. "I thought you were out for revenge, no?"

"Revenge against the assassin," Zarina corrected.

"Adajin kills daily, but you care more about someone who kills once."

"If that once is my life, then yes, I care more about that."

Rana's familiar pout appeared, though her eyes were sharp.

Zarina turned a hard eye on the snarling heap that was Adajin. "Are you the assassin whose family has hunted my own for thousands of years?"

He spat blood at her feet. "Why should I tell you anything?"

She fell to her knees and gripped the collar of his robes. "Because if you don't, I'll tie you to Nefertari's tomb myself and let you starve with only my ancestors to laugh at your demise."

He ran his tongue over his teeth and smiled.

"Tell me who you are!"

"You waste your breath. Let me cut the flesh from his bones piece by piece until even his mother does not recognize him." Rana raised her blade, but Richard stepped forward, placing a hand on her wrist. She hesitated.

Zarina pounced on Rana's opening. "Tell me who you are, or I will let Rana have you."

Adajin eyed the glittering blade, and Zarina leaned in close. She could not miss his answer.

"I am the master of your old servant." Adajin's bloodshot eyes turned to Farak. "A worthless piece, he is. Always wetter than he is dry. I can see why you left him to die." He chuckled, flashing his bloody teeth in cruelty-laced mirth.

Zarina slapped him, and his laughter turned into heavy breathing. Adajin pulled himself up onto his elbows and scooted back.

"Tell me once and for all, Adajin. Are you Maathornefurer's heir and assassin of the queens?"

Even injured and filthy, a sneer lived on his lips. He opened his horrid mouth to answer, and a blade plummeted into his throat.

Twenty-Eight

"No!" Zarina cried, falling back on the grainy stone floor of Nefertari's tomb.

She reached forward to—what? Scoop the blood back into Adajin? She gagged, her hands fluttering above Adajin's twitching body like lacewings after the harvest. She had to do something.

She could do nothing.

Richard's strong hand stilled her.

"It's done," he said. "Let him go."

"But how will I know?" she whispered. Her eyes trailed the flecks of crimson on her hands and Adajin's robe, then lighted on the matching red gems in the dagger in his throat.

Her dagger.

She pushed Richard away.

"You!" she cried, jumping to her feet and turning on Farak.

He stood silent, his throwing hand empty. She stepped towards him, then stopped. She had just begun to trust him again. Had just started wanting to. And they—they had kissed. The heat drained from her face. Had that just been a distraction? Her chest tightened, making it hard to breathe.

Adajin no longer seemed like the clever assassin who left death threats in Nefertari's tomb. And she had not considered how many men he had lost in the market. Her stomach twisted, shooting pain into her liver. Did Farak change loyalties and decide to save her instead? Or was Adajin not the assassin? But then why not wait to kill him until he spoke? And if Adajin *was* the true heir of Ra Farak had decided to protect, why did he slice his throat?

"How could you?" she sputtered at last, boring her eyes into Farak's. "He was about to confess his identity. He was about to give me the peace I needed. How could you take that away from me?"

She braced herself, then ripped her dagger from Adajin's throat. The sound made her gag, and she turned away from the sight, finding her hands, instead. They were covered now, coated in red even her lenses couldn't hide, and completely unrecognizable. The smell of iron was too much, and she pressed her lips into the crook of her elbow to keep her insides from spewing.

Who was she anymore?

She shivered with disgust and ripped off her vest.

She used the tattered cloth to clean the sticky hilt of her dagger and wipe the crimson guilt from her hands. With each wipe, a glimmering ruby reflected her distorted image.

Death.

That's who she was now. But without knowing who to kill, she would end up destroying everyone. She had become the very thing she was trying to avoid. At this rate, she was no better than the assassin. She needed it to stop. She had to be free.

There was only one way to know the truth now, to keep her rage contained. She gripped the ruby handle and slowly raised her eyes to Farak.

"You did this." She jumped to her feet and advanced toward him. "And you will fix it."

"Hey, ho," Richard said uneasily, stepping between her and Farak. "We came to kill Adajin. Mission accomplished."

"No." Zarina cut him short. "We came to kill the assassin, and instead, Farak killed Adajin—the man he's been serving like a dog the past year." She flipped her dagger and re-secured her grip, ready to attack. "Tell a blood-sealed truth, Farak. Was the man you killed the assassin?"

His bronze eyes found hers, and the corners of his lips softened. "Please, don't do this."

"You saw the assassin in the market near Rana's shop."

Zarina turned to Rana, but only darkness rested where she had stood. Rana must have taken off as soon as Adajin perished. Her chest tightened with worry. Rana was the only semblance of a family she had left.

"Richard." she turned to look at him while blood soaked her sandals. "Go after Rana. Make sure she is safe. Tell her to wait for me, that I'm coming for her."

"I'd rather not leave you—"

She held his gaze and softened her voice. "Please. I can't lose her. Not now."

Richard looked between her and Farak, his lips curling. He pressed them together and nodded. "I will be right back. Don't try to kill each other while I'm gone or you'll end up with more than your blades locked."

Then he darted up the stairs and into the black after Rana.

Zarina turned back to her new target.

This time, she would not forgive.

"Tell me who Adajin is, Farak, or my rubies will garnish your throat next!" She stabbed her dagger at him.

"It's not so simple, Zarina." He raised his empty hands in front of him.

"Why won't you draw your weapon?"

"You know why."

"Draw your weapon!"

Farak eyed her wearily before pulling his blade and holding it loosely at his side. "I am sworn to protect you."

"Then why do you protect the assassin?"

He gestured at Adajin on the ground.

"Don't." She shook her head. "Don't do that to me. I know he's not the assassin, now. You wouldn't have killed him otherwise, would you have? Not since you decided to protect the person trying to stab me in the back."

"You are wrong about all of this, Zarina. A too-willing believer that things are out of your control. A participant in a perceived fate even though you have no more power to see the future than you do to discern the past."

"Things *are* out of my control!" She snapped and gestured at Adajin's lifeless body and his contorted face. "If I had been in control of things,

Adajin would be alive and I would have answers. But you stole that chance from me and cut its throat."

"The only thing I did was eliminate one of the forks in the path you're already on. You decide what comes next. But you can't see it. You never could. You just stand at the center of the intersection and wait for a stampede to force you one way or another."

"Not true," she challenged, his words thistles coating her heart. "I chose my own path when I asked you all those years ago to forsake the curse and love me. It was you who told me I had no choice, and now complain that's what I believe."

Farak shook his head and slapped the broadside of his sword against his calves. The metal caught the light of a dim lantern sitting in a pool of Adajin's blood by the stairs, flashing and flickering to keep the shadows at bay. "For all your talk of rebellion, you're still here in the tomb of your ancestors making decisions based on some ambiguous idea of fate."

"I am here *because* I am fighting my fate. I'm fighting to live."

"What is living for you, Zarina? Running from shadows as you flit from tomb to tomb? Forsaking those who care about you as an unnecessary martyr? You're not living, Zarina. You're existing. And of all the lives you could endure, that is the one I wanted for you least."

A soft thud and clattering sounded up the stairs, and she glanced back, her heart picking up its pulse. Had Richard found Rana?

"You are not your curse, you know." Farak's gentle timber pulled her attention back.

"My ancestry is everything I am, Farak. It's my pride and my people. It's my purpose and the way I perceive the world. I am so much of what my mother taught me, and I love as much as I hate the pieces that make me whole."

"Zarina . . . ." He stepped forward, and she shied toward the stairs. His shoulders slumped, and he stopped his approach.

Sand glittered in the light around his feet everywhere but where he shadowed. It seemed they were being watched—by the painted eyes of the white-robed priests on the murals, by the ocular gemstones on the jackal urns and hippopotami statues that lined the walls in regal stature.

She, too, watched Farak as he watched her.

"You don't have to give up your culture or your past, your mother or your ancestors to live for you. You just have to choose, everyday, to focus on the power you do have and not the power you don't."

Another sound emanated from up the stairs, a sharp *clang* that sent her heart racing. She glanced at Farak and his outstretched hand, then back into the darkness up the stairs.

Her anger was slipping, and she was desperate to cling to it, to never let anyone betray her again—especially Farak.

"You're just trying to distract me from why you killed Adajin," she spat, attempting to stoke her rage and keep her blood running hot. But the sounds up the stairs diluted it with worry.

Had Richard and Rana run into more men? Did they need her help?

Farak sighed deep and heavy. "It doesn't matter, does it?"

"What?"

"What I say to you. You'd only listen to Ra himself at this point, and even then you'd give him sass."

She bristled. "Maybe you just give terrible advice."

"Maybe." He shrugged, and that made her even angrier.

"You know what, you're right. I'm not going to listen to you. I shouldn't. Because even though I left you in the desert, you were always whispering in my head and needling at my heart. My dependence on you holds me back." She hefted the snake-twined dagger from her hilt and shook it so it glistened in the light. "You want me to make choices for myself, then I will. Starting with letting go of you." She threw the dagger at Farak's feet. "Take this with you. It only holds me back."

His eyes widened. "You—"

"Had it the whole time." She nodded. "And a lot of good it did me."

Zarina slipped the blood reflection of her mother's ruby dagger into her scabbard, then turned and headed up the stairs.

"Zarina!" Farak called behind her.

"Just go, Farak." She fought the urge to return to him with each step. To yell and scream at him and to cry in his arms. But he could not be trusted. Ever again.

"It's not safe," he said, his voice rapidly growing closer

She hurried faster, breaking into a run. He would not stop her, not draw her in with his secrets and history and warmth and jasmine. And she knew then that if she didn't get away from him, she'd be with him forever.

"Zarina!"

She picked up her pace, doubling the stairs she took with each step. The flicker of fire below and the glow of lanterns above cast strange shadows on the wall, stirring memories of everything she had seen and felt and heard the last two days and years before.

Farak seeing the assassin and refusing to tell her.

The discovery of the Hittite queen's line.

Adajin's blood on her hands.

The portrait of Nefertari with the assassin behind her back, that ominous symbol hanging over her head.

And Rana showing up, the mark of Hathor gleaming on her hair clip. On her dagger.

The mark with two long lines and a ghostly moon in the center. The same mark that covered The Seeing Eye in the secret chamber and the one that shadowed the murders of her family.

"Rana!" she gasped as she hit the top step.

Before her, Richard lay on the floor, a sapphire blade in his side. Rana stood tall, her azure cloak dipped in his pouring blood.

"*Nuur.*"

Twenty-Nine

Zarina ran toward Richard. Rana yanked her dagger from his side and blocked her way. Zarina pulled back and eyed him desperately, praying to Ra and Ma'at and any other god she could think of for signs of life.

"Rana," she whispered, though no word had ever hurt so much to utter. "How could this be you?"

Rana raised her knife and lunged.

Zarina swung her ruby hilt up just in time. Their blades caught and slid off each other with a *shing*. She spun around and thrust her hilt against Rana.

Contact.

Blood burst from a fresh welt on Rana's delicate cheek.

Rana touched a hand to the wound. She pulled a red-coated finger back and looked between it and Zarina. A tender frown marked her lips before her eyes hardened. "You fight like a baboon, slashing every which way. It's a wonder you can hit anything."

"I've hit you." Zarina cocked her chin. "Twice."

She pulled her shoulders back and hardened her face, hoping to appear menacing, but her eyes kept slipping back to Richard and the copious amount of blood on the floor beneath him.

Rana sighed. "I'm about to kill you, and you can't even focus."

Just then, Farak burst forth from the stairwell and into the middle of the room.

Zarina's nerves ran raw. She wanted to scream and yell like she had earlier. But all she could muster was "Rana . . . she's the—"

The extra light from his lantern broke into a dozen shimmering angles. Her vision blurred white-hot around the edges, and she stumbled back, catching herself against the wall. Farak's face appeared before hers, but even blurry, she could see the betrayal written in his eyes.

"You knew," she accused weakly. "You knew it was her."

"I'm sorry," he said. "I will make this right."

"There is nothing you can do here," she said, and her heart stung knowing it was true. Zarina pressed her goggles against her eyes so the white edges retreated, then pushed herself upright. "No man can serve two masters. Is this not true for you?"

He lowered his kilij, glancing between her and Rana.

Zarina pressed on, following the snake-like suspicions that had grown the past two days. "Why did you keep Rana's secret in the market? Why did you kill Adajin to keep it, too? What—" She pressed a hand to her sickened stomach. "What did you do to owe her such loyalty?"

Rana's sharp eyes turned to Farak. "Tell her."

"What did you do to him, Rana?" Zarina asked. "What did you do after I left?"

"Tell her," Rana said again through clenched teeth.

Farak's muscles tensed, ready for battle, but he did not raise his sword. "I can't."

Rana clenched her fists and pointed her dagger at him. "Tell her!"

"No."

Rana stormed over to Farak, but he did not move, not even to wince. She was tiny next to him, small like Zarina with softer hips and lips and sighs. Her current face, however, was anything but. In all the years Zarina had known her, she never would have guessed there was so much rage hidden beneath Rana's charm.

"You are a coward," Rana hissed and slapped his cheek.

He stared at the wall, and Zarina dashed toward Richard. Rana swirled around and cut her off.

"Move, Rana," Zarina seethed.

"No. No one gets a happy ending."

"Then kill me already!" Zarina spat. "You've had the chance. Over and over again you've had the chance to kill me. Why not just do it?"

"I gladly would," Rana said, hefting her dagger. "But it's not so easy." She drove the blade toward Zarina, and Farak's kilij appeared between the two, cutting her off. "See?"

"Stand down, Farak," Zarina commanded with a hard look.

She stared at him until his sword lowered and he took a step back. Now she would confirm what she suspected. She pulled her dagger back, one eye still on him, and flung it at Rana, who stood defiantly. Farak waited until the last second, then moved like a crocodile, swiping Zarina's blade off its course just before it hit a smiling Rana.

"I knew it," she whispered as the icy truth fell upon her.

He would not break his oath so he could love her, but he would break his oath for Rana. And Rana knew it, too.

"You're still protecting her even when you're sworn to me!"

"Zarina—" He pleaded, reaching a hand toward her.

She stepped back with a scoff. "You've refused to play your part up to this point, what gives you the right to start now? Do you plan to referee our fight until we die of old age?"

Richard groaned behind Rana, and Zarina dove for him. Rana's blade once more blocked her path, Farak's own not far behind to ensure no blood was spilled.

"Enough," Zarina seethed, pulling back and wiping sweat from her brow. "Why do you protect Rana, Farak? Do you—Do you love her?"

Farak's face fell. "Zarina—"

"What Farak and I have is far more complex than mortal love," Rana said, turning her nose up to the side.

"A—a baby?" Zarina whispered, eyes wide.

Farak nearly choked. "No. Of course not."

"Then what is going on?" Zarina cried. "And so help me Farak, if you try to weasel or kiss your way out of this—" She tipped her knife toward his heart to finish the threat.

"Kiss?" Rana's cool demeanor shattered. Her voice cut like shards of sparkling glass. "You've been playing favorites, Farak."

Rana dashed forward, and they locked blades, Farak's sharp watch on them both. As their eyes met, Zarina felt her resolve waiver. She knew those honey-brown eyes, even through two-toned goggles. She had known them for decades. And right now they shimmered with hurt.

"I don't understand." Zarina breathed heavily and met Rana's hard gaze. "After all these years of friendship, you're killing me because of Farak?"

Rana puckered her lips, creasing her eyes in the corners. "Don't be ridiculous."

"Then why now?"

"Because I didn't know." Rana swiped her dagger to the side. "I didn't know who you were. I suppose I should have; the very first time we met as children, Farak followed you like a puppy. But I was so little then. So alone. It made me weak. And stupid as you. Then you showed me the map, and I've been hunting you since."

Zarina released the tension in her blade and stumbled back. "But down in the caves—that was after the map. It was just me and Richard, why didn't you do it then?" Zarina asked, clawing against the stupor that clung to her mind like wet fabric. "And in Alexandria," Zarina exhaled, catching another of Rana's blows with a *zing* of her dagger. "You wanted me to leave with you. To become blood sisters."

Rana spun, carving a half-moon in the air with her blade, and came down against her. Zarina met her advance, ruby red against azure blue as the hilts of their dagger danced back and forth.

"A moment of weakness, no?" Rana pulled back and kicked Zarina in the stomach. "A confusion about who is really my family and who is not."

Zarina stumbled back, clutching her liver. Rana lunged again, and Zarina met her just in time. She pressed her whole weight into keeping Rana back. Sweat trickled from her brow and underneath her goggles, and Farak moved closer.

"I don't believe that."

"Why does it matter?" Rana said, pushing harder and harder against her. "You said no."

"I was trying to protect you—"

"You were trying to kill me."

Zarina couldn't hold the pressure any longer, but she'd rather die than give up and have Farak intervene. She mustered her strength and shoved Rana back so she could dodge left.

"I wasn't trying to kill you. I was trying to kill the assassin and find justice."

"We are one and the same." Rana slashed her blade down by her side, the sapphires catching the eerie light in glints of deep blue.

Zarina's hand relaxed around the hilt of her dagger. She could not keep her thoughts straight, not with her eyes betraying her.

Rana, her friend, stood before her.

Rana, the assassin, also stood before her.

She was fighting fate for family, but fighting fate meant fighting the only family she had ever known.

And with every long shadow that fell across Rana's face, Zarina knew even less what to do. Rana's resolve, however, seemed to crystalize.

She hefted her sapphire weapon into a fighting stance and walked toward Zarina, sure as the moonrise.

Zarina skirted the edge of the tomb, keeping a sketchy distance from Rana's resolute eyes. Richard groaned, and she tried twice to make her way to him, to catch a glimpse of something, anything to ease the pinch in her thundering heart, but Rana blocked her and forced her back.

Farak positioned himself between them, a hulking shadow in a fight he should have no part in. He was humoring them, Zarina was sure. Maybe he thought if they fought enough, they would feel better, make amends and be friends again. But his presence only made things worse. Especially since she still had no idea what he owed to Rana enough to give up his eternal salvation. The only thing she did know was that this fight could only end in death. Zarina looked down at the shine of blood in her dagger's rubies.

Her whole life revolved around death.

Her reign as queen of Aegyptus was drenched in it. And if Nefertari's body laying in the tomb below meant anything, it was that death could only be conquered by dying. Only, Rana would be the one to die this day.

She had to be. It was the only way to save Richard. It was the only way to avenge her mother's cruel end. Justice demanded that Zarina end the cycle or herself this day. And there was no greater force in all of Aegyptus.

Zarina glared at Rana, whose eyes grew wide. Then she came, blade flashing against the man-made light. Back and forth and across and down, her blade whipped like a storm's wind. Rana's sapphire dagger nearly cut Zarina's cheek, Farak's blade glancing it back at the last second. Instead, the sharp metal ripped through Zarina's sleeve, shredding the thin fabric into pieces. Cool air brushed her newly exposed skin, and she staggered back with a gasp.

She had never seen Rana fight so. Not in Alexandria, nor earlier here. Zarina had easily beaten her both those times.

A chill ran along Zarina's bare skin. "You let me win all those times we've sparred."

"You're as smart as a baboon, too," Rana said.

Zarina looked from her sliced sleeve to Rana and back again. "Why would you do that?"

Rana's frown deepened. "Because I forgot who my family was. And then I remembered."

"Family? What do you know of family? It was your father who killed my mother." Zarina pulled her shoulders back. "I have no family because of yours. And you must pay for what they've done. It is the only way."

Rana wiped the thin trickle of blood from her bottom lip. "I have already paid my price."

"You have paid nothing!"

"I lost my mother that day, too!"

"What does that have to do with anything?" Zarina pulled back and nearly lost her balance.

Rana's face crumpled. "Your family can't see past their own noses! Though it's no wonder why, considering their size." Rana's sorrow morphed into something cruel and coy.

Zarina's hand shot up to the long bridge that sat upon her face. "If we do miss anything, it's from looking at the knives *your* family throws in our backs."

Rana looked at her dagger, rolling it back and forth so it twinkled and sparked in the dimming light. "Nefertari's children have always been stupid."

Zarina raised her dagger when Richard moaned from the corner. Relief flooded her frame, and she fought everything in her not to run to him. She had to focus. She had to finish. She had to—to slit Rana's throat. Her chest squeezed so tightly, she could barely breathe, the thought crushing in on her.

Fate truly mocked her. Her existence had come down to avenging her past family or her potential to create a future one. Her history or her future. Her oldest friend or her . . . her Richard. The weight of her dagger never felt so great, the red of the jewels never so blinding.

She looked to Richard, the wild curls splayed about his head sticky with blood. An innocent felled by the hand of the assassin. Her determination resolved.

She couldn't kill Rana with Farak standing guard, and he would always be standing guard. She turned her eyes to her Guardsman and took a slow breath. The answer stared back, cold and black as the desert night.

She couldn't kill Rana with Farak alive.

Thirty

Zarina took a deep breath.

As long as Farak insisted on protecting Rana, she would never be able to resolve her fate. He had to go, even if the thought made her physically sick. He was bound not to harm her—though that no longer mattered—but she had never been under the same obligation. And now, he stood in the way of justice.

She looked at his clavicle so she didn't have to see his eyes and raised her dagger. Then, she dashed forward, feigning a strike on Rana.

Farak lunged to protect Rana, and Zarina slashed for the same place on his chest he had held her against in port, pulling back as she pushed forward. Farak twisted out of her way just in time, eyes as wide as the noonday sun. She stumbled with a grin. Finally, she had surprised him. But she would not get an opening like that again, and she had wasted it with hesitation.

Farak did not draw his blade.

She gripped the hilt of her dagger so hard, the rubies imprinted themselves on her skin. What was wrong with her? Even as Richard lay dying, she could not kill her Guardsman.

"Farak," she said, tremors shaking her body. It took all the queenly hypocrisy within her veins to ignore the splintering in her heart every time she said his name. "I invoke the oath you made with Ra and command you to stop Rana."

He didn't move.

Rana smirked.

"Fine." Zarina ground her teeth together. "I was giving you one last chance not to face an eternity of darkness. If you can't do what you were born to do, then at least stay out of my way when I do things like this." She grabbed a broken crane head from off a nearby vase and hurled it at Rana. The jagged end smacked a surprised Rana across the brow, and another trickle of blood marked her lovely features.

Rana glared. "I would not do such things if I were you."

"I thought you weren't afraid to fight a baboon."

"What?" Richard asked, his voice cracking. He pushed himself up from the floor and onto his elbow with a grimace. He pressed a hand gingerly to his side and exhaled sharply through his teeth. "Who's the baboon? Or is my Arabic getting worse? I did take quite a hit to the head."

Zarina's chest ballooned with air. It was the first time she could breathe since she had entered the tomb. She would not be the cause of his death. Not unless Ahmet was prepared to take her as well.

"Are you okay?" Zarina asked around her endless dance with Rana. She wanted to throw her arms around him.

"Ay," he said unconvincingly in sloppy English. "But I have terrible news."

The desert air left her lungs.

Richard dropped his voice to a loud, raspy whisper. "I think Rana is the assassin." He gestured his head in her direction, then winced.

A smile slipped from her lips. He was either making jokes again or completely bonkers. Either way, the tomb seemed brighter. "Thanks for the heads up."

Rana sighed. "Enough of the talking. And enough of your secrets. Farak." She tilted her chin up, "I command you to stop Zarina."

Zarina raised a brow.

"Farak," Rana's sing-song voice turned as sharp as her blade. "Do as you're told."

It was Zarina's turn to smirk. "Why would he ever listen to you?"

"Because I'm a queen of Aegyptus."

"A Hittite queen has no place in Aegyptus."

"I am Ramses's true heir and Ra's deified descendant," Rana challenged.

Zarina should not have laughed.

This much she knew.

But she did; a long, bitter laugh at the preposterousness of Rana's declaration until she saw Farak's face crumple.

"Farak?" she scoffed.

"The day I found you . . . ." he reached into a pouch on his belt and, with much hesitation, pulled out another sapphire Finder.

"How?" Zarina's hand darted to where hers hid in her pouch. Her other hand wiped her green lenses clean with her sleeve. "How do you have that?"

"It is mine." Rana declared, pulling her head back so she looked far more regal than Zarina ever could. The firelight illuminated her spectacular frame and accented the blue in her flower barrette.

"Both buriers arrived on my doorstep the same day eighteen years ago," Farak said. "As the only living Guardsman, I . . . I had to choose who to find first."

Zarina shook her head. Dread and hope mixed within her, making her sick. "What are you saying?"

"That he doesn't belong to you." Rana cut in. "That he can choose between us and still avoid Ahmet's jaws."

"Farak?" Zarina clamped down on her trembling jaw. "Is this why you hid her identity in the market? Did you know she was a royal then or . . . was it your past with her that shut your mouth?"

He turned away from her pleading eyes. "I've always known the assassin was a royal."

"All those years together when I told you of my wish for family and mourned my potential demise at the hands of the assassin, how could you not tell me the person who fulfilled each criteria was one and the same?"

"I did what I thought was best!" He turned to her, stepping to his full height. "And Rana's an eternally distant cousin at best. I knew the assassins descended from the Hittite queens, but I did not know their daughters could bind me with the curse. I did not know the other princess I was supposed to protect was also the assassin. I thought it impossible. And I didn't know—" He choked on his words. "I did not know she lived." He turned his golden bronze eyes on Rana. "I did not know you could live without a Guardsman by your side."

"But you did not care, either," Rana said. "Not once you saw her."

"He's *my* Guardsman," Zarina said. "And he always has been, so why would he care about you?"

Rana shook her dagger. "He should never have been *yours* to start with. It is my scarab he holds in his hand."

"And it is my *Finder*," she emphasized the correct name and pulled hers out, "that he handed back to me when he found me as a child outside the cellar of a pistoria."

"My gentlewomen," Richard said, gesturing weakly between the two.

Zarina and Rana glared.

"My apologies," he tugged at his red, soaked collar. "I have lost a great deal of blood. What I meant to say was my dagger-wielding demi-goddesses, why are you fighting about this when Farak should have the answer?" He paused to catch his breath and touched a tender finger to the wound above his eyebrow. "Was it not his sword the little machinations scurried to? He should know which one arrived where."

Zarina sank onto her heels, a mantle of realization weighing her down. "*Ya msebty.*" She turned wide eyes on her Guardsman. "That's why you're stuck, isn't it, Farak?"

"There is no stuck or not stuck," Rana said impatiently. "Which one of our beetles found your kilij?"

"It is not his kilij," Zarina said at last. "Not all of it."

Rana and Richard looked to Farak.

"The blade is mine," he said. "The hilt is my twin brother's. My mother made it so after he had passed. In his honor. And just in case."

"There was another Guardsman?" Rana's voice was soft.

"He died as a baby," Farak said stiffly.

"How?" Rana's moon eyes narrowed. "How could this happen?"

"We thought it was the gods correcting a mistake," Zarina offered weakly. "That there was not a second queen born and therefore no need for a Guardsman."

"But I *was* born," Rana said. "And the gods must have recognized that because Farak's brother was born, too."

"Until they realized you were a fraud and fixed the error," Zarina said.

"How dare you," Rana challenged. "For all we know they killed *your* Guardsman because they knew you weren't worthy of your ancestry."

"Ridiculous," Zarina countered, but Rana's words snaked through her, burning her with venom wherever they touched.

Rana whipped back her cloak and turned to Farak. "So will we never know? Are we stuck in this limbo forever?"

They stared at Farak who looked past them all, refusing to answer. The silence grew increasingly palpable until Richard's practical voice stirred the dust.

"Separate the blade from the hilt."

Farak flinched.

"Then you'll have the answer," Richard said. "It's simple enough." He used the wall to pull himself to his feet then held out his hand for Farak's kilij.

Farak frowned. "You can barely hold yourself up."

"Right-O. Saw through that, did you?" Richard offered a pain-tweaked smile. "Pay no mind. If the buriers are drawn to each Guardman's sword, and Farak's kilij is made up of both, then whichever beetle goes to the hilt is his brother's charge, and whichever trundles to the blade is his. Easy enough, that, though I don't understand the science behind it at all. Go on then. Pop it off and let's be done."

"No." Farak placed a hand on the hilt of his kilij but did not unsheath it.

Zarina grabbed his hand, trying to free the weapon. "No? What do you mean no?"

"I will not do it."

"You *will not* do it?" Rana asked, shaking her dagger in his direction. "You will not free us from this eternal uncertainty before I slit her throat?"

Farak's frown deepened with Rana's words. "I cannot."

"Then what *can* you do?" Zarina threw her hands up. "If you are protecting both of us, you are protecting neither of us. If you refuse to dismantle your sword, you have already betrayed your oath and promise to the gods."

Zarina shifted her weight to the balls of her feet, hoping her words would provoke him into action.

Farak's shoulders sank. "I cannot unsheath my sword and break it into pieces because it would break me with it. The day I found you, Zarina, is the day I betrayed my oath." He turned his golden eyes on her, sincerity filling the worry lines that creased his face.

"Is this true?" Zarina asked.

She tried to ignore the duplicitous fire building within her, for it was filled with hope and longing and the jasmine scent of togetherness that she both loved and hated. She felt a protectiveness stir within her she had not felt before. She did not want to lose her shared past with Farak. She did not want to lose him, even after all this, because it meant losing a part of herself.

But she also had to know.

She scanned his face and braced herself. "Am I not the one you were sent to find?"

"I do not know," he said with gravity.

"And he never wished to," Rana added, her face a mixture of terrifying and pitiful.

"How would you know?" Zarina asked.

"You remember how we met?"

"Of course, I do."

"The day after your mother died along with mine, you remember this, yes?"

"We ran from those boys in the street and hid in a barrel." How appropriate it seemed now that even as they met they were already running. Only then, it had been together.

"We became friends instantly, unaware that the day before our mothers had fought to the death as enemies. It is too bad we did not know better then, I think." A glimpse of true sorrow crossed Rana's face before vanishing.

"Don't talk about my mother," Zarina said, her horrid death reminding her why she came.

"And why shouldn't I? Their fates were tied. Our fates are tied. We are the same."

Zarina shook her head. "Your mother and father were murderers, and Maathornefurer's line was never cursed. You *chose* your wretched fate. *That's* why we are not the same."

"We were given the greatest curse!"

"To be liars who attack young girls and kill their mothers?"

"To be forgotten!" Rana cried. "To be forgotten and unloved. Our fate has not changed. My mother did set a trap to kill yours for what she did to our family. But she changed her mind, became weak-hearted, and tried to save her, then drowned with her in the burn of hot sand. Mercy killed my mother. Mercy and the scourge of your family."

"Your mother?" Zarina scrunched a brow.

She had been such a fool to assume the assassin would be a man just because the few who had been seen by her ancestors were male.

Rana continued, her voice as hard as steel, "I dug and dug as the moon waxed and waned in the sky until at last, I felt her fingertips. Cold, like my heart. But only my betraying father came to take me away. He drank himself to death a year later. I guess he did not love me enough to stick around or finish his job and get rid of you."

Zarina saw once more her dear friend before her.

The one who stood by her no matter what. The one who risked her life for her and did her best to offer her freedom. And the one who was just as bound to feckless fate as she and Farak. She had stood at that same sand pit that same day, but when Farak had arrived a week later, he had carried only Zarina away from the carnage that lay beneath. She could not imagine bearing that burden alone.

"I love you, Rana," she said quietly.

"Not enough to give up your silly hunt. Not enough to forsake your revenge and be my sister."

Zarina opened her mouth, but what could she say? What Rana said was true. She had chosen revenge and fear and the hopeless fight against fate over Rana's offer of family. She was not like her mother at all.

"What is funny, yes," Rana continued, one finger on her pouty lips, "is that we already were blood sisters."

"What?" It was Farak who Rana caught off guard this time.

She shot him a clever smile. "My father was a philandering man. He was married to my mother and starting a family when he met who I now know was Zarina's mother. She was beautiful, he told me in drunken slurs. A desert rose kissed by sunlight."

Zarina frowned. That sounded more like Rana than her.

"I guess he decided one daughter and wife was not enough. So he laid with your mother and made it two, which is why my mother laid a trap to make it one again."

Zarina's mother had told her many times about the roguish man she had barely known as a young child. Dark, handsome, dangerous, the desert moon who chased the sun. "So . . . my mother fell in love with the assassin's lover?"

"No." Rana shook her head and tucked a silky wave of hair behind her ear. "She fell in love with the assassin."

Thirty-One

Zarina's mother had fallen in love with the assassin? In *love*? After everything she and her family had been through?

Did that mean she and Rana were half-sisters?

And if that was the case, what did that make her? Half-martyr, half-assassin?

The tomb darkened, the shadows crushing down oh her. No lens could change what Rana had said. No color could brighten reality. Zarina's blood pulsed as a headache behind her eyes. It could not be true. Her mother could not have betrayed her so.

"Blimey," Richard mustered a reply, and Zarina was grateful.

She could barely grasp hold of the slippery truths spilling from Rana's lips. They couldn't be sisters. *Rana* was the assassin. Her arch-nemesis. The very reason she lived alone and in fear.

Farak crossed his arms. "Your shared parentage must be why the burier worked."

"It worked because I'm Maathornefurer's current princess," Rana said, her sharp eyes flicking to him.

"No." Farak clipped. "It is not enough for your murderous ancestors."

Rana scowled.

Farak continued, "There were no Guardsmen for Maathornefurer's line. It is one of the reasons your family started hunting the others. Your ancestors saw the scarabs as the official sign of nobility and would stop at nothing to get one. And your family nearly succeeded with the end of Isetnofret's line, but her Guardsman activated the beetle with his blood and sent it back to the Guardsmen as his final act. For millennia it lay hidden and protected from your line. It seems your father found out its secret location and managed to steal it anyway, then gave it to you."

Richard leaned back against the wall, his face a sheet of white. "The science behind that is—"

"Ancient," Zarina said, furrowing her brows. Then it hit her. "Cairo! The sacred Finder beetle was stolen from the library. But how? The contents of the chamber and how to get in were a secret known only to my ancestors—"

The answer hit her, and her eyes widened.

Rana smirked. "Looks like both your father *and* mother betrayed their families. It makes sense why you would refuse my offer, now."

Zarina's stomach squeezed.

"We make our own paths, love." Richard smiled weakly. "So my Zarina's a double princess—one of Nefertari's *and* Maathornefurer's lines," he mused. "That explains that nose of yours."

Zarina glowered at Richard.

"I don't care how many ancient queens she descended from." Rana bristled at his words. "The burier worked with my blood, and I am owed a Guardsman. I am owed the life Zarina squandered!"

"A life of fear and inbred headaches? A life on the run with a man I—" Zarina caught herself, glancing between Farak and Richard. "You do not want this life."

"A life with someone is better than a life alone. Something you did not believe, *Nuur,* leaving god's gift of companionship to die in the desert. You are truly more of an assassin than I. But that, too, is in your blood."

Zarina lifted her dagger, but her mouth ran dry. "I . . . I am no assassin."

"You are as much assassin as I am." The glint in Rana's eye held far more than Zarina could bear.

Her knees trembled, and she was instantly grateful for Richard's hand steadying her back. He had been right all along. She was far more involved in her fate than she ever could imagine, and the gods had been laughing at her the whole time.

Her entire life, she had been running from herself. She had been hating herself. All this time she had been declaring her ancestry with pride when she didn't even know who she was.

She was truly lost.

She dropped her dagger and bent over, hands on knees to catch a breath.

Her mother—the woman who had kept her safe until the day she died—had kept her in the dark. But why?

The words she had uttered on their way to Cairo all those years ago swirled in the scattered sand of her mind.

A place to call home.

A place for family.

And the one that snagged at Zarina's mind and tore it in half. *Perhaps another little girl just like you to be sisters.*

Her mother must have known the assassin was the same man with whom she shared a bed. Which meant her mother had had a chance to end their generational torment and reclaim her fate. Instead, she had chosen to make a family with the murderers and steal the burier for the assassin . . . for Rana. To make her a princess, too.

But no family came of her sacrifice.

Blood and vengeance and death would always win out.

And now, Zarina was condemned to live as a murderer and die as a victim. As half assassin, she was truly the curse on everyone she had feared she'd become. Maathornefurer and Nefertari battled within her, and her fate never seemed so unclear.

"Too bad your mother's Guardsman was as poor at his job as Farak is," Rana continued coldly. "Wasn't it his job to keep her out of trouble?"

"It's his job to keep trouble *away* from her," Farak said, pushing his way past Rana.

He knelt on the ground next to Zarina and placed a hand on her free shoulder. It was little comfort, even with both men at her side.

"It doesn't matter," Rana huffed and marched up to Farak, "all this lying and hunting and killing for generations. The Royal Guardsmen still spurn our family. Even being a blood sister to Nefertari's very line, I was not enough for you."

Zarina lifted her head and studied the sorrow in Rana's eyes.

Genuine.

Real.

But the words made no sense. "What are you talking about?"

"What I've been saying this whole time, and what you have never cared about. Farak found you first," Rana said, shoving a finger at his chest. "He found you first when we were little girls and never came to find me. You were all he needed; the pure princess he was looking for. And I wasn't worth the trouble."

Pain broke across Farak's face.

"Tell her I'm wrong, Farak." Rana's honey-brown eyes fell to the floor.

He raised his hands in defense, leaving Zarina's shoulder cold. "It is not so simple as all of that."

"Because you love her, don't you?" Rana accused, not waiting for him to explain.

"I—" he stuttered and stood, stepping away from Zarina.

Zarina leaned in, holding her breath for the answer and trying not to see that Richard watched her, trying not to feel his tightened grip on her skin.

"Don't you?" Rana challenged again.

"I am forbidden!"

Zarina exhaled. It was the answer he had always given.

"And yet you stayed with her," Rana said, the pitiful softness in her eyes sharpening into something far more severe. "Her pet. Her whipping boy."

"Farak and I were more than servant and master." Zarina's temper rose. "We have a bond you wouldn't understand."

But Rana had no time for her. She leaned against Farak, standing on her tip-toes, so her red lips hovered just below his. "I could have made you so much more, Farak."

Hot pink bloomed across Farak's cheeks. Zarina's knee-jerk reaction was to rip her off his breathless chest, but Richard's hand slid down her arm and grabbed hold of her wrist, pulling her back as she stepped forward. She bit her lip and looked at him, his face uncharacteristically stern.

She was a monster, loving them both. And he was beginning to see it now, too.

Rana had been wrong. A broken relationship was even worse than being alone.

"I waited for you, you know?" Rana said, her voice a mixture of bitter and coy. "I waited years for you, Farak. But you never came." A single tear escaped her moon eyes, trickling down her cheek.

Zarina pulled her hand from Richard's and pressed against the bridge of her nose to keep back a headache. It was the most she could do without looking desperate. "If I had known, Rana—"

"You would have what?" She fell back on her heels and turned her fierce eyes on Zarina. "You are just as much a slave to this whole thing as the rest of us."

Unease spread between them. The lantern cast shadows across their faces, the chill of Rana in front of her and the warmth of Richard behind. And then there was Farak. Her usual stay of safety was now as fickle as the wind.

"Let's go, Zarina," Richard said, holding out his hand.

His gentleness startled her after everything that burned inside the tomb. "What?"

"Let Rana have Farak. It is her right just as much as yours. Besides, you hate your life as Ra's heir, whereas Rana wants it. Come away with me and leave all this behind. Rana will leave you be, won't you?" He flicked his eyes to her *sister*.

The word felt foreign even now.

"Yes, *Nuur*," Rana chimed, her voice coated in too much sweetness. "Leave, and I won't kill you . . . today."

Zarina looked at Richard's hand. At the sincerity and warmth that exuded from his helplessly kind eyes. She wanted to take his offer. She wished she'd taken his first offer. With all she'd done to him, this would surely be his last. She willed herself to take his hand. To reach out and grab his offer of freedom. But she could not. Ma'at's mercy, she could not do it.

He deserved more than an assassin. More than blood-filled secrets that she did not even know. Secrets that revealed an uglier version of herself each time. And he deserved more than half her heart. Afterall, he could not compete with the gods; he said so himself.

"Zarina?" Richard took a step closer, the strain of the effort clear as the sweat on his brow and the blood pouring from his hair and side. His smile held fast, but the shine in his eyes was beginning to dim. "Do you love me?"

She wanted to affirm him, to throw her arms around him. To fly off with him into the night. But she could not hurt him anymore. She would not.

Zarina dropped her gaze to the ground, silent.

"Do you love Farak?" he whispered, searching her face for an answer she knew he would not want to hear.

"Yes." She looked up as she said it. "Though I wish I did not."

"Ah." Richard leaned back against the wall and tilted his head up toward the painted stars.

Did it matter that the dark azure and glow of white were naught but paint on stony walls?

Twice she yearned to reach for him, and twice she pulled back. The pain in his eyes poured coarse grains of sand into her being, filling her heart and swallowing her up. She could not survive leaving another love in the desert. But her decision did not change. There was no other way to spare Richard the agony of her curse. Who she loved was the one thing left she could control. And she would protect him from her.

"It is like you said, Richalala. I'm not sure there's a place for you in my world."

"You know fate isn't—that you aren't—?" Richard's shoulders slumped, and his face fell into his palm. He slowly ran his hand through his curls.

"She cannot choose you, Richard," Rana said. "You are not revenge nor justice. You are not Ra. You are nothing here in Aegyptus. Zarina chooses to be a slave to fate. And you are not fate, no?"

He lifted his crushed eyes and looked between them, landing on her last. "Goodbye, Zarina."

Richard slinked out of the chamber, pushing her helping hand out of the way as he passed. Zarina watched her future—her escape from this nightmare—fade away, leaving her in the teeth of darkness. She splayed her hand upon the wall by the stairwell to stay upright and stared blankly at the hole where Richard had stood. There was a matching hole within her.

"You could have spared him that, no?" Rana's voice broke the silence when the last of his footsteps faded. "If you had just died in the alleyway."

Rana's barbs fell on nothing. Zarina's soul was hollow, her heart inky black after a life of lying to herself. She thought she knew what suffering was. She thought she knew what it was like to lose what she loved most. She had known nothing.

"You could have spared everyone their pain and ended both curses, both cycles, as the daughter of both the assassin and the queen."

Every twist and knot and snag inside her smoothed into a cold sheet of glass.

Numbness.

Zarina could only imagine herself floating, floating down the waters of the Nile, and disappearing through the gates of death.

Her limbs weightless. And heavy.

Oh, so heavy.

Her heart a black hole that dragged her ever closer to nothingness.

Down, down, down.

No one would watch as she passed into the next life.

Not on this side or the next.

She fell to her knees, her hands open and upturned on her blood-stained clothes. Then she leaned forward and lay her head on the sandy floor. Let Rana end her now. Death was the only choice she had left to make.

"Do not pity her," Rana's brittle voice cut through the ensuing silence. "She treated you no better than Adajin. Even my blade is too good for her back."

"Rana!" Farak said sharply. "You have done enough."

He stepped between them, so she could see only a sliver of where her half-sister stood. Where the assassin stood. One of two assassins. And her oldest friend. She had become the sister her mother had spoken of, yet learning they were actually sisters had destroyed it. How was that so?

"*I* have done enough? *I* have?" Rana's eyes caught the white light, making her look otherly. Unreal. Like the gods lived within her. "Unsheath your kilij, Farak, and declare so again." She lifted her sapphire blade and pointed it at him.

"I will not fight you," Farak said, irritation clipping his words.

"Then shall Zarina and I pay for your mistakes? You are just as guilty as the rest of us."

Farak sighed. "The answer to death is not more death. Revenge only begets more revenge and hate more hate."

For the first time since Richard left, Zarina's heart stirred. Not with love. With something sticky and hot that wanted to burn, that wanted to see everything burn.

Fate was nothing. An idea. A figment. An unseeable force. But Rana and Farak lived and breathed before her, ruining her life.

Richard said to fight a person. Well, there they were, and they would pay for this. One way or another and with Ra as her witness, they would suffer this curse with her.

Thirty-Two

Every injustice of Zarina's life lay bare before her, and Farak and Rana were at the heart of it all.

Rana was right. Farak was just as guilty as she and Rana, if not more so, because he held the answer that haunted them both.

She muscled her way out of Farak's arms. "Rana's right."

Farak's eyes widened. "Zarina?"

"Fight her."

"I will no—"

"You will!"

"Don't do—"

"Enough!" She cut off his plea. She was done listening. "I will do as I please. And *you* will do as I please. And if I'm not your master, she is. So you must fight."

He rose to his full height, the golden bronze of his eyes glinting. She would not back down.

"Fight Rana."

His jaw muscle twitched.

"You said you defied the curse the moment you met me. But that's a lie you tell yourself. Because the second you knew who Rana was, you wouldn't slay her for me. You never really chose anything. You just hid. You are worse than I."

"You do not know of what you speak," he whispered dangerously.

"Draw. Your. Sword. And fight her!"

"No."

Zarina seethed at his insolence. At his lying. At Rana's stupidly petite figure watching them fight.

"Then tell me why you spared her."

"Because of my oath."

"Lie," Zarina said.

"It is not—"

"Do not lie to me, Farak! You could not have known the second she showed her face as the assassin that she was the lost princess, not after so many years of not knowing."

Farak fell silent as some of the fire in his eyes melted into surprise.

Zarina bared her teeth. "Did you think I would not realize that? Did you think I was stupid?"

"Of course not."

"Why did you spare her?"

"She is your frien—"

Zarina kicked sand at him. "A Royal Guardsman cares not for friends. Only duty." She leaned forward, challenging his flickering gaze, and dropped her voice low. "So, why did you spare her?"

"I—"

"Why?" she cried.

"Because I cared for her. Too much. After you left, she and I, we—-"

Zarina fell back on her heels, tired from the angry nothing nipping at her hollowness. "So it is."

Rana moved closer to Farak and laid a hand on his shoulder. "It is good she finally knows."

He kept his eyes on Zarina. "It was brief."

She stared at the wall.

"I was lost without you."

"You mean without a cause," Zarina said coldly.

"You betrayed me in the desert. I took time to heal."

"With Boozah."

"No," he argued half-heartedly.

"With Rana, then."

"Well, yes. But I left soon after to search for you once more. And when I realized it was her in the market—I should have killed her. You're right. I still had feelings for her, but those ended then."

Rana's grip on Farak tightened, so her fingers puckered his shirt.

"And yet she lives." Zarina turned her icy gaze on Rana.

"I cut her as we fought in the streets of Alexandria, pulled her cloak from her back. When I hesitated, she twisted away and grabbed my pouch. It broke open onto the streets, and the summoning burier came tumbling out. She picked it up, blood on her fingers, and it activated, scurrying for me as it had when we were all children. I was lost in that moment. I didn't know what to do."

"You kill her." Zarina lunged forward and grabbed the hilt of his sword.

Farak held the blade tight through his scabbard. "Do you still believe that, knowing she is your sister?"

Zarina faltered.

"And shouldn't you be happy?" He asked, his muscles straining against her pull for the first time. "You despised my loyalty. You spurned my desire to protect you." The resolve in Farak's face cracked, but his grip on the kilij held strong.

"I wish I were happy to hear it," Zarina spat. "I'm cursed to be hurt by you. And all because of Merytamun's pathetic mercy."

"Was your life with me that terrible?" Farak asked. "Was my desire to care for you such a burden?"

"Yes!" She cried and was filled with regret. "I wish I had been Rana and she had been me."

Farak stared at her, eyes wide and broken. She had never felt worse in all her life. Not even when she left him the first time. She was twice bereft this time, having lost Richard and Farak. But the sticky anger inside would not release her.

"Let us see who you belong to so we can free ourselves from this torment!"

She pulled on his blade. He held. Then, hands enclosed around hers.

Rana placed her foot against Farak as she yanked back with Zarina. Farak's grip tightened, the muscles in his arm bulging from the strain.

Pulling alone would not be enough. Then she saw it on Farak's belt. The key to the hidden chamber and a perfect tool for bludgeoning a sword in two.

Zarina released her hold on the hilt and snatched her throwing stick as Farak tumbled back. Before he could rebalance, she grabbed hold of the kilij once more. Rana met her eyes and nodded. Zarina bashed the end of the stick into where the metal and hilt met just above Farak's fingers. His grasp tightened, but it was too late. A crack formed, and the sword split in two. Rana and Zarina fell back, the hilt in Rana's hands and the throwing stick in hers.

"No!" Farak cried, getting up from where he had fallen.

His eyes darted between the hilt and the throwing stick.

Then he dove.

Zarina jumped back and barely made it out of his grasp. Surprise rattled her resolve. He had come for her and the key instead of the hilt.

Why?

Was the secret behind the Singular Eye more important than the answer to all of their fates? The thought chilled her despite the smoky heat still wafting from downstairs. She had to find out what it was. Her eyes met Rana's, just as round with the same realization. Rana nodded again.

Farak lunged for the stick, but this time Rana blocked his path.

"Run, Zara. Find out his secret."

"*Now* you two work together?" Farak asked, his face a mask of incredulity.

Zarina did not wait for his frustration to overtake Rana. She flew down the stairs, nearly tripping over her heavy boots. Breathing hard, she skidded into the secret chamber.

Farak bellowed from the stairwell behind her.

She shoved the key into the hole in the center of the eye and twisted. Zarina jumped back, expecting the walls to shift. Instead, the stone broke around the Singular Eye and popped open. A simple scroll rested in a cylinder just big enough to hold the ancient papyrus.

She tugged it out, Rana and Farak's blades clashing in the background.

She forced her nervous fingers to unroll the scroll. Brittle bits of paper crumbled on the edges, already turning to dust. She read the ancient Aegyptian, devouring as many words as she could with each thrum of her heart. It was the curse Ramses placed upon the queens in the name of Ra. It was no secret. She knew it all by heart by the time she was three. Her eyes reached the bottom of the scroll. Her heart caught. The last line was a part of the curse she had never seen nor heard.

Farak's hands reached past her and snatched the scroll from her hands. But it was too late. She had read it all.

She turned, stone against stone. Wide-eyed, she removed her mismatched goggles so she could see things as they were. Farak's eyes were upon her, filled with pity. She dropped her gaze slowly, taking in his battered features. The cut along his brow. His chapped and torn lips. The bruises covering his hard muscles and soft skin. Hands that saved her. Feet that ran to take her in. She loved him. Every bit.

And now she knew why.

Rana tumbled into the room, her nose crinkled beneath fiery eyes. "Did you read it?" she asked between breathless gasps. She grabbed for the scroll, and Farak let her have it, his eyes still pitying Zarina.

One glance, and Rana rolled it back up with a snap that chipped away at the tattered edges. "It is too long and my ancient languages are as dusty as this old scroll. What did it say?"

"That we have no say in our fates at all," Zarina said, her voice surprisingly steady. "In our lives. In our love. We never had a chance."

"What is this you speak of?"

"Farak."

Rana leaned in. "Yes? What about him?"

"One servant for every master."

"What are you talking about?" she asked, shaking Zarina's shoulders. "And why are you so calm? Look at me."

Zarina blinked and turned her gaze to Rana. Without the tint of goggles, she seemed more human. Still beautiful, but with a freckle on her nose and creases by her eyes.

"The Guardsmen are sworn to protect but never confess love to their charges, as we all knew. While we princesses are fated to love them with all our hearts, our real curse is generations of unrequited passion for Merytamun's failing. An ache in our chests that can never be soothed." She let the words sink in, watching as Rana's face fell. "The gods control our blood, our family, and our hearts. All of it."

"And you knew this?" Rana asked, glancing at Farak.

"I have always known," he said, his voice gruff and his eyes downturned. "We Guardsmen are warned from the first breath we take as babies to the last one we take before leaving home that our princesses will love us. It is our greatest temptation and a burden that we must carry. To protect and serve but never act on the growing feelings inside us, lest we condemn to Ahmet's darkness both our soul and that of the one we care for."

"And how many queens have known this?" Zarina asked, her mind in a cool daze.

He shifted his weight. "None. Until you two."

A flicker restarted in her chest, and the roar of fire grew within her.

"It can't be true," she said, clenching her fingers tight against her palm. "My mother loved another. The assassin, even! That flies in the face of fate."

"I don't think your mother cared much for fate, to be honest." Farak sighed, heavy and thick. "And her Guardsman died long before you were born, as you well know. The heart can heal and move on if given enough time."

"Can it?" she spat.

His eyebrows softened, and she had to look away.

"If my mom didn't believe, why did she teach the will of the gods to me? Why did she let me believe if she didn't herself?"

Farak's shoulders slumped. "The same reason as I did. She was willing to risk her eternal soul, but not yours in case she was wrong. I think she was trying to *show* you a new life so you could choose for yourself, she just didn't get the chance."

Zarina shook her head, rage and logic battling within her.

"But all those years—All those years you let me believe I was crazy. You let me think I was in love with you, that I would give my life for you!"

"Would you not?" he whispered.

His simple question stilled her.

She had not given up her life for him. When she left him in the desert, she had given up her *eternity*.

"But how?" Her glass wall shattered as the inferno engulfed her. "How can that be if these feelings are all fake?"

"Fake and god-decreed are two different things," he said matter-of-factly, boiling her ancient blood. "The effectiveness of the curse is that your feelings are very real."

"You should have told me."

"What good would it have done?"

"I could have fought my feelings for you instead of nursing them. And I would have known that the pain I feel every time you betray me is not my fault." Zarina shook her head and started pacing the chamber. "And what of Rana?" she finally asked.

He cast his gaze to the floor once more, and her sister shifted beside her. No longer the assassin, but a hurt girl who had been forsaken long ago.

Zarina hurt for her just as much as herself. "How could you do that to her?" She punched the wall, so pain spidered across her fingers.

Farak shifted his sorrowful gaze. "If I had known who you were, Rana. I never would have—We never would have—" He rubbed a thumb along the pinch in his brows. "May god burn my soul for eternity if I have jeopardized your eternal life in any way."

Rana put up a hand to stop him. "I don't want to know anymore. I cannot bear it. You. My sister. This pain." She touched a hand to Zarina's shoulder, her eyes dark crescents. "I have to leave this place and this life. If I am already cursed and my soul sealed, then let me at least live the rest of my life in peace." Then she disappeared up the stairs.

Another person lost from Zarina's life.

She should follow. Forsake fate, too, but a fire still burned inside her.

Farak's bronze eyes lingered on the stairwell before sifting back to Zarina.

"This is why I turned you away all those years ago, Zarina. You're so devoted to the gods and the curse; I didn't want to break you if you ever found out. And I didn't want to take advantage, not when you believed so ardently and I did not."

"But you kissed me," she said, touching a hand to her lips. His warmth had vanished from her skin, leaving stinging in its place.

His voice cracked. "*'arğūk sāmiḥnī.*"

She turned away from his pleading eyes.

"*'atawassalu 'ilayk,* Zarina. Please."

"How can I forgive you? You knew my feelings were not my own, yet you still . . ." She could not finish, could not process what had happened. Her chin quivered, and she fought to hold it still.

"Because Rana was right," he said softly, running a hand through the wispy ends of her braids. "I've loved you from the moment I saw you. And I'm selfish and weak, and I couldn't resist anymore. I couldn't be around you one more second without pulling you close, without touching your skin and tasting your lips. I was going mad."

She wanted to turn to him, to soothe his sorrows and wrap herself in his warmth. But this feeling was a lie. She knew that now, though it did not stop the tearing pain.

"And because," Farak continued, his fingers softly pulling at her hair, sending tingles across her scalp. "I stopped believing in the gods long ago."

Her breath caught. "Then why did you protect me all those years?"

"Because I love you."

"How could you let me control your life in the name of the gods when you didn't believe at all?"

"Because I love you."

"Then how," her voice caught, and she took a moment to breathe. "How could you rebuff me when I offered you my love?" She turned to look at him, and he caught her face in his hands.

"Because I love you, Zarina Nefertari. And I knew you believed the curse was true. I didn't want to do that to you. To do this." He leaned in and kissed her long enough for a tear to wet her cheeks before she turned her head away. "I am not a divine servant of the gods. I am just a man."

Did no one believe in fate as she did? Her mother had given it up for the assassin, and he for her. Farak had never believed, and Rana, too, had been able to walk away. But how? How could they ignore a thorn burrowing into the middle of their backs?

The ground rumbled.

She froze.

The sand shifted beneath them. She looked up at Farak. His eyes were wide, and his muscles tensed. Not good. A blast sounded, muffled somewhere in the distance, and the walls shook once more. Dust and debris trickled down from the ceilings coating their clothes and hair.

The gods had judged them and decreed their fate. For defying the curse, they were forsaken. Blast after blast shook and shattered the tomb.

She would die here after all.

Thirty-Three

Zarina ducked, and a block of ceiling shattered at her feet, obliterating Nefertari's as they hit the sandy floor. The whole tomb trembled, the anger of the gods unleashing around them. Urns fell. The jackal's head tumbled and broke into a dozen pieces. She grabbed the gas lantern from where it rested on the floor before it was taken by the dark.

"Adajin's men," Farak said. "They were instructed to blow the place if anything happened."

"Well that would have been good to know sooner," she snapped, dodging a shelf full of hippopotamus statues as it crashed to the earth.

She grabbed the lantern and dashed for the stairwell that led to the entrance. The floor groaned. A long crack split the plaster on the wall. White stars and azure sky fell from above, and Rana with it.

"Rana!" Zarina dove for her and broke her fall. "Are you okay? What happened?"

Rana coughed and scurried to her feet, yanking Zarina up with her. "I did not have time to escape with the tomb surrounded."

Another blast shook the tomb, and they stumbled.

The hilt in Rana's hand tumbled free, getting lost in the crumbling stone. Zarina held tight to the lantern and splashed its light across the debris, searching for the answer to their fates. A glimmer caught the hilt, and Zarina reached for the metal, clawing as dust and brick cut her fingers.

"Leave it," Rana hissed through her teeth.

"But—"

"It is better your fate remain hidden than to find it out by dying," Rana snipped, staring at her.

Zarina's fingers curled into a fist. That had to be true, didn't it? She had spent her whole life not living because she feared how she would die. In the end, it had served her not one wit and hurt those she cared about it. She needed to focus on living not just being alive. And that meant letting things go.

Zarina took a deep breath and nodded. She let Rana pull her up but hesitated when she pulled her toward the back of the tomb.

"You're going the wrong way."

"No, you are." Rana grabbed her wrist and ran with her into the secret chamber. "The upstairs is completely blocked by debris and Adajin's ugly men."

"They are ugly," Zarina agreed. "But how will we get out? The entrance I used to get in is up those stairs."

"I'll go up," Farak said, flexing his muscles and cracking his neck. "I'll clear the way so you can escape."

"We do not need you," Rana cut. "You have done enough. Just stay alive, yes? So we can kill you later."

He reached for the hilt of his kilij, ready to defy their orders, and found only air. His shoulders slumped. "As you'll have it."

Rana ran her hands along the wall until she found a picture of Hathor's symbol on Queen Nefertari's white hedjet crown. She slipped her barret free and placed it over the symbol. A straight line cut down the wall, revealing a thin, dark entrance into the unknown.

"Of course, your family of assassins would have secret exits out of this tomb," Zarina muttered.

"Entrances," Rana corrected. "Which also serve as exits. And you're part of the family of assassins, too, remember?"

Zarina bit her lip. "I guess that doesn't sound *so* bad."

The ground shook with an aching groan, so hard this time, that it knocked them off their feet. A large pillar broke at its apex and careened toward Zarina. She fell back, not far enough. She shielded her neck and face and braced for the pain. Instead, Farak stepped in front. The stones struck the corded muscles of his back, and pain tore through his face.

"Go!" he cried and nodded to where Rana disappeared into the wall.

Part of her wanted to flee. Ra, it was true. She wanted to ignore her pounding heart and searing worry and let the stick of rage wash over her and leave him there to die. But the cursed part of her wanted him to live.

Zarina helped push the heavy stone off his back and grabbed his shirt. She dragged him toward the crack in the wall, through crumbling floor and falling ceiling, through smoke and flame, and through the bodies of dead men that slipped through the cracks from the floor above. They reached the sliver of hope that was the crack Rana had escaped through, and horror washed over her.

Farak's broad shoulders would not fit.

"Go," he said.

"I cannot."

"Fate does not decree you protect me, Zarina. Quite the opposite." He softened his face with a tenderness she had not seen since he cradled her on the ship. "You may leave."

"I don't want to," she said, her lip quivering like she was seven again, standing motherless outside the sand-filled pistoria.

"And what good is you staying?"

Another blast engulfed the tomb, and more plaster coated the air around them, shaking the light of the gas lantern she held in her sweaty palms.

"So I can save you."

A flash of mirth smoothed his creased brows. "I should have protected you better—from your delusions."

Zarina cracked a worried smile that pulled at her chest. "Was that a joke?"

"What do you think? Did I pull it off?" His grin widened, but the shine in his eyes was not happiness.

She brushed the white from his hair and cheeks. "I shouldn't have abandoned you in the desert."

"You never looked so beautiful as when you flew away that day," he said, wiping away a smudge of black from her cheek. "I wanted to die."

"I'm sorry," she whispered between the rocking *booms* that quaked through the earth.

"I love you," he said, his eyes glowing in the enclosing dark.

"You stupid man."

He chuckled. "Thank you."

"For what?" She placed her hands on his cheeks.

"For letting me spend my life with you."

"What are you—"

Farak pulled her close and kissed her one last time. His fingers pulled gently through her hair. His breathing matched hers, lips soft and arms strong around her.

The whole tomb rocked and swayed. Plaster burst. Urns crashed to the floor. And her heart burned so fiercely, she thought it would consume her. She didn't even care. She didn't care that she was cursed or that her feelings were contrived by a god because it was her heart that felt them. Fated and fake were different, but they were also the same. Things that didn't matter if she decided it be so.

Farak pressed in harder, stronger, like he was afraid she would slip away. She wrapped her arms around his neck and allowed him to come closer. Then his lips became more fervent, as if consuming her taste one last time. Her fingers tightened on his skin, too late.

"Go." He pulled away with a heavy breath.

"I can't," she said.

But his eyes looked past her to someone else. A hand grabbed her arm and pulled her through the crack as Nefertari's tomb collapsed between her and Farak in a flash of fire and light.

Zarina cried and screamed and tore at the arms that held her back until the explosions had completely sealed them off from the tomb. Another large crack split on the opposite side. Dazed, she allowed herself to be dragged away, the warmth on her lips cooling as Farak began to fade into a memory.

After several turns and twists past dry rock, she emerged into a cavern. The lantern in her hand pitched to and fro, revealing bursts of colors and pharaonic faces upon the walls of an unfamiliar tomb. The flash of lights brought her back to the present. She looked at the hand on her wrist and followed it up to find its owner.

"Richard?"

She blinked, and he remained.

"Richard! You're alive."

Zarina dropped the lantern with a crash and threw her arms around him. She breathed in his reedy, ink smell and pressed herself closer, but he was unyielding. His shoulders went taut, and he pulled away.

"Come on, then," Richard said tersely. "Let's find the exit before Rana slits our throats."

Zarina's surge of warmth froze. "She went this way? You saw her? Is she safe?"

"Is she *safe*?" He shot her a scathing look.

"She *is* my sister."

"Ha!" He grabbed the lantern from her hand and began his search of the tomb walls.

"And she has forsaken fate."

He scoffed but averted his eyes.

Zarina frowned, following close behind him to stay in the light. He had clearly not forgiven her, and the realization that he might never forgive her sank deep into her bones like a chill after getting caught in the rain. Still, seeing him eased the weight on her heart and warmed the numbness just enough that she could carry on.

"What are you doing here?" she asked to keep her mind from wandering.

"You brought me here," he clipped.

"I meant, what are you doing here in this other tomb?"

"Adajin's men took the entrance before they blew the place. But they used way too much charge and destroyed the foundation of this entire section of tombs. When I tried to double back, the wall and floor split and cracked into two. I fell through and ended up here. I believe it is whatever tomb was adjacent to Nefertari's."

Zarina tripped behind Richard and fell to her knees, cutting a gash in her pants. Pain bit at her skin and bone. She looked down. The flowering red of the cloth blurred and brightened. She looked up. Richard was beside her. Or two Richards.

"*Ya msebty*," she said, holding in what little swirled within her stomach. "This tomb was sealed, wasn't it?"

"The fumes?" Richard's face washed in and out of focus.

She nodded.

"Ruddy timing," Richard said and scooped her into his arms. "Why aren't they affecting me?"

"Because you are strong."

He ran from wall to wall and up and down stairs looking for the way out. His biceps bulged with her weight, and his chest rose and fell heavily against her cheek. She nestled in and listened to his heart pounding, quick and steady. His surging life would probably be the last thing she heard before she died. She had maybe half an hour. She was glad to spend it tucked close to Richard. She couldn't help but think about what awaited her on the other side or whether Farak and her mother would be there, both having laughed at the gods as they tried to defy fate. Wherever they were, she would join them, and that would be enough.

Richard went to the highest landing where the entrance should be, but the door was still sealed as tight as the day priests shut the heavy stone thousands of years before.

"You will not find a way out there." Rana's crisp voice came from the shadows behind them. Even swallowed up in the murkiness of poison, Zarina knew it was her.

Richard shuffled Zarina around in his arms and turned to face Rana. She could hear the tight smile in his voice. "Rana, my dear, are you offering to show us the way out? 'Tis very noble. I offer you my thanks."

"Why are you helping her?" Rana's voice cut through his charade.

Zarina held her breath to keep out the poison—both in the air and in Rana's words. Why *was* he helping her?

"What would you have me do?" He asked, dropping his voice low as if that would stop her from hearing.

"You help her after all she's done to you?"

"She's only human, Rana. Same as you."

The ache in Zarina's heart roared over her stupor. All she wanted her whole life was to be a normal human, not a demi-god or a cursed heiress. But when Richard said it in the way he did—like he didn't care for her at all, like she was pathetic and weak and not worth his time—she curled into a small ball, hugging her knees close.

Rana sighed. "Come," she said, and her shadowy blue figure disappeared.

Richard followed silently, leaving Zarina to think. To think of all the things she had done wrong. How she should have treated Farak better all those years and would never have a chance to make amends. How she should have fled with Rana, her unknown sister, to live a new life. How if she had just chosen Richard—her belabored breath caught in her throat—if she had chosen *anything* but fighting uncontrollable fate, she could have been spared death and Farak with her. They three, her only friends and family in the entire desert, had been the escape she had been searching for her whole life.

She just hadn't been able to see it.

At last, they had walked the entire tomb and arrived back at the same dark gash in the wall that led to the chamber. Hot, thick air poured from it, but at least it wasn't tainted with anything more foul than smoke. Richard set Zarina down inside and stood a stone's throw down the passage.

"How is this way out any better?" Richard pinched the bridge of his nose, leaning his back against the rough wall with one foot propped against it.

"Do you have a better way, foreigner?" Rana snipped. "At least the walls through here are not so solid, yes? We cannot travel through rock unless you're as ghostly as you look."

"Are you going to carry her through all that?" he asked like Zarina wasn't there, but she could not protest. The spinning torrent in her head had just started to slow.

Rana waved him off. "We both know I will not."

"Then how are we getting through all this?"

"I know not. But in Aegyptus, a partnership means both people contribute."

He sighed. "I finally make it inside the ancient tombs and instead of sketching, I'm fighting brutes and babysitting."

"Where's your sense of adventure?" Zarina cracked, finding a thread of thought at last. "Where's your yarn and donkey leg?"

Richard released his nose and looked up, a quirk on his serious brow. "I wasn't doing all this for adventure."

She studied his face.

He studied the ceiling.

He was right again. He had gone through all this horror for her, and she had thrown it in his face. Rana had been right, too. She had been cowardly when he had been brave. And she had been cowardly when Farak had been brave. And even Rana had faced her doubts and decided while she had just kept on running from an ancient, unseeable curse and fighting things she didn't even understand.

It was time she found the courage to be like them. Fate or not, they were what mattered to her.

Zarina pulled the shining burier from her pouch and held it out to Rana. "This is how we will get out."

Rana touched the iridescent wings. "How will this help when both pieces of the sword are lost?"

"That is exactly why it will work."

"Nuh-uh." Richard crossed his arms. "I'm not encouraging this madness."

Zarina leaned in closer to him. "It has to be done."

"What?" Rana asked, coughing delicately from the acidic air, so her gold bracelets tinkled on her arm. "What are you talking about?"

Richard's lost smile hid beneath thinly-pressed lips, and he refused to look at her.

Zarina ignored him, though the prick in her heart was much harder to forget. "You dropped the hilt by the stairwell that heads toward the entrance of the tomb, so when the ground stops shaking, it can help lead us to the way out."

Recognition lighted in Rana's eyes. "And what of the blade? Where is Farak?"

"He fell." She spat out the sand coating her mouth, the pointed claws of misery raking at her heart. Even Richard held his tongue. "With the blade still in his scabbard. If we use the other burier, we can see if Farak lives. He deserves that much."

The word "if" felt like a firebrand on her tongue. It implied hope when she knew there was none.

The scowl on Rana's face softened.

"Do you have your burier?" Zarina asked.

Rana nodded and pulled it out of a pocket within the folds of her dress. "Are you sure we should do this?"

"No." Zarina tried to grin, but her lips split, and she winced. "But no matter his part in all this, Farak must be found. And it's time we reveal the truth and end this. You deserve answers as much as I do."

"Not that it will change anything," Richard muttered under his breath.

Zarina shifted so that all she could see was him. His eyebrows cinched together with hurt, and his ragged curls hung limply around his face. He pushed his glasses up his dirty nose and stared at her with eyes dipped in hopeless resignation.

"I have already decided that it will not."

"It's comforting to know I've lost even to a dead man," he said dryly.

Zarina sighed. "That's not what I meant."

"Yes," Rana interjected with an air of haughty helpfulness Zarina could already tell would be trouble. "It is not her fault she loves Farak."

Zarina flinched.

"She is cursed to love him."

"Or you are," Zarina added hastily to keep the shadow that had fallen over Richard's brow from deepening.

"Of course," Richard laughed bitterly. "Choosing Farak is not even your choice anymore. How convenient a way to get out of responsibility."

"That's not what I meant at all," Zarina said, her temper sharpening as her faculties returned.

He scoffed. "Right-O. I'll just believe you on that, will I? Believing in you has really been working out for me." He gestured wildly around the cracked and crumbling tomb.

"Richard—"

"I know what it's like to be picked last for cricket. No thanks."

Zarina sighed. Richard was angry, and she didn't blame him. It would be better to show him her sincerity rather than make more promises he didn't believe she'd keep.

She held up her beetle and turned. "Here, Rana."

Rana's delicate brow raised.

"You deserve both the beetles. You act more like a descendant of Ra than I ever have. I'm sorry I didn't leave with you when you asked. I would have loved sailing the skies with you."

Rana smiled softly. "I'm sorry, too, *Nuur*, for trying to kill you. But I cannot take your burier. We shall each take our own fate and choose what to do with it."

Zarina nodded and swallowed her fear along with the dust and smoke coating the air. "And then maybe make our own fate?" She asked in tones filled with hope.

Rana paused and looked at her. "I think that time has passed, no?"

Zarina's chest tightened, Ra crushing her heart in his hand.

"Fate already belongs to my *Nuur 'innaya*," Rana said. "Though you are not that to me, anymore. Or not *just* that, my *'ukhti alhabiba*."

My dear sister.

A strength Zarina had never felt buoyed her with Rana's words. "I am glad to have a sister, *'ukhti jamila*."

Rana pricked her dainty finger on the tip of her burier and set it into the sand, then kissed Zarina's forehead. She grabbed the gas lamp and, in one fluid movement, jumped through the crevice toward her fate.

It was Zarina's turn to do the same.

Thirty-Four

Zarina watched Rana go, her heart twinging with hope and love and fear and excitement.

She threw the beetle in her pouch and pulled out her foxfire beads, then rubbed them hard against her hands and arms, against her cheeks and pants and the ridges of her collar bones. They were stubs when she was done, but she glowed like a lost star searching for light. She tossed the stubs into her pouch and slipped her goggles on to keep the acrid smoke from stinging her eyes. The lenses were still mismatched, but any clues that could lead to the way out were worth the disorienting difference in color.

Ready to venture into chaos, she turned to Richard who still leaned against the cool wall of the tomb, soot smeared across his nose. She slipped the beetle in hand and tried for a tired smile.

"Ready?"

"I think I'll wait here," Richard said, kicking a pebble down the dark of the crevice.

"I've learned something about you, you know," Zarina said, trying to imitate Richard's missing charm.

Kick.

"You care far more than you let on."

His bright eyes met hers, jewel-hard. "I think I made it perfectly clear exactly how much I cared. And a lot of good it did me."

Kick.

Her smile slipped. She could not put on a face of joy in front of such sadness. How had Richard done it these past few days?

"Shouldn't you be getting on, then?" he continued tersely. "Farak's as strong as a bull. Or he is a bull, I never sorted that one out, but even he will need rescuing this time."

She grinned. "I knew the old Richard was somewhere in there. That's why . . ." she steeled herself in the dim blue of the cave. "No, that's one of the *many* reasons I—"

"Don't," he said, and whatever glimmer of comradery had surfaced faded once more into tension-filled gloom. "Don't say something you'll regret."

She opened her mouth to protest.

"I deserve that, at least, don't I?" He cut her off and ran a hand through his wild hair. "Some peace after everything you've put me through? So don't go saying something you won't mean once you find out Farak's alive or what your *fate* is. There is no room for me in your world."

Richard's eyes flashed with something forlorn and distant and utterly lonely. He pulled her in tight, so her face was just below his. She gasped, then greedily took in his inky warmth. He leaned in close, his lips a whisper away, and ran his fingers down her arm and to her hand, sending thrills up her spine. When her heart thrummed so hard she thought it would burst, he plucked the burier from her hand and swiped it across her bleeding lips.

"Let's finish this," he said, expressionless, and threw the scurrying beetle into the black.

"No!"

She bit her lip, hastily glancing between Richard and the tomb. If it was just fate—-she could overcome her impulsive need to fulfill or fight it and leave with Richard. But Farak was in there, and if there was any chance he lived, she needed to find him. He was part of her family—the circle of people she loved and would fight for.

She crawled out as gracefully as a donkey, collecting cuts on her already damaged skin. The rubble was so thick, in many places there only stood a yard or so between the carnage and what was left of the ceiling. She crouched and lurched forward. The blue of the beetle vanished beneath a column. She pulled at a small boulder, clearing stones and chipped plaster from around its base. The beetle's iridescent blue popped up a few yards away, near the shattered head of a jackal urn.

She stumbled after it, desperate to catch up and grateful for the distraction it gave from her bursting heart.

Richard.

She stumbled and hissed out a breath as a new well of blood poured from her leg.

Farak.

She shimmied under a leaning pillar and held her breath like it would keep her from getting crushed.

Rana?

Rana's silky robes swooped over and under a star-smattered piece of ceiling and disappeared once more.

Zarina's burier paused over a stone cast with Ra's image. *Of course.* The small, metal scarab took to work for the scarab to bury down, down, down. Zarina followed suit.

A half-meter in, she could feel it.

The buzz of a Guardsman's sword.

But which piece was it? Hilt or blade? With the terrible and destroyed state of the tomb, she couldn't tell if she was near the stairs or not.

She stopped her frantic search and held her bloodied fingernails in front of her. She didn't recognize them. She didn't recognize herself. And what if what she found changed her even more? What if Richard was right? Because of the way she had so far lived her life, there was no room for her either.

She would have to make room.

Zarina squeezed her hands tight. Released. And kept digging. The buzzing hum rattled the sand off a brick at the bottom of her hole. The final brick. She was sure of it. She shoved her fingers into any crevice she could find, ignoring the bite against her skin, and heaved.

Zarina squared her shoulders and pulled with everything she had. She strained so hard, she swore she heard something in her knee pop. The rock remained steadfast. But she couldn't give up.

Should she ask for Rana's help? Would the outcome of the scarabs ruin what they had built together as children, as sufferers of fate in this tomb? She bit her lip and turned to where the soft bob of Rana's orange lantern touched the walls.

It didn't matter.

They were family. Sufferers of the same self-inflicted mindset and only newly recovering. And they loved each other. That was something she could feel here in this life, something good that lifted her up. Cursed or fated, it didn't matter. She wasn't alone in any of it, and that mattered more than anything.

She straightened up and stretched her back, then called "Rana! Help me!"

A faint call returned over the dusty silence. "I cannot, *'uhkti!* I am in the throes."

Zarina swallowed a thick helping of sand-coated pride and prayed to Nut. There was only one other choice. "Richard?" She called with less gusto.

The soft scurry of Rana's feet met her ears. Then nothing.

"Richard?"

"You're skinny, little arms aren't very strong are they," he said, startling her from behind. She turned to see him hovering over the hole she had dug.

"Did you follow me?" She took a step towards him and slipped, falling backward. Before she hit the sharp corners of debris, he caught her sleeve and pulled her back up.

"Look at you. Truly a disaster." He released her sleeve.

"Richard . . . ." she said, voice soft. She wanted to reach out and touch him, but still felt the burn of his words from within the crevice. "Why did you come when I called?"

His lip twitched, eyes trailing the chaos around them and refusing to look at her. "I had no intention of following, mind you. But after the fifth or so cry of pain emanating from your corner of the tomb, my gentlemanly upbringing tutted that I was in need of reproach. I would be remiss if I allowed you to die and then haunt me my entire life."

Zarina did her best to hide her smile. "I never thought I'd be so glad for your foreign upbringing."

"Indeed," he said and crouched down, placing one hand on each side of the rock.

"You always come for me, you know?"

He glanced away, his green eyes catching the light. "A terrible habit."

"*Indeed*," she imitated him, but her heart bloomed.

He *did* always come for her, regardless of fate or fortune or Farak. He stood by her side even when he didn't believe in fate. He showed up even when she told him to leave. And even when death was on her tail and in her hands and below her feet, he did not flinch and run away.

"You ready to seal your fate?" Richard asked, pulling her from her thoughts.

She looked at his sunburnt face and wild curls and couldn't help but smile.

"I'm ready to face it and do what needs to be done."

He looked as if he were about to say something more, then shook his head. "As you wish."

She grabbed the free sides of the rock, and they pulled together.

Thirty-Five

With a heave, she and Richard chunked the rock with the image of Ra to the side where it shattered with an underwhelming *chink*. Zarina bit her lip and looked into the hole. She gasped and fell back.

A hand.

Motionless.

Farak's.

Bile climbed up her throat, and she spat the side.

"Oi," Richard said, dropping to his knees. "You going to leave him like that? His fingers are moving?"

She nearly cut her cheek scrambling back over. Farak's hand moved ever-so-slightly, stirring the smoke-swirled air.

"Farak!"

She and Richard dug furiously, throwing stones and pottery shards and plaster pieces behind them in their effort to hurry. They found his elbow. Then his shoulder. She and Richard strained to remove the pillar that lay atop Farak. Finally, it rolled over with a groan. And there he lay.

She dropped down beside Farak and brushed the dust from his face. "Are you okay? Farak? Are you awake?"

His eyelids fluttered. She sighed with relief. Then he grumbled something low and gravelly.

"What?" she asked, leaning in closer.

"Boozah."

She scrunched her nose but did as he asked, finding the leather-bound flask at his waist. She popped it open and poured some of the foul-smelling liquid past his dry lips. He spluttered as the alcohol burned his throat. Thank Nut he was alive.

Zarina looked up at Richard, but he was gone. A shadow moved through the debris and up the opening for the stairs.

She wanted to run and catch him, but what about Farak? She couldn't leave him to die. Not again. Though she did not want Richard to leave her either, not without him hearing what she had to say. She owed them both so much, how would she ever repay it?

She swallowed her worries and turned to her Guardsman.

One thing at a time.

It was all she could do.

"Good news, old friend," she said as Farak coughed through the bad-smelling liquid. "You did not waste your entire life serving me."

He raised a brow. "I'd beg to differ."

"I meant the beetle." She plucked it from off his scabbard, then poked him in the ribs so he gasped. "Mine was meant for you."

He dropped his head down and shut his eyes. "So, do you wish I were dead?"

"No," she said and stretched her legs out beside him.

Shattered columns and flaky plaster poked through her leather pants. One long trail of blood ran past her knee and looked like the scar on her ship—like the Nile. She smiled to herself. She *was* in a rebirth.

"Do you wish I were?" she asked.

"Never," he coughed in reply.

They sat in silence. Only their tired breathing swayed the air.

"Where's Rana?" he asked at last.

"With the wind."

"And Richard?" He looked past her.

"Him, too."

Farak took another swallow of boozah, then rasped, "When you pulled that stone from off my eyes, I thought Nefertari herself had come to save me."

"I glow far more brightly than any mummy would. And you're remembering the story wrong. Nefertari would want you dead. It was Merytamun who spoke out against Ramses."

"And you who spoke against Ra," Farak said, his voice steady at last. He lay his head on a shard of stone and closed his eyes.

Zarina grabbed the flask from Farak and took a big whiff. She gagged. "That didn't work out so well for either of us."

"It did not work out for Merytamun because she only did half the job. In the end, she submitted herself to Ramses' will."

"And saved her friends," Zarina defended half-heartedly. "Along with her lover."

His eye peeked open. She met his gaze and held it.

"In the end, she lost them all, anyway," Farak said, his voice gruff and tired.

Zarina sighed. She knew more than ever how her ancestors felt. Still, she did not like the feeling that she was being lectured. "Is this because your belief in Ra was all a big charade?"

He winced again, though she had not touched him. "I may have fibbed on that, a bit."

"What?" she shoved his arm.

"Stop touching me," he wheezed. "You're as handsy as a baby baboon."

She raised her brows expectantly.

"The curse . . . it lives in me. I was raised as the grand protector. The one who would save our family from eternal damnation. Even as I doubted it, I had to believe. Because they did. And I couldn't let them down."

"You got a little Christ complex going on, there?" She shot him a rueful smile.

"Definitely not," he said. "His god knew better than to rest anyone's fate on a petulant princess."

She raised her hand to hit him again, but her threat fell flat. "Be careful, or I might not help you out of this tomb."

"Ra help me," he said and smirked.

"Let's pray he doesn't."

Zarina set to work freeing his legs and feet and helping him limp out of the hole. There, in the center of the wall to their left, lay a lonely lantern blinking in the dark. Rana had found the exit.

She and Farak made their agonizing way across the rubble and out into the fresh air. It was morning. The arid wind whipped fresh around them and the sun was not yet too hot. She changed out her glasses for a soft yellow. Not the best filter, but one that always made her feel a little happier, a little more light.

She scanned the hills, what was left of Adajin's abandoned camp, and the valley that spread before them. No sign of Richard. No sign of Rana. But at least she had Farak.

They sat in the glistening sand and lay, arms over eyes, as they warmed the chill of the tombs out of their bones. Farak groaned as he stretched his bruised muscles. He cast a shadow over where she lay, so she peeked out from her hiding.

Zarina ran her toes through the sand, her boots discarded next to her. She smiled under the sunshine, unburdened for the first time in her life.

"Be honest, Farak, how terrible do I look right now?"

He squinted at her in the light, pulled his boozah out and took a heavy swig, then squinted at her once more. "Bad enough this won't help." He drained the last of it and tossed the flask in the sand. "You look like a wet owl pellet."

She punched him in the shoulder. "You don't look so good yourself."

"Ay."

Zarina looked at Farak. He had his knowing face on, all arched brows and flat lips and bronze eyes with flecks of haughty gold. She had missed this face. She would miss it.

They started their trek over the backside of the hill.

Zarina slid down the last of the hill, boots in hand for when the sand grew too hot. "Without fate chasing me down in a black cloak, I'm not sure how I'm going to get where I need to go. Everything has always been so dependent on things outside of my control."

"That depends on you." Farak pushed himself up so they were eye to eye and leaned in close, awakening the fire they had always shared. The fire that was as real as it was decreed. It burned hot, and she couldn't tell if what she felt was pain or something else.

"I choose you, Zarina," he whispered and pressed his forehead against hers. "And if you'll let me, I'll be forever at your side. I am entirely, desperately at your command."

She bit her lip, taking in the cinnamon breeze between them and drinking in each fleck of gold in his earnest eyes. She had spent years alone wishing, wishing he would say these very words to her.

"So," he whispered. "Cursed or free? What will you choose your fate to be?"

Zarina yanked the lever next to her helm so that the ship's sales whipped and snapped against the headwind. An ugly iron beast flew ahead of her, barely afloat under its strained balloons. If needed, a minute of her heatglass on the tethers, and the ship would hit the earth. She set her course and turned up the steam, then jumped down the few steps to the main deck and centered the magnifier on the ship ahead. She caught the tethers in her crimson-tinted sight but shifted lower. Lower and lower until she found what she sought.

With a measured tilt, the thick glass caught a taste of sun and beamed it across to the deck of the other ship.

There he was. Spotlighted by Ra himself. And practically melting under the heat.

Richard spun around. She could see his tiny face clearly skewed with confusion even from this far away, his arms full of his usual mound of paperwork.

Zarina smiled, spun the magnifier off, and jumped back to the helm. Her narrow ship cut easily through the fighting gusts of desert wind until she pulled up alongside the roughly-laid wooden deck Richard stood upon. She tossed a rope across the railing and around a hook, tethering the two ships together so they were only a meter apart. The captain of the flying hunk of junk cursed at her, stomping his way from the upper deck down to chastise her.

She took a deep breath. It was now or never.

She had missed him so much, even seeing his sour face made her feel light. But they had not left on good terms. And his shirt was entirely drenched, which meant he probably hadn't appreciated her little tease with the heatglass. Who knew he'd melt so fast?

Still . . . she had come all this way.

"Brit," she called, leaning across the railings towards him.

"Zarina." He nodded once. It was the sharpest thing he could have said. The cruelest. Was she no longer his princess? "I see Rana let you live."

She stifled a scowl. "Rana and I have put the past behind us. She's family now." The thought flew like a songbird in her chest. "Real, living, not painted-on-the-wall family. She's leaving Aegyptus for a while. Heading to Europa to make some black market inroads. We're choosing our own fates."

"Right," Richard said it like he had a locust in his mouth. "What are you doing here?"

"I hear there are pirates about. I thought you might need some saving."

Richard pushed up his glasses with one finger. "I'm certain I can manage things without your help."

The wind rustled by, and several of his pages took to the breeze. He reached for one in vain, losing several more pieces in the effort. A large scroll tumbled out from his elbow and rolled toward the edge. It flew off the side and into the air.

Zarina grinned. "And who shall rescue these?" She snagged the scroll with one swipe and held it out to him.

"What do you want, Zarina?" He tilted his head down and looked up through his lashes, green against brown like the Nile through its reeds.

She wanted to swim.

Instead, she tossed the scroll from one hand to the other and back.

"You're the most unforgettable man I've ever met, so I came for you." She put up a smile and swallowed. Her throat had never felt so dry. Why was talking to him so hard? She never used to give it a single thought. "Just for you."

"Did you stow your bodyguard under the deck to spare my feelings?"

"He'd hardly fit," she said, trying to imitate one of Richard's classic grins.

He sighed, shifting his papers so they obscured pieces of his face. "I don't want to do this Zarina. Go home."

"I am home."

"I don't mean Aegyptus."

"Neither do I."

The papers stilled, and Richard peeked over the top.

Her cheeks warmed. So did his.

"Where's Farak?" he asked.

"I don't know." Her grip tightened around the scroll. She met his peeking gaze. "Using his big muscles and surly temper to run the parts of Adajin's empire that Rana took over. Hopefully, wooing some brown-eyed maiden."

"You're a brown-eyed maiden."

"We are through, Richard. Farak and I."

"I've heard your declarations before."

She laid one scroll-filled hand atop the railing and leaned close enough to join him in his fray of papers. "You haven't heard my declarations for you."

"I certainly did not hear a declaration for me when I asked if you loved me."

She winced. "I thought I needed you to go. I didn't want you to get hurt."

"You said I don't belong in your world." He looked at her with pained eyes, then dropped his gaze to his feet. "And—And maybe you're right. I can't compete against the eternal curses and mysterious gods that guide your life. I don't even understand a lot of what I've witnessed these last few days." His voice drifted off, but his eyes reached shyly for her own.

"You belong in my world because I choose you. And I will continue to every day. Everything else we can figure out as we go."

His eyebrows sunk, a look of doubt clear in his slack lips.

She reached out and smoothed his furrowed brow with her thumb. "I'll tell you the same thing I told Farak when I left him to live his life."

"The first or second time?" Richard asked with his brow arched.

"The second," she couldn't help but sass back.

His shyness soured. "I'd rather you not."

"He asked me if I wanted to live cursed or free. And I said free."

Richard's face softened.

"You make me feel free."

"Because you see me as an easy way out of your curse?"

"My curse is over as much as it can be." She smiled saying the words, the warm desert breeze brushing her skin and weaving through her hair. "Rana and Farak and I took care of that ourselves. With no assassin, I am able to live my life without fear of dying. Though I will only be able to have daughters. I've decided that's not such a bad thing . . . as long as you agree." She offered him a wink.

The pink in his cheeks deepened past his sunburn. "And what of fate?" he challenged, eyes watching her carefully through his wild stack of parchment. "Of the gods?"

"The gods will not begrudge me living the life they granted. As for fate . . . it's as real as what we make of it. It's changeable. Like you. And like me. And like the world around us. And if it isn't, it can come beat me with the gods in the afterlife."

"With a throwing stick?" The corner of his lips twitched.

"Like I'm a duck."

His terse lips broke in a small grin.

"For now, though, I'm going to embrace the parts of my heritage and family that are best for me and live and love the way I want to. Just like my mother tried to, only I'm picking a much better partner. Though you'll really need to get better at Arabic. I'm not talking in your baboon tongue the rest of my life any more than I'm giving up my goggles or leaving Aegyptus." She tapped a finger on his nose. "Now, are you going to head back to balmy Britannia or come on an adventure with me?"

"An adventure?" Richard shifted his pile to one arm and ran a hand through his curls. "Where are you headed?"

"*We* are headed to Alexandria," she said resolutely. "I need to do a few things for my sister, first. Then we're headed to Cairo after that. Since I'm not running from my heritage anymore, I figured you'd want to help me dig it up and then overpay me for it." She flashed him a smile.

"I thought you hated Cairo," Richard said suspiciously, though his teasing grin had returned, filling her heart with light.

"Everyone hates Cairo," she said with a grin.

"So it is," he said, then dropped his papers in a billowing heap on the deck.

He jumped over the railing and scooped her up into his arms. He swung her into a dip, then paused when his lips were a breath away from hers.

"I'm going to call you darling princess."

"What?" she balked. "In front of people?"

He smiled and nodded. "I helped you fix your assassin problem which means I get to call you whatever I want.

"I—you—"

Then he kissed her, and nothing else in all of Ra's desert mattered.

Curious what happens when Rana, our mysterious Aegyptian assassin, is assigned a job that involves tight-laced Phillip Sheffield from Book 1? Get the Rogue Royals: Book 3, *The Earl's Assassin* and join in on all the rorty fun! (turn page for excerpt and link!)

Excerpt from *The Earl's Assassin*

Rana stayed upstairs, comfortable in the shadows as she watched the sway and shift of the room below. The crisp music clicked like heels on tile. Unimaginative. Stuffy. And the women in the room seemed only to swoosh around in circles tittering in high voices while doing nothing of importance.

At first, Rana kept waiting, waiting, waiting, for the women to prove her wrong, but then she realized: the women were part of the decorations and ambiance. They were the commotion needed to cover up the far more serious, shadier conversations the hummed between the pockets of men smattered around the room. It was not a dress she should have considered wearing to this party, it was a pair of slim, woolen pants. Which made what she had on perfect. A blend of the two roles, soft and flowy and down for business.

Still, she would draw heated stares, so she put up one of her more radiant smiles. It would be better to soak in the fire than to let it burn her up. She held up the silver comb to catch a reflection of herself and had to practice five times before a confident smile with a hint of demure came naturally to her lips. Perfect.

Then she bent over and twisted half her hair up, twining it around the coil of her hairband so it looked loosely like a braided crown. Not all the way up in a ridiculous turban of hair like the women below, but not so wild that it would scare people away. She used the snatched bobbins to hold it in place.

Already she could tell that Britanians grew wary of anything completely free from a cage.

Ready, she walked down the stairs, careful not to sway her hips as much as they wanted to. Two steps from the bottom, heads started to turn and the hum of gossip died down to startled silence. By the last step, the women were louder than crickets at sundown, gathering closer and closer until even the men in the room had to take notice.

Rana put up the smile she practiced and bounced into a curtsy. She had only a moment left to complete the setup. If she didn't snag a secure place within the social circles of this room, Phillip would have her kicked out again. And there was no safer place when fighting a tiger than riding on its back.

She stared at them with large eyes, trying to look innocent. The nearest gaggle of women mercilessly thrust forward an anxious-looking girl with frizzy red hair. Their sacrifice to the gods.

"I am lost," Rana said, speaking loud enough for everyone to hear. "I am looking for my Phillip." She dropped her heavy black lashes and forced a blush. "I mean, Earl Sheffield."

The crowd gasped, and her habib showed up right on cue. When he saw her, the glint in his eyes turned to monsoon lightning.

"Habib," she cooed. "I was about to tell them how we met so they would help me to find you."

He stiffened. Every eye slid to him, leaning into his unspoken words. Gasps waited on wagging tongues.

"There is nothing to tell," he said. She could see each twitch of his cheek as he tried to stomp down his growing irritation. "We met in port to—"

"He picked me up, knowing I would need him after such a long journey."

He ground his jaw. "To discuss a business arrangement."

She gasped lightly, shaping her mouth into a perfect 'O', eyebrows knitted just a little. "What a cold way to describe your offer of marriage."

The ladies in front all gasped, their faces mirrors of her own. The group of Os snapped between her and Sayid Phillip, not sure who to watch more.

"Now, wait just a minute, Lady Maathornefurer—" he started, his face paling.

"What did I say about my name?" She raised her brows and quirked her lips.

His eyes managed to burn like ice when he looked at her. "Rana," he said through clenched teeth.

The hoard of women broke into a hushed titter.

"May I speak with you in private?" he muscled out.

She forced a blush into her cheeks. "Now?" she asked and looked askance.

"Not that private!" He could barely speak the words, his face was so tight.

A few men chuckled behind him.

"For my love, my habib, always." She smiled sweetly and waited.

He gave a tiny, hard bow and swept his hand for her to follow.

She continued to wait, smiling sweetly.

The ice in his eyes fractured with rage, but he straightened and offered her his hand just as she wanted. Lighting her fingers gently on his, she followed, bobbing her head with a demure fluttering of eyelashes at the women they passed. She had expected him to take her to the exit or a curtained corner of the room, but he veered down an airy hallway and to an open parlor.

Then he yanked her inside and slammed the door.

Want a stream of free books, exclusive content, and info on Kyro's next releases? You can sign up for her newsletter here and be part of the community fire!

Interested in seeing more books by Kyro? Check out her website, or www.eightmoonspublishing.com!

Aegyptian Arabic

ʿĀbiṯ - mischievous

Abaya - head covering
Aibtisamat Rae - Ra smiles
Almaealij - healer
Alwaghad - villain
Ana aelam an hadha sahih - I know this to be true
'arğūk sāmiḥnī - please forgive me
'atawassalu 'ilayk - I beg you
Dabit - Officer
Dewa-net jer - term of endearment
Djellabas - long, loose-fitting unisex outer robe or dress with full sleeves
Eh akhbaar? Are you okay? Is all well?
Eid al-Adha - Holiday of Sacrifice, the 2nd largest of the two main holidays celebrated in Islam.
Habib - lover
Haga tehar'a el dam. There will be nothing left before long.
Hedjet - type of crown worn by Egyptian pharaohs and their queens
Hemars - donkeys
Iḥras - Be quiet, shut up
Jahanami - infernal

Kassabah - an Islamic measurement of distance
Khali - uncle
Kirat - smallest unit of measurement for length
Laki alaka - None of your business
La ijre - "To my foot" which means "I don't care"
Khayin - Traitor
Mahbub - unit of money
Majnun - crazy
Manaf lileaql - preposterous
Marha - hurrah or bravo, an expression of excitement
Mazeaj - mischievous
Nar - fire
Najah bahir - splendid prosperity or holy treasure
Nuur 'innaya - light from the gods, radiant gift from the gods
Niqab - Islamic head covering and robe
Pistoria - Bakery
Ohkti - sister
Rech-kwi tju, rech-kwi ren-ek - ancient protection uttered against death and Ahmet
Sayidi - Sir
Shurta - Police
Tāgir - Merchant
ukhti alhabiba - my dear sister
'ukhti jamila - my beautiful sister
Wadi festival - The Beautiful Festival of the Valley, a celebration of the dead
Wahsiratah - Alas, oh woe
Wlih - an expression of surprise that is sometimes used to indicate people will get hurt
Ya 'iilhi - Stop
Ya dahwety - an exclamation used when overwhelmed by the situation
Ya homaar - Son of a donkey
Ya khabar abyad - an exclamation used when you feel the pain deep down in your liver

Ya kharaashy - an exclamation used when in need of help
Ya lahwy - an exclamation of surprise
Ya maraary - Oh bitterness!
Ya msebty el sowda - Oh my black catastrophe! Woe is me!
Ya nhar eswed - Oh black day!
Ya rab - Oh, Lord! An expression of exasperation
Yjb 'an nadhhab alan - We must go now.
Zeri-mahbub - one quarter of a mahbub

Arabic Numbers

Wahid - One

Itnan - Two

Talata - Three

Arba'a - Four

Hamsa - Five

Translations are a thank you to my sensitivity readers, google translate, and https://sajjeling.com/2014/03/18/how-to-omg-like-an-arab/

Aegyptian Gods

Anubis - God of the dead and deity of cemeteries and embalming as well as the protector of graves.

Apep - Apopis/Apepi/ Rerek (see below) is the serpent god of death and demon of chaos who represents evil. Foe of the sun god, Ra, he represents all that is foreign or outside the ordered cosmos.

Baal - The god of thunder and rider of clouds considered to be lord of heaven and earth.

Babi - Or Baba is the bull or chief of baboons. He represents the deification of the baboon.

Ba Pef - Minor god of the underworld worshipped in the Old Kingdom who is the malevolent deity of misfortune.

Hathor - Depicted wearing a headdress of cow horns and a sun disk, she is the mother of Ra and goddess of sensuality, music, dancing, maternity, and womanhood.

Horace - Heru/Hor is god of kinship, healing, protection, the sun, and the sky.

Isis - Great Mother Isis or Aset is the goddess of healing and magic.

Ma'at - The goddess of justice, truth, balance, and order. She is the gatekeeper to eternal life.

Nut - The sky goddess, mother of Isis, Set, and Nepthys.

Ra - King of deities and father of all creation and give of power and light. He is the patron of the sun and can take on its physcial form.

Renenet - Renenutet/Ernutet/Renen-wetet is a goddess from the Old Kingdom who governed the harvest and subsequent nourishment.

Rerek - (See Apep above)

Shay - Shai/Schai/Schay is the ancient goddess of wisdom and keeper of books, she also governs fate and destiny. Ancient Egyptians believed she existed as a deity but also that she was born with each individual to help govern their lives.

Victorian Slang

Balmy - eccentric, foolish, or full of barm. In other words, freothing, excited and flighty

Bit of jam - shortened from the jammiest bits of jam, which indecite the best part of something or the most beautiful young woman

Bang up to the elephant - perfect, complete, unapproachable/beyond compare

Bloke - man, fellow, guy

Bobbies - police

Damfino - a condensed version of damned if I know

Dapper - neat, trim, smart

Foozler - a bungler, or one who does things clumsily

Gibface - an ugly person, especially one with a heavy lower jaw

Off the chump - to be crazy. A form of 'chumpy' which is someone who is a mild sort of lunatic and "off his head" which means the same as the first.

Podsnappery - a person who is determined to ignore the objectionable or inconvenient while assuming airs of superior virtue and noble resignation.

Rorty - boisterous, rowdy, or saucy

Ruddy - an expression of irritation

Scurf – an exploitive employer or gang leader

Shoddy – of subpar quality

Umble-cum-stumble - thoroughly understood

About the Author

Kyro Dean has written over 20 novels and loves writing as an escape. She owns and edits for Eight Moons Publishing and for the blog, Vanilla Grass Writing Resources. She loves to speak and present and has shared her knowledge at many conferences. When not writing, she loves spending time with her delightfully curious children and talking with her plants, though they often give terrible advice.

Check out her website www.kyrodean.com. Or check her out on social media (Twitter and Insta): @kyro_dean!

I love my readers!

Join my mailing list for to get all the latest and tons of free reads!

Thank You!!

Another big thanks to my wonderful **Kickstarter chuckaboos**! I couldn't have done it without you!

Melissa Brown, Kellen Nelson, Jeremy Kowalski, Adrienne Hiatt, Andrew Kaplan, my darling Dita Bachi, Elesa Hagberg, Thomas 'Kranodor' Hahn, Engineer Ed, Travis Fonseca, Bella's Realm, Michael Hayes, Vixen Rue-Aurora, Derek Egerman, Eron Wyngarde, Tracy L, Nikole, Josh McGinnis, Justin A. Rosenbaum, James Rowland, Coral Hayward, K. Seery, Alex M, M. L. Hutchins, Chris Hubbard, Riki, Golinssohn, Oleksandra, Isaac 'Will It Work' Dansicker, Rachelle Funk, Megan Frank, Michael Webber, Molly Celaschi, Steve L., Richmond, Alison Woods, Mary Ann, John Wesley Dean III, TJ Nichols, Mary Ann, Josh Wilcox, Michelle L, Sergey Kochergan, Jennifer, and all the amazing backers who wished to remain anonymous!

And, as promised, they're written in ink, not blood.

Want in on my next kickstarter so your name can appear in the books, too? Don't forget to join my mailing list!

Warning: You *will* hear about my copious plants!